ANAM

Book III of the Marysvale Trilogy

JARED SOUTHWICK

Prologue

Wood creaked as the barrel lid was pried up and removed. Even though thick, gray clouds continued to blanket the sky, filtered sunlight pierced the darkness, blinding the boy in his watery prison. How long had he been locked up? Certainly, not more than thirty minutes, as revealed by the light; however, it felt like hours to his cold, cramped body. All around him, a chorus of water drops, finding their way down from the tops of trees, sang the grand finale of a spring symphony. It made the forest seem hallowed, fresh, and still.

Too still.

Where are the birds that carol their gratitude after the storm?

They weren't there.

The boy blinked and squinted in an effort to take in the world once again.

Above him, a cloaked figure materialized and hovered over the opening.

From his vantage point, the boy could see most of the man's thin face, sculpted cheekbones, and long nose.

Under the folds of his cloak, the man produced a soft, refined hand and reached down into the barrel.

The child cowered, afraid of what it might do to him.

The man stopped.

"Do not be afraid. I will not hurt you," he said calmly.

The boy didn't move.

The man did not withdraw his hand but kept it there, waiting patiently for the small, trapped figure to take it.

"I must apologize," he continued serenely. "I assure you, I had no idea that you would be placed in such a deplorable situation. Had I known, I most certainly would have forbidden it. Will you forgive me?"

The boy said nothing.

Terrified, exhausted, hungry, and very cold, the child suddenly became aware that his body was shaking uncontrollably.

Still, he hesitated.

Inside the barrel, he was alive. He wasn't sure what would happen outside of it. He feared the men, but even more so, he feared the monster.

"Come now," the man coaxed gently. "Surely, you cannot stay in there forever. You must be famished. Ah, I can see that you shiver. Come along, and I will wrap you up in a blanket. You may dry by the fire while you eat."

Something inside the boy warned him to be afraid, and indeed he was. But when his only other option was to remain in the biting water, with his stomach all tied up in painful knots, he felt his only real choice was to take the stranger's offered arm.

This man seems nice enough, he reasoned with himself. *Besides, what else can I do? If he wanted to kill me, he could've done it by now.*

For just one moment longer, the boy wavered.

Then he grasped the outstretched hand.

With a smile devoid of all warmth, the man pulled him up. "There's a good fellow."

Trembling, the child climbed out of the barrel, and the man placed a thick, wool blanket around his shoulders. He drew it tightly around him.

"Come," said the man.

In long strides, he walked over to a small fire where a kettle sat on the coals. The boy stumbled after him on numb, stiff legs.

Gesturing to a log lying horizontally on the ground, the man said, "Sit down and warm yourself by the fire."

He obeyed, nearly collapsing as he took his seat.

"What is your name, son?" queried the man.

"John, sir."

"Have you no surname, John?"

"John Stone, sir," he corrected.

For a brief moment, the man hesitated, and his eyes narrowed.

Then, taking the kettle from the coals, he poured John a full tankard of cider and handed it to him.

After carefully testing the temperature of his drink and finding it to be just right, the boy drank deeply. The warm liquid flowed down his throat and into his belly. The chill that had previously settled in his bones began to fade, as did the shivering. He drank a bit too fast, and a trickle of cider overflowed out of the corners of his mouth and down his chin and neck. Pulling the mug away, John wiped his face with the sleeve of his wet shirt and blinked at the imposing stranger looming over him.

The man studied the child with sharp gray eyes. Without looking away, he reached down into a sack and withdrew a small loaf of bread enfolded in cloth. Unwrapping it, the man tore the loaf in half and handed it to the boy.

"How old are you, John?"

"Ten, sir."

"I have a son about your age; his name is Lyman. Do you know him?"

John shook his head.

"Ah, perhaps you will someday. I'm certain you two would get along famously. Do you have family, John?"

The boy nodded and bit off a rather large mouthful of bread. He chewed, swallowed, and took another long draft from the mug.

The man patiently waited for him to finish and then pressed, "Tell me about your family. Do you have a mother and a father?"

John licked his lips and answered, "Yes, sir. I have a grandmother and auntie, too."

"How splendid. What are their names?"

"Grandmother Stone and Auntie are both named Sarah. My father is Richard, and my mother is Mary."

"I know those names," he mused.

John took another bite of bread. And then it dawned on him that they were alone.

I wonder where the others are? he thought.

While chewing his food, John looked around and then behind him.

A small, involuntary gasp escaped his lips.

6

The other robed figures were nowhere to be seen, but the monster was.

Standing motionless, under the protective branches of a nearby tree, it watched silently, with piercing red eyes.

Instantly, the frightened boy dropped the mug and shot to his feet, preparing to run.

The man placed a restraining hand on his shoulder.

"Fear not, John Stone; he will not hurt you. He is as harmless as a deer. Have you ever seen one like him before?"

John, almost imperceptibly, shook his head.

"Not until today," he squeaked.

He had heard of them before. Even Aunt Sarah had claimed to have seen one, but John thought she had been jesting.

Tremulously, John turned and stared at the monster. A jolt of anxiety and realization shuddered through his body.

Before being forced into the barrel, John had suspected that the beast's eyes had changed from a deep black to somewhat crimson in color. However, he couldn't be entirely sure then because the difference had been too subtle.

But now, he was sure. These eyes were undeniably red.

Standing just behind him, the man purred, "You must trust me, John. No harm will come to you. You simply surprised us earlier as we were unprepared for a visitor. You see, what we were doing here today was meant to be a secret. Have you ever held a secret, John?"

"Yes, sir," he replied in barely a whisper.

John continued to stare at the monster, transfixed by those tantalizing red eyes.

The man asked another question, but John didn't hear it.

Giving in to the overwhelming compulsion to look, the boy had leapt into the monster's soul.

Expecting to find the same opaque mystery he found in other animals, John was amazed to discover that this creature was unique. The animals that he had read before made no sense to him at all. This soul was different. It felt human in some ways, but in others, it was completely foreign.

John was mesmerized and wanted to see more. Gathering his strength, he prepared to dive deeper.

Suddenly, a beam of light shot past him and plunged deep into the monster's soul. Startled, the boy felt his tentative hold begin to slip, and he struggled to remain attached. He had never held on before with so much effort.

Loosely regaining his grip inside the monster, John realized that the light was less like a beam and more like a twisting tube of illuminated glass. It looked alive. Pulsing images seemed to flow through it as if something was moving through a tiny forest. The boy drew closer, fascinated by its presence and by its beauty. He felt curiously drawn to it.

All fear melted away, leaving him spellbound. John felt an intense yearning to touch it with his consciousness.

So he did.

And when he did, pandemonium unleashed its terrible ferocity.

A string of events occurred so rapidly that they seemed to happen all at once.

The boy's soul connected with the tube and all of his senses were immediately overwhelmed. Sight, smell, and hearing all intensified and astounded him. Looking down at his hands, he realized that they were no longer his, nor was this his body. A sense of power rushed through him. Yet, strangely enough, he felt timid at the same time. He also seemed to have grown very tall. Long, mangy hair covered every inch of him. Amazed, he studied his hands and turned them over. Massive, black claws protruded out the tips.

In reality, the child wasn't looking down at all. His eyes were still locked with the creature's in front of him.

In the same instant, a tremendous tremor shook through both him and the beast. The monster bellowed a horrifying roar that rolled across the ground and washed over him, penetrating his own soul with a deep, cold terror. The power of it racked the boy's small frame.

The tube John was connected to suddenly cracked and, with it, the monster's roar immediately changed to a pleading yelp. Was it a yelp of fear or pain? Perhaps it was both; the boy couldn't tell, and he didn't have time to contemplate it.

In one terrific boom, the tube exploded, literally throwing him backward. The monster was hurled back as well—both tossed by some great, invisible force.

The man caught John in his arms.

Nothing caught the monster.

After crashing to the ground, it rolled onto its feet, howling.

Instantly, the monster turned and ran. Smashing through branches and trees, it quickly vanished into the forest.

Greatly frightened, John jumped to his feet, spun, and stared wide-eyed at the man. He, too, appeared wholly bewildered.

The man said nothing for a moment, as he looked at John, then to where the monster had disappeared, and then back to

John. And then the man began to pace back and forth a few times.

Finally, he stopped and, facing the boy, slowly asked, "What did you do?"

"Nothing," John replied lamely.

There was no anger in the man's voice, only wonder. "Clearly, John, something just happened that you were a part of. You *must* tell me."

John hesitated. "I…I can't. I promised I would never tell."

"Tell what? Tell whom?"

Looking down at his feet, the boy remained quiet.

Regaining control, the man coaxed, "To whom did you promise, John?"

With great apprehension, John replied, "My father."

"Ah," the man said kindly. "Yes, those can prove to be difficult promises to keep, can they not?"

The boy nodded.

"Nevertheless, John, I am now in a tight spot because of you. You see, I have a secret, too—a secret that I swore to keep. But now you know my secret. I am afraid that if it is revealed, people will unavoidably get hurt."

"I don't know your secret," the child protested.

"Oh, but you do. No one was supposed to see us with that Brean. But you have."

He paused and then asked, "Does anyone know you are out here, John?"

The boy nodded. "Father will come looking for me if I'm gone too long, maybe even Mother and Aunt Sarah."

"Then, more people could find out. Now we mustn't cause all that trouble, must we, John?"

The boy shook his head.

"Of course not. But if I allow you to leave, I can do nothing to prevent you from divulging my secret—unless I keep you. You wouldn't want that now, would you?"

Again, John shook his head. "But I won't tell. I promise."

"Ah, but parents have a way of getting things out of you that you may not want to tell them. Do they not?"

The child agreed but said nothing.

"If only there were *some* way that you could guarantee your word."

Significantly, the man paused while tapping his finger on his lip.

"How about this? If you tell me *your* secret, I will be certain that *mine* will be safe because we'll both know about the other. That way, I can trust you because you don't want your secret revealed. And I vow to remain quiet, to ensure your silence. Now, does that sound fair to you, John?"

The boy thought about it. *It does sound fair. But what if I get in trouble?*

"Come now, John. I cannot permit you to leave without some assurance. And I don't want to keep you; you seem like such a nice boy—a boy who is interested in doing what is honest and good. Am I correct in my beliefs?"

John nodded. "Yes, sir. I suppose…"

He stopped.

"Go on," prodded the man. "I will not say a word. I promise."

He sounded so nice.

Do I really have a choice?

Finally, John blurted, "I...I can get into people."

"What does that mean?"

"I read things about them. I can tell if they are lying and things like that."

"How fascinating. Is that what you did to the Brean?"

"Yes, sir."

"Do the people you read react the same way?"

"No, sir; that was different. I don't know what went wrong. I didn't mean to hurt it!"

"Not to worry. I think your gifts are wonderful."

Thoughtfully, the man added, "It is a pity they cannot be used to their fullest potential."

After a brief pause, the man casually inquired, "And have you read me?"

Surprised, the boy realized that he hadn't even considered it.

"I can see you haven't. Let's keep it that way, shall we?"

"Yes, sir."

"You are a good boy, John. And I *know* you will keep my secret safe. You had better run along now before anyone comes searching, and you get yourself into trouble."

The child hesitated only for a moment before turning and sprinting away.

Behind him, the man looked on until the boy had disappeared from view.

From the darkness of the woods, a hulking beast slinked back toward the cloaked figure.

"You already know what he can do, don't you?"

While tapping a finger to his temple, the monster growled in a deep, guttural voice, "Felt him here."

"Who would have believed it?" marveled the man. "To find two of you, so different, yet the same. Pity we don't have time to train him."

The monster snarled.

"Very well," said the man. "Now is *our* time to act. Follow him. Find out where he lives, and you will find who you seek. Kill them all."

Chapter One: Reunion

A gigantic plume of black smoke choked the sky, casting the early dawn into gloomy darkness. Like unwanted interlopers, a few lazy snowflakes danced among the heavy rain of gray ash.

Scattered in groups across the vast fields of Alyth, mourning villagers huddled in stunned disbelief as they watched ravenous flames devour their dying town. The skeletal remains of their homes still stood as hollow shadows of their vibrant and happy dreams.

Many villagers embraced one another as tears flowed freely. Others sat like silent statues on the ground. The grim job of burying the dead had begun, and family members wept over the bodies of their fallen loved ones.

A gathering of villagers had formed around the twelve newcomers from Syre. The strangers stood in some surprise as they watched one of their own embrace a lady they had never seen before. With his head buried in her hair, James Shepherd, the blacksmith, enveloped the slender body.

Wrapping her arms around his broad neck, the lady held him tightly. Neither one dared to let go, afraid the sweet vision would end, and the other would disappear.

After a long while, Sarah finally pulled away. Placing both hands on James' red-bearded face, she lifted it and looked into his eyes. Tears streaked down both their cheeks.

"Oh, my love!" she exclaimed joyfully.

Seeing him for the first time, Angus gasped, "Jimmy?"

James turned at the sound of his name and saw an old man. His face was black with soot, his hair was singed, and he was missing an eyebrow.

"My son!"

Instantly, a quiver formed on the old man's lower lip. His eyes moistened as tears welled into little pools and broke free, streaming down his dirty face.

Dropping his cane, Angus took one faltering step toward him and then another.

At first, James appeared confused.

Then, all at once, recognition dawned, and his expression turned to joy.

"Father!" he cried in wonder.

James ran to Angus and caught the old man up into a giant bear hug.

In a quavering voice, Angus said, "I pray my eyes do not deceive me, for it would be a cruel trick. I believed ye dead, my boy."

"As did I believe of you."

They embraced for a long moment before Angus released him.

"Where have ye been? What kept ye away?"

James hesitated, still clearly overwhelmed. Walking to this side, Sarah slipped her hand into his and squeezed it reassuringly.

James cleared his throat. "I…I thought you and Sarah were both dead."

"Why would you think that?" asked Sarah.

15

"I was told the Brean had killed you."

"And what foul bein' told ye such a lie?" spat Angus.

"Why, Jex. Jex told me."

"Jex!" cried Angus in disbelief. "But he was the very body which bore the news of yer death!"

Angrily, he continued, "To think I thought of him as a son! And a trusted member of the council!"

"It is an evil web he weaves," said Sarah. "His treachery bites deep."

Waving her arm at the burning village, she added, "This destruction is his doing."

Sarah explained the depths of Jex's betrayal to a dumbfounded father and son.

Both James and Angus shook their heads incredulously. Their mannerisms removed any doubt of their relationship. Now that they were side by side, it was uncanny how alike they were.

Thomas, wielding his way between Hannah and me, rested a hand upon the back of my shoulder and asked, "Who's Jex?"

I winced ever so slightly under his weight. Though somewhat masked by the now permanent shaking of my ravaged body, it was enough. If anyone were to pick up on it, it would be Thomas.

He removed his hand and, without waiting for the answer to his first question, asked another.

"John, what's wrong?"

From the tone of his voice, it was clear that he knew very well what was wrong, having suffered it on many occasions by the hand of his own brutal father.

This question, while not loud enough to draw everyone's attention, nevertheless drew Sarah's. She released James' hand, turned to me, and waited for my reply.

"Nothing that you haven't been through before," I said, trying to manage a smile.

It was a pathetic attempt to reassure them that I was fine. But in truth, I was not fine. The vigilance in using my gifts, the wet and cold, hunger, fatigue, beatings, and battles had all taken their toll. Even as I stood, I felt my muscles threatening to give way and refuse their support.

"What, praytell, does that mean?" probed Sarah.

"It means," said Jane, "that he has been whipped quite savagely."

Sarah's face turned hard and menacing.

It matched the edge in Angus' voice when he asked, "What wicked scoundrel would dare to do such a thin'?"

"This one," grunted Sabin, stepping forward.

We all turned to look at him.

"But why?" asked Angus.

"Because I was a fool. I believed John to be evil and you all under his spell. I was wrong."

"Is that all ye have to say for yerself?" bellowed a red-faced Angus. He trembled with anger. "Good heavens, is nobody loyal? How are we supposed to fight our enemies when we have to worry about our friends?"

Sabin stood and stoically bore the abuse without complaint as Angus continued to rail against him.

Sarah looked like she wanted to shoot him.

"Were they going to try you for witchcraft?" whispered Thomas in my ear.

I nodded.

His face flushed with anger. "Men who accuse innocent people like that should be the ones to burn."

"Uh, Thomas?"

"Yes?"

"Perhaps there is something you should know. I'm afraid it may change how you think of me."

Just then, the old man finished his tirade and turned to me. "Well, laddie, what shall we do with him?"

I stopped talking. Bewildered, I looked at him and then at Jane.

She shrugged.

I turned back to Angus. "Why is it up to me?"

"Ye are the body he has offended," Angus reasoned.

Sabin took a step forward and cleared his throat. "I will agree to whatever punishment is decided. If I may be permitted, however, I beg your indulgence for just one moment. First, I plead for mercy on behalf of my men and request that they be left unmolested. This act was all my decision and my wrongdoing. Whatever they did was under my orders. I deserve the punishment for the entire affair. Secondly, I want you, John, to know that I now see what Angus and Sarah see in you."

He swept his arm over the groups of villagers. "Whether they know it or not, we all need you now. I will help you in whatever way I can."

Sabin nodded and stood erect, with his hands held behind his back, waiting for his sentence.

I remembered my plan to punch him in his broken ribs. But there was no anger left in me. It had been replaced by exhaustion so complete as to render everything else trivial. I had no desire for any more fighting.

"I think," I stated, "that we need all who are willing. If Sabin is on our side, then we are the better for it."

Sighing, I looked around. "Besides, we have more pressing things to attend to."

"Well said, laddie," exclaimed Angus. "Nevertheless, Sabin, ye arenae gettin' off so lightly. I deem some punishment is still in order. When the council is formed, I shall offer up somethin' fittin'. John is right; there is much to accomplish while the daylight lasts. Now go round up the council—or those who are left. We'll need to take stock of the supplies we have, organize the villagers, and assign chores. While you're out there, recruit help and fish what ye can out of the river. There also may be useful things lyin' at the bottom. See if ye can find someone brave enough to dive in and retrieve anythin' down there. We need to know what we can salvage."

"Beginning with you, John," said Sarah. "Come with me. I want to examine your wounds and warm you up. You look like death himself."

"What about Smoke?" I asked.

"Stop worrying about the horse."

"I'll take care of Smoke," Thomas said brightly. "I miss him. And I'll groom the other horses, too."

"See? You have nothing to worry about." Turning to Thomas, Sarah asked, "And your name, young man?"

"It's Thomas Martin, ma'am," he said, tipping his hat.

"So nice to meet you, Thomas. Now, John, Thomas will see to Smoke while I see to you. Jane, Hannah, come along. You too, James, I'll need your help."

Following in her wake, we walked along the bank to the backside of Alyth, where the items saved from the fire had been tossed.

"We need a shelter," stated Sarah.

"I'll take care of that," James replied, and he promptly set off toward their packhorses.

"Hannah, please help me find our bundles."

"You were able to get our things out?" I asked in amazement.

"We didn't have much to begin with. However, you don't live in a town like Alyth without planning on the possibility of fire. I had time to wrap up some of the more important possessions in blankets and tie them up—items I deemed we would need the most. Let us hope our bundles are still dry. I tossed them over the river." Sarah shrugged. "Still, they may have been kicked into the water during the fighting."

Hannah moved off to search through the scattered items from the town.

"Jane, will you please procure some dry clothing for John? I had meant to put a change in for him but didn't have time."

"Where shall I look?"

Sarah stared out over the fields littered with the bodies of the Brean and, to a lesser extent, the villagers that had yet to be buried.

Jane followed her gaze. Comprehension dawned, and she simply replied, "Oh."

"You can't," I argued. "It will be desecrating the fallen."

"I don't believe they will mind. We will not leave them disrespected."

But seeing the horror still haunting my face, Sarah suggested, "Perhaps you'll find something amongst the supplies, Jane."

"What about the villagers?" I protested. "Many of them are wet also. You're wet too."

"Angus will see to them. You just need to worry about yourself. You are the most important person here."

"I don't agree with that."

"Yes. You are. Now stop arguing with me. Your trembling comes from more than just the cold. We need to find a suitable place to set up camp so you can rest."

Sarah and I walked around the village until we found a spot closer to the gate, located away from the supplies and the dead.

James trotted up on his mount, leading another three horses laden with provisions. A man from Syre, whom I recognized as Eric Johnson, accompanied him.

They both dismounted and quickly went to work unloading the first of the pack animals.

I moved to help, but Sarah thought otherwise.

"Sit down, John, before you fall down," she said sternly.

I didn't argue.

The men carried over a white tarpaulin and unrolled it. In a few minutes, they had raised a tent. Ropes and stakes secured the corners. The opening faced the blazing town. James carried in an animal skin that looked like it had once been a bear. He spread it across the cold ground. Eric went to work, starting a small fire just outside the opening of the tent.

Soon, Jane returned with Hannah, each carrying a bundle. Jane also brought dry clothes draped over her arm.

Sarah took the garments from Jane and handed them to me.

"Go inside and put these on. But leave your shirt off and wait for me."

While holding my newly acquired raiment, I watched her lift the first of the bundles, untie the rope, and unroll the blanket, revealing the contents. It contained clothing for the women.

Sarah turned to me and chided, "Well, what are you waiting for? Go inside and change."

I ducked inside the tent and closed the flaps but didn't tie them off. From the loose opening, a sliver of light illuminated my surroundings.

While making the change, I listened to their conversation.

"Ah, good, here they are."

"What are those pouches for?" asked Hannah.

"They contain various herbs and plants that I use for medicines. I had to pester Angus incessantly to obtain them for me. From how difficult they were to find in the first place, I daresay it would be impossible now. There are some I wish I had, especially at this time, but they were not to be found."

"Hannah, here are your clothes. Jane, will you unroll that other bundle? There should be a small pot inside. Very good.

Now, will you please fill it with water and put it on the fire to heat? I have clothes for you as well, my dear. I know you aren't wet, but they are here if you choose."

"I believe I will. And then I shall wash our laundry in the river," said Jane.

All fell silent for a moment, leaving only the sound of things being opened and organized.

After I finished changing, I folded my wet garments and set them aside. It felt good to be dry. While I still shivered, it wasn't as violent as before.

Reaching up, I flipped one of the tent flaps open and peered out. The bonfire that was Alyth still awed me. It was hot enough to warm the whole of its homeless residents.

Sarah was on her knees, rummaging through the bundles. She pulled out dried food, washcloths, a large knife, and a small wooden bowl—these items she set aside. Then she went to work inspecting the contents of several small leather pouches, which I assumed contained the herbs and plants previously mentioned.

I flipped the other tent flap open and caught sight of Hannah fidgeting with a makeshift sling that cradled her wounded arm.

"Stop messing with it," instructed Sarah.

"I wish you wouldn't make me wear this. I look ridiculous. My arm was good enough to shoot with."

"That was out of necessity. You need to let it heal completely."

Jane walked back from the river, carrying a small pot filled with water. Using a stick, she moved the logs, made a flat space, and placed it on the fire.

A few feet away, James and Eric were unloading the other pack animals.

Sarah took one of the blankets that had held the items, stood, and passed it through the tent flaps.

"Wrap yourself up in this. While we wait for the water to heat, you may as well warm yourself by the fire. In the meantime, girls, you can change inside the tent."

I took the blanket, draped it gingerly over my back, and stepped outside.

Stooping, Sarah picked up a cloth and the wooden bowl. She dipped the bowl into the pot of water and drew some out.

Handing them to Jane, she said, "As we've already bathed, more or less, during our swim, you may appreciate this." Then pausing, she added, "I suppose you could wait for the water to warm if you desire."

Jane took it.

"This will be fine, thank you."

Together, Jane and Hannah retreated into the tent and closed the flaps.

With his work finished, James joined us by the fire while Eric took the horses to where the other men of Syre were constructing a corral.

Sarah looked at James, and he returned her gaze. They exchanged a solemn but tender expression, filled with questions and feelings that only a lifetime apart could convey.

She took a deep breath and then let it out. "What thoughts fill your head, James Shepherd?"

He paused for a moment before replying, "Too many to count, but mostly sorrowful ones. Sorrow for the lost time. Sorrow for what could have been."

"There is also joy," added Sarah. "For what was lost is now found."

He smiled. "There is that."

"Tell me, James, what happened those many years ago when you and the others went for help?"

He broke his gaze and looked off to some unseen place, accessing memories from the recesses of his mind.

"I tell you, Sarah, it was uncanny. The Brean shouldn't have found us. We were extremely careful. No fires, only six men, no direct route. We minded our tracks. We did everything we could to disguise our trail and our scent. It was thoroughly planned out. Of course, you know all this."

"So did Jex," added Sarah.

James nodded. "Aye. Been thinking about that, too."

He fell silent.

Sarah let the silence hang for a moment and then asked, "And what have you come up with?"

"I don't fully know. We weren't terribly close before the end, Jex and I, yet we weren't terribly distant either. Just something between us had cooled. I could never understand it then. We squabbled a wee bit, but nothing that far out of the ordinary. I'm finding his betrayal difficult to accept."

"Mmm, we all are," Sarah replied.

After a brief pause, she asked, "How about in retrospect? Knowing what you know now, does anything seem clearer?"

"Aye, I suppose *some* things *are* a wee bit clearer. The way the Brean found us made no sense, and there wasn't just one, but many—too many. One or two scouts, sure. The six of us could have handled that—perhaps it was even expected—but not a dozen or more. It happened at dusk when the light was growing dim...."

Shaking his head at the memory, James continued, "It was over before it began. We came over a ridge, and," he spread his arms wide, "there they were, already upon us. The horses panicked. We did our best to form up. Got our shots off fair enough. But there were just too many, and they were too close. None of us had time to reload our guns."

James shrugged. "I don't remember much after that. Not even sure how or why I survived. I either fell and hit my head, or a Brean bashed it."

After a moment's pause, James asked, "Remember Alexander, Sarah?"

She nodded. "I didn't like him much."

One corner of his mouth turned up in a half-smile, perhaps remembering that indeed she hadn't.

"I woke covered in blood, with a nasty wound on my scalp and one across my chest. I found Alexander lying on top of me, still alive but unconscious. He never came around enough for me to ask him anything. I don't know if he somehow fought them off? Doubtful. Perhaps the Brean passed us over, taking us for dead. Regardless, I lived through it.

"I searched for the others. William and Edward were nowhere to be seen. I have no idea if either man survived; I never saw them again. Brandon and Hyrum were lying close by; it took me quite some time to bury them.

"With our horses gone, I had no way of moving Alexander. I probably should've left him, but I couldn't bring myself to do it. I sat with him for three days. At first, he did wake up a few times; but something wasn't right. He didn't respond to anything I said. He mumbled at times, but he made no sense. It was like he was talking to somebody else, but there was no one there."

James took a deep breath and let it out. His shoulders sagged as if under a tremendous burden. "On the third day, my fears were realized, and the Brean returned. I didn't have much warning, so I climbed a tall tree and hid. And they did what I couldn't bring myself to do…"

A shudder ran through his body. "I like to believe that Alexander saved my life. If the Brean returned and saw fewer bodies than they had left, they might have deduced that one of us had survived and hunted me down. But when they found Alexander still breathing, they assumed he had buried the dead. Of course, I'm not certain, but I think of it that way. It gives his death meaning."

Sarah took one of his great hands and cradled it in hers. "I am so sorry you went through that."

He patted her hands with his other one.

"I'm sorry any of us have."

"What happened next?" asked Hannah.

I felt mildly surprised to see her and Jane standing by my side. I hadn't noticed them emerge from the tent.

"Well," continued James. "I stayed up in that tree all night. To be honest, I was scared witless by what I saw them do to poor Alexander. But come morning, I noticed a rider approaching in the distance. He was leading a few of our stray horses."

"Jex," whispered Sarah.

James nodded.

"He had said he had a bad feeling," explained Sarah.

James nodded again, agreeing with that sentiment.

"It was far too early to expect any of you to return," she continued. "But he insisted on going after you. He felt sure something had gone wrong. I wanted to come, but he said it was too dangerous to risk any more lives."

"Do you think he was going to warn you? To try and stop what happened?" offered Hannah.

With a sad expression, James shook his head. "Nae. As I said before, some things *are* clearer. Knowing what I know now, I believe he was surprised to find anyone alive. His joy felt unnatural, not genuine. His sorrow also seemed forced when he bore the terrible news that you all had perished."

Addressing Sarah, James continued, "Jex told me that you and Father had been killed while scouting a location for a new settlement. I had no reason to doubt him. Upon reflection, everything about our meeting felt off. I presumed he was suffering from shock—the shock of losing so much. Now I know it was all a lie."

"Why do you suppose he came after you?" asked Jane.

"I believe," offered Sarah, "that he intended to make sure the desired outcome had been secured."

"But then why didn't he kill you?" Jane pressed.

"The surprise of finding me alive may have thrown him off a wee bit. I was also wounded and extremely weak, not having had anything to eat or drink for a few days. I was as near to death as I ever was, and that's no lie. Jex told me that he was going to look for the missing men and that I should wait for him with the horses. He said he would return in an hour and help me get back to Marysvale. From what I know now, my guess is that Jex had no intention of coming back, thinking it likely that I would die shortly on my own, or knowing that the Brean would return, and they could easily finish me off.

"Before he left, Jex gave me his canteen and some food. I took them gratefully, but I was too overcome with my own shock and grief to respond to the terrible news of your deaths. As I let that seep in a wee bit, I decided there was nothing for me back in Marysvale. I planned to wait and tell him that I wouldn't be returning with him, but I had a queer feeling inside urging me to leave right away. I feared that the Brean would return before Jex could, so I heaved myself onto one of the remaining horses and set out to find him.

"Oddly, the uneasy feeling persisted and intensified, so, before I got too far, I turned my horse about and fled the other way. The interesting thing is, I sensed I was being followed. I thought it might've been a Brean or just my nerves getting the better of me. Perhaps it was Jex. For the first little while, when I believed I was being tracked, I went to great lengths to hide my trail. I wanted to die, but not by the hand of a Brean. I rode long and hard, hoping that I would succumb to my wounds and join you, Sarah."

"But Jex came back wounded," said Sarah. "As if he had been in a fight."

James shrugged.

"I don't know about that. I suppose he could've inflicted the wounds himself to make his story more believable."

"Or Lord Wright punished him for his failure to find you," suggested Hannah.

"Perhaps," Sarah agreed. "What did you do then, James?"

"I rode nearly all day. Eventually, I came upon a farm and collapsed in the field before I could make it to the house. The farmer, a good man by the name of Grant Stewart, found me. He and his kind wife nursed me back to health. I was there for about four months before I felt strong enough to move on. After a year of drifting, I decided it was time to head back to Marysvale. However, when I reached Syre, I stopped. I just couldn't face life back there without you, so I stayed in Syre and started over. I had lived there for many years when John and that great horse of his arrived."

Addressing me, James said, "Children can change so much in that time; I wasn't entirely sure it was really you. You gave no inclination that you recognized me or knew anything about Marysvale. I hinted at it a few times, but to no avail."

Thomas walked up then and stretched his hands over the fire, warming them.

"I didn't say anything because I didn't remember anything of my younger life," I explained. "I still don't, really, just fragments and occasional flashes of memory, nothing too specific. Most of what I know has come from Sarah and Jane."

"What happened to you? Why don't you remember?" asked Thomas.

"I was attacked by the king of the Brean and hit my head. I had no recollection of anything. And my father, for whatever reason, never told me about it."

"Brean? Are those the dead animals lying all over? Are they the ones you told us about Mr. Shepherd?"

"Aye. We didn't see any of them on our way here. I wondered if they'd all been killed off over the years."

"Sadly, no," said Sarah. "They were most likely all here, attacking Alyth. There is much you and your men should know about them and Merrick Wright. However, that can wait for nightfall. There is still much work to do before then. And John needs medical attention, food, and rest."

"But I can help," I protested, even though I felt like I couldn't.

"No, you cannot," Jane stated emphatically.

"Jane is right, my dear," agreed Sarah. "You are in no state to do anything. With little food, little sleep, fighting off the Brean, and torture, I believe you have earned a rest. Besides, I have a feeling that there will be plenty for you to do in the coming days."

Reaching down, Sarah retrieved some dried apples and venison and handed them to me.

"Now off you go into the tent. Eat while I get a poultice ready for your back. You too, Jane, you've earned rest as well."

I glanced at Hannah, expecting some kind of objection. A look of disapproval flashed in her eyes, and for a moment, I expected a complaint about impropriety. But she didn't say anything.

Clearing his throat, James said, "Well, I best find Father and see what needs doing."

With my blanket still wrapped around me, I slipped into the tent to lounge on the bearskin. Jane followed me in and sat with her legs crossed on the corner of the rug. I divided the food between us. Hungrily, we devoured our meal in silence.

Through the flap, I watched Sarah pour a small amount of hot water into the bowl. Then, she took some herbs, crushed them up, and dropped them in. She stirred it using a stick, alternately adding plants and water until she had the concoction just right.

Together, Sarah and Hannah entered the tent.

"Now, let me have a look," ordered Sarah. "Remove the blanket and lie on your stomach."

Hannah sat down next to Jane, and they both turned to watch.

I obeyed.

"Oh my," gasped Hannah. "That doesn't look good. Sabin has *not* heard the end of this."

Sarah and Jane wore expressions that seemed to agree.

"I'll be fine," I reassured them.

Sarah began spreading the warm paste over my back. "Now, tell us what happened on *your* journey."

Jane began with the silent, awkward ride out of Alyth and her description of how the men turned on us when we were not far from the village.

While Sarah attended to my back, I listened to Jane's tale and gazed out at the fire. It crackled and popped near the tent entrance. I could feel the heat radiate through the air, or perhaps it was the intense heat given off by the still-burning town. My eyes grew heavy, and by the time Jane told of our first camp, I had slipped into a deep, exhausted sleep.

Chapter Two: The Chief Captain

My eyes blinked open in the dimly lit tent. I still lay on my stomach, in the same position where I had fallen asleep. A yawn escaped as I stretched my arms over my head. I then attempted to rub the remaining sleep from my eyes. Looking around, I found that I was alone.

I pushed myself up onto my knees, and I discovered the burning in my back had subsided some. It still stung, as cuts do, but the pain had greatly diminished. There was no doubt that Sarah's concoction was indeed working.

Seeing my shirt folded neatly by my side, I threw off the blankets and slipped it on. A coat had also been laid out for me. It didn't look like mine, and I wondered if it had been taken from the dead. I stood up, shrugged into it anyway, and left the tent.

Hannah sat alone by the fire, poking at it with a stick. A pistol occupied her lap.

Noticing me, she looked up. "Feel better?"

I nodded and sat down next to her. "How is your arm?

She lifted it a little in its sling. "It's still sore, but I can use it."

"Where are Jane and Sarah? Have they been able to rest?"

"Jane and I slept some, just not all day as you did. I'm not sure about Sarah. They're at a town council meeting right now. I volunteered to stay behind."

"Volunteered?" I asked doubtfully.

"Well, not entirely. I did want to go, but someone had to stay here to watch over you. And I could see it was more important for Jane and Sarah to be there."

"Do I *need* watching over?"

"Yes, you do. Not all the villagers trust you. We thought it best if you had a guard. We sure wouldn't want someone sneaking in and killing you."

"No," I agreed. "We wouldn't want that. Where are they meeting?"

"In the stable."

"What?" I asked, looking around. "Something survived?"

"Not much."

Surveying the scene, I could see that nearly the entire village, including its protective walls, lay in a charred heap. The wasted remains of some homes still stood; however, in their weakened, smoldering state, they would soon succumb to gravity and collapse.

Everything was a loss, save the bridge, a small section of wall, and a stable. They were black and scorched but still intact. I supposed that the open space between the walls and town had allowed the villagers to save that small section. Salvaged barrels and other items had been stacked and organized by the bridge. Near the stable, the livestock was contained inside a makeshift corral made of tree branches and rope. It looked like any of the animals could easily escape if they wanted to. But they didn't know that, and two guards were standing by just in case.

A few other tents had been erected as close to the smoldering fires of Alyth as possible for warmth. No one had set up camp near us, however. We were all alone.

Thomas walked up, carrying a load of wood cradled in his arms.

"Oh, you're awake," he commented, dumping broken branches onto the ground.

Then, picking up a few pieces, he laid them on the fire.

"You didn't want to go to the meeting?" I asked.

He shook his head. "I wasn't invited. Besides, I didn't want to leave Miss Wolfe alone."

"There is no need to concern yourself over me. I am very capable," Hannah replied politely.

"Oh, I don't mean that, Miss Hannah; I'm very sure you are. I would just feel more comfortable. You're far away from the rest of the group, and those dead monsters make me very uneasy. No one should be alone."

Monsters. I haven't checked to see what's out there yet, I thought guiltily.

Opening my supernatural sight, I scanned the woods. A mile away, two Brean perched in different trees a half-mile apart from each other.

Hannah, noticing what I was doing, asked, "Do you see anything?"

"Yes, two of them."

"What?" asked Thomas. "What do you see?"

"There are two Brean. One over there," I pointed in the general direction.

"And another there." Swinging my arm, I again indicated the spot.

"Alive?" he asked, a bit panicked.

"Yes, alive."

Thomas reached for his musket.

Trying to reassure him, I said, "I don't think they will be much of a problem."

"You don't *think?*" he repeated, unconvinced.

"Well, one doesn't truly know. But based on past experiences, I wouldn't panic just yet. They are only scouts. Although last time there were two, Sarah felt nervous; and for good reason—we were attacked shortly after that."

"How *shortly?*"

"That very night. One tore out the window in my room, trying to get to me. The girls and I fled to Marysvale right after it happened."

"We went there, too," Thomas declared.

"And they let you go?" blurted Hannah.

Then regaining some composure, she added, "I'm just surprised. They usually don't allow anyone to leave."

"Oh, they didn't even let us enter the town. We showed up at night, and a Captain Smith, who seemed to know Mr. Shepherd, wouldn't open the gate. He told us to keep on going to the next settlement. Said it was for our own good. Mr. Shepherd asked if he had seen you, and Captain Smith confessed that you had been there but weren't anymore. He indicated the general direction you had gone, so we decided to follow. A few hours into our ride, we noticed the smoke and came to investigate. That's when we found you with the soldiers."

"You arrived just in time," I acknowledged gratefully.

"Tell John what happened after he was forced to flee Syre," encouraged Hannah.

"You know about his father?" I asked quietly.

She nodded. "Thomas told us. You forgot to inform us of that little detail, did you?"

"Must've slipped my mind," I muttered.

"Truthfully," Thomas confessed, "I'm relieved he's gone. I feel guilty about that, but I am glad. My mother? It's hard to say. I don't understand it, but in some strange way, she misses him. Still, I also see the relief in her. She seems happier.

"One thing is for sure, that night blew the top off a powder keg that I'm not sure anyone knew was there. Of course, there were many calls for your blood, but not as many as you'd think."

I cringed inwardly.

Thomas continued, "When you didn't show up with the hunting party as expected, Mr. Shepherd came back to Syre to look for you. And when he found out what had happened and how they had planned to kill you..." Thomas blew out a soft whistle. "I would not want to cross that man when his blood comes to a boil. Mr. Shepherd gave them a dose of their own medicine. The very night he got back, Mr. Shepherd organized a surprising number of willing people and rousted Governor Potts and many others out of their beds in the dead of night. He took their weapons by force and marched them down to the town hall to have a talk about how things were going to be from there on out. Of course, gossip woke everyone else almost instantly, and the whole town showed up to witness the event. There was a lot of pent-up anger amongst the townspeople. A good number of them wanted to put a noose around Pott's neck right then and there. Mr. Shepherd had a hard time putting a cork back in what he'd started, but he finally did. It became clear enough to the old regime that there was plenty of support for Mr. Shepherd, and change was there to stay. Those who didn't like it were strongly encouraged to leave. Though emotions were pretty tense for a while, eventually, things settled enough that I was able to convince Mr. Shepherd to organize a search party to see if we could find out what happened to you."

I sat in stunned silence.

Sensing my unease, Thomas changed the subject. "How do you know the monsters are there? I can't see anything."

I inhaled deeply and then slowly let it out. I knew there was no getting around it. As much as I didn't want to tell him, eventually, he would find out. It would be better coming from me than from a villager who might blame me for what happened here.

"Thomas," I began slowly. "There is something you should know. I have certain abilities, one of them being that I can see very well and far in the dark."

"That's putting it mildly," said Hannah.

Scratching his head, Thomas said, "I don't understand. I can't even begin to make them out. Not in the slightest."

I hadn't really considered what this moment would mean to me—or to Thomas. He had always been genuine, but I hadn't always been entirely open with him.

How could I?

I had never supposed I'd get the chance to explain. Or rather, I had never dreamed that I'd *have* to. But here I was.

"That's not exactly what I mean. I don't see them with my natural eyes; it's more of a second sight."

Taking another deep breath, I pressed on. "And that's not all. My second-sight also enables me to see other things."

I paused again as Thomas looked on expectantly.

"I can read people's souls."

Thomas hesitated. "What does that mean?"

"It's hard to explain, but it basically means that I can tell things about a person's character, like if they are honest or deceitful. I can look past the public image and see who they truly are on the inside."

There was a bit more to it than that. Sometimes I could tell what others were thinking, but that was hard to do, and it could be misleading. When I was young, Jane had employed such tactics only to deceive me. Besides, what I had already shared was probably more than enough for him to digest.

After all, why overwhelm him with everything at once? Just let him get used to this first, and then I can ease him into the rest later.

"Can you read minds?" he asked.

Oh, blast it!

I sighed.

"At times," I replied honestly. "It's a bit more difficult to do, so I don't try very often; and if I do, I can only really see what one is actively thinking about."

"And you can keep him out," Hannah added earnestly.

Thomas didn't ask the obvious question of how to do it; instead, he asked another.

"Have you ever read me?"

I hesitated a second before nodding once.

"What did you find?"

"I found genuine goodness and a desire always to be better. Those traits endeared me to you."

"John?"

"Yes?"

"Don't do it again," he said, with a hint of steel in his voice.

Inwardly, I winced. Outwardly, I simply replied, "I won't."

We fell silent as Thomas concentrated on the flickering firelight. His face appeared troubled.

"So, they were right," he finally said. "My father and the others were right about you."

"They were not right," Hannah said flatly. "John is no more a witch than you or me."

Thomas looked up at me and then to Hannah.

"But what else could it be other than witchcraft?"

He looked back to me with a curious expression, doubt perhaps.

"What if my father really wasn't himself?"

Frustration began to well up inside of me. I never liked being accused of witchcraft, but hearing Thomas consider it was especially hurtful.

"Thomas," I said, with a hint of steel in my own voice. "I am not a warlock. I have never practiced witchcraft at any time. Your father was the way he was long before I got there."

I could tell from the look on his face that he knew I was right.

I sighed, and with it, tried to release my rising irritation before it could turn into anger. I understood the confusion Thomas must be dealing with. I had killed his father, and his father had been accusing me of witchcraft.

"Does it really change things?" I asked. "Would you have been better off not knowing me?"

He didn't say anything.

I wished that, just once, someone would believe that I was good.

But I was wrong; not everyone had believed the worst in me.

"I think I finally see why you don't like sharing anything about your gifts, John," said Hannah. "At first, I thought it would be wonderful to have your abilities. But seeing what you have to put up with makes me feel differently. I even feel sorry for those who persecute you. I can't help but wonder how many other extraordinary talents we miss out on, simply because those with them may be afraid to share. I suppose I just don't understand, and I hope I never really do."

Addressing Thomas, Hannah continued, "I noticed that you, Thomas, have brown eyes. To me, your judgment of John is like me wanting to try all people with brown eyes for witchcraft because I have green, and I consider brown eyes to be a sign of the devil."

"It's not the same thing," Thomas stated flatly.

"Really? How is it different?"

"Well, everyone has eyes. And I don't have any control over my eye color."

"It's the way you were made?"

"Yes."

"John can't help the way he was made. Why should he be burned for God's gifts to him?"

"You're assuming they come from God."

That triggered a fire inside Hannah. But before she could jump to her feet, I placed a restraining hand on her shoulder and gently kept her down.

"It's all right, Hannah."

"It is not all right!"

"What I mean is give him time. Thomas has been forged in the refiner's fire and has been through more than you know. Plus, I've just given him a lot to digest. He is a good man, and I trust that he will treat me fairly. So just give him some time to think about this."

"Give who time to think about what?" asked a deep voice behind me.

I turned and saw James, Sarah, and Jane approaching us.

"Give Thomas time to think about what we told him."

"And what did you tell him?" asked Jane.

"About me."

"Oh," said James.

"You know about John?" asked Thomas.

"I've known for a long time that he has certain abilities; I just didn't know what. But Sarah has informed me of them."

"And that doesn't bother you?"

"Nae, quite the contrary. I see the potential, and I'm very grateful we have him now. Only wish we had him a long time ago."

Thomas looked confused and conflicted.

Sarah walked over and patted his shoulder. "Don't fret and don't force it. Just be patient and fair-minded. In time, you will understand what your heart is already telling you. It won't be long before you see what we see."

"Yes," added Jane. "And if you do what John says, you might even live through the next few days. Which should be easier to do now that John has been chosen to be our chief captain."

"What?" Hannah and I exclaimed in unison.

"I knew I should've gone to the meeting," muttered Hannah. "I could have been a great general."

"You can have it. I want no part!" I exclaimed.

"General would imply that you have an army, which you do not," informed Jane. "What you have is a group of ragtag villagers who are far from soldiers but are excellent marksmen."

I felt panic rise to my throat.

"Can't I have a say in this? I don't even know what I'm doing!"

"We need you," said Sarah. "You're the only one who can get us safely to Syre."

"We're going to Syre?" asked Thomas.

"Aye," replied James. "I have discussed it with the men, and we feel that the good people of Syre would all be willing to house a refugee family for the winter. The plan is for us to travel together until we reach Sarah's cabin; there, the villagers will stop and recoup for a wee bit while we go on and prepare our neighbors for their arrival."

"What about Marysvale?" asked Hannah. "I thought we were going to help them."

"We discussed that possibility as well," said Sarah. "We feel that to try and take a fortress like Marysvale at this time would be futile. We are destitute with many women, children, and wounded in our company. We need to first get them safely to Syre before coming up with a plan for Marysvale. Besides, Syre must also be warned about what's coming, so they can prepare. Considering what John has seen, Merrick's tyranny could spread to Syre and the rest of the country all too soon."

Seeing Hannah's disappointment, Sarah added, "Don't you worry, dear. We will not forget our friends in Marysvale."

I considered the people who would be depending on me. It was one thing to watch over Jane and Hannah, who really didn't need my help. In fact, I was indebted to them for saving my own life. It was quite another to be responsible for the fate of hundreds of individuals. My breathing sped up and came in quick gasps of anxiety.

Reading my panicked expression, Sarah consoled, "Never you fear. You will do fine. You proved that in the forest. Your defense of the men was quite ingenious. It may seem overwhelming now, but you will grow into your assignment."

"What about Angus?" I countered. "He's the leader of this village."

"Angus will organize the moving of the villagers and supplies," said Sarah. "All you have to do is plan our defenses—how to get us there safely."

"Oh, is that all," I grumbled.

The weight of the responsibility fell gravely upon me. I grew lightheaded, and my chest felt tight like something was crushing my lungs.

"Don't you remember how I nearly got us killed coming to Alyth?" I protested. "I can't possibly do it."

Jane shrugged. "That was through no fault of your own. Sometimes things are simply out of your control, no matter what you do. The pieces were already in motion; there was nothing you could have done differently. Sarah is right; you are a great leader, John. You got us to Marysvale, and past the Brean, safely. And you got us out of Marysvale. You were also the key to saving the expedition, at least most of us. We probably wouldn't have lost anybody if they hadn't been so intent on burning you for witchcraft."

"But most of the villagers still want to kill me," I complained.

"Not most," corrected Jane. "Only some. You have more allies than you know. And who would have thought Sabin could be so persuasive?"

"That is not very comforting."

Jane knelt beside me, took one of my hands in hers, and looked up into my face.

"Please, John. We need you. You understand the Brean like no one else. I don't know how, but you do."

She gazed at me with her big green eyes.

"Oh, that's not fair," I muttered.

She smiled. "Shall I take that as a yes?"

"As I don't have a choice, I suppose so."

"Oh, you always have a choice. We can't force you. But we do need your heart in it, or you won't be much use to us."

"You know what I mean. How would I be regarded if I turned it down? What would *you* think of me? Right now, I wish I didn't care, but I do."

Jane put her mouth next to my ear and whispered, "I know. That's why I love you."

Then loud enough for all to hear, she added, "Besides, it won't be so bad; you have all of us. Can we count on you?"

"Again, not fair…but…" I sighed. "I promise I will do what I can."

Jane stood up, turned to Sarah, and smiled. "See, I told you he would do it."

Chapter Three: The Fastest Brean Ever

They may have believed in my abilities, but I didn't. The knowledge that they, and the villagers, were putting their lives into my hands completely terrified me.

What if I make a mistake? What if I end up getting us all killed? Not only must we bypass the Brean safely, but we also need to skirt Marysvale without being caught!

I felt sick.

The danger I was personally facing in returning to Syre was also not lost on me. I had killed the magistrate and would be tried for murder—something that could see me at the end of a noose.

The old desire to run away flared vigorously back to life. More than ever, I wanted to take my friends with me and flee as far away from this cursed region as possible.

However, as much as I desired to run and save my skin, I also knew that my friends would never leave the others to their fate. They would never give up, no matter what happened. And because of their determination, I knew that I would fight right alongside them.

I surveyed the group. Thomas' expression was unreadable. Mr. Shepherd looked stoic and more like a leader than I ever would. Jane and Sarah both smiled reassuringly. As for

Hannah, although she tried hiding it, I could tell she was crestfallen.

Hannah loved to strategize, and I needed help. Perhaps she lacked experience, but I knew her mind was swimming with ideas.

"Don't look so forlorn," I said. "You're not getting out of things that easily. I still need a superior strategist by my side."

Hannah's face brightened.

"Not that I'm promising to follow everything you suggest, but, as my tactician, what would be the first thing you would do?"

"Well," she said thoughtfully, "darkness is falling fast, and there are still a lot of things that need to be completed. However, I believe the first thing I would do if I were you is to start looking at our situation as a war. They fired the first shot and, with it, they decimated the town. Of course, I suppose you could look at it as Lord Wright fired the first shot a long time ago when he joined forces with the Brean. Either way, being in a war, would you allow two of the enemy scouts to constantly watch your forces and always be informed of your movements?"

"No, I don't expect I would."

"Then there are two scouts that are watching us right now that need to be dealt with."

"Very well, General Hannah."

I turned and studied the position of the two Brean. Their location was such that one would have to pass between them to get to Marysvale.

I looked back at my friends.

"Thomas, if my memory doesn't fail me in my old age, I seem to recall that you are a decent shot from horseback. Care to come with me and see one of those beasts up close?"

Thomas hesitated, looked at the dark woods, and then replied, "No, not particularly."

But he couldn't suppress a grin and stood up anyway, lifting his musket with him.

"Jane?"

She nodded and stood.

"I want to come," pleaded Hannah.

"Oh, don't you worry," responded Sarah. "There will be plenty of opportunities to have your turn. For now, however, you would be wise to use that arm of yours as little as possible."

"I suppose," she said begrudgingly.

I stood up.

"We will need our horses. Thomas, how's your mount?" I asked.

"I'm on Shade. He's the best one we have. He's not as swift as Smoke, but he's fast enough."

"Good. We'll also need two rifles each and two pistols. Between the three of us, we'll have twelve shots. That should be enough. And if someone knows where my crossbow is, I'd appreciate taking it, too."

"Leave the weapons to me," said Sarah. "I'll fetch them and meet you at the horses."

With that, we separated.

Sarah and James went to get the needed weapons while Jane, Hannah, Thomas, and I set off to the makeshift corral.

"Thomas?" I asked.

"Yes?"

"There are a few things you need to know about the Brean. Despite their size, they are very swift and nimble; Shade will have to dig deep to outrun them. And their strength is lethal. They are also smart, but they can be tricked. Shoot them in the head if you are able. It's your only real chance of getting them with one shot. Otherwise, it will take at least two or three to drop one. Be prepared with your other weapons, should you miss."

He nodded.

"Jane, can you see well enough to shoot from a distance?"

She peered out into the growing blackness. "I don't know; it's getting awfully dark. It depends on how close we are."

"Thomas, how about you?"

"I'm with Jane. I can't see very well; but, I expect if we got close enough, I could hit it."

I sighed. "I was afraid that was the case. I suppose it'll have to be me then. I don't want to get too close if we can help it."

"Won't they charge when they see us coming?" asked Thomas.

"I don't think so. These are just scouts. From what I've observed, they don't do much other than watch."

"In that case, what if they run when they see us?"

I contemplated his question for a moment before responding, "How about this? Let's ride between them both as if we were on our way to Marysvale, pretending that we don't see them. After we've passed the one farthest away from Alyth, we'll turn, and I'll shoot. If I miss, and it charges, I'll try again. In case of another miss, then you two will be my backup. I don't know what the other Brean will do, but if it runs, we'll be in a position to intercept it."

"Sounds like a good plan," said Thomas.

"Jane?" I asked.

After a brief consideration, she replied, "Your idea is as sound as any I can come up with."

"Then that's what we'll do."

Arriving at the corral, I saw Smoke in the herd. As much as it pained me to leave him behind, I wouldn't be taking him. He deserved a good, long rest.

Selecting a bridle, I searched for the horse Hannah had ridden to Alyth. Spotting him, I ducked under the rope and headed in his direction. Smoke trotted over and greeted me.

Patting him on the neck, I said, "Sorry, big fellow, not today."

Turning, I walked through the midst of the other horses.

Smoke nudged me with his muzzle.

Stroking his cheek, I muttered, "Get some rest, Smoke; I won't be gone long. Besides, we won't be separated much over the next few days."

Turning around again, I continued over to the other horse. All the while, I could hear Smoke following, his warm breath washing over my neck and shoulder.

Again, I turned to face him.

As I was about to scold him, I stopped. He stared at me with big, dark eyes, looking as if he wondered what he had done to displease me. Why else would I be taking another horse? Of course, he may not have been thinking that at all, but after having lived with him so long, that was my impression.

I sighed. "Well, I suppose it's not that far. You can come if you insist."

Leading him out of the corral, I found Jane and Thomas already in the process of saddling their mounts while Hannah looked on. I dropped the bridle that I had selected earlier and, after a brief search, located Smoke's tack.

"I wish I could ride him," confessed Thomas. "It's been a long time, and he's the kind of challenge I like."

"I'm sure you'll get another chance fairly soon," I said.

"I haven't had another chance yet," Jane said wistfully.

"Wait, John *and* Smoke let you ride him?" asked Thomas in astonishment.

"He didn't have much choice…and neither did Smoke. It was a bit of a battle at the beginning, but after a short war, I won."

Thomas laughed. "That's how it was for me, too. Except I had to beg John to let me try."

"You didn't have to beg," I said defensively. "I was just concerned that you didn't know what you were getting into."

"That's probably true. Smoke did put up quite a fight, but it was sure worth it."

"Well, don't you worry; there will be plenty of opportunities to ride him."

Hannah snorted. "You can all have him. He scares me."

"You don't like to ride?" asked Thomas.

"I don't mind riding. Smoke just makes me nervous."

"He probably senses that," said Thomas.

"Probably," Hannah agreed.

Daylight had nearly deserted us. I peered into the forbidding woods.

"I suppose we best get this over with," I sighed. "No sense in waiting."

"Except you may want to wait for the rifles," said Jane in a teasing manner. "Unless you plan on killing them with your bare hands again."

"You killed them with your bare hands?" asked Thomas incredulously.

"I didn't hear about that," Hannah chimed in.

"I only killed one, and I didn't do it with my hands. I had a hatchet."

Hannah let out a slow whistle. "Still, that's amazing. I don't know anyone else who's been able to kill one without a musket or something like that."

"I know someone else," I replied.

"Who?" asked Hannah. "He must have been strong."

"Yes," I agreed. "She is."

Her eyes narrowed. "Well, who is it?"

"Your sister," I answered.

Jane shook her head. "That's hardly the same thing. I just tricked it and then shoved it over a cliff. The lake below is what killed it."

"Well, I think it still counts," I said. "Anyway, I haven't forgotten that we need our weapons. Where is Sarah?"

I looked around and found her walking toward us.

"Oh, there she is with Mr. Shepherd…and Mr. Shepherd."

Apparently, Sarah had ministered to Angus' burns since his arms were wrapped up in fresh bandages. We led our horses to meet them.

"Ah," said Angus. "I can see we made a smart choice in our chief captain. Already you're goin' to work."

"Actually, sir, it was Hannah's idea."

Angus peered at her. "Oh, it was, was it?"

He smiled. "There's some spunk in this wee one; we need that around here."

Then, chuckling softly, Angus murmured, "Though her future husband might feel differently."

He winked at me conspiratorially.

"Yes," I agreed with a grin.

Then, whispering to Jane, I added, "I can hardly wait to see it."

Jane stealthily jabbed me in the ribs.

"Ouch! You know you are just as curious as I am," I complained.

She hissed, "Perhaps, but I wouldn't say it like that."

Still, despite her tone, a smile crept across her face.

Hannah furrowed her brow and glared at me.

"What?" I said defensively. "You didn't hear me say anything."

"I don't have to hear you say anything to know what you said."

I muttered something unintelligible, which may or may not have contained something about women and no sense of humor.

And with that, I swung up into the saddle.

Thomas and Jane followed suit.

James and Angus handed us each two rifles while Sarah passed out the pistols, adding the crossbow to my load. I accepted it gratefully.

After we secured our weapons, Sarah looked up at us. "It always seems a bit silly to say be careful, as if you were planning otherwise. But, please, do be careful."

"Don't worry," replied Jane. "I'll keep an eye on him."

"Comforting that we have at least one adult on this venture," added Hannah.

"What about me?" Thomas asked defensively.

Hannah smiled playfully. "Yes, well, you *are* male *and* the friend of a witch, so naturally, you have two things working against you. I suppose we'll just have to see."

"Warlock," I muttered. "At least get the term right."

I nudged Smoke into a trot and angled him toward Marysvale.

The others caught up quickly.

"Is she always like that?" asked Thomas.

"Unfortunately," I replied.

"John!" scolded Jane.

"Oh, very well," I conceded. "Not always. There are times when she surprises me. She is remarkably strong. And I do like having her around. However, if either of you dare to repeat it, I will deny everything."

Both Jane and Thomas smiled, and then Thomas turned to look at me, his face suddenly serious.

"Where are the monsters?"

"In front of us, not far. There is one on our left and one on our right. Both are perched high in trees."

We traveled a short distance before Thomas asked another question. "Do you think the Brean can understand our speech?"

I looked at Jane for her thoughts. She shrugged.

"I don't know," I confessed. "I know that their leader can, but I don't know how well."

"Perhaps we should treat them like they do understand," he suggested. "And remember that most animals have excellent hearing."

"That is a good point, Thomas," agreed Jane.

We each fell silent.

When we passed under them, I opened my vision again and tried not to look up. A mild jolt of surprise passed through me as I discovered something I had never noticed before. Although the Brean were on opposite sides of the path, a half-mile apart, I could see both of them just as well as if I were looking directly at them. I recalled the times I had used my gift in this way and realized that it had never dawned on me that I didn't have to move my eyes to see everything. I did move them, of course, but that was just out of habit.

We kept going until they disappeared behind us.

"Almost time," I said quietly. "The one on our right first."

Thomas withdrew a rifle. Jane and I hadn't bothered stowing ours; both were respectively resting across our saddles. She merely lifted hers as I did mine.

I nudged Smoke forward and turned him toward our chosen target, positioning him so I could take a shot and not hit Jane or Thomas in the process.

The Brean watched our approach.

As we continued towards it, the monster shifted its stance from a leisurely position to a ready one.

When I judged we were close enough, I reined up Smoke.

At that exact moment, it made a decision. In one swift movement, the Brean squatted and jumped. As it fell, it twisted so that it had its back turned toward us.

I brought my rifle up, aimed, and followed its path through the air.

The Brean dropped adeptly through the branches and caught a limb. Using its momentum, it swung its feet in an arc, somersaulting away from the lower branches and trunk.

It landed in a squat and then sprang up, preparing to flee.

I squeezed the trigger.

The rifle belched its deadly little projectile. The ball hit, catching the Brean in mid-leap, square in the back. It yelped and tumbled to the ground.

I spun my head to the left. The second monster was already down from the tree and sprinting—straight away from us.

I turned to tell Jane but then observed that my first shot hadn't been fatal. The Brean had regained its footing and was preparing to run.

"JANE, THOMAS!" I shouted.

"We have him!" yelled Jane, not needing any further explanation.

I kicked Smoke into action and charged after the second monster.

As we galloped away, both Jane and Thomas' rifles fired almost simultaneously.

I didn't bother looking back.

The fleeing Brean was fast, really fast.

We hurtled through the forest after it. Smoke seemed to revel in the chase. His strides were powerful, not tired like I had feared. The wind rushed by, causing my eyes to moisten in protest. Tears streamed back across my face.

I ducked my head and looked back at Thomas and Jane. They had successfully dispatched the first Brean to the afterlife, its spirit visible to my sight. Though they raced toward us, in the wake of Smoke's pursuit, they rapidly fell behind.

My heart pounded as the excitement of the chase pumped through my veins.

We gained on the monster, but not as quickly as I had expected.

It was definitely the fastest Brean I had ever seen.

The woods thickened, forcing Smoke to slow—a problem the Brean didn't seem to have. It used its long arms, knuckles, and hands to propel it over logs and around trees. At times, it ran on all fours, ducking under branches.

I hunched low in the saddle as twigs reached out and snagged at my clothing.

The impossibly fast Brean abruptly altered course and angled back toward Marysvale.

This was its first mistake.

And the second was closely related to the first.

It ran through a patch of woods where the trees were thin, giving me an opening for a shot. But in that same instant, I realized what it was planning and that my chances of killing it were speedily drawing to an end.

Ahead was a thicket. If the Brean entered the dense foliage, it would be free. Smoke would surely charge in if I desired, but it would be a struggle to merely penetrate the first few feet, let alone maneuver a gun. The vast entanglement of twigs would make any shot impossible for a rifle and a crossbow. Using the pistol, I'd have to land both shots perfectly. And with my aim, well, that would be a miracle.

I had one slight chance and little time to take it. I turned Smoke and mentally plotted where to intercept the monster.

We angled toward it from the side.

Smoke galloped hard, and we closed in on the beast.

Standing up in the saddle, I took aim and squeezed the trigger.

The rifle boomed and bucked in my hands. White gunsmoke blasted out the end only to swirl around us as we galloped through.

The Brean yelped.

I felt triumphant. I had hit it! But I didn't know where or how badly.

My victory was short-lived.

The yelp turned into a menacing snarl.

Suddenly, the monster dropped down on all fours—hands and claws dug into the ground, and with a twist of its body, it sent its feet skidding around.

It ended its slide in a crouch, facing us.

Instantly, my triumph turned to terror.

The Brean roared and sprang.

Using its arms like paddles, it rowed forward as it gathered speed.

I stole a quick glance behind me.

Jane and Thomas were too far away to help.

Facing forward, I turned my attention to the problem at hand. With me bouncing up and down on a galloping horse, I reasoned that the pistols would be equally useless since I had missed with the rifle.

The gap between us was closing much too fast.

Smoke didn't yield one bit in the face of the charging monster. If he felt any fear, he didn't show it.

I took my best chance.

Dropping the rifle, I snatched up the crossbow, aimed at an eye, and pulled the trigger.

The bolt shot toward the monster, past it, and disappeared into the woods.

The Brean had seen my movements and had leaped sideways.

Now running a parallel course, we drew closer.

I let the second bolt fly.

It sailed through the air, twirling as it flew.

The bolt's wicked tip plunged into the Brean's shoulder near its collarbone.

The monster howled in pain and rage.

Without missing a step, it reached up and tore it out.

The Brean was now close enough to smell its dank and unwelcome scent.

Our eyes locked, and, in an instant, I saw my fate and knew there was no time to change it.

Chapter Four: Confusion

The monster's black eyes burned with fury as it again dug its hands and claws into the ground. Colossal muscles rippled with raw power, tearing the earth as it altered course. Its feet skated sideways, but this time, it only made a quarter turn.

Dropping the crossbow, my hands dove for the pistols in my belt.

The beast sprang into the air like a mountain lion pouncing its prey.

While still fumbling with the pistols, I rocketed forward in the saddle, hunching down in a desperate attempt to save myself.

The monster shot towards us.

Smoke, still in a gallop, took another stride. I could sense the beast passing behind me.

It worked! I thought in jubilation.

But then it came.

The mammoth arm of the Brean collided with me and ripped me up and out of the saddle.

With its massive arm around my chest, the monster drew me in tightly, squeezing me against its body and filling my nose, mouth, and lungs with a choking, putrid stink.

As we plummeted toward the ground, the Brean's crushing force intensified, growing so strong that breathing became difficult and then impossible. The air was literally squeezed out of me. My ribs and arms felt like they would break at any moment from the tremendous pressure.

With the agility of a cat, the beast landed on its legs and free arm.

My hands still fumbled on the pistol grips, frantically trying to maneuver them against the devastating embrace of the monster.

The Brean stood up and wrapped its other arm around me. Its chest heaved as it drew in a great breath of air. In a moment, I knew that building power would translate into terrible strength, and the monster would pulverize me.

I was able to move one of the pistols over the top of my belt. It came free but was immediately smashed between our bodies.

The sucking intake from the monster reached its pinnacle. I could feel the beginnings of a dreadful roar rumbling deep in the chest of the beast as its muscles began to contract.

Angling the pistol at the belly of the beast the best I could, and, hoping I wasn't shooting myself instead, I pulled the trigger.

The blast was muffled between our bodies, but the roar of pain from the Brean wasn't.

Its crushing embrace slackened enough so that I could get the other pistol free.

Without hesitation, I turned it, pointing up into the monster's stomach, and fired.

The Brean let go.

I fell, my legs buckling underneath me as I hit the ground.

Blessed air rushed into my lungs, and I inhaled hungrily.

The monster stumbled back.

Incredibly, it hadn't fallen. It lurched about, grasping its stomach and side.

Uncontrollable panic welled inside me.

The Brean still lived, and I was out of shots.

The only thing I could think to do was to run. I leaped up and sprinted away.

After a few yards, my brain slowly kicked in.

Where are you running? it asked.

In truth, I didn't know. I hadn't thought about it.

WELL, THINK ABOUT IT!

In a split second, I took in my surroundings and situation. I'd been running straight away from the monster, but that was across the open. It could easily catch up with me.

I scanned for Smoke and found him. He had galloped away from the thicket.

The Brean noticed my glance and realized my intention. It stopped staggering and rushed to put itself between us. Though its movements weren't as sharp and swift as before, there was still power and purpose in them.

The thicket, run there!

It wasn't much of a plan, but I wasn't going to lie down and make it easy, at least not any easier than it would already be for the gigantic brute.

I turned and sprinted as fast as I could for the dense bushes. My feet beat upon the ground, and my lungs burned as they tried desperately to keep up with the demands of my legs.

I sensed the beast pursuing. It gave a small, labored grunt with each footstep as it ran.

Though wounded, I knew it would catch me.

That thought filled me with dread.

How long would it take to catch up? Would it just bash me on the head? Smash me between both hands? Kick? Bite? Claw? Would it toy around with me?

Fear coursed through my body. My heart pounded so furiously; it felt like it would leap from my chest and sprint away on its own.

The thicket loomed in front of me, and I threw myself into it.

Branches and twigs lashed out at my face. I raised my arms in an attempt to keep them at bay.

A few steps later, the monster crashed in behind me.

Baleful sounds resonated all about me like thunder.

I envisioned the Brean simply reaching out and pinching me between its thumb and forefinger and then lifting me from my feet like a mouse.

Turn now, and run to Smoke!

I decided to listen to the voice in my head and spun around. Shoving my way through the undergrowth, I half ran, half stumbled. Even with my forearms protecting my face, twigs still whipped my cheeks and ears. A few times, even my hair got caught. I didn't stop. Whatever discomfort or pain I felt was still better than the fatal sting of claws in my back.

I continued on in terrified desperation, driving my protesting muscles, heart, and, especially, lungs.

Suddenly and without warning, I burst into the clearing.

Without the expected resistance from branches, I stumbled and fell.

This is it, I thought. *It has me.*

For the briefest of moments, I considered staying down. But then Jane flashed in my mind, and I continued my roll right over and rose to my feet.

I whistled for Smoke. Blessedly, he came running.

As he approached, I reached up and grabbed the saddlehorn in one hand and a fist full of mane in the other. I took a step and launched up, pulling myself into the seat.

Grabbing the reins, I turned Smoke away from the thicket.

Stealing a look back—

I stopped, frozen in my tracks.

The Brean was no longer chasing me.

It still moved toward me, but it was no longer running. In a futile effort to staunch the flow of blood, the Brean pressed one hairy hand to its side and another a little higher up over its stomach.

But that wasn't what stopped me.

I stopped because the dark vortex of the monster had disappeared.

In its place shone a soul.

How is this possible? Is the transformation just part of their death process?

The creature stumbled and collapsed to its knees, lurching forward. Involuntarily, a hand left one of the wounds and kept it from falling flat.

The Brean rested for a moment; its breathing labored.

This is the end, I thought.

But I was wrong.

With tremendous effort, the Brean pushed up off the ground and continued staggering forward.

Hearing the sound of horse hooves thudding behind me, I turned.

Jane and Thomas pulled up, one on each side of me.

"Sorry that it took us so long," Jane exclaimed. "We lost you and had to follow your gunshots."

A rustling came from the thicket.

Both Jane and Thomas immediately drew their rifles.

I held my hands up. "Don't shoot."

The Brean pushed through the last of the undergrowth and into the clearing. It still held one hand to its stomach, but the other hung loosely by its side.

"You *don't* want us to shoot it?" Thomas asked incredulously.

"No," I replied. "It won't harm us now. Its fight is all gone."

Jane lowered her rifle and rested it across her saddle. Thomas started to but instead decided to keep it ready just in case.

"How do you know?" Thomas asked doubtfully.

"I've seen it before. I believe when the Brean are mortally wounded, and they know their death is near, they give up."

"How many times have you seen it?"

"Once or twice."

He didn't seem placated.

But then, the Brean fell to both knees.

It hesitated there for a moment before collapsing onto its side.

And then, the Brean did something odd. It looked directly into my eyes, pleadingly.

"Should we go?" asked Jane.

"In a moment," I whispered curiously.

I leapt into its soul.

The first thing I noticed was that it felt pain. And at that moment, the Brean was consumed with it. I couldn't feel it, but I knew it was there—like watching a storm through a pane of glass. I supposed that, like the images I'd seen in Naehume, feelings were universal. They were physical, tangible, and common between species. Of course, the Brean were the *only* animals I could read in some fashion. Any other animal was a mystery to me, like looking into a muddy river. Well, muddy wasn't quite the correct term. They were beautiful in their own right but still impossible to understand. Perhaps the similarities between our shared physical structures allowed me this link.

Thoughts, on the other hand, made no sense to me. They were there but in a different language; I just couldn't interpret them.

After a moment, I realized that it was repeating the same thought over and over again. I still didn't know what it meant, but the patterns were definitely the same. Occasionally, it would reflect on something else, which felt different than the repeated one. Then it would refocus and echo the familiar patterns.

The Brean's life force ebbed away slowly, and the link between us grew weaker. A searing surge of pain rolled through its body, and with it came something else unexpected.

The thought returned, but this time its eyes grew more concentrated, more penetrating. They narrowed and felt like they were boring into my soul.

I flinched from the intensity, and the link broke—but not the gaze of the Brean. Its eyes still fixated on mine.

Jane, studying me, asked, "What is it? What do you see?"

Her question piqued Thomas' curiosity. He glanced between the Brean and me, still not trusting that it wouldn't jump up and attack.

My eyes furrowed. "I…"

Hesitating, I looked at her. "I don't know for sure. But… I think… I think it wants help."

"It looks beyond help to me," said Thomas.

"Yes," I agreed.

I reached out a hand to Jane with the palm up. Instinctively, she knew what I wanted and handed me her rifle.

The Brean watched as I lifted it to my shoulder.

Suddenly, its eyes rolled back into his skull, its chest heaved, and it seemed like it had wholly given up the fight.

Its end was only a matter of time.

Aiming the rifle at the Brean's head, I hesitated.

The beast had regained focus and was again beseeching me.

I closed my eyes, unsure of what to do.

But there was nothing to do; the Brean was dying. The only question was how long it would take and whether or not I would leave it there to suffer.

My feelings confused me. Mere minutes ago, I had believed it to be a terrible demon—as it still could be. But at that moment, all I saw was something as helpless and innocent as a wounded fawn.

Finally, opening my eyes, I aimed and pulled the trigger.

Immediately, I looked away, unable to meet the gaze of the specter that stood over its former body. I didn't want to see it—to meet its questioning stare, especially after it had tried to kill me.

Correction, said my inner voice, *after you had tried and succeeded in killing it.*

You're not helping, I argued back.

Without a word, I turned Smoke and set off. The other two followed and fell in at my sides.

"Is that what it wanted?" asked Thomas. "For you to put it out of its misery?"

I didn't answer. I didn't truly know.

Locating my discarded crossbow, I slid off Smoke and retrieved it.

Jane, sensing there was more, asked, "What is it? What bothers you?"

Shrugging, I answered, "I don't know what it wanted. I just didn't want to see it lying there suffering."

She peered at me through the darkness. I didn't meet her eyes.

I found the rifle, picked it up, and then remounted.

"There *is* more, isn't there?"

"You're becoming like Sarah."

"Thank you; that is a compliment. I have also been around you long enough to pick up on things. Like the way you keep your head down when you're avoiding something."

I looked up.

"Too late. I already know there's more."

I sighed and let my shoulders sag a bit.

"See? I was right."

"It's just not supposed to be like this."

"What do you mean?" asked Thomas.

"The Brean are such vicious fighters—like they enjoy it. When evil people die, their souls are in turmoil. It is not a peaceful experience. But it's different when good people die; it's very serene. It's even beautiful to watch them move on to the next phase of their existence."

"And the Brean?"

"It's peaceful."

I shrugged my shoulders again. "I don't know; perhaps Naehume is right. Maybe they truly believe they are fighting for their existence."

"Who is Naehume?" asked Thomas.

"He is the king of the Brean."

"And you can talk to him?"

"We all can," answered Jane. "He is able to speak our language. Well, more or less."

"I've been connected with him in some of my dreams," I confessed.

Instantly, I wished I hadn't said that part.

Thomas let out a low whistle. "Boy, this just keeps getting better by the minute."

"Glad you came?" I asked.

"Heavens, no."

"Well, I'm glad you're here," I said sincerely.

"You are? Why?"

"Because you're my friend, and I need as many of those as I can get."

"I haven't forgotten about your witchcraft," he said pointedly.

"No," I said. "But here you are by my side, and that says something for you. If you weren't my friend in some capacity, you wouldn't be here now."

Thomas looked down. "You're right. I've been thinking. It isn't even really about your powers or my father; if it truly were, I wouldn't have come out here with you. I suppose I'm hurt that you wouldn't trust me enough to tell me about yourself. That's what is getting to me."

"I'm sorry," I replied regretfully. "I was so afraid of being driven out of Syre that I did everything I could to hide my true self. Beyond that, it's not a topic most people warm up to, and I didn't want to risk losing your friendship. Looking back, I should have trusted you."

Thomas deliberated for a moment and then added, "Well, I suppose I can understand your fear. And I'm glad you didn't use it against me. You could play some cruel tricks with those abilities."

"Oh, you have no idea how tricky he can be," said Jane.

"I am not," I replied defensively.

"No? What about the time you tricked Hannah when we first met and took her pistols? When we feared you might have killed Sarah."

"You were going to kill me!"

"Was not. And then you tricked me into allowing you to escort us back to Marysvale by making me believe you couldn't shoot a crossbow."

Thomas bobbed his head in agreement. "Yep, I fell for that one once too. Ended up mucking out a barn."

Again, I protested, "That was Sarah's doing; she wanted me to go with you. And I didn't really trick you; you just assumed I couldn't be that skilled."

"You evaded a whole army of soldiers in Marysvale. You also tricked the slave minister and sold two soldiers into slavery."

"We couldn't afford to be found out. Plus, they were beating an old, defenseless man. It was more out of desperation than craftiness. Besides, I'm sure once the mistake was discovered, the soldiers were freed."

Jane waved her hand dismissively and turned to address Thomas.

"And then he orchestrated our escape out of an impossible fortress, as well as eluded the soldiers that pursued us all the way to Alyth. And that was after wreaking havoc on their ranks."

I raised my finger to protest and then put it down.

"Well, that actually is fairly accurate. But, I did have some help from a pretty good marksman."

"*Pretty* good?"

"Very well, one of the best I've seen," I added with a grin.

"That's better."

Thomas' face held a look of complete astonishment.

"I haven't heard about any of this," he said in wonder. "Maybe I am glad I came with you after all. Just start from the beginning."

And so, for the rest of our ride back, we related the events from Sarah's cabin to the present day.

Chapter Five: Whom to Trust

I knew I should've joined you," said Hannah as we trotted up.

James and Sarah were also waiting.

"I don't believe it would've made much difference," I replied while dismounting Smoke.

Noticing the scratches on my face, Sarah asked, "What happened?"

I shrugged. "I had to run through some bushes."

"Tell me about it."

And so I did, while James and Thomas led Smoke, Ember, and Shade away to be cared for.

By the time I had finished relating the events, with the usual interruptions and clarification requests from Sarah, they had returned.

Coming from the direction of the supplies, I noticed Angus shuffling toward us, carrying a brightly lit torch. Sabin walked by his side.

Following my gaze, Jane said, "They will want to know your plans for defending the villagers."

Instantly, the familiar, sinking feeling of incompetence overwhelmed me.

Don't worry. I tried telling myself. *Just because there are a host of men, women, and children depending on you doesn't mean that you will lead them all to their doom...*

Stop it! You're not helping! I chided myself.

Sarah, seeing, or perhaps sensing, my conflict, said reassuringly, "Calm your fears. I know you can do this, John. Trust your instinct."

Angus, closing in, shouted enthusiastically, "Been doin' a wee bit of huntin'?"

He raised his cane and aimed it like a musket.

"Is he always this cheerful after a disaster?" I muttered to James.

Smiling, James replied, "Aye. He would say, 'There is good in everythin' that happens. Our job is to find that good and build upon it.'"

"Even when there is only bad?" I asked doubtfully.

"Especially then. Every trial has the potential to either make you or break you. It's all a matter of choice."

"Comforting," I muttered, not sounding a bit convinced.

My mind scrambled for a plan, searching its catacombs for something, anything that could protect such a large number of people.

Nothing.

It was one thing to defend myself, or perhaps even a small group of people, but an entire village? Now that was truly daunting.

I sighed and turned, surveying the wreckage of Alyth, the surrounding fields, and the dark, skeletal forest beyond.

Sabin and Angus drew up to our little gathering.

"Did ye go after the beastie in the tree?" asked Angus.

I nodded.

"Thought ye might have from all the rifle commotion," he said.

"There were two of them," I remarked.

"And what about the others that are still out there?" asked Sabin, sweeping his hand toward the woods. "How shall we proceed to protect the town?"

What town? I thought.

There was no town, no homes, no buildings. But I knew he meant the villagers, so I kept my tongue.

Closing my eyes, I deliberated for a moment.

And then, turning to Hannah, I asked, "Well, what do you reckon? Suppose they'll be back again tonight?"

Without hesitation, she shook her head. "No, I don't believe so."

"Neither do I," I agreed.

"Why wouldn't they?" asked Thomas.

"Do you want to explain?" I asked Hannah. "Or shall I?"

She jumped at the invitation and said, "Well, I suppose the Brean *could* attack again tonight, but why? Although our village is lost to us, we still hold an excellent defensive position, at least for the moment. With the flames dying, we can enter what's left of Alyth and stay warm. We will still be surrounded by water, so their only point of advancement is across the bridge—something we can easily defend. Why take on that obstacle when they can simply wait and come after us in the unprotected forest? They know that, with winter setting in and our food stores burned up, we need to leave *now*. They will expect us to evacuate to Marysvale or perhaps push on to Syre and beyond. Regardless, they know the direction we will be traveling.

"I agree with Hannah," I said. "However, since we can't be entirely sure, we will need to take some precautions. Have all the villagers moved inside the town?"

"Aye," said Angus.

"Good. This journey is going to be perilous. With so many in our company walking, I'm calculating that it will take us two weeks to reach Syre. By then, we'll likely be fighting the weather as well as our hunger. Do the people know the plan and what we are up against?"

"Aye. The council called a meetin', and we filled them in."

"Did you tell them about the Brean's alliance with Lord Wright?"

"Aye."

"How did they take the news?" I asked.

"Ah, they were heartsick about Jex and his treachery. The Brean's connection with Merrick was also somewhat disturbin', but I'm nae sure all are quite believin' it yet."

"We will be in danger from both Brean and the soldiers of Marysvale, especially when we near the town. Are they willing to defend themselves against men and monsters?"

"Aye. They'll nae soon forget what happened here. I believe they will fight."

I nodded.

Taking a few steps forward, I took Angus by the elbow and said, "May I ask you something in private?"

Sarah raised an eyebrow but said nothing.

"Of course," he replied, a bit confused.

We stepped away from the group.

When I felt sure we were out of earshot, I asked quietly, "Will you release me from my promise?"

"What pledge is that, laddie?"

"The night of the council meeting, you sent Jex to secure a promise that I wouldn't use my gifts to read the villagers."

"Oh that," he waved his hand dismissively. "That was more of Jex's idea than mine. Of course, we know now why he asked."

Angus paused, peering at me with keen eyes. "Laddie, we need yer talents now more than ever. Don't hold back. As long as it is in the interest of doin' good and gettin' us safely through this, by all means, use everythin' available to ye."

Then, with a wry look, he asked, "Would ye truly nae have used them if still bound by yer word?"

"I don't know," I replied honestly. "It may have depended on the situation. But with a release, I won't have to grapple with my conscience."

Angus regarded me shrewdly. "Oh, ye most certainly will; it is part of bein' a leader during such times. Lives are at stake, and lives will be lost; it is unavoidable. Ye will have to bear them on yer conscience. And I know they will be in yer thoughts. I believe it is one of the qualities that will make ye great. Nothin' worse than a leader who cares more about himself than the lives of the people he is about to change. However, with that said, don't let it paralyze ye."

I remembered Sabin and the words I had spat at him in anger.

I chastised him and said that he would have to account for the men who had died because of his poor decisions. He must have believed that he was doing the right thing, but it was still wrong, and the consequences were devastating. I wondered if he felt the bitter sting of regret.

Then, I wondered how I would feel when my turn came to tell a family how their loved one had died under my charge. Will they look at me with understanding, or will it too be in anger? As I considered this, much of my resentment toward Sabin melted away.

Angus watched me silently with knowing eyes—filled with wisdom and compassion. He patted my arm and then returned to the group.

I lingered a moment longer. Sabin's men had followed his commands, even though he was wrong. Whom could I trust to stand by me? My position was a precarious one. I had been chosen to lead the villagers to safety. The problem was, many of them still felt that I was the enemy. Would they be working to subvert our cause? No doubt they would believe they were doing the right thing.

I shook my head at the thought and walked back to the others.

Jane, Sarah, and Hannah looked at me questioningly. I knew they all wanted to know what I'd asked, but I decided to ignore them for the time being.

Approaching Sabin, I inquired, "How are your ribs?"

Sabin had been hurt during our fateful expedition for the sulfur. However, I also had an ulterior motive in asking. I wanted to see if I could trust him. My feeling was that he had changed toward me. There wasn't the same animosity between us as before. After all, he had come to my defense when the villagers wanted to kill me and taken full accountability for my unjust flogging.

Still, I needed to be sure.

He felt this side absentmindedly and replied, "Hurts to move my arm on that side."

"Are they broken?"

He fingered his ribs again. "Don't know. Thought I might have at first; now, I don't think so. I can't feel anything definitive. Perhaps cracked or bruised. Either way, I'll do what needs to be done."

While he answered, I took the opportunity to read him.

I could sense his heavy burden. He indeed suffered great remorse over the expedition. I also sensed hatred, but it wasn't aimed at me. Sabin abhorred those responsible for the destruction of Alyth. There was no deceit in him. In short, about what I expected and certainly hoped. I could trust him.

I let it close as he finished.

"Very well," I said. "If you feel up to it, Sabin, have Sam, Ben, and Matthias help you round up the best shooters in the village and arm them. They will need to position themselves at the gate and sleep there tonight. If I see anything, I will alert them, most likely with a rifle shot."

I paused, and Sabin nodded once, indicating that he understood.

"In the morning," I continued, "the four of you will organize the villagers into teams of three. We'll follow the plan we already worked out in the forest. Assign the strongest of the

82

three to be the primary shooter, and then assign a secondary, and then loader. Form as many teams as we have weapons."

Considering further, I added, "For every rifle, assign backups from the rest of the villagers, in case a shooter falls. Every able person should know what they are to do should there be an available rifle. Organize them in such a way that they will travel with their prospective shooter, so they are prepared to step in should the time arrive."

"And then what? How will we proceed once the teams are formed?"

"I'm still figuring that out; I'll instruct you tomorrow. This should be enough for right now."

Sabin nodded once. "I'll see to it."

With that, he turned and walked away.

"Now what?" asked Jane.

I turned to Angus. "Are we prepared to move in the morning?"

He hesitated before answering, "We're still workin' on that. We have one wagon."

"Was it fixed?" I interrupted, remembering our damaged wagon from the expedition.

"Aye, but we have wee more supplies than space, and there are the wounded too. Many of them aren't able to walk. There's some disagreement over what to do about them."

"Food, gun powder, and balls are the essentials. Everything else can be left behind."

"Aye, we know that already. And I agree with ye. Still, it is easier said than done. The council is divided over what is essential."

"Can't you make them do what they're told?"

Angus rubbed the back of his neck and replied, "Perhaps so, but I don't rightly know. Some blame me for the destruction of Alyth. They believe I was foolish in my trust of ye. My authority at this point is a wee bit shaky. They will do what I say as long as they agree with it. Any blind trust at this point is over."

I nodded in understanding.

"Mr. Shepherd?" I asked James.

"Aye," he replied. "Now that my father is here, call me James. Less confusing."

"Very well. Are you willing to help?"

"Aye. It is why I'm here."

"Though some of the villagers may remember you, it's been a long time, and they don't know your men, which means that the men from Syre are not conflicted by personal feelings for the people. Do you believe your men will do what I, or *we* say?"

James nodded.

"Even when they hear that I'm a warlock?"

He hesitated.

In that reluctance, I learned what I already suspected.

Not bothering to wait for his reply, I asked, "Will you go and bring your men to me? They will find out eventually, and it's better that they hear it from me rather than from the villagers and their half-truths—or outright fantasies—if they haven't heard them already."

James nodded. "Aye. I think that best as well."

He excused himself and, accompanied by Angus, went to find his companions.

"What are you going to tell them?" asked Thomas.

I shrugged. "The truth. Perhaps not all the details, but I will tell them enough. They need to know what's at stake, and I need them to be untainted by lies. Then, if they choose to reject me, at least it will be in full knowledge of what's real and not rumor."

Thomas nodded in agreement. "In that case, I think I'll go help James."

He turned and ran to catch up with the Shepherds.

"You should try not to ruffle feathers," instructed Hannah.

"In other words, don't be me," I said dryly.

"Exactly."

Jane asked, "How do you think they'll take it?"

"From what I know of these men, I believe them to be just and good. I trust they will do what is best for all of us. In fact, I'm counting on it. The point that they are here shows that they aren't afraid of doing what they believe is right."

Hesitantly, she then asked, "May we know what you talked to Angus about?"

"Oh, that," I replied. "I just wanted to be released from my promise not to read the minds of the people."

"Well, I don't release you!" cried Hannah, taking a step back.

Using her good arm, she made a slithering motion as she added, "I don't want you snaking through my mind and looking at all the secrets of my soul."

I waved my hand dismissively. "I don't need to read you; I already know what there is to know."

Hannah folded her arms and retorted, "*What?* I am a *very* deep person. It would be a pleasure to read me."

"No, thank you."

"I wasn't giving you permission," she snapped.

"All the same."

"Now, children," Sarah reproved. "I am sure John does not need to read any of us."

"But he called me shallow," interrupted Hannah.

"I did not."

"You implied it!"

"Did not," I reaffirmed. "I just agreed with you."

Jane sighed. "And we are putting our fate into the hands of these two."

"I believe your hands are in here just as well," I remarked.

She smiled. "Thank goodness for that."

I watched the men's shadowy figures walk across the open space, led by James and Angus.

"Yes," I replied vaguely.

The others sensed the change in my tone and turned to see what caused it.

I hated this moment. My breathing quickened, and my anxiety escalated. I took a few deep breaths and tried to calm my body and mind.

Chapter Six: Decisions

The men of Syre strode over and halted, patiently waiting for me to speak.

Gathering my courage and hiding my shaking hands, I asked, "Did James tell you why I wanted to speak to you?"

They shook their heads.

"First of all, I wanted to thank you for coming after me. It takes character, especially when I never took the time to get to know any of you."

"Was nothing," muttered a tall fellow who I knew by the name of Ted.

"Well, it's not over. And it *will* be something when it is. You all saw the Brean?"

Again they nodded.

"I thought James was a bit tipsy in the head when he talked about them. Never saw one until we got here," commented Eric.

"You were lucky," I replied. "I suspect it was because they were busy with us. Managing to avoid them completely is a phenomenon that won't be repeated. Odds are, there will be scouts all over the forest watching to see which direction we go."

"What do you mean?" asked Thomas.

"He means," joined in Hannah, "that while they believe we will travel by way of Marysvale, they don't know for sure. We may try to go around and bypass the town altogether."

Thomas scratched his head. "And why would that matter? Why would they care?"

"Because Lord Wright wants to make slaves of us," explained Hannah. "And he can't do that if we skirt past his empire to Syre where we can join forces with other free people. We are a threat to him."

"We can take down a few overgrown bears," interrupted Ted.

"Yes," I agreed. "But these are not bears. And there aren't just a few of them."

I turned to James. "You know this all too well, don't you, James."

He nodded his head and sighed. "I should never have brought you all here. I wrongly supposed that the blood feud with the Brean would be well over by now, and it was safe to return. Since leaving, I never saw another one of them, just heard rumors of an occasional strange beast in the forest. You heard them as well. I believed we had enough of us to take care of a straggler or two, but I had no idea of the magnitude. I should've never brought you all with me."

"How would ye have known?" asked Angus. "I don't think any of us believed it would last this long or go the way it has."

"Sarah?" I asked.

"Yes?" she answered.

"I think they should know everything. Will you tell them?"

"Of course," she replied.

Sarah started at the very beginning when the Brean first showed up. Then she quickly moved on to how Merrick Wright struck a deal with Naehume, how they plotted and coordinated the Brean attacks to create panic and imprison the people within the walls of Marysvale, and how Wright slowly gained control and unaccountable power through his treachery and deceit.

Although Sarah told them how I knew of Wright's secret, she left out any mention of my abilities. I supposed she was saving that for me to share how I saw fit.

She related the circumstances surrounding my arrival at her cabin and our midnight flight to Marysvale. She also recounted how Lyman had murdered Mr. Wolfe, the torture inflicted upon Hannah and herself in the dungeons, and our escape. She ended her tale with the betrayal of Jex and the fall of Alyth.

When Sarah finished, Angus confirmed Sarah's story, as did James. Jane and Hannah also added their testimony to the truthfulness of the events.

I could sense the men felt overwhelmed. Some struggled with it more than others. It was so far outside their realm of reality that their minds had a hard time grasping the certainty of it all. They didn't particularly doubt the story; they were just astonished by this extraordinary tale. If the corpses of the Brean hadn't been scattered about, I suspect they would've thought the whole thing merely a crafty yarn at best; at worst, they would've believed we were lunatics.

Nobody said anything.

I knew my friends were waiting for me to share my part, but they couldn't see what I saw in the men.

I delayed a moment, allowing time for the story to penetrate and sink in.

When I found that most had come to some state of acceptance, I cleared my throat and plunged into my disclosure.

"There is something else you need to know."

Every man looked up and gave me his full attention.

"Lord Wright has his eye beyond Marysvale. The only reason you haven't heard from him yet is that he had his focus on Alyth. With Alyth now destroyed, I fear that Syre is next in line. Like it or not, this is a battle you will face sooner or later. It's coming."

"How do you know this?" asked Eric.

"You're going to find out sooner or later, and likely most of what you will be told will be false. However, some of it will be true, and I want you to hear it from me first in the hope that you will keep an open mind."

I faltered for a moment, searching for the right words.

In that brief indecision, the panic surged inside of me once again.

How do I tell these men from Syre that, although I certainly wasn't in league with the devil, I was indeed different? Would they understand? Or, would they come to the horrible conclusion that Martin was a victim and that *I* was guilty of murder?

They all waited patiently, and I realized they could plainly see the conflict etched on my face. I relaxed my tightly pressed lips and eased the tension in my facial muscles.

I inhaled deeply and then began. "This is not easy for me...."

After another brief hesitation, I finally blurted, "I have certain abilities. For much of my life, I believed them to be more of a burden than a blessing. However, in this country, I'm finding them invaluable. They have indeed saved my life and the lives of others, and they may come to save your lives as well.

"I can see into souls and have a keen intuition about people. I can read their intentions and know if they are honest or deceitful. Another ability I've discovered is that I can see rather far and extraordinarily well in the dark."

Of course, there was more to it than that, but I decided that this simple explanation was enough to convey the essentials without betraying the magnitude of my gifts. I wanted the men to know enough to be aware of what I could do, but not so much as to seriously concern them.

One of them let out a low, slow whistle. "So that dastardly Martin was in part right. Oh, beg your pardon, Thomas."

Thomas didn't seem bothered.

The man wasn't saying it as if he believed Martin. He said it more in wonder at the implications—that perhaps there was something about this that required some pondering.

"No," I replied. "He was in no part right. I am no more a warlock than someone who can touch the hearts of others through music or words, has an eye for beauty, or a way with animals. These are simply the gifts and abilities that *I* have been given. I did not seek them."

I paused then continued, "When I lived in Syre, I left well enough alone, worked hard, and bothered no one. Any evil brought upon your town was done so at the hand of others. As you will recall, the vast majority of it happened well before I arrived."

I could see that they knew this to be true. They all recognized that Martin and the other Syre leaders were tyrants. It was comforting to realize that they hadn't been shaken in their knowledge of them by my revelation.

It also appeared that my fears of being treated as a murderer were unfounded, and I relaxed somewhat. Still, I knew that I wasn't out of the woods yet. We had a long journey ahead of us, and tensions could flare. As James had said, every trial can make or break us. Whether I ended this journey with enemies or friends, only time would tell. Nevertheless, I knew that I had successfully blunted any blow to my reputation that the citizens of Alyth could inflict. I set to work dulling it further.

"The people here are suffering. Their safe haven has been destroyed. The man truly responsible for this disaster is a traitor who fled to Marysvale. The people are looking for someone to blame and to punish. As the odd newcomer, I am an easy scapegoat."

"And you want us to side with you?" asked Ted, with raised eyebrows.

I could tell that he was growing suspicious of what I was setting up. But his suspicions were wrong.

"No," I replied flatly.

This response raised more eyebrows, but in a different way. The men were curious.

"I want you to side with the victims," I continued. "But not necessarily in the way they may wish. I want you to do what is best for them."

"Well, then," replied Ted, "we want the same thing. I don't see the problem."

"I do," replied Eric. "What's best for the villagers and what they want may be two very different things. Emotions are high, and it's plain there are not enough wagons, medicine, or supplies, in general, to go around; fights are bound to break out. That's what you mean, isn't it, John?"

I nodded.

"You need us to be lawmen of sorts."

I nodded again. "You can see the problems we face. We need men who will be able to enforce hard decisions."

"What if we don't want to help?" asked Ted. "Why don't we just leave?"

"Haven't you been listening?" Jane asked incredulously. "Whether you like it or not, your fate is bound to us, and we are bound to John. He is the only one who can detect the danger before it is upon us."

I could sense that Jane's line was pushing the man into a corner. He had just been exploring the possibility, whereas now he seemed more interested in arguing with her. Of course, she didn't know that.

"Listen," I explained. "If you want to leave, we won't stop you."

I pointed at the dark woods. "I doubt you'll make it far. We just killed two of them that were spying on us. There will be more."

I could see what one man thought. And without thinking, I responded, "It's true you have muskets, but unless you get in a good headshot, it will most likely take upward of three balls to kill one. How are you going to do that when you can't see them in the dark? And what if they send fifty after you? If you haven't already done so, go look at one of those monsters up close. They have claws, teeth, speed, and the strength to rival bears, with the brains and dexterity of a human.

"I'm not trying to scare you." (Although I very well was.) "I'm trying to save you like I'm trying to save the villagers." (Which was also true.)

"You can take your chances out there alone." I again motioned to the black forest. "You may get lucky. Then again, you might not."

I had reached the men, at least most of them.

Ted, who still wanted to argue with Jane, was being stubborn.

"He's just tryin' to scare us, boys. We'll be fine."

"You will have to go without me," James stated bluntly. "I'll be staying."

"And me," added Thomas.

The others hesitated.

I gave them a long moment before pleading, "We want *and* need you, but the decision is yours. Since we're all going to Syre, it seems wise that we travel as a company. However, if you stay, I need to know that I can rely upon you and that you will do what is right."

Another long moment passed before one of the men finally piped up.

"Aww, come on, Ted. We all know you're just arguing like you always do. I'm staying too. What say you, boys?"

Some took a bit longer than others, but in the end, they all agreed.

Except for Ted.

"I don't know," he said, scratching his beard. "I just don't know. You've said a lot, and I'm wondering if we *are* doing the right thing. What if we're wrong? What if *you're* wrong? One moment Martin was proclaiming you a witch; next, he's dead. And now you're saying that there might be something to it after all."

I couldn't help the tinge of anger growing in me. Even worse, I could sense his argument was changing the minds of some others. Though none of them voiced it just yet, they were wondering if they shouldn't have agreed so quickly.

Stifling my irritation, I ventured, "I know how my actions toward Mr. Martin must look to you all. I never planned to bring anyone into this. When I put my back to Syre, I believed I would never have to answer for what I had done. I must admit, a part of me feels shame and deep-seated discomfort facing you now.

"No matter what you think of me, I couldn't leave Syre knowing what I knew *or* what Thomas and his mother knew too well. Magistrate Martin was not guiltless. He had innocent blood on his hands, and you all know that he would *never* have faced justice, not *ever*. Even if I have to hang for killing him, my action most likely saved lives. Even *your* lives. With Mr. Martin unchecked, more would surely have suffered."

I shook my head. "But this isn't about me, or even about you right now. It's about the lives of these people." I motioned toward the burning fires of Alyth. "They need our help. I'm not asking you to do this for me. I'm asking you to do it for them.

"That being said, I do not ask you to follow me blindly. If *anyone* has a right to see me hang, it is Thomas. He has no guile, and I know he will be fair, so I trust him. I know you all feel the same way. I will listen to him if you will. Thomas, what do you say?"

Thomas scratched his head uncomfortably.

"I'm willing," he said. "I'm just not sure what you mean, John, or why the others would even need me. Seems to me they are capable of deciding for themselves."

Ted answered for me. "He means if anyone has a fight with him, it would be you. None of us have had someone hurt by him, only you. If the one person who could demand justice isn't, what right do we have?"

"Oh," replied Thomas.

"That's part of it," I admitted, "but not all. It also means that tough times are ahead. When things get difficult, and they will, you are going to hear a lot of complaining and accusations from the people of Alyth. Understand their grief and desperate situation. However, also be aware that there is a strong possibility that they will turn their anger against me, which could prove devastating for everybody. I am asking you to stay the course with us. If you find yourselves agreeing with the villagers, and don't feel that you can tell me your grievance, then Thomas will be the one to confide in. I trust that he won't inflame the situation, and you know that he will listen and act according to your best interest."

I turned to Thomas.

"I know you are able but are you willing?"

He nodded. "I'll do what I can."

"Well," replied Ted, scratching his beard, "I can live with that."

I sighed quietly, releasing tension that I hadn't realized I'd been holding.

***

The night had grown cold and dark. Clouds blanketed the sky, blocking the moon and stars. Occasionally, the wind shifted slightly, blowing smoke from the smoldering ruins. The villagers slept close to the remaining coals, huddled together in families.

Near where the gate had been, I perched atop a rickety, makeshift tower. Angus had the foresight to have it built from some of the more salvageable pieces of lumber. It was only a platform, about the length and width of three adults lying side by side. Luckily, two of the large timbers used for legs were taller than the others. They continued up past the floor, giving a place to rest one's back. Overall, the structure wasn't terribly tall, about the height of three men.

Because of the hasty erection of my roost, it seemed that every time the breeze shifted, so did the platform. It was nerve-racking at first. However, as the night progressed, my fear of falling had given way to the sensation of being rocked to sleep, which made staying awake difficult.

Jane had remained with me a short time, but I sent her off to curl up with Hannah and Sarah as she had nearly had no rest in two days.

While, to the naked eye, the forest seemed to be still and lifeless, with my eyes, I could see otherwise. Larger animals were nowhere to be seen, but smaller animals were on the move. Night birds searched for their prey while others scurried hither and thither.

I was pleased to discover that, with all the practice I had received of late, it was possible to keep my vision open more often without feeling too fatigued. It even seemed that my range of sight had grown. As Sarah had predicted, I was definitely becoming stronger with my gifts. Still, they weren't limitless, and I was obliged to pace myself and only check every so often.

As the night wore on, my drowsiness increased. Even with the rest I had received, I still felt exhausted.

My eyes swept across the swarm of people slumbering below. It was indeed sobering to ponder their vulnerability. Men, women, and children were all putting their trust in me to protect them—to stay awake and raise the warning call should the need arise.

With such a burden placed upon my mind, I resorted to all sorts of tactics to remain alert. I slapped myself, tried humming a tune, and literally counted sheep, then cows, then goats. They all worked for a time, but eventually, I had to move on to something else.

Once, I even stood and jumped up and down—until the sudden shifting of the tower re-instilled my doubt in the integrity of its construction. Finally, I took off my coat. The uncomfortable cold washed over me and invigorated my senses—for a time.

In the throes of fighting sleep and losing, I felt the tower sway. Someone was carefully climbing the ladder, and I became instantly alert.

My concern vanished when Sarah's head appeared, and then the rest of her, as she crawled up and onto the platform. She wore a coat and carried a blanket.

"Can't sleep?" I asked.

"No, quite the opposite," she replied with a tired smile. "I meant to get up some time ago, but I couldn't keep my eyes open long enough."

"You *should* be sleeping; everyone else is."

"Not *everyone* else."

I smiled wearily.

"I'm supposed to be awake. Who else is going to be able to keep watch?"

"I can. My gift may not be as strong as yours, but it will suffice. Now, go get some rest."

I didn't move.

Carefully, Sarah sat down by my side. Together we dangled our feet over the edge.

"I dream of the bed at your cabin," I said. "I miss the porch and watching the sunset sweep over the trees in the evening. I even miss your bathing contraption. Even though I wasn't there very long, it felt like home."

She patted my arm.

"So do I," she confessed. "And it will be home again someday."

I smiled sadly. "Will it?"

Sarah looked at me with compassion and knowing wisdom. "It's not only the journey there that you are worried about, is it?"

I silently shook my head.

"The trial?"

I nodded.

Placing her hand on my back, Sarah said, "James believes that you have a solid case for self-defense, and he's not the only one who supports this sentiment. Come what may, John, we will stand by you."

I looked into her eyes and said, "Thank you."

I shrugged my coat back on, then reclined on my side. Using my arm as a pillow, I closed my weary eyes. Although I hadn't intended to, a split second later, I'd fallen promptly to sleep.

Chapter Seven: So It Begins…Again

I woke, finding myself covered with a blanket, still lying on the platform. Clouds continued to smother the sky, hiding the sun and time of day, but it was decidedly morning.

Oh no! You can't afford to fall asleep! I chastened myself.

I sat up a bit too quickly; my head swam, and my body protested from the sudden movement. Though my back still burned from the lashings, the intensity was gone.

Thomas sat by my side, watching me without expression.

"Not the most comfortable place to sleep," he commented.

"I didn't plan on sleeping here," I replied through a yawn and a stretch. "Sarah showed up and told me to lie down. I guess that was all it took. Where is she?"

"She's helping to get the villagers and supplies organized."

Looking about, I noticed that a lot of people were standing around. Although some moved about, carrying items here and there, most appeared lost, needing someone to tell them each little thing to do.

Out in the field, I observed Sabin and Jane, each working with several groups of three. The shooting teams had been formed and were now practicing drills.

"How are the villagers doing?" I asked as if I really didn't want to know.

I imagined fights breaking out and tension everywhere.

As if reading my mind, Thomas replied, "Not as bad as you think. Sure, there have been some disagreements—there are some headstrong folks down there—but nothing too dramatic. See for yourself."

His arm swept behind us, and I followed his motion. Animals of all types were either laden or in the process of being laden with packs.

"The wagon will transport the wounded," he explained.

Then, with a slight grin, he added, "It's been interesting to watch them place burdens upon the backs of the livestock. Some animals take to it better than others."

Indeed, it appeared that those most willing were the goats and mules. I even saw a dog carrying small packs, being led around by a young girl. A rag doll, tucked securely under a rope, added to the load.

It appeared that most of the horses were being saved for riders.

I started to stand up. "I should help."

"No," said Thomas with a restraining hand on my shoulder. "They want you right here keeping watch. I'll go and let them know you're awake."

I sat back down while he flipped a leg over the edge and shimmied down the ladder.

The tower swayed from the movement.

Taking advantage of his absence, I scanned the forest for any sign of the Brean. Something I should've done the moment I woke up. Rebuking myself for the oversight, I made a mental note to get into the habit. Now that there were no walls, lack of vigilance could quickly get a number of us killed.

There were none.

My attention returned to the ruins of Alyth. The charred structures had completely smoldered away to dust. Small clouds of ash swirled about as little gusts of wind carried away any evidence that a village had existed here. I wondered how long it would be before nature completely erased the remaining wall, the bridge, and the stable. All it would take would be a spring storm and a swelling river to weaken the ground and topple them.

Alyth would now be lost to history, surviving only in our memories.

My mind drifted back to relive our stay. It had been a happy little town, more so than most. Despite my troubles, it also held something special for me. I wasn't alone. Family and true friends had filled my void, and I wanted more of it. It was a hard thing to see its death.

Thomas hadn't been gone long before he returned. He threw a cloth bundle up onto the platform. It landed with a thud. After scrambling up, he then tossed it into my lap.

"What's this?" I asked.

"Food," he replied as he flopped his legs over the edge and sat down.

I opened the sack and found some freshly cooked (albeit cold) beef.

"One of the more stubborn cows met its fate on behalf of the town," he explained.

I felt grateful for it, and the meal disappeared rapidly.

Thomas watched me silently while I ate.

When I finished, he asked, "Do you truly believe all that about me?"

"All what?"

"What you said last night."

"Yes," I replied. "I trust you completely."

He hesitated and then ventured, "Even though I'm still sore that you kept your secret from me?"

"I know. And I'm sorry," I replied. "Still, I suspect you're beginning to understand."

"Not fair!"

"Not fair what?"

"Not fair using your knack on me."

With a slight smile, I explained, "Thomas, special gifts are not always required to know where someone stands. The fact that you are sitting here relaxed says a lot. If you weren't experiencing a change of heart, you wouldn't be next to me now."

"Well, I still haven't completely forgiven you," he said firmly.

"I won't rush you."

I continued eating in silence, wondering how to bring up the subject of Mr. Martin.

Finally, I ventured, "Thomas, I want to apologize to you for any pain I caused you with my actions. When I took the life of your father, it was out of my love for you and not my hatred of him. Does that make any sense?"

Thomas was quiet for a few moments before he spoke.

"When news came of his death, all I felt was relief. I was so grateful that Mother would never have to suffer again at his hand. But I also felt concerned for you. I knew that you would be a wanted man now, and I didn't want anything bad to happen to you. I was on pins and needles, not knowing what I could do for you. When Mr. Shepherd returned and took control of the situation like he did, I knew that I could trust him to help me find you. And here we are. Mr. Shepherd invited the men from the hunting party to join us; everyone came without hesitation. John, we all know you did the town a favor, and none of us want to see you hang for it. I'm going to stand up for you when the time comes."

I was speechless. Gratitude for his frank forgiveness washed over me. All I could squeak out was, "Thank you."

We sat together with our legs swinging over the side of the platform and watched Sarah, Jane, Hannah, both Shepherds, and Sabin walk over to the base of our little tower.

I climbed down, and Thomas followed.

"Good to see you're nae dead, laddie," said Angus with a grin. "I was beginnin' to wonder; ye were slumberin' so deeply."

"Sorry," I said sincerely, rubbing the back of my stiff neck. "I didn't plan on it."

"Don't apologize, laddie. Take the sleep when ye can get it. Heaven knows when yer next chance will come."

"Angus is quite right," added Sarah. "But that is not the reason we are here. There is a bit of a dilemma as we have lost valuable time preparing for our departure, and we need your opinion. Should we stay another night, in the safety of the town, and get an early start in the morning? Or do we leave now?"

I stroked my chin.

"What do you think, Hannah?" I asked.

She couldn't help beaming, relishing the opportunity to share her astuteness.

"Well," she began, bubbling with importance. "I don't believe staying here another night will serve us; if we leave now, that gives our enemies less time to prepare a surprise attack, if that is their scheme. All waiting does is prolong our stay in the cold and give them more time to plan."

"I'm inclined to agree," I said.

In truth, I didn't know what was best. Both choices seemed sensible.

After another moment and not seeing any better alternative, I finally made a decision.

"As soon as we're ready, we'll set out."

"Aye, we will see to it," Angus said enthusiastically.

Then turning to James, he added, "Come along, Jimmy."

Together they peeled off to get things moving.

"In the meantime," I said to Sabin, "I want to talk to the shooting groups, including the men from Syre."

"I'll fetch 'em," he grunted and then departed.

"Do you really think we'll be attacked?" asked Thomas.

As soon as he said it, I could tell that he wished he hadn't.

"Sorry, I suppose I already know the answer to that."

He swept his arm across the fields, still littered with dead Brean.

"It just doesn't seem real to me—like I'm living in a dream. I expect to wake up at any moment."

"No," I agreed. "It doesn't feel real at first. It takes some time."

"At least you weren't surprised by…well, by *you*," he added a bit sheepishly.

"That is true," I admitted.

"Don't worry," said Hannah. "It *will* set in. Probably about the time one of those brutes gets set to club you."

"They use clubs?" Thomas asked in amazement.

"Yes," replied Sarah. "But they *can* be killed."

"What if they come in the numbers they did when Alyth fell?" asked Thomas.

"We fight," Sarah answered simply.

"Not that we have much choice," he murmured.

"Oh, we have a choice," countered Sarah. "We could send word to Marysvale that we surrender. However, I, for one, will not surrender."

Thomas appeared thoughtful.

"Can we win?" he asked.

"Yes," Sarah said firmly. "But winning is as much a state of mind as anything. An army that is defeated within has already lost. Keeping spirits up and believing that we will overcome will be our greatest challenge."

Thomas pondered this as the shooting groups began to arrive.

"Plus," added Jane, "we have something any army would love to have, and that is John."

I couldn't help blushing and feeling rather uncomfortable.

"That's what I keep hearing," muttered Thomas.

Jane looked at him sympathetically. "The reason Lord Wright wanted John to lead his army is because of his abilities. He can track enemy forces from afar and avoid being detected. He can get into their minds and discover valuable information. He is not a small advantage, but a substantial one."

"It's also why, when John refused Lord Wright, he tried to have him killed," added Hannah.

"You mean while in the dungeon?" asked Thomas.

"Yes," replied Hannah. "And a few times in Alyth."

"I got this," she continued, holding up her bandaged arm, "saving him once from an assassin."

"Amazing," exclaimed Thomas. "You threw yourself in the way of a musket?"

"Much worse. A crossbow bolt, actually—quite a nasty one, too. But John would do the same for us. *Wouldn't you, John?*" she said threateningly.

I laughed. "Well, for most of you."

Hannah broke into a grin.

Then, seriously, I said, "Of course, I would for any of you."

"Very touching sentiments," commented Sarah. "But how about we stop planning on dying for each other, shall we?"

We agreed and, with the shooting groups now fully assembled before us, I climbed back up the tower to get a better look and address them.

Both my natural and extrasensory eyes swept across the gathering. There were about sixty shooters, making up twenty shooting teams, not including the men from Syre. They were less than I'd hoped for and far less than Lord Wright would have, but as most of the weapons had been lost in the inferno, it was likely all the firearms we had.

Still, I reasoned with myself, *it could be worse.*

With proper instruction, we could lay down a constant barrage of fire upon the enemy from the best marksmen around—not something to be dismissed.

Then again, beside the Brean, Lord Wright had hundreds of soldiers, possibly even thousands. Naehume had shown me others like Lord Wright. Did his garrison include men from those places or men recruited only from Marysvale? I made a mental note to ask Jane about it later.

Among the shooters were several women. Like Sarah and Jane, they, too, wore men's clothing.

I shouldn't have been surprised. Alyth was an odd little town. In another place, no women would be included in the group, even if they were the best; and certainly not dressed like men. Trial and necessity had a way of changing people, sometimes for the better. I reasoned that to be true in this case as well. After all, the three women in my life were the best marksmen I'd ever seen; and I felt a wave of comfort and strength having them by my side.

Sabin, noticing my hesitating eyes on the women, called up, "You did say the best shooters."

"Yes, indeed; I do want the best. And if these people are the best, then they are needed and welcome."

I continued my inspection. Several emotions were represented throughout the group: grief, fear, and anger being the dominant ones. These people had witnessed the number of Brean we were up against, felt their brutality, and suffered the loss of loved ones. To be facing them again, without the protection of walls or water, would be terrifying. I could sympathize.

Some of them directed their anger towards me—not much I could do about that. The question I had was whether or not they would follow my commands.

I decided to find out.

"Have you organized them into groups of three?" I asked Sabin.

He nodded. "Yep, set 'em up the same way as before, with the same instructions."

"Good."

I briefly reviewed the roles of the primary, secondary, and loader.

"Form up into your shooting groups, so I may get a better feel for what we have."

A few of the people started to move, but most stood still.

One man, rather large, stepped forward, folded his arms resolutely, and spat defiantly, "Why should we take orders from a *witch*? It's you who have brought this evil down upon us. Sabin had it right before you possessed him."

Then addressing the group, he reasoned, "Don't you see? If we are to have any hope of survival, we need to rid ourselves of this devil. Evil begets evil."

I studied the group. Many wouldn't meet my eyes. Others shifted nervously and glanced from me to the man. Some glared at me, and others glared at him. This response from the villagers didn't surprise me in the least. However, what did surprise me was the reaction inside of me. In that moment, something inside me suddenly grew cold, faded away, and died. Any concern I had felt for these people was instantly snuffed out like a candle.

I felt no fear from his accusation. Instead, I felt an overwhelming surge of hostility. Far from wanting to be accepted by them, I no longer felt the need even to be part of them. I was sick and tired of trying to help where I was not wanted, and I had no desire to continue. The only reason I was standing here now was to appease Jane; it certainly wasn't out of love for these people. Their stupidity in shunning my counsel, without any thought to their real danger, incensed me.

All of the fear, the torture, the trials, and near-death escapes had slowly but steadily changed me. I had been forced to use my powers, and I had seen the worst in men.

I saw how evil imitated virtue. It cloaked itself in the robes of justice; it was the most respectable person in the room, draped in the mantle of leadership, in a position of trust. It had a gilding of gold and a gilding of friendship, but they were illusions. Strip away the lies, and you're left with lust: lust for power, wealth, self-gratification, and sometimes, even lust for blood.

I knew pure evil, and I was not it!

The man's words struck like flint on my heart, igniting the tinder that had been building inside me.

In place of fear, anger flared to life, filling my whole being with intense energy.

Not even bothering to use the ladder, I leaped down off the platform and, in the same movement, broke into a quick stride.

I approached the man.

111

He had a thick, scraggly beard and a long, black, curly mane of hair tied behind his neck.

"Let him have it, Charles," cried someone in the crowd.

Charles swelled out his chest and exclaimed, "If it's a fight you want, then I'm happy to…"

My fist crashed into the side of his jaw so swiftly that he had no time even to throw up a feeble defense. It connected with such force that the man flew back and fell in a daze.

My vision burst open, fed by such raw emotion that it refused to be kept inside. The colors and auras of all living things spread before me, unconstrained. Rage and power coursing through me.

"Get him, boys!" someone shouted.

Chapter Eight: The Tables Turn

My vision drew me to four particular individuals, two of them immediately to my right.

They rushed me.

I turned and saw one of them swinging a fist.

In a lightning-quick movement, I sidestepped away.

His blow struck air just as his friend took a swing.

I grabbed the first man by the hair and positioned his head just enough to intercept his comrade's blow—the fist connected with the man's head.

I shoved the falling man aside while unleashing a particularly savage undercut on the second.

The second man's head snapped back, and both men crumpled to the ground, moaning.

I stepped back and away, placing the fallen pair between me and the two other charging men.

Jane had maneuvered herself in a position to stick her foot out, tripping one.

He fell, sprawling in the dirt. A string of profanity escaped his lips.

The fourth man lunged in a rage.

However, he didn't make it far.

Sabin took the opportunity to smash the butt of his rifle in the back of the fellow as he passed. The man stumbled for a few steps and then fell flat on his face.

Drawing up to my full height, I looked down at the four with uncontrollable anger blazing in my eyes, accompanied by a fierce determination. I seemed to swell even larger than I was. I felt invincible.

"Is that all?" I growled in a guttural and menacing tone that even took me by surprise.

Something about me gave them pause. They were unsettled by my appearance and by the change that had come over me.

Far from being flustered, I towered threateningly, ready for them to stand and try again.

My gifts seemed to consume my whole being. Every muscle throbbed with power. I felt incredible—like I could tear trees out with my bare hands.

My eyes swept over the rest of the gathering, daring anyone to step forward.

"Is there no one else?" I hissed with disappointment.

The power of my vision swelled, and their souls lay bare before me. I could not only see their auras; I could read every one of them at once.

I sensed a few others who had been prepared to join in the fight, eager to take out their misdirected rage and hurt on me a moment before. Now, they were filled with uncertainty.

They felt fear.

I bore into each one of them in turn, waiting for a reply.

They gave none.

I shot a warning glance at others who thought I was to blame for their misfortune.

In a look, I did my best to convey that I was done with their foolishness. Whoever stood against me would be summarily dealt with.

I felt dead sure of that.

No one moved. No one dared, for fear it would be taken as a challenge.

I could sense their awe.

After a long moment, I strode over to Charles, the very first man I had hit. He sat on the ground, looking fearfully up at me. A trickle of blood oozed out the corner of his mouth.

Without stopping, I walked over, bent down, seized him by the coat with both hands, and jerked him roughly to his feet. I spun him around and pushed him through the crowd. They parted as we passed.

When there was nothing but the forest in front of us, I shoved the man forward. It wasn't violent enough to cause him to fall, but he stumbled a few steps before catching his balance.

Charles stopped, turned, and looked at me dumbly.

Without saying a word, I pointed into the woods.

He looked multiple times between the forest and me.

When I finally spoke, my voice was low and resolute, filled with authority. Everyone hushed to listen.

"There. There is your enemy."

I turned to the rest of the people.

"Your enemy is out there, both beast and man, waiting and plotting. And I am *not* one of them. I do not need you; you need me. If we work together, we can end the oppression of evil men and monsters once and for all. Those that are *with me* will reclaim their lands and be free.

"I don't care if you think I am the very son of the devil—and some of you do. I only care that you stand with me for this cause. If you cannot, then take your family and leave now!"

I crossed my arms and waited.

No one moved.

More time passed, and still, no one moved.

I waited some more.

After a long while, I stated, "Very well, then."

With the excitement over, the weight of my powerful vision came crashing down. I felt incredibly exhausted. Nevertheless, I forced myself to remain erect and command an authoritative tone.

From the crowd, I singled out five men. They were not chosen randomly. I knew these five men had something in common. They were passionate, both for the cause of justice concerning Alyth and the protection of her people. Of course, they were not the only ones to feel that way; but I got the impression they would be among the most vocal and undaunted in their convictions. With that determination, they could inspire the others when the situation grew dark and the hearts of their fellowmen faltered.

Along with Mathias, Ben, Sam, and Sabin, I chose Charles.

"You five, and you men from Syre, stay here. The rest of you go and make ready to leave."

As the crowd dispersed, Thomas said, "John?"

I looked at him.

"Yes?"

"I'm glad you didn't join Lord Wright. I'm glad you're on our side."

"I agree," added Hannah. "You were terrible—but in a good way. I've never seen you like that before. Imposing." Shaking her head, she added, "I'm sure glad I wasn't one of those men."

I looked at them with a sly grin and admitted, "I know. I scared myself a little, too."

When everyone else had gone, I addressed the men.

"You five are to be captains. Each of you will be over your own shooting group, plus three others. The twelve individuals in your charge will make up a unit. Sabin will assign the groups to you. You will carry out every order and make sure those under you follow the instructions given. Do any of you take issue with this?"

None did, so I continued.

"Very good. Although we are not a regular army, we do need a defensive strategy. If the Brean are in a full outright sprint, my warning will only give us a short time to act. Just like you, I can't see over hills, so our time may be shorter depending on the terrain. That means we'll have just enough time to form up if we're fast."

I wished it were different. I wished I could tap at will into the power that seemed to release with anger, but, as I hadn't learned how, we couldn't rely upon it.

"How will we know where to form up?" asked Matthias.

"I was just about to explain," I replied.

I showed them different hand signals, shouts, or whistles that would instruct them where to assemble in relation to the main group of villagers. One set of signals indicated the front, another set for the back, the right, and the left. We practiced slight variations, such as forming up on the left side but towards the front, the right rear, and so on. Once I explained all that, I had each captain repeat the signals to make sure they understood.

I then assigned each shooting team a number. From there, I could adjust individual shooting teams to other locations should the need arise.

"What about those of us from Syre?" asked Ted. "We aren't in teams."

"You are all team six, and Thomas is your captain," I explained. "You have a different function than the rest. As you all have horses, you will be outriders. My sight has limits, and if I'm scouting in front, I may not be able to see far enough in the other directions. Spread out, with some distance around the group, and move along with them, acting as lookouts. If you see an imminent attack, fire a shot, preferably into a Brean. If you can, ride back and notify me or whomever I leave in charge. Once I have the chain of command decided, I will inform the rest of you, and you may apprise your groups. Questions?"

"What about at night?" asked Thomas. "How will watches work?"

"I'm the best one for night watch; as we won't be moving, I can handle that."

"Even you need to sleep," countered Jane.

"I know, but one thing at a time. I will have a plan by then; for now, it's important that we get moving."

"What about our families?" asked Ben. "Are they to struggle along without us?"

I shook my head. "Shooters should stay with their families, but make sure you travel with your team. When it's time to form up, I'll give the signal. Anything else?"

They shook their heads.

"Very well, go instruct your people and prepare to leave. Sabin, as you know these men and the teams best, will you organize them into units?"

Sabin nodded and, with the other four, walked off toward the main body of villagers.

"Thomas, have your team organize yourselves however you all think best; then go see what you can do to help the Shepherds."

He, too, nodded and left.

I started walking back to the tower.

Jane, Hannah, and Sarah fell in by my side.

"What about us?" asked Jane.

I looked at Sarah. "What do you think you should do?"

"John, you are doing a fine job, and we are here to support you in any manner."

"That isn't much help."

"What I mean is, don't be afraid to use us where you need us."

"But it doesn't feel right ordering you about."

"You don't need to order," said Jane. "You just need to ask."

"Very well. I'll need your help as messengers."

"That doesn't sound very important," murmured Hannah. "What a huge waste of our talents."

"Hannah!" chided Sarah. "We said we would help where needed. In *whatever* capacity that may be."

Hannah looked dejected.

I smiled. "Well, there's that, and I need you by my side to make up for my bad shots."

Hannah brightened and nodded. "Oh, yes, I can see that."

Reaching the tower, I succumbed to fatigue. I sat down and leaned against one of the legs, using it as a backrest. Exhaustion washed over me.

"Did it take much effort?" Sarah asked, concerned.

"You wouldn't believe it," I answered. "It's very tiring—that episode particularly so. It feels like I did half a day's work in just a few minutes."

"You're getting stronger," she observed. "I could feel it."

"I did too," added Jane, with a bewildered expression.

"Yes," I admitted. "But that intensity only seems to release under extreme anger. I wish I could get it open like that at will."

"Anger can indeed be potent," said Sarah. "And you can accomplish incredible things with it. However, it's an emotion not to be trifled with. It has a voracious appetite. It will never be satisfied; it will only demand more and more until it consumes all of you."

"I don't know how else to tap into that kind of power," I admitted.

"There is an energy already within you that is immensely more powerful than rage."

"I can't imagine what that could be. I have never felt anything stronger than that. What is it?"

"Love," answered Sarah.

She went on to explain, "Where anger breeds apathy and cruelty, love inspires compassion. It heals, unites, and frees us from the paralyzing bitterness of hate. Be careful, John, the one you nurture is the one that thrives. If we ourselves are not free, how can we free others? Love should not be underestimated; it *is* the most powerful force."

"I'm not sure it would have the same effect," I said doubtfully. "Because that was very intense like nothing could hide from me. I've never felt that way or been able to see like that."

"There *was* something about you during that experience..." Jane hesitated, trying to figure out what it was.

Hannah, picking up where she left off, said, "I know what she is saying. There was no hiding from your authority."

"Jane is right," said Sarah in agreement. "We could feel your anger, but it was more. Confidence and surety..."

She frowned.

"Yes," Hannah added excitedly. "It was all of that, but it was pure. I don't mean pure as in innocent, but pure as in clear, defined. We could *feel* your intentions, your sincerity, your drive, and even your power. We knew you were unconquerable—that anyone who stood against you would regret it in the harshest terms."

Her eyes widened. "It was like your soul was opened to *us*."

That comment struck a chord with the other two, and all three women wore expressions of wonder.

"John," said Jane, in nearly a whisper, "Hannah's right. It was a window to *your* soul. I think you projected yourself. You showed us what you were really like in that moment. There was something different about you, and it wasn't just your physical presence."

She hesitated and then asked, "Is that what it's like for you to read us?"

"I…I don't know…I suppose."

That troubled me. To have my soul visible to everyone, even just a sliver, felt like an invasion.

"What's wrong?" asked Sarah.

"It's a bit disconcerting to be exposed like that."

Hannah grinned. "And now you know what it's like for us to be around you."

"I have a newfound empathy."

Chapter Nine: Unfazed

It turned out that getting the villagers organized and where we needed them took longer than I'd hoped. Tasks, such as lashing barrels and packs on animals, were a slow process. The little rope we had was quickly used up. After it was gone, cloth was torn into strips and braided. However, there was a disagreement over what should be sacrificed to make rope—blankets or clothing? It was a trivial matter, but one where feelings and passions ran high. The men of Syre decided it best to use some of both, thereby making everyone on the two opposing sides angry with them.

On top of that, the villagers had a tendency to talk with one another instead of getting ready; or they would stop what they were doing and stare at nothing for minutes at a time. It seemed like tree sap in winter could move faster.

Still, I did have some compassion, as I suspected that most of the feet-dragging came from their obvious state of shock and disbelief. They were being forced to leave everything—their homes, property, and, in some cases, their dead. Understandably, they were clinging to what little they had, which were mostly memories. Grieving took priority, despite the dangers that waited for us in the dark.

Consequently, it was well past noonday before we mournfully put our backs to the ruins of Alyth and set out for Syre.

The three women in my life led the main group with me at the front. They rode the horses we'd fled to Alyth on—the only difference being that Jane rode Ember. Seeing Jane's attachment to her mare, Sarah suggested trading, which Jane readily accepted.

Thomas had organized the outriders. He decided to take the lead himself, riding far in front of our company, out of everyone's eyesight, except my own.

The pace was slow. I figured this first day would be more of an experimental run. Tomorrow, if Angus didn't drive them harder, I would. A lackadaisical approach in this dangerous time and season would certainly cost us lives.

After conducting a brief sweep of the forest and checking on the outriders, I decided to drill the shooting teams. I didn't want the villagers to panic, thinking it was a real alarm, so I had Jane and Hannah inform the captains of my plan.

When the word had been spread, I gave the signal for the shooting teams to fall to the right of the main body. And, as I had feared, confusion ensued. Some grumbled and moved slowly. Some ran to the front. More ran to the left, with only half actually arriving at the designated spot. Eventually, the lost discovered their mistake and joined the group at about the same time as the lazy, who simply strolled to their positions.

"You all must not like your own hides very much," I told them. "If that had been a real attack, the Brean would be picking their teeth with your bones about now. Our defenses would have collapsed before you even got into position."

They didn't like the rebuke, but they bore it.

As soon as the shooters returned to their families, I called another location. Much of the same occurred.

The third time, they all moved faster, albeit with a few more grumbles.

The fourth was even better, but with more protests.

With the fifth drill, though nearly everyone complained, we finally saw success. All but a few shooters found their positions quickly.

Every time we stopped, so did the rest of the company. They, too, were beginning to take things seriously. Without any orders to do so, the men and strong young men formed a protective barrier around the women and children.

Unfortunately, it wasn't much of a defense. If we fell, the Brean would break through with little trouble. However, it did give me an idea. If the villagers had weapons, spears, perhaps, it would help. It still wasn't much, but at least it was something to fight with. More importantly, it would give them a sense of control over their own fate.

As a result of the drills, our advancement moved at a snail's pace.

While most grew to appreciate their importance, some did not. One man in particular, whom I recognized as a member of the town council, grumbled about the constant interruptions. On the fifth stop, he grew extremely vocal and insulting, questioning Angus' sanity and the other council members' decision to place me as chief captain.

As I dismissed the shooters and trotted back to the front, he stopped me.

"This is all a gross waste of time," he loudly complained while puffing out his chest. "Everyone knows we should be pushing ourselves as hard as possible to reach safety. All you want to do is march around importantly, pretending like you actually know what you're doing. You obviously have no training or skills in such critical matters. If the Brean attack, none of these fanciful drills will matter in the least."

I simply sat atop Smoke and looked down at the man.

He might be right. If the Brean attacked in the numbers we'd seen before, we would probably lose. But then again, he might be wrong. If things went in our favor, and every shot found its mark, we stood a *slim* chance—but at least it *was* a chance. If we did nothing, we had no hope.

The man was also wrong about something else: the drills weren't wasting time; they were empowering the people. Through their practice, the villagers were gaining confidence in their ability to move as a body and unitedly defend their loved ones. Even if our efforts did fail, at least we would go down fighting. Better to battle to the last man than to lie down and be slaughtered to the last man.

Too tired, too sore, and too hungry to care much of what he had to say, I fiddled with Smoke's reins while he verbally unleashed.

My lack of interest made the man even angrier.

He folded his arms across his chest and spat, "Well, what do you have to say for yourself?"

I looked down at him expressionless and, with a slight shake of my head, said, "Nothing."

Giving Smoke a nudge, we started walking past the man. His face took on a look of shock, and he placed his hands on his hips.

"Well, I have *never* been treated so rudely in all my life!"

"I have," I calmly replied over my shoulder. "My advice is to get used to it."

I could sense his anger. He couldn't decide what to say. Half-spoken insults and curses sputtered out, only to be cut off and replaced with another.

He finally settled on one.

"WITCH!" he cried.

I halted Smoke and lazily turned him about to face my accuser.

Curiously, I felt no anger like before. Possibly because I still felt exhausted from the last episode. Perhaps it was something else. Regardless, his slander didn't bother me at all.

I felt pity for the man. He was most likely weary and hungry. Winter was around the corner, and he had no place to go. Certainly, he had lost his home and security. Perhaps he had even had to bury his wife or a child.

Even more, he was afraid—afraid for his own life.

Everyone looked at me, wondering what I would do.

Dismounting, I approached the man.

He nervously took a step back and clenched his fists.

"What is your name?"

"Henry," he said stiffly.

Henry looked to be about forty years of age. He had no beard, except for the stubble that grew from lack of shaving. His hair was graying, especially near his temples and above his ears. His eyes told the tale of recent grief, deep and heavy.

"Well, Henry, would you like to hit me?" I asked.

There was no arrogance, anger, or resentment in my tone, only exhaustion.

"Pardon?" said Henry bewildered.

"You have gone through a great deal, and I can sympathize with your loss. I've had everything taken from me too. Multiple times, in fact. If it will make you feel any better, you may hit me."

The man looked confused. This clearly wasn't the reaction he'd been expecting.

He looked at the crowd questioningly, as if they would explain what was going on and tell him what to do.

Nobody said a word.

He turned back to me.

I continued, "Sometimes you just want to take your anger out on something, someone—anyone. I am giving you that opportunity."

Henry hesitated, then his fists unclenched, and his shoulders sagged.

In a sigh, he replied, "No, I don't want to strike you. What would be the point?"

"Very well, then."

I turned and remounted Smoke.

The villagers still watched.

Addressing them, I explained, "I meant it when I told Henry to get used to rough treatment. If it goes badly and you are captured, you will certainly be a target for cruelty in Marysvale. Perhaps even slavery."

I studied them for a moment and then continued, "I know that many of you don't believe me. You can't trust the stories. You think it impossible. Well, I don't care to convince you. If you are ever unfortunate enough to set foot in that town and see the looks on the people's faces—the hollowness in their eyes—you will have all the testimony you need.

"I want one more point to be clear. When the Brean attack, there won't be any room for error on what to do or where to go. These shooting teams will be the only thing standing between you and destruction. I advise you to help them get it right.

"Those of you who have been assigned as backup shooters need to be just as prepared. Even though you aren't drilling with them, watch and learn, so you are ready to act when it's your turn.

"One last suggestion: use this time to prepare spears, slings, and any other weapons you can think of. When the time comes, you will wish you had something to fight with. It may not be much." I shrugged. "But you never know. There are a lot of you; it can add up."

With that, I signaled another drill.

This time, with the aid of the villagers who had picked up on our system, they all made it exactly where I wanted them to be in record time.

When we were finally moving again, Sarah, Jane, and Hannah trotted up to me.

"You are filling your leadership role quite nicely," commented Sarah.

I snorted my disagreement.

"I feel like a mess; one moment I'm furious, the next, I'm calm."

"You're under a lot of stress, and you're tired," said Sarah. "Don't be too hard on yourself; what you are doing seems to be working. Just look at them."

We all turned to see villagers scurrying about, collecting fallen branches, and sharpening the ends into spears.

"Do you think the weapons will do much good stopping the Brean?" asked Jane.

"No," I admitted. "But that wasn't the reason why I suggested making them. For one, it gives the people something to do and helps keep their minds off their weariness and hunger. Hopefully, there will be less complaining. Secondly, it will help them feel like they have some control over their safety, even if it's only in their minds."

"Winning is as much a mindset as anything," mused Hannah, repeating Sarah's remarks.

Sighing, I muttered, "I should call for another drill. I want to make sure they have it all down."

Hannah disagreed. "Don't you think we should get some miles behind us? It won't be long before we have to stop, and we've just barely left Alyth."

I shook my head. "It's more important that they're prepared. The Brean will come. If they are running full out, I won't be able to give much warning."

"And what if men come instead?" asked Hannah. "What will you do then?"

"I don't reckon they'll send men. At least not until we're closer to Marysvale."

"You don't know that. Why not use men during the day, and Brean at night?"

"You're right; I don't know," I admitted. "I just can't believe that men have it in them to slaughter defenseless people. The Brean wouldn't have any such reservations."

Suddenly, I reined up Smoke and stopped.

"What is it?" asked Jane.

"I just remembered something; I'll be back in a minute."

I whirled Smoke around.

When the role of chief captain was thrust upon me, I decided to memorize the unique auras of as many people as possible, so I would be able to locate whomever I needed to in the dark. It was helpful to me now as I scanned the throng of villagers.

Locating the person I sought, I trotted over to where he walked with his wife.

Sam watched me draw up and came when I signaled.

"We're going to need bonfires. Will you recruit as many people as necessary and make fire bundles again so they're ready in case of an attack?"

"I will," he agreed hesitantly. "But it's a long way to carry a bunch of sticks. And there are wounded in the wagon. We can't just pile it on top of them."

"Just prepare the fire bundles. When we get closer to camp, then you can start collecting the wood. We'll be stopping just before dark. With all these people, it shouldn't take long to gather fuel."

"We will need campfires, too," said Sam. "We need to stay warm."

I agreed but added, "Those fires come after the wood for these defensive fires are collected. Warmth is for comfort; these are for our lives. You'll need to see what to shoot at."

"Like last time."

"More or less."

"How many do you need?"

"At least four—a fire in each corner, with the villagers in between. The more you can make, the better."

He nodded, and I returned to the women.

"Where did you go?" asked Hannah.

"I needed to talk to Sam." I then explained the fire bundles and the need for the shooters to see in the dark.

"Jane, will you instruct the captains on how it works? Tell them to stand with their backs to the flames. It's too large a group for us to construct any barrier, and I don't want their night vision compromised by the light."

She nodded and then turned Ember toward the company.

Snapping my vision open, I did the usual quick scan of the forest. I found Thomas some distance out.

"I'll return shortly."

"Where are you going?" asked Hannah.

"To scout a good long way in front of us and to find a place to camp for the night."

"I want to come."

I shook my head. "There's no need; I'll take Thomas. I want you to rest your arm."

"It's fine," she said. "I was able to shoot the Brean with it, you know."

"There are no Brean yet. When the time comes, you may give them your best; but I don't want you using your arm before then."

She opened her mouth to protest, but Sarah cut her off.

"John is right, Hannah; you must rest as much as possible. Let those who are well take their turn for now."

"But John isn't fully healed," she complained.

"You have a point there," I admitted. "But the answer is still no."

Without further argument, I nudged Smoke into a trot.

Then, calling back, I yelled, "Oh, and tell Sabin he's in charge while I'm gone."

"Sabin!" Hannah cried incredulously. "What about me?"

"I don't think anyone will listen to you," I answered.

She didn't like that. But it didn't matter; it was true.

Before long, I caught up with Thomas.

He turned and, upon seeing me, he halted and waited.

"Very brave to be out here all alone," I said, drawing up to his side.

He grinned. "I can shoot. And Shade here is the fastest one from our stable."

Thomas patted the horse affectionately on his neck.

Together we continued on at a brisk pace.

"I never understood why he was named Shade," I commented.

"Me neither. Knowing my father, both the horse and the name probably came from a shady business deal."

I wanted to chuckle, but I still didn't feel comfortable around the topic of his father.

Thomas, however, wore a grin. I settled on a half-smile.

"Well," I said, changing the subject. "Are you up to exploring with me?"

"Of course," he replied. "Where are we going?"

Waving in the general direction in front of us, I replied, "Oh, just up the trail. I want to scout out some distance ahead of the company. I figure if there is an ambush, it will most likely come from the front. I also want to find a good place where we can stop for the night."

"And what constitutes a good place?"

"Somewhere close to water, with a depression in the ground, large enough for our entire camp. I want us down some, so we aren't that easy to spot. We'll also need a hill close by where I can keep watch in all directions."

"Mmm," Thomas replied thoughtfully. "Might be hard to find all that together.

"Probably," I agreed.

"There is a stream," said Thomas. "But I think it's rather far away. We won't reach it by nightfall."

"Yes, I remember, but I don't recall its location. Last I saw it, we were moving a lot faster, and I was focused on the soldiers chasing us."

"Is Marysvale really as dreadful as you all make it out to be?"

I took a long time before replying, trying to think of where to start or how best to answer.

Finally, I said, "They have slaves, Thomas. They take citizens who have supposedly committed some crime, drag them out of their homes in the middle of the night, and sell them."

His initial reaction was abhorrence. But upon reflection, Thomas asked, "Are they guilty?"

"Does it matter if they are?"

He shook his head. "No, it doesn't. If true, it is still horrible."

The '*if* true' upset me.

I stiffened.

Apparently, I was still not a person to be trusted—at least not fully.

I tried to stifle my irritation.

"You saw the place. What did your intuition tell you?" I asked.

He thought about it and then replied, "I must admit, it did feel ominous. I was glad when we were denied entrance."

We continued in silence for a long while.

A few times, Thomas asked if I saw anything. I simply shook my head.

In the silence, I looked up at the sky. A sea of clouds cast the bleak forest in a dismal, gray light. It was a depressing sight—no color, no life, no warmth. A chill filled the air, making our breath visible.

I speculated on what Wright was planning for us now.

What if they are planning something we haven't considered?
I wondered. *Very possible. Why not wait until we are close to*
Marysvale and then attack with their whole force? We would be
crushed between the Brean and the soldiers with no way out
but to surrender.

The lack of men or monsters concerned me. I expected to
see a scout at the very least.

Our enemies will need to see what kind of a force we have.
I'm sure losing the battle for Alyth wasn't in their plans. So,
they know we have some fighting capability, but they don't
know how much. The Brean scouts we killed certainly got a
look at us, but they still wouldn't know anything other than that
Alyth was a complete loss. They didn't have enough time to
discover much else.

I let the thoughts drop for the moment and focused on the
task at hand.

Thomas ventured, "Sarah is your aunt?"

"Yes," I replied, without looking at him.

He knew that she was.

"Did you know about her?"

"No."

Another stretch of silence.

Finally, he said, "John, I'm still the same Thomas. You *can*
talk to me."

I softened a bit and let out a sigh.

"I'm not so sure, Thomas. Perhaps too much water has
flowed under the bridge for us. I'd hoped differently, but I
don't feel entirely comfortable around you. I did what I did,
certain that I'd never have to face you again. And you aren't

completely trustful of me. The accusation of witchcraft is a powerful one. Once leveled, it taints you. As you said, to find out that I am different…"

I shrugged.

"Well, what do I say?" I continued. "For the first time in my life, I'm not sorry for my abilities. It's as much a part of me as your thumbs are part of you. You didn't choose them, but there you have it. And wishing it away is pointless. I've spent my whole existence hiding who I am. It's a practice I no longer participate in. With these gifts, I have saved the lives of those I love and others, too.

"I *am* different, very different, and that can be scary for some. You wouldn't be the first friend to turn your back on me, and you won't be the last. Thomas, I know you are a good man, and the world needs more people like you."

Thomas looked down, perhaps searching inside himself, perhaps feeling ashamed.

Either way, I decided to leave him to himself.

Then, looking forward, I inhaled sharply and reined up.

Chapter Ten: Something New

 What is it?" Thomas asked in alarm, his hand instantly reaching for his musket.

I also went for my rifle.

"Brean!"

"Really? Where? How many?"

"Only one, but one is enough. It's some distance off."

"What is it doing?"

"Coming this way."

Excitement, apprehension, and fear all played across Thomas' face, mirroring what he felt inside.

"What do we do? Should we turn back?"

"No, this is actually good news."

"It is?" Thomas asked doubtfully.

"Well, I suppose it is not great news. Having one show up never is. However, there's usually always one around to keep an eye on things, and I find it odd we haven't seen one before now. I suppose I'm just glad that it's something expected."

I reached back and strung up the crossbow.

"Still, I'd rather they didn't know where the company is, nor how well armed we are."

"Or lack of it," corrected Thomas.

"That would be more accurate. Let's get this over with, shall we?"

He nodded.

Kicking our horses into a canter, we angled off slightly and set a path to intercept the beast.

Quickly, we closed in.

The Brean stopped.

Hearing something, it trained an ear toward us.

A brief moment passed, then it tilted its great head up to the sky.

Oh, wonderful. I thought dryly. *Just what we don't need—for it to call in a bunch of its mates.*

However, it didn't give the high staccato-like cry for help. It simply sniffed the air, perhaps trying to catch our scent.

We drew closer until we could see the Brean with our natural eyes, and the Brean could see us.

For a moment, we stared at one another.

It didn't move.

We continued our slow charge.

Then, it gave a small cry, turned, and fled.

"It's running!" shouted Thomas in excitement.

Instinctively, he broke into a full gallop, like a predator, knowing anything that runs must be prey. Smoke, not to be outdone by some newcomer's pony, or so I suspected, galloped forward without being told.

It was one of the things I didn't particularly like about Smoke. He hated any horse leading him, especially one who was running. I only wanted him to run when *I* said he could. Normally, I would've stopped him and forced him to do it right, but I allowed it this time.

However, I wouldn't let him outpace Shade and Thomas, which bothered him. Secretly, I enjoyed his agitation and thought, *Serves you right for trying to be the master.*

I also had another reason for holding him back. Remembering my lesson from the previous night, I didn't want to be alone again in a face-off. The Brean made a slight course adjustment. We followed suit and charged right on after it.

A short distance later, I signaled to Thomas to rein up.

"Why are we stopping?" he asked, confused.

"I don't think we're really gaining on it."

"We were," he insisted.

"Perhaps, but not fast enough. Eventually, we could probably catch up, but then we'd be too far away from the main group. If we had to run at that point, our horses would be tired. It's not worth risking that just for this one."

"Couldn't you just detect the danger with your sight and keep us away?"

"Detect, yes. But I still feel uneasy about it. If more showed up and came at us from the side, they could cut off our retreat."

"Won't we just have to deal with it sooner or later?"

We both looked at the monster. It had stopped and was looking back at us.

Thomas had a point. We would indeed have to deal with it at some point.

"Yes," I admitted with a sigh. "We will. Very well, but let's see if we can draw the beast in. I don't want to go galloping across the countryside, tiring out our horses. Follow me, and let's see what it does."

Thomas gave me a doubtful look, but we turned Smoke and Shade around and started back toward the company.

He fidgeted in his saddle while gripping his musket tightly.

"I don't like having our backs to that thing," he confessed.

"Neither do I."

In unison, we both turned to look behind us.

The Brean followed but did so cautiously, only matching our pace and not gaining any ground.

We faced forward.

"What is your plan?" asked Thomas.

"Don't have one," I admitted.

"I thought you said you were going to draw it in."

"Yes, but I don't quite know how to do it. I've never been in a situation like this before. You?"

"No."

"I mean, do *you* have a plan?"

"Oh." Thomas thought for a moment. "No, can't think of anything."

We looked back again.

This time, the monster was closer.

Again we faced forward.

"Well, your lack of a plan seems to be working," he whispered.

In a hushed tone, I replied, "It's only because I have a tendency to attract trouble. I believe this qualifies."

Thomas nodded enthusiastically in agreement.

Another look back.

The Brean was a tad bit closer.

"Can you get it?" I asked.

"You mean shoot it?"

"Unless you can throw a knife that far."

Thomas shook his head. "Not close enough, and there are a lot of trees. Can you?"

I nearly laughed out loud but stopped myself out of sheer self-preservation. "No."

But to be fair, I doubted even Hannah would be successful. The monster seemed to realize the limits of our weapons.

We traveled a few more paces and then looked back.

"No closer," whispered Thomas.

Then, "Wait, why are we whispering?" he asked out loud.

"I don't know," I replied. "You started it.

Another look back.

Still no closer.

"Shall we go after it?" asked Thomas, gripping his musket for emphasis.

"Might as well. I can't think of what else to do."

In unison, we turned and charged.

As before, the monster fled.

We galloped neck and neck, dodging and weaving through the barren trees.

Thomas rose slightly out of the saddle, reins grasped in one hand and his musket in the other. He gazed intently on the fleeing Brean.

Loosening the tension on Smoke's reins, I let him pick our path.

The monster raced around trees and over logs with the dexterity of a deer, never slipping, stumbling, or falling.

The distance between us gradually shrank, but not as quickly as I would have liked. I was ready to call off the chase when, presently, we came upon a gentle hill.

As the Brean ran up, it began to tire. Its pace slackened, and it slowed dramatically.

We thundered easily up the slope, gaining significant ground on the brute.

The monster crested the hill and then disappeared over the top.

Instantly, Smoke's ears flicked up, and I sensed a change in him and his gait. It was a subtle change, but I knew he was nervous.

I reined him up.

"It must be waiting for us just over the ridge," Thomas said breathlessly, coming to a stop.

Shade snorted nervously.

Patting his neck soothingly, Thomas said, "It's okay, boy."

"We'll go around the hill and come at it from the side," I suggested.

Fortunately, the horses obeyed, albeit reluctantly. We went across the hillside and around to the back.

I expected the Brean to either have a significant lead on us or, more likely, be setting an ambush out of sight, just waiting until it could pounce.

However, I was wrong on both assumptions.

The monster was standing at the base, looking at the top of the hill, waiting for us to crest. It appeared to be resting. Its chest heaved as it stooped over with a hand resting on a knee.

Almost like a man, I thought.

It noticed us quickly enough.

Signaling Thomas, we reined up.

"Quick, try shooting it with my rifle," I said, tossing it over to him.

Thomas caught it adeptly and tossed his musket back to me.

The Brean, sensing our intentions, stood and looked ready to run.

In a flash, Thomas quickly drew and fired, seemingly without aim.

Fire and smoke exploded out the end of the rifle.

The monster's head wrenched back violently as the ball slammed into its skull, right between the eyes. The rest of the body followed, and the whole hairy beast fell in a splayed position on its back. It had died before it hit the ground.

"That was some shot!" I said in admiration.

"Indeed," Thomas said breathlessly. "Especially since I was aiming at its chest."

Upon reflection, he added, "Don't tell the others that."

Grinning at him, I promised I wouldn't.

We trotted over to the beast and looked down.

Thomas crinkled his nose. "Awfully smelly. How do they…?"

But I wasn't paying attention.

Smoke was still agitated. His neck bolted straight up, ears swiveling.

Thomas had noticed something in our horses too. "John, I think something is still out there."

"So do I."

"Can you see anything?"

"No, nothing."

"I thought you could sense these things."

"I can."

Again, I scanned the trees.

"I've been keeping a lookout nearly the whole way. There is nothing else."

"Perhaps they are still upset over this one," ventured Thomas.

Shade whinnied as if in response, but that wasn't it.

My heart skipped a beat.

A sound.

But what?

"Did you hear that?" I asked.

"My horse?"

"No. I'm sure there *is* something else."

Thomas patted Shade, calming him slightly.

"There it is again!" I exclaimed excitedly.

"I heard it that time."

"Leaves rustling?"

Thomas nodded in agreement.

"But I don't think it's coming from our horses," he said, confused.

"Nor from that dead Brean," I added.

Turning my head from side to side, I searched for whatever it was.

Nothing!

I couldn't see anything that should cause such fear.

Suddenly, everything felt cold, like a chill had settled all around us. Something about the forest had changed. It felt as if

145

the woods sensed something too. The whole forest seemed to hold its breath collectively.

Fear gripped me—not only from what was out there but from the fact that my vision couldn't detect it. I'd grown accustomed, even dependent upon the ability to see with my gifts. The possibility that it was failing terrified me as much as whatever was out there. It was an odd feeling, considering I'd spent much of my life wishing it away.

"Do you see it? What is it?" asked Thomas, his voice high and tense.

"I don't see anything."

"I thought you could see living things."

"I can…or I could a moment ago. I saw that Brean you just killed."

To say the horses shuffled nervously was putting it mildly. We had to hold the reins mightily to keep them from bolting. Leaves rustled and crunched under their hooves.

And then I heard something else.

I froze.

This sound, I recognized.

Chapter Eleven: Nowhere to Run

The memory of my flight from Syre flashed into my mind. It felt like ages ago, though it wasn't quite two months—the very night when I had killed Mr. Martin. It was of a mist-filled clearing bathed in moonlight. While the circumstances between now and then were very different, the sound was the same.

A slight rasping noise again reached my ears.

No, I was wrong; the sound *was* different. In that clearing, I had only heard one rasp.

Now, I heard two. No, three. Or was there more? I couldn't tell. They were very slight.

The sound came again from behind us, and a decaying odor filled my nostrils.

With my heart racing, I spun Smoke to face the beast, but it wasn't there.

Again I heard it, and like before, it came from behind me.

No matter which direction I turned, it always seemed to be at my back.

Another spin.

Again I saw nothing.

"What do we do?" asked Thomas.

His eyes were wild with fear, reflecting my own.

"We run!"

"But where? What if we run right into whatever it is."

"I don't know," I admitted.

I closed my eyes and took a deep breath, trying to smother the panic that clouded my reason.

We could go back the same way, I thought.

But somehow, that way didn't feel right.

An idea flashed in my mind. I was about to discount it, but the feeling that Smoke knew the answer persisted.

I hesitated, reluctant to trust our fate to a horse.

Finally, more out of desperation than submission, I gave in.

"Follow me," I said.

Patting Smoke's sweaty neck and trying to sound calm, I said, "Okay, boy, show us the way."

I let go of the reins.

Smoke put his nose to the ground and sniffed like a dog. He took one step and then another, all with his head down. Then he raised his neck, turned, and, like a cannonball, he took off.

A twig snapped, loud and unmistakable. But it didn't come from us.

Smoke ran in a wide arc to our right, although there was nothing directly in his path that I could see. Finally, he turned and galloped straight and fast.

Looking back over my shoulder, and for the briefest of moments, I thought I saw a sliver of the dark vortex of a Brean. It flashed so quickly that I couldn't be sure.

The only thing I could see now was an extremely terrified Thomas galloping after us on top of Shade.

We ran fast and far.

When I felt safe from the danger, we slowed our pace. After a while, we stopped, gave our horses a rest, and waited for the caravan to reach our position.

"What do you think that was back there?" ventured Thomas.

I shook my head. "I don't know for sure. I think they were Brean."

In frustration, I shook my head again. "I don't understand it. I've always been able to see them, but not this time."

Feeling deeply troubled, I started pacing.

Is my vision failing me? Is it possible to use up? Are they able to hide from me? Is this a trick of Naehume? Perhaps, when we were linked, Naehume did something to me, and now he can hide the others from my sight. But that doesn't make sense, Naehume couldn't have influenced Thomas, and he couldn't see them either.

The only one I saw was the one that we had chased.

But maybe he wanted you to see it.

I paced some more.

The women, being the forward scouts, were the first to arrive.

Immediately upon seeing me, Sarah could tell something was wrong.

"What happened?" she asked, concerned.

The women dismounted and came to stand by us.

Anxious to hear what she made of the matter, I related the events that had unfolded with as much detail as possible. It must have been enough for once because she just listened without probing for more.

When finished, I asked, "What do you think?"

"I'm troubled by the whole thing," said Hannah.

"As am I," Jane concurred.

Hannah, furrowing her brow, said, "It sounds like the monster was leading you into a trap."

"It would appear so," I agreed.

"Yes," said Thomas. "Its actions certainly seemed deliberate."

"But if it were a trap," I mused, "how come they didn't spring it? Why let us leave?"

"Perhaps they weren't waiting for you," suggested Jane.

I paused. "I hadn't thought about that. You suppose they were waiting for the villagers?"

"If not you, that only leaves the villagers."

Doubt gripped me.

Sarah remained in silent contemplation.

"What do you think?" I asked her. "Were they waiting for the villagers?"

"Tell me about the hill," she said while tapping a finger to her lip. "You said that you suspected an ambush at the top?"

I nodded.

"Therefore, you went around?"

I nodded again. "I was afraid we'd walk right into it otherwise."

"The one Brean that you could see, it was just waiting for you?"

Again, I nodded.

"Yes," said Thomas. "It looked like it expected us to come over the hill, not around it."

Bugger, I thought, *I did leave something out.*

"Thomas is right," I said, trying to correct my omission.

Sarah stopped tapping and pressed her index finger to her lip.

"What does it mean?" asked Hannah.

"I believe," responded Sarah, dropping her hand, "that going around the hill may have saved your lives. Perhaps the reason they didn't spring the trap is that they weren't ready."

She hesitated again before adding, "But I am not certain. They could also have been waiting for the villagers. Perhaps they moved into position, hence the rustling you heard, but then decided not to do anything. It could be either, or something else entirely."

"What do we do?" I asked.

"What can we do?" returned Jane.

"We can't let them ensnare the villagers," said Hannah. "If that *is* their plan."

"No," I exhaled. "I suppose we do have to find out what they are up to. I don't like it, though."

Jane squeezed my hand consolingly. "None of us like it when those beasts are involved."

"Or when Lord Wright is involved," added Hannah.

"Well, John," said Sarah. "The course of action is up to you."

I thought for a moment and then said, "Very well. Hannah, will you go back and inform Sabin of the Brean and have him dig up at least a dozen men with horses? Preferably ones who are handy with rifles."

"I'm coming as well," stated Jane.

"Me too," said Hannah.

"No, you're not," Jane and I said in unison.

Hannah looked defiantly at us. "And why not?"

"For the same reason as last time," I said. "You're not healed, and there are others who can do it."

"Oh, I like your reason much better," said Jane.

"Why? What was yours?" I asked.

"Just that she is my younger sister, and Father wouldn't want her risking her life unnecessarily."

I smiled at her. "I think that would've been good too."

Having none of it, Hannah asked Jane, "Well then, why do you get to go?"

"Because someone has to keep John alive."

I nodded my head. "That's a good one too. She can't argue with that. However, I can."

"And you would lose," said Jane.

That was almost certainly true.

Hannah turned to Sarah. "Are you going to let them do this?"

Sarah took Hannah's hand in hers and patted it affectionately.

Hannah glared. It was clearly not the answer she was hoping for.

But before she could say anything, Sarah said, "Now what we need you to do, my dear, is to carry the message to Sabin."

Hannah looked like she was about to argue, but then she pulled away from Sarah, walked over to her horse, and flung herself up with extravagant flare.

"See," she said. "I have plenty of strength and am perfectly capable of saving John."

She turned around haughtily and trotted off.

As soon as Hannah had left, Sarah turned back to us and asked, "Where did this take place?"

I pointed in front of us and off to the left while explaining the approximate location.

"I believe I shall join you as well, but I want to talk to James first. He has more experience than just about anyone else in fighting the Brean, and I want his insight. Don't wait for me; I will catch up."

"Don't you think you should rest?" I asked.

"Yes," she said. "And you should as well. However, these are the circumstances in which we find ourselves."

***

I was glad to see that Mathias had joined the group of riders. He flashed me a big smile, and I returned it.

Sabin had sent exactly twelve men, all with muskets and pistols. Seeing them, I wished I had more, but I was afraid of leaving the villagers unprotected.

Mathias rode up and asked, "I hear there are Brean out there waiting for us. What is your plan?"

"Don't have one."

He paused and said with a grin, "I think I liked your last plan better when we fought them around the wagon."

"Well," I said, smiling. "You may not like my primary plan, but I think you'll like my backup plan if it all goes wrong."

"And what's that?"

"Run away as fast as we can."

"Against those beasts, there is no shame in that."

Turning serious, I addressed the men.

"The Brean are out there, and I'm afraid we don't know what they are planning. That is why you are here; I want to put a stop to whatever their scheme is. If we can't accomplish that, then I would like to at least know what they are doing. Better for us to find out than for your families."

They nodded in agreement.

After relating the details of our strange encounter, I said, "Since we don't know what they're up to, it's difficult to come up with a plan. However, I don't want to charge in there aimlessly: this is what I propose. When we get close, I want you to spread out in groups of two, with a large distance between you. That gives you two shots to bring down one of those brutes. The better marksman between you takes the first shot; aim for the head if you can. The second one will be there if he fails, and your pistols will be there if you can't do it with rifles. Those who have horses that tend to get spooked take the outside. Any questions?"

Ben asked, "What if they all charge at one team?"

"Then run."

A few of them laughed.

I went on to explain. "You should be far enough away from each team that it should force the Brean to spread out. However, there shouldn't be so much distance where another team can't help, should you need it. Understand?"

They did.

"How many are there?" someone asked.

"I don't know."

"I thought you could see them."

"Well, I can't," I snapped.

I wasn't sure if I felt more agitated at the question or the fact that I couldn't detect them.

Calming down, I explained, "I don't believe there are many. It would be too tricky for the Brean to hide in large numbers, and Thomas and I not to see them."

Unless Naehume has found some way to force our minds to ignore them, I thought.

But I didn't say that.

Instead, I explained, "They could be anywhere. Hiding behind trees…"

"Or holes in the ground," suggested Mathias.

"Perhaps. There are a lot of leaves covering the forest floor, but I didn't see any mounds of dirt suggesting they dug holes. I don't know when they would've had time to do that or know where to dig them."

"They could've guessed our path and dug them somewhere along the way and then lured you there," he reasoned.

I shrugged. "That is true. Since we couldn't see them, anything is possible. All I know is that we were close enough to hear them breathing and smell their stench. As such, if any of you have a plan you would like to offer, I'll listen."

I waited. No one said anything.

"Very well."

And with that, we set out with Thomas, Mathias, Jane, and myself leading the way.

"Do you think they are still waiting?" asked Mathias.

I shrugged. "Don't know."

"Can you find the spot again?"

I nodded. "Just follow our tracks."

Mathias looked down. "Oh. I suppose that's easy enough."

We rode through the forest while I kept a lookout. Before long, I saw what I was expecting to see—another lone Brean stalking through the woods.

It hadn't seen us yet, but it soon would.

Halting, I turned and addressed the men. "It won't be long now. Stay behind me, and when I give you this signal," I waved my arm one direction and then the next, "spread out. I want three groups on each side."

They nodded in acknowledgment.

Nudging Smoke into a trot, I took the lead.

Thomas, Jane, and Mathias followed closely behind.

I adjusted our course and rode toward the monster.

The beast stopped. Tilting its head, it strained to listen to the faint sound made by our approach.

A few moments later, it saw us, and we saw it.

Letting out a small cry, it turned and ran, but not quite in the same direction as before.

Thomas, drawing up by my side, noted the difference.

"What do we do?" he asked.

"Follow it."

We increased our pace to a gallop.

I had an idea, and I wanted to test it. If there were an ambush waiting for us, the monster would lead us right to it. If not, it would try to lose us at any cost.

We'd know soon enough.

I began to slacken our pace.

After a moment, the Brean noticed that we had slowed, and it too slowed.

My heart rate quickened, and my hands felt clammy.

Now what?

I began to have doubts. We still didn't know *how* they were going to attack. All we knew is that they would.

"What is it?" asked Jane. "Why are we stalling?"

"See how it slows?"

She nodded.

"It wants us to follow."

Jane's eyes opened wide with comprehension.

I added, "There is no sense in making our horses any more tired than they are."

"How will we know when we're there?" she asked.

"Our horses will be the first to detect it," I explained. "Watch for the signs."

After a few more minutes, the Brean stopped on a rise.

Before us, the terrain was relatively flat, other than the usual muddy mounds and depressions that accompany an uneven forest floor.

The beast turned and looked at us.

Smoke's ears flicked up.

"We're here," I said.

I gave the signal.

The men spread out.

Mathias and another man took the position to my immediate right.

Jane and Thomas stayed with me while the rest spread out as instructed.

I checked my crossbow, pistol, and rifle. The latter one I kept in my grasp.

I noted the others similarly checked their own weapons.

We advanced cautiously, one step after another.

The horses grew anxious, snorting, stamping, and hesitating.

As we progressed, so did their agitation.

Some whinnied, others faltered, throwing their necks back and threatening to buck their riders.

The men comforted them the best they could while scanning the forest, trying to detect anything.

My vision, like the last time, was useless. I couldn't see any Brean, other than just the one.

I scanned the tops of the trees, perhaps expecting them to jump down from their perches.

Nothing.

It had to be the forest floor.

Although the leaves were dead and covered the ground, they didn't seem thick enough to hide Brean. Even if they could somehow huddle under the dense foliage, something *would* show—a finger, an ear, a partial foot—something would show.

But there was nothing.

They could have dug holes, but then where were the mounds of dirt? The leaves would also have been disrupted where they had been moved and then spread again over the holes.

There were no such signs.

Still, the floor had to be the only answer. Didn't it?

I considered Naehume. He was powerful, but what was the extent of it? He had been able to reach me in my sleep. Perhaps he could reach the others as well and tell our brains not to see the Brean.

Cold settled around me; it seeped into my fingers and toes. I shivered.

The dread of an imminent fight, or, as I was beginning to believe, our imminent doom, felt suffocating.

A putrid smell permeated the air, and I wrinkled my nose at it.

The ground. They have to be in the ground, I thought. *But where? Perhaps we should retreat while we still can.*

A rifle cracked to life.

It was the man next to Mathias.

"What are you shooting at?" Mathias asked excitedly.

"Just trying to flush them out," said the man. "I suspect they may be hiding behind the hill, like the one that Brean is standing on."

"He could be right," said Thomas, his voice filled with tension. "There was a hill at the last spot too."

I agreed. Still, this was a very small hill; there couldn't be many Brean if that were the case.

Does there have to be very many? I asked myself.

A sound reached my ears.

But it wasn't a rasp.

"Someone is calling to us," said Jane.

I looked around.

Far behind, I saw the tiny figure of Sarah waving her arms and riding furiously toward us. James was with her, as were another dozen or so men.

Letting out a sigh of relief, I asked, "What is she saying?"

"I can't quite make it out," replied Jane. "She's too far away."

Jane cupped a hand around her ear. "I can make out the word, *around*."

"We already know they are around here," said Thomas.

"To the front? To the side? Where?" I asked.

All the horses were jumpy.

One horse whinnied and reared.

"Shhh, there is more. I can't make it out; the horses are too noisy."

Jane put her rifle across her saddle and cupped both ears with her hands.

I swung my rifle around, looking for the slightest movement, anything to suggest where the attack would come from.

Smoke stamped, wondering what we were doing. His ears swiveled wildly.

Suddenly, Jane snatched up her rifle, her eyes wide and her face white with fear.

"What is it?" I asked before she could explain.

"Sarah says they're all around us!"

Chapter Twelve: Lambs to the Slaughter

Without warning, the Brean, standing atop the hill, abruptly dropped down on all fours. Opening its mouth wide, exposing long sharp teeth, it bellowed a bone-chilling roar that caused its entire body to shake.

Suddenly, the ground about us heaved skyward.

A torrent of leaves flew into the air as if kicked up by a gale-force wind.

But there was no wind.

The trap was sprung!

All around us, Brean seemed to magically appear from the swirling leaves, the ground, or both.

Our poor horses were terrified beyond reason.

Some bolted in panic, their riders clinging desperately to stay on.

They were the lucky men, the ones who would survive.

Thomas and Matthias were thrown clear off their rearing horses.

Mathias' rifle fired a wild shot as he hit the ground.

Jane managed to stay mounted despite Ember's distress. She struggled to aim her rifle even as she fought to keep Ember under control.

Smoke jumped and lurched sideways, but he did not rear or flee.

Some weapons erupted, but they were too few.

The monsters were upon us.

It was then that I realized we'd already lost.

All around me, I heard the screams of men and the snarls of Brean.

The boom of Jane's rifle thundered from my immediate right, causing my ears to ring.

Snapping my head around, I saw a monster fall in a bloody mess.

Thomas screamed.

I spun, frantically trying to find him.

A Brean had picked him up by his leg.

He looked like a ragdoll in the monster's hand.

Dangling Thomas over its head, it then whipped him down toward the ground.

Jane's pistol cracked.

The head of the Brean rocked back as it was struck in the face by the ball.

Though the monster wasn't killed, he did let go of Thomas, lessening the intensity of his destruction.

Regardless, Thomas still hit the ground with a sickening crunch.

He lay motionless.

The Brean lumbered away, covering its face with its hands in an effort to staunch the blood that flowed from its wound.

My frozen body finally defrosted, and my mind snapped into action.

I saw Mathias fleeing from a pursuing monster.

I snapped up my rifle just as the Brean slashed at his back with its powerful claws.

Mathias screamed a heartrending cry. He fell forward, his tattered shirt exposing four long, deep gashes.

My rifle thundered to life, and the shoulder of the monster exploded.

The Brean bellowed in pain and fury, unsure whether to retaliate against me or its original prey.

Using his arms, Mathias tried dragging himself away from the snarling beast.

Snatching the pistol from my belt, I kicked Smoke into action.

Fearlessly, he burst into stride.

As the monster leaped for Mathias, Smoke charged forward with a terrific surge of speed, intercepting it.

The hulking beast crashed into us, knocking Smoke off balance.

I raised my pistol as we hurtled to the ground.

The monster roared; its putrid spittle washed over me.

Shoving the pistol in through its gaping jaws, I pulled the trigger.

The roar cut off in a choked gurgle.

My leg came free of the stirrups as we hit the ground, and I fell flat on my back, unable to breathe.

Trying to suck in air that refused to come, I gulped like a fish out of water.

The carcass of the dead Brean landed on top of my horse.

Wrestling under its weight, Smoke soon extricated himself and stood up.

I spotted Jane. She had retreated a short distance and was reloading.

Finally, slowly, blessed air began to return to my starving lungs.

As soon as I could, I frantically crawled to Mathias.

He was facedown and motionless.

"Mathias!"

His breath came in short, ragged, shallow wheezes.

"I…" he labored for another breath. "...can't…" Another breath. "...move."

Gently, I rolled him onto his back and pulled his body into my lap, cradling his head in my arms.

The sounds of the battle, or rather the massacre, fell all around us.

Snarls, roars, cries, and a few pistols could be heard.

I couldn't look; I didn't want to see the devastation.

I had led these people to their slaughter.

My attention and my head were bowed over the man cradled in my arms when a cacophony of rifle fire erupted around us.

Sarah and the men from Syre had joined the fight.

I didn't care.

Thomas and Mathias had both defended me, and this was how I repaid them.

Mathias looked up at me. His eyes were dull and wide with fear. His light was fading.

Between labored breaths, he said, "I can't…feel…my legs."

Tears welled in my eyes.

"Don't worry," I said soothingly. "They're still there. You're going to be all right."

Neither of us believed it, but the words, although shallow, seemed to comfort him.

"You might have to rest for a day or two," I said, continuing the lie.

My tears broke free and streamed down my cheeks.

"Is that...all?" he asked.

"Maybe three, but no more."

He smiled weakly.

"Does it hurt?" I asked.

"No."

There was a rattle in his voice now.

"John...I'm scared."

"Don't be," I said, but I doubt he heard me.

The light in his eyes had extinguished.

Burying my head in his chest, I drew him up and held him tight.

"John," he said.

I didn't move.

"John, look at me."

I still couldn't bring myself to do it. I felt too guilty.

"I'm sorry," I sobbed. "This is my fault."

"No, it's not," said Mathias. "This was done by the hand of others. John, you have to listen to me; I don't have much time. Thomas isn't with me. He needs your help."

I looked up at him.

"The battle still rages," he said. "If you fail, you both die. Look!"

Mathias pointed with an outstretched arm.

At that moment, the black eyes of a wounded Brean fixed on me. Its hand clutched its side while blood seeped through its fingers.

"Take up your bow," said Mathias. He pointed to the ground not far from me.

There lay my crossbow, knocked loose from our fall.

Another figure appeared next to Mathias, but I didn't watch the reunion. My failure to keep him safe cut to my soul and I couldn't bear to look on anymore.

However, I could do what he said. I could show him some honor in that.

Wiping my eyes with my sleeve, I scrambled for the bow.

The monster charged at the same time.

Reaching the crossbow, I snatched it up, aimed for an eye socket, and let the bolt fly.

It sliced through the air.

The bolt struck its thick head, tearing open a long, wicked gash across the side of its face.

The Brean yelped in pain, turned its head, and covered the wound with a hand.

I had missed the vulnerable eye socket, but the movement exposed another target.

With a quick pull of the trigger, the second bolt cut through the air.

It struck and buried deep into the monster's neck.

The beast's hand shot up and tore the bolt out.

It was a mistake. Its lifeblood gushed from the wound and oozed from its mouth.

Reeling, the monster stumbled forward and then staggered sideways toward Thomas.

Dropping the bow, I ran past the monster and dove for Thomas.

Wrapping my arms around his torso, I half rolled, half flung him free from the falling brute.

The monster crashed to the ground, whipping up leaves all around us in a gust of wind.

Even though we were within its reach, it made no attempt to lash at us. The brown eyes of the Brean looked at me and blinked.

The raw brutality from the moment before was gone.

I didn't watch its last moments.

Hooking my hands under Thomas' armpits, I dragged him away.

And then, like Mathias, I cradled him in my arms. His eyes were closed, and blood trickled from his nose and mouth.

After a few minutes, the sounds of fighting died down, and the forest fell eerily quiet.

Either we had won—if you could call it that, or I was the last one left alive. In which case, my time was short.

I didn't care. I just held onto Thomas and waited, with my head bowed.

There I sat until a hand touched my shoulder.

Looking up, I met the sorrowful eyes of Jane.

Sarah stood by her side, and James stood by Sarah.

Silently, Sarah knelt and pried open one of Thomas' eyes. She peered into it and then let it close. She placed a hand on his chest and, with her other hand, felt for his pulse of life. Then she proceeded to open his shirt and inspect the damage underneath.

While Sarah appraised Thomas, I looked around for the first time.

Unmoving men mingled with dead monsters. A few horses added to the casualties.

"How many?" I asked somberly.

"Eight dead, five wounded," said Jane.

She knelt by my side and placed a reassuring hand on my shoulder.

I felt anything but comforted.

My eyes fell upon a few pieces of upturned earth.

Jane followed my gaze.

"Blankets," she explained. "Thick blankets caked with mud and leaves. They simply carried them here and hid under them. Remember how the first monster gave a small cry before it ran? That must have been their signal."

I didn't say anything. I felt hollow, certain I could never feel joy again.

These men had followed me right into an ambush. It was a trap that we knew about, and still, I led them like lambs to a slaughter. I had innocent blood on my hands. Because of me, these men would never see their families again. Their wives would now have to face this terrifying journey alone. I wondered how many had children.

Under the tremendous weight of guilt, my head bowed, and my shoulders slumped. I looked down at the young, battered face of Thomas. I thought of his mother and how she must be waiting for him to return home.

"Jane," said Sarah. "Return to the others. Tell Angus where we are and explain what happened. Have him bring the company to us. When they arrive, it will be time to stop for the night. In the meantime, we'll get some campfires going and see what we can do for the wounded. Will you also please fetch my bag of herbs?"

Jane nodded and stood.

Reaching a hand up, I grabbed her sleeve.

"No, you stay here. This massacre is my responsibility, not yours. It is I who must bear the news."

"John, you don't have to…"

I cut her off and said resolutely, "I do."

Gently, I laid Thomas back on the ground and stood up.

"Then I'm coming with you," said Jane with an equal amount of determination.

I didn't argue. Instead, I found Smoke, mounted, and set off for the company, with Jane on Ember by my side.

We rode in silence. I stared at the ground feeling heavy and numb.

After a long time, Jane finally spoke.

"It's not your fault, John."

"Yes, it is," I snapped. "I am the fool who led them into that ambush. Even worse, I *knew* it was a trap."

Jane didn't seem fazed. "And what could you have done differently?"

"I could've kept them away, kept them safe."

"And risk the entire company? The Brean *were* looking for us. They would have found us all before nightfall and set their trap. It was only a matter of time. If you hadn't done what you did, we wouldn't be talking about just eight dead men but the massacre of a whole village."

"We could've done it another way."

"And what way would that have been?"

She waited for a reply.

I said nothing. I didn't want to be consoled. In my heart, there was no meaning to the deaths of these men.

I had killed them.

Jane fell silent.

We passed an outrider without saying a word. He didn't ask any questions.

I rode straight past Hannah, without meeting her gaze, and on to Angus.

Jane stayed with me, and Hannah fell in behind on her mount.

I slid off Smoke, turned, and faced Angus, unsure of where to begin.

The look on my face must have said it all.

Angus took my hand, cupping it in his, and patted it. He regarded me with eyes filled with sorrow, compassion, and understanding.

"Oh, laddie, I know that look. I am very sorry, indeed."

I said nothing.

"How many?"

"Eight dead. Five wounded."

"Jimmy?"

"Alive."

Angus couldn't hide the relief on his face.

"What about Sarah?" asked Hannah.

"She's fine."

"And Thomas?"

I looked away.

Hannah grabbed my arm. "Tell me!"

I looked at her and said, "Not dead…at least, not yet."

She leaped down off her horse, ran to a goat that Angus had been leading, and removed a satchel.

I recognized it as the one containing Sarah's herbs.

Hannah flew back onto her horse, wheeled him about, and sped off following our tracks. Her dark hair streamed out behind her.

"Where did it happen?" asked Angus.

I explained.

"And the names of the dead?"

"The only one I knew is Mathias. I never bothered to learn the rest."

And I felt horrible for it. I should know the names of the men I had sentenced to die.

From now on, I vowed, *I will take the time to learn them.*

Jane spoke up, "Rick, Ammon, and Jace are the ones I know."

Angus nodded. "Keep this news to yerself for now. I don't want villagers runnin' through the forest in a state of hysteria and gettin' lost in search of loved ones. They will find out soon enough. Now, my dear Jane, fetch blankets and water flasks for the wounded. They will be cold and thirsty."

Jane obeyed and set off in search of the supplies.

As she walked away, Angus regarded me with keen eyes.

Placing his hand on my shoulder, he said, "Laddie, we all knew there would be the work of death in this matter. It is inevitable when dealin' with monsters and tyrants. Don't let it paralyze and destroy ye."

I said nothing.

The last thing I wanted was forgiveness. I wanted to feel every ounce of the guilt and pain that I deserved and suffer the full wrath of my inexcusable folly.

Without another word, Angus patted my arm, and I left to help Jane.

Once the needed supplies were strapped to our horses, we returned to the others.

Upon arriving, I saw that the wounded had been moved together and far away from the dead Brean.

Our dead had also been gathered and placed side by side. Their faces were covered respectfully with their hats.

Able men either stood guard or gathered wood. Two campfires were already blazing near the wounded.

Jane and I dismounted.

After unloading the blankets, Jane quickly went about wrapping the wounded in them.

Hannah knelt by a still unconscious Thomas and held his hand in hers.

Sarah moved about the men, administering various herbs. She also bandaged their wounds from torn strips of cloth.

I felt utterly hopeless.

James came and stood by my side but remained silent.

"It's a good thing you and Sarah came," I finally said. "There wouldn't have been anyone left."

He hesitated a moment before replying slowly, "Sarah blames herself."

I scoffed at the idea. "Nonsense, we all know whose fault this is, and it's not hers."

"Are you certain that it's yours?"

He didn't wait for a reply.

"She came to me for help…"

"I know," I interrupted. "She thought you would have some ideas."

"Aye. But it took time to work it out. Once I learned that you couldn't see through dead things, I reasoned that the Brean would try to conceal themselves. It took us a wee bit longer to round up more men. Sarah was desperate that we find you before you found the Brean."

"It wouldn't have mattered. I already knew it was a trap. We are all fortunate that you weren't caught in it. It allowed you to actually get off some shots. If you all had been here, then you also might have died in the surprise."

"If Sarah had been here, there wouldn't have been a surprise. Dead things cannot confound her gifts. Did she not tell you?"

James' implication made me pause.

"I did know," I admitted. "But I never considered it."

"Aye, unfortunately, neither did Sarah, at least not at first. She could've detected them when you could not."

I looked at Sarah and saw her with newly opened eyes. She moved from patient to patient, administering with deftness to their needs, but her face was pale, and her shoulders sagged as if yoked under a great weight.

"These deaths are not hers to own, and they are not yours. Lord Wright and Naehume are the guilty ones. This blood is on their hands. Not yours. Not hers."

I looked at him. "You sound like your father. Perhaps you're right."

James smiled, but it wasn't happy; it was tired and full of weariness from this whole messy business.

He nodded toward Sarah. "If only I could convince her of that."

"I know what she is feeling."

Leaving him, I walked over to Sarah. She was kneeling by a man who appeared like he wasn't long for this world.

She looked up at me.

Without a word, I knelt beside her and threw my arms around her.

At first, she did nothing. Then, Sarah buried her head in my shoulder and wept.

Chapter Thirteen: No Ordinary Dream

The clouds were breaking up. They floated hurriedly across the night sky, momentarily covering the moon and then moving to reveal the pallid white light.

The villagers now slumbered next to scattered fires. They had mourned the fallen in their own way. Many were bitter and angry with me. Most didn't say anything, which is what I preferred. A few were grateful that the whole company didn't blunder across the trap.

But the more I thought about it, the more I had my doubts.

I suppose the Brean could have tried ambushing the villagers; one never knows. But then why lead a small group of men to them? It didn't make any sense. Although, perhaps, they planned on using the same tactic on the villagers after they killed us. With no survivors, they would be none the wiser.

Earlier in the day, I had shown the outriders what the blankets looked like so they knew what to scout for. Whether they could spot them, however, was questionable. The blanket disguises were so ingenious; they would have to probe every mound of mud and leaves from here to Marysvale.

Sitting upon the same hill where the Brean scout had signaled the onslaught, a shiver ran through my body. It was cold, and now, without the clouds, the temperature was sure to plummet.

All three women had offered to take the watch, but I insisted on doing it myself. The Brean were cunning. If they attacked, and the women didn't see them coming, I didn't want them living with that burden on their conscience. Others offered as well, but I declined for the same reasons. And I didn't want it on *my* conscience that, if I hadn't been asleep, I could've given a proper warning.

So, there I sat.

Under the pale illumination of the moon, I looked upon the carcasses of the Brean still scattered about. I could also see the new cemetery where eleven makeshift crosses marked the resting place of those who fell during the fight and the three who later passed away. Angus had promised that, when able, they would return and set proper headstones.

The whole scene had a chilling, sobering effect. It was not that I didn't feel that way before, but now, in the dark, its gravity set in.

I laughed mockingly at our childish naiveté. The hope that a displaced group of cold, hungry, and poorly armed people would make it unmolested past Marysvale was absurd.

And to put their trust in me. What were they thinking? What was I thinking? There is no hiding from them.

I realized that they were simply toying with us.

At any time, Naehume can assemble an army of Brean as he did in Alyth, attack us during the night, and we'll fall. Attack us during the day, and we'll still fall. Throw disciplined, trained soldiers into the mix, and the battle will last only a few moments.

Again, I laughed bitterly.

We'll probably surrender at first sight.

The villagers were frightened, cold, and beaten. All they wanted was a warm shelter, a bed, something besides meat to eat, and the opportunity to mourn. I couldn't blame them. That's all I wanted as well.

Sarah's cabin was constantly on my mind, and I longed for it.

A figure walked up the hill towards me. I recognized her aura, and I rose to greet her.

The girl I loved came and stood by my side. Taking my hand in hers, she looked up at the moon. A passing cloud had just uncovered it, bathing her beautiful face in its light.

I watched her breath, visible in the chilly air, and noticed her shiver slightly.

"Cold?" I asked.

"Aren't you?"

"In more ways than one."

Opening the front of my coat, I said, "Come here."

Jane encircled her arms around me, turned her head, and pressed her cheek to my chest. Wrapping my coat around her, I returned the hug.

"Better?" I asked.

I could feel her head nod against my chest. After a few minutes, her shivering stopped.

"I can hear your heart," she said softly.

"What's it saying?"

"It is sad."

"If that's all it is, then that's good news, for there are many hearts tonight that are broken."

Jane sighed sorrowfully. "It pains me to see the torment on your face—and on Sarah's. Death is part of dealing with those beasts. It is unavoidable. And it's not over."

"I think this whole plan of ours is a mistake."

"Really? What would you do differently?"

"There are already grumblings that we should go to Marysvale and just throw ourselves at their mercy. We can't win, Jane; they are too powerful. And they aren't going to simply let us go; we know too much."

She hesitated a moment before replying carefully, "The villagers think it cannot get any worse. They believe anything would be better than this. But they're wrong. I know what awaits them. Have you forgotten? You experienced the oppression of Marysvale for only a couple of days. Imagine living like that for a lifetime—to have tyrants controlling your destiny. Yes, you may be alive, but what of your soul? To be free to chart your own course is always worth the sacrifice. It is better to die free than to live as a slave. The difference between you and Sarah at this moment is that she understands this."

We stood for a long time in silence, embracing one another, while I contemplated what she said.

Another person walked up the hill.

Jane released me as she heard the footsteps through the leaves.

"It is a cold night," Sarah observed knowingly and without reproach.

Another cloud passed by the moon, plunging us into darkness. And, just as quickly, it departed again, illuminating the forest in the pallid light.

"How are you?" I asked Sarah.

"I was about to ask you the same thing. My sleep wasn't restful, and it *is* cold. Nevertheless, I feel somewhat better."

"I'm glad," said Jane.

"Now it's your turn, John," said Sarah. "How are you?"

"Don't know if I feel much like sleeping."

"I can understand your position. However, rest is essential. Not only will it freshen your outlook, but I also don't want you faltering from fatigue when we need you most."

"Isn't that time now?" I asked.

"No, I can take over. There is no guarantee that they won't use coverings of some kind again."

"I certainly hope they don't all start walking around the forest hiding under blankets," said Jane.

I agreed.

"I suppose Jex told them that you couldn't see through dead things," mused Sarah.

"Most likely," I acknowledged.

"I just don't know how they made them so fast. It hasn't even been two days since Alyth was destroyed!" said Jane.

"They had time," I reasoned. "I'm certain Jex told them that night when I saw him with Naehume, and whom I suspect was Lord Wright, in the forest."

"Jex has a lot of blood on his hands," observed Sarah.

"Do you think he will ever face any justice?" I asked.

She hesitated.

"That's what I thought," I said dryly.

"No, it's not what you suppose. I don't know what will happen to Jex. Yet, in my heart, I trust we will prevail. I told you in those first days that your presence here changes everything. I still believe that, and I believe it is for the good."

I gave a short, contemptuous snort. "You've been driven from your home; Jane's father was murdered; Alyth has been burned to the ground; dozens of people have been killed. I don't see how any of that is good."

"Did you imagine it would be easy?" asked Sarah. "Did you once believe that Lord Wright would simply give up now that you are here and let us all go on our merry way? That he would not fight to keep what he took? Did you think that there would be no price to pay?"

"I…I don't know," I admitted.

"Perhaps the things that have happened are exactly what is needed. A lot of walls have been built up in both towns and in ourselves. We build them for comfort and safety, and security. So much so that we never want to venture outside of them. Sometimes those walls have to be torn down by circumstance for us to realize that life without walls is much better."

"And what if the people don't want it?"

"Then it is up to us to show them a better way and convince them. Most people are followers. They want to do what everyone else is doing, wear what everyone else is wearing, and think what everyone else is thinking. It takes exceptional individuals to enact change, and there aren't many of them. They face difficulties, challenges, persecution, and even death. However, the rewards for the brave are vast and worthwhile.

Even if they aren't around to enjoy the fullness of their sacrifice, they leave a great legacy for those who come after."

I didn't know what to think. Confusion racked my soul.

How did I get myself into this? I had no desire to help people who resented my help themselves. And I didn't like the pressure of leading these same people to an unknown end. I didn't want the guilt of failure, and I begrudged the foresight of knowing that some failure is inevitable.

I felt stuck and despondent.

"And you believe I am one of those people?" I asked, not knowing what else to say.

"The question isn't if *I* believe. The question is, do *you* believe? Everyone can be one of those people if we choose to, and do not fear the scorn of men."

"You didn't answer my question," I said stubbornly.

"Yes. I believe you were preserved for just this experience. Your being here with your gifts, at this time in history, is no accident, John."

We stood for a long time before Jane finally said, "Go and sleep, my love. Everything will seem better in the morning, and you do need rest."

Reluctantly, I obeyed.

Jane, of course, didn't know how wrong she was.

***

I walked through the moonlit streets. The air was cold and the ground frozen. I was alone, but it didn't matter; I was always alone. I preferred it that way, as there were no others

181

like me. I was different. My powerful strides carried me over the bodies that lay heaped in the streets. Brean, humans, they were all the same to me.

Looking down, I beheld their frost-covered faces. Most of them I didn't know. I didn't care.

I continued stepping over corpses, out through the battered gates of Marysvale.

Soon, I came upon two lifeless girls. These I recognized. The younger one stared up into a sea of stars with vacant green eyes. An old wound had been healing on her arm, but it was nothing to the ones in her chest. The older girl lay with her head across the breast of the younger one; her arm draped over her waist—sisters from what I remembered. Marks on the ground suggested the older one had dragged herself to the younger. Four deep slashes on her back told me how she had died.

They meant nothing to me.

Breaking into an easy lope, I cleared the field of the dead and slipped into the trees. He would be hunting me when he was finished with the soldiers in the keep.

Our eternal hatred would have to wait another day. For now, I wanted to wash the blood off of me and rest.

Keeping up my steady gait, I ran long and far.

Far away from him.

The sun was waking, bringing its brilliant warmth to the wintery day.

I'd grown to hate the light.

Ahead of me lay a pond. My mouth felt dry, so I slowed to drink from its clear, cold water.

Drawing up to the edge of the still pool, I knelt down and bent over, ready to dip my head…and stopped.

Staring back in the reflection wasn't me, but that of a hairy, red-eyed monster with wicked scars across his face.

I cried out in terror, but the monster in the reflection simply laughed.

The red eyes faded away as I jerked awake.

**

In my conscious state, the horror of the dream crashed over me. I recalled all the dead people lying on the frozen ground, slaughtered at the gates of Marysvale. Like a hot iron, the haunting images of Jane and Hannah burned into my memory and harrowed my soul. It felt so real.

A long shiver ran through my body, but not from the cold.

Villagers, whom I had awoken with my shouts or who were unable to sleep, looked at me strangely. They seemed to regard me as if I were truly possessed with a demon.

I sprang to my feet.

I had to see Jane. I had to see the light in her eyes, not the dull, hollow, lifeless ones that plagued my nightmare. I wanted to feel the warmth in her hands, to see her chest rise and fall with life.

I had to see her smile, the one that could melt the ice from my heart.

I needed to keep her safe, safe from the fate that awaited her at the gates of Marysvale. The villagers could not go there; I had to make sure that the future I saw would never come to pass.

I ran to the hill.

The clouds had returned with reinforcements, blocking out the moon. The wind had also picked up and was now whistling through the trees.

In the air, I smelled the scent of impending rain. Or worse, snow.

The two women who sat huddled together watched me approach.

"I hoped you would sleep longer," said Sarah.

Sitting next to Jane, I took her hand in mine.

She looked at me curiously but did not pull away. I continued to hold her hand, turning it, feeling it. It wasn't warm, but it was alive.

I touched her cheek.

Sarah, too, stared at me oddly.

"John," said Jane. "What bothers you? Why are you acting so strange?"

Meeting her eyes, I pleaded, "Jane, come away with me. Let's leave tonight."

"What brought this on?" Jane asked in bewilderment.

"I saw your fate—the one that will surely come to pass if we go to Marysvale. Jane, we can't go. I can't bear the thought of losing you like that. Nor Hannah."

Looking down, I closed my eyes as if I could block the searing images from my mind.

Jane's hand touched my chin and raised it. Opening my eyes, I gazed into hers.

She smiled. "It was only a bad dream. We are not going there."

"No," I shook my head. "It was more; I know it. I can feel the power of that vision. It was no ordinary dream."

"Tell me about this dream," Sarah urged.

"No, it's too horrible to relive," I replied with a shake of my head.

"John," she replied. "Your dreams tend to be important. It would be best if you could share it with us."

Again, I shook my head. "I don't want to; it's bad enough. But this I will tell: I saw villagers slaughtered at the gates of Marysvale by the Brean."

"Were there soldiers involved?"

"No. At least I didn't see them; I only saw the results of the massacre."

"And what about the people of Marysvale? Could you see them? Was I there?" pressed Sarah.

"You plan on dragging this out of me no matter what, don't you?"

Sarah smiled. "That's what aunts do."

I sighed and told her the whole nightmare, including seeing Naehume's reflection in the water instead of my own.

This bit of information troubled her deeply.

"Aren't you bothered by the death of our friends?" I asked, a bit perplexed.

"Of course I am," Sarah replied soothingly. "But I'm more troubled by what you experienced and saw in that reflection. You have a very disconcerting and dangerous relationship with that monster."

"But what about the rest? What else matters if you're all dead?"

"It *may* matter. However, you have been known to misinterpret your dreams."

"Perhaps," I confessed. "But this one is different. If we go to Marysvale, everyone will die."

"Let's not worry about that now," said Sarah. "The people are just scared, and any talk of that is only born of grief. No one seriously wants to go there."

A small raindrop fell upon my face and ran down my cheek like a tear. The image of Jane and Hannah filled my mind as I again replayed the horrible nightmare.

A moment later, the clouds broke open, and sheets of rain pelted our company. Instantly, the whole camp was aroused, and villagers scurried about trying to seek shelter. However, being in a forest with leafless trees brought few options.

Some of the luckier ones had oil-skinned coats or fur that kept them dry, but the majority had nothing. The blankets, which were too few to go around as it was, were soon drenched.

A heroic effort was made to keep the fires going. However, after a few short minutes, only two campfires blazed hot enough to keep lit. Yet, even those looked like they would soon lose the battle.

Presently, it became apparent that the only way to keep the villagers warm was to get them walking. With so few possessions, you would think that breaking camp would be effortless, but, alas, that proved not to be the case. Muck from the rain-drenched forest floor slowed everyone down to a snail's pace. The villagers were not used to such difficulties, and many of them made the worst of it.

As the early gray of dawn began to cast away the pitch blackness of night, I stood on top of the hill with Jane, Smoke, and Ember, waiting.

Hannah, who had not left Thomas' side, came running toward us.

She was smiling.

"He's awake. Thomas woke up."

I let out a huge sigh of relief. Jane threw her arms around Hannah and embraced her.

"How is he?" asked Jane.

"Talking and hungry. Come see."

"That's a good sign," I said. And, together, we led our horses down to the camp.

Thomas sat with his back against a tree. He was one of the lucky few with a good oil-skinned coat. He sat wrapped up in it, sipping a cup of something hot. And by the face he made, I guessed it contained something from Sarah to make him feel better.

James and Sarah squatted by his side.

When he saw us, he flashed a weak but happy smile.

"How do you feel?" I asked.

"Like I jumped off a cliff."

"Well," I replied, "if it helps, you look like you jumped off a cliff. It will be a special girl who will want to marry you now."

He started to chuckle, but it got caught in a groan of pain.

Which made the rest of us laugh.

"Ouch," he said. "Don't say things like that; it hurts to move. How's Shade?"

"Alive," I answered. "He has a cut across his neck, but he fared better than you did."

"Did you get the bugger who did this?"

I nodded. "Thanks to Jane. I don't think you would be alive right now if she hadn't shot the monster when she did. It slowed down your fall."

"Thank you, Jane," he said solemnly.

Thomas looked around. "It appears like you're getting ready to head out."

"We are," I confirmed.

"Then will you get Shade ready for me, John?"

"It would be better if you rode in the wagon."

Thomas turned his head to appraise it. "Where? It's all filled up."

"We'll make room."

He shook his head. "No, I'll ride."

Turning to Sarah, I asked, "Any broken ribs?"

"Possibly. I don't know for sure. He is, however, pretty black and blue on his chest."

"Might be more comfortable in the wagon," I said to Thomas. "Riding is going to hurt some."

And that was putting it mildly.

"I can ride. Others need it more."

"You sure?"

He nodded. "Unless you can conjure up some shelter and a soft bed for me. Oh, sorry, John; I didn't mean it like that."

Smiling, I replied, "I didn't take it that way. Leave Shade to me."

I turned, ready to retrieve his horse, but stopped.

Something in the mist caught my attention.

I peered at the form curiously.

It was a large form. No, multiple large forms.

I ran to Smoke and drew out my rifle.

The others looked surprised and anxious.

"What is it, lad?" asked James, reaching for a pistol in his belt.

"Riders."

Chapter Fourteen: The Welcoming Party

Jane reached for her pistol. "How many?"

"Three for now, but I'd wager there are more out of sight."

"How far?" asked Thomas, trying to stand. His face grimaced in pain.

James placed a restraining hand on him. "Stay down, laddie. We can take care of these few."

Gratefully, Thomas sagged back against the tree.

Studying the figures for a moment, I said, somewhat bewildered, "They seem to be in no hurry."

"Best get my father," said James.

Hannah volunteered to fetch Angus, and, after retrieving their rifles, Jane, James, Sarah, and I walked out to wait for the incoming riders.

Angus, Sabin, and Sam, along with a few others, soon joined us.

Silently, standing in the pouring rain, we watched.

And, through the mist, they came.

Three soldiers drew up in front of us.

Jane stiffened.

I studied the lead man more closely, trying to figure out how I recognized him.

"Matthew," whispered Jane, jogging my memory.

"Ah, Lyman's crony," I whispered back.

I recalled seeing him with Lyman when we first entered Marysvale.

Jane nodded. "He's a nasty one, every bit as mean as Lyman. They were together so much that they even sound the same."

"Wonderful," I muttered.

"Greetings!" Matthew declared loudly and extravagantly.

It drew the attention of some villagers.

"State yer business," growled Angus.

Matthew looked at me. "Ah, John, how nice to see you again."

He said it graciously enough, but the quick flash of a sneer betrayed his true feelings. Well, that, and the fact that I could see contempt and malice in his soul.

Matthew then tipped his hat to Jane. "Miss Wolfe, always a pleasure."

"Yer business!" Angus roared.

"Now, there is no need for that, I assure you. We come as friends."

Matthew removed his hat and placed it deliberately over his heart. Standing up in the stirrups, he called loudly so all could hear.

"My name is General Matthew Pierce, but please just call me Matthew. As the general in charge of Marysvale's defense, let me be the first to express our deep condolences for your losses. When we heard of the tragedy that befell Alyth, we were indeed horrified."

His eyes swept over the assembling crowd.

"Liar," I hissed low and threateningly.

If Matthew heard, he didn't acknowledge it.

He continued, "As neighbors, our thoughts and prayers are with you. We have come to offer our help during these troubled times."

"By sending three riders?" I asked doubtfully.

He gave a little laugh. "Oh, heavens, no. When he heard of your dreadful misfortune, Lord Wright personally organized a relief effort. We have a camp waiting for you with shelter and hot food, and you will also find plenty of warm blankets, welcoming fires, and hot cider to ease your discomfort. Plus, there are fifty well-trained soldiers to offer you their protection and aid in escorting you to the safe haven of Marysvale. Come, it is not far."

"What do you hope to gain by leading us to Marysvale?" asked Sarah.

By now, the whole company had assembled.

Matthew placed his hand over his heart. "Why, the only thing we hope to gain is friendship. We wouldn't dream of forcing you to do anything against your will."

I gave a contemptuous little laugh.

"You should tell that to the people already living there."

Matthew smiled condescendingly as if humoring a child. "The people of Marysvale are quite content. They are not the ones suffering in the wet and cold at this time."

"The only reason these people are suffering now is because of the treachery of Lord Wright!" I spat.

Matthew's smile vanished. "Those are quite serious accusations to be thrown about by an *outsider*. Where is your

192

proof? Treachery may be at play, but it was not at our hand. We have been peaceful neighbors for a very long time. No, this evil came to you in *recent* days."

He placed a finger to his lips and glared at me. "I wonder who could have brought it upon you?"

I clenched my fists and gritted my teeth. I wanted to tear him and his sanctimonious tone down from the saddle.

"I have a wee question," said Angus, with a hard edge to his voice. "How did ye find out about our calamity? The fire was deliberately set by the hand of a traitor named Jex. I believe he had accomplices, friends he could run to when the deed was done. Have ye heard of him?"

Matthew tapped his finger to his lips as if in contemplation.

He replied slowly, "No, I don't believe I am acquainted with anyone by that name."

"Odd," said Angus. "Then how did ye learn of our misfortune?"

He has him there, I thought triumphantly.

I couldn't help the slight grin that spread across my face.

"Oh, that," replied Matthew, with a dismissive little wave. "No, that came from a concerned citizen of yours. He goes by the name of Daniel. Do you know him?"

My smile vanished. How could I forget the wagon master? I despised that man—the way he looked at Jane and how he restrained her while Sabin inflicted his injustice upon me.

Matthew continued, "From what I understand, he was on some expedition when the unfortunate fire broke out. When he saw and understood the inevitable consequences for your village, he came to Marysvale, asking us for our help." He

193

paused dramatically. "We all assumed he was acting on your behalf."

Looking as dumbfounded as I felt, Angus simply gave a small shake of the head.

Addressing the whole company, Matthew said, "I assure you, good people, we are more concerned about your wellbeing than words and silly accusations. At the very least, come and warm up with us. It is hard to make sound decisions under such taxing circumstances. After you are taken care of, we may discuss whatever you desire. Then we can clear up all misunderstandings and false information you have been told about Marysvale, her citizens, and her leaders. After that, if you choose to go your own way, we will, of course, wish you well and assist you on your journey as best we can. Now, what do you say?"

Henry, the disgruntled village councilman, said, "I'm cold. I'm hungry. I see no reason why we shouldn't go. It's on our way, and a hot cup of tea and a warm fire would go a long way right about now."

Sarah spoke up. "I know what you are all feeling, and I know how tempting this all seems, but I've lived there. So have Jane and Hannah. We can all testify that Lord Wright does nothing unless it is for his benefit. It all starts out very innocently, and then, before you know it, they have all power over you. They offer assistance in exchange for your freedom. This is a trap."

Matthew laughed. "I know of Miss Stone here. She probably hasn't told you that she was found guilty of inciting discord and encouraging rebellion in Marysvale. It would appear to me that she hasn't changed her ways."

Sarah's face turned red, and she clenched her fists in anger.

"Tell me," continued Matthew. "What did these so-called tyrants do to you for your crimes?"

"They threw me out."

"That's not entirely true now, is it Miss Stone? Did they not build you a farm? From what I understand, it was quite large and very nice. They gave you animals, planted orchards, and fully equipped you to make more than a healthy go at it. Isn't that true, Miss Stone?"

Sarah hesitated, unsure how to reply.

Matthew again addressed the group. "Now, doing all of that for a criminal doesn't sound like the actions of a villain to me? Does it to you?"

The villagers looked uncertain.

"They put me where the Brean could keep an eye on me," said Sarah. But she said it, knowing how it must sound to the unwitting villagers.

He laughed. "You chose the location."

"It wasn't like that," she retorted.

"Now, now, Miss Stone," Matthew crooned condescendingly. "How can we trust you when you haven't been entirely truthful with us thus far?"

"Then what about my father?" Jane spat furiously. "Your friend, Lyman, murdered him!"

"And who murdered Lyman?" he asked.

"He was trying to kill us!" she shot back.

Matthew smiled compassionately. "Miss Wolfe, I am deeply sorry for the loss of your father. But, we both know that he died from natural causes…"

"That's a lie!" cried Hannah. "He was shot right before our eyes."

Matthew, with a sad look, nudged his horse past us and up to the company.

"Good folks, I did not come here for this, and I am truly sorry you were made a part of it. It is obvious to me that you have been misled. Miss Wolfe and her sister have feelings for this strange fellow." Pointing to me. "Distressing grief and *other* forces may be at play here. However, it is not for me to judge."

He turned his horse around.

"I am finished discussing the past. We only desire to help. But, as our aid is unwanted, we will now take our leave."

"Wait," called Henry, walking forward.

Matthew took a few more steps before stopping. He turned around in the saddle and looked at Henry expectantly.

"We need help, and we would be foolish not to investigate your offer." Then addressing the crowd, he suggested, "We can easily find out if this is a trap by sending a scout."

"Unnecessary but wise," said Matthew with a smile. "In light of what you have undoubtedly been told, I would do the same. Send as many as you would like. We would enjoy the company."

"This is a mistake," I said.

"What is one more in a long list of deaths?" Henry said pointedly.

"It will be all right, John," Angus said reassuringly. "Send one of the lads to check it out."

I turned to James. "Will you send one of the…"

"Don't bother," interrupted Henry. "We will send someone *we* can trust."

"Albert!" he called.

A tall, lanky man in his late twenties stepped forward.

Henry turned to him.

"Find a horse and go see if it is safe for us to follow these gentlemen."

Albert nodded.

Why do I care? I thought. *After all, I don't want to be part of any of this. I didn't ask to lead these people; why should I care what they do?*

As I contemplated this turn of events, I glanced up at Matthew. He looked at me with contempt etched on his face.

There was no doubt he was hiding something. The question was, what?

I leapt into his dark soul.

Promptly and unexpectedly, he shoved me out!

It startled me.

A quick sneer flashed across his face, and he quickly turned away from me.

He knows! He knows how to keep me out! That traitor, Jex, had to have shown him that.

What I hadn't told Jex, or anyone else for that matter, is that I could break through those defenses if properly motivated. To my knowledge, the only one who knew of that was Sarah, and I doubted that she had told anyone. Not even Jane knew I could do it.

Feeding my internal anger, I glared at him, eagerly waiting for him to expose the windows to his soul. He would look back and gloat; surely he would; it was in his nature.

However, Matthew did no such thing. He simply kept his back to me.

This act infuriated me even more.

Albert returned with a horse, and without any further exchange, they trotted off.

Henry, newly bestowed with a sense of authority, addressed the villagers.

"We have some decisions to make. We have been given a glimmer of hope. Now, I know what Angus and those with him have told us. Granted, he has been a good leader, and I don't want to diminish that, but times have changed. An unexpected opportunity has presented itself. Now, I am not saying we should run off with our eyes shut, but we must face reality. And the reality is we have little to no options. I propose we march to their camp, ask some tough questions, and hear what they have to say. If something is amiss, or Albert does not return or bears bad tidings, we continue with what we have planned. It is the wise thing to do."

Henry looked around, importantly. "So, what say you? Do we continue on this path of misery, or do we take the hope offered?"

Sarah stepped forward. "You have lost much, perhaps everything dear to you. I understand how you are feeling."

She touched the base of her neck. "I, too, have lost much in this conflict. Like you, I have lost a home, a mother, a brother, his wife, and many friends. We are indeed living in dark times. All may seem bleak and hopeless, and I do understand what a glimmer of hope this appears to be. However, unlike you, I have been down the path of Merrick Wright, and I know where it leads. You are free now, but you won't be if you accept his help. And it is only a gilding of help he offers. Beneath the thin surface lies despair, and it won't take long to get there. You will see it only too quickly after the gates of Marysvale slam shut behind you, and your freedom is gone."

"And why should we trust you?" asked a young mother; she carried a toddler in her arms. "Matthew is right. Bad things started to happen when you all showed up. Angus should've thrown you out the moment he learned of a devil among us."

Her eyes flashed to me and diverted away quickly.

"Now, Lucy," said Henry. "What's done is done. Angus has tried to be fair, perhaps to a fault at times, but he is still a good man. Let us wait and see what Albert reports."

Angus stepped forward, his hand clutching his cane. "This is foolish. Ye are nae already in Marysvale because ye didn't like the way things were goin'. Ye know what it's like there…"

"No," interrupted Henry. "All we know is what you have told us. All we have are the testimonies of these four people, which were built upon rumors. We have heard nothing solid. There is no proof."

"Many of ye know what Merrick was like back then. How has he changed?" pleaded Angus.

"That was then," said Charles. "This is now."

A bruise had formed upon his face where I had struck him.

"Things have changed since these soldiers appeared," Charles continued. "From what we were told, we were expecting oppression and tyranny. Now we see mercy in a time of need. What are we supposed to believe? Are we supposed to believe the word of someone who has admitted to having unnatural powers? How do we know he hasn't used those powers against these women? Deceived them as well as us?"

"You have my word to add to theirs," growled Sabin. "John may be unnatural, but he is good, and we owe our lives to him."

"Exactly," jumped in Henry. "You yourself, Sabin, were convinced that he was evil. And you convinced many of us as well. You gave compelling evidence. Then you leave with him in the woods, come back, and now you're an ally. That doesn't just happen. From our standpoint, it looks like he got to you as well."

"He didn't," said Sabin in a low and menacing voice. "But your stupidity is getting to me. I was going to kill him. Despite that, he still saved us from the Brean."

Lucy's voice rose angrily. "You claim the Brean attacked the settlements to help Merrick Wright, but you could make the same argument about John. Think about it. When things are going badly, whom do we run to? How is it that he, and those he loves, survive the attacks when my Philip does not? Perhaps the *assassin* that we heard about was trying to save us from *him!* We have no proof of anything other than his word and those who may be under his spell."

"We are not under his spell!" Hannah shot back hotly. "And he is trying to save you. He was the one who warned us of the Brean attacking the town the night of the fire."

"Convenient," scoffed Lucy.

Hannah clenched her fists tightly, the blood draining from them. She shook with rage and appeared like she would fling herself at the poor woman.

The back and forth continued.

Jane put herself into the argument only to be told she was under a spell.

I felt hurt, angry, frustrated, and tired, but I also felt relieved.

As much as I wished for them to believe me, I knew that changing their minds was impossible when they wanted to believe the falsehoods.

I also saw this as my way out. There was no shame now. We tried to convince them, to show them, and save them, but if they were determined to go to Marysvale, well, who were we to stop them? Perhaps if we weren't with them, the future would be changed. Wright would win, so what would be the point of killing them? No, he would just add them to the rest of his subjects, and they would get what they deserved.

It was Henry and his newfound power that finally put a stop to the arguments.

"This is all very silly. Matthew is right; we will see more clearly once Albert has returned. And if it is favorable, we will warm ourselves, fill our bellies, and then discuss our next move in a proper state of mind. I put the question to the remaining council. Do we blindly follow Angus and simply pass by without a look, or should we do the prudent thing and at least investigate the possibility?"

An old man from the town council, who I knew by the name of Marcus, came forward. He was the one I had read in the council meeting as proof that I could read their souls. I still remembered the images of his dying wife and felt some compassion toward him. His face looked even older, and his frame even frailer. I suspected the exposure from the journey was taking its toll; perhaps it would even take his life before the end.

"I am sorry, Angus, but Henry has a point." Marcus raised his frail arms in the rain and shook his head. "We are not cut out for this. Perhaps it would be different if we had more provisions. But to see women and children in this misery..."

He cast his head down, unable to meet Angus' hard glare. "I side with Henry."

Out of the twelve councilmen, only eight now lived, excluding the traitors Jex and Daniel. One by one, each said their peace, with similar arguments to Marcus', and sided with Henry. The two dissenters of the council were Sam and Sabin.

And just like that, the mantle of leadership passed from Angus to Henry.

Angus said nothing.

I expected him to look dejected. On the contrary, fire blazed in his eyes. It could've been mistaken as anger. But knowing Angus, I knew it was determination that fueled him. I suspected that he refused to go through all that he had, simply to end up back at the beginning. Which, for him, was under the subjection of Lord Wright.

Taking charge, Henry decided that the company should immediately set off for Matthew's camp. He reasoned with the villagers that Albert would return long before they arrived. And if he didn't, they would have plenty of time to mount a proper defense, although he thought it highly unlikely that would be necessary.

After commandeering a horse fit for his new position, Henry took the lead.

Nothing was spoken, but I sensed that allegiance had changed. The shooting teams would be reluctant, if not outright refuse to take orders from me now. Angus was yesterday's leader, and those of us he defended were relegated into the distrusted category. The company was far from unified, but there was agreement that they should at least reserve final judgment for a later time. They wanted to see if a warm fire, hot food, and a cup of cider could be attainable.

I felt oddly torn between anger at their hostility and ingratitude, and compassion. In this state, I watched the sorry group trudging through the mud. They were cold, miserable, and defeated. I couldn't blame them. Although I knew the horror that awaited them, under the circumstances, perhaps it was the best decision.

Our group fell back to the rear. No one felt like talking.

Listening to the sound of the rain falling to the forest floor, we plodded along in silence. Ahead of us, we could hear the occasional baaing of sheep, the mooing of cows, and the snorts of horses. The only constant sounds were the never-ending rain, the trudging of feet through the mud, and the whimpering of cold and hungry children.

Time slowly passed as we slogged through the gloom.

Finally, Hannah broke the silence. "Don't you think Albert should be back by now?"

"It depends on how far away their camp is," replied Sarah.

"But the soldiers got here fairly early, and Matthew made it seem close. Do you think something happened? Can you see anything, John?"

I shook my head and muttered, "No."

"Perhaps they are planning an attack," suggested Hannah. "What should we do?"

No one answered.

"John?" she prodded.

I shrugged. "Form the groups up; that is if they'll listen. They'd assemble for the Brean, I'm certain. But for the soldiers, I'm not so sure. They're stubborn enough to believe that the soldiers would just be charging in to save them."

While shaking a fist, Angus blurted, "How could they forget Merrick's deception so quickly? We have to make them see what is really goin' on! Make them see reason!"

"What do we do?" asked James.

Angus tugged on his beard. "Been ponderin' that, Jimmy. I must confess that I don't rightly know. But there has to be a way! Every problem has a solution."

"And vice versa," added Hannah under her breath.

Thomas cracked a smile.

I was still conflicted. Part of me wanted to help, and part didn't. Mostly, I just felt miserable.

"I should never have told them about my gifts," I muttered without really thinking.

Angus looked over at me with a mixed expression of defiance and sorrow. For a moment, I wished I hadn't said it. After all, there was no going back and changing the past. What was the use of pining over it?

Angus simply replied, "Ye may be right, laddie. Ye may be right."

"Perhaps," added Sarah. "But the outcome would be the same. It wouldn't have prevented the fire, and we would still be right where we are now."

"So, what's to be done?" asked Jane.

"What can be done?" I retorted. "Henry shouldn't be trusted, that much I can tell you. He is caught up in the euphoria of power. As for the others, you can lead a horse to water, but you can't force it to drink. If they don't want our help, then I say we leave."

Everyone looked at me aghast.

"We can't leave them here," scoffed Angus.

"They would be destroyed by those wolves in sheep's clothing," added Hannah.

"I don't know how we can prevent it," I replied. "The way I see it, we have two options: one, go to Marysvale with them. They may let the villagers live, but you all know they aren't going to forget what *we* did to them."

"And the other option?" asked Jane.

"We leave right now. We all have horses; we can make out quickly enough."

"We can't leave before the villagers make a decision whether or not they'll actually go to Marysvale," Jane declared.

"For all we know, they'll get some food in them and see reason again."

"And what if at this very moment the soldiers are planning their attack?" added Hannah. "You talk about leaving before we even know what they are going to do with our friends."

"Hannah and Jane are right," agreed Sarah. "We have to at least find out what they plan to do with the villagers. After that, we may decide what we do next."

Hannah nodded in agreement.

"You sound like Henry," I muttered.

Sarah heard me. She raised an eyebrow and shot me a withering glance.

Instantly, I regretted saying it.

Again, we fell into silence while the rain continued pouring down upon us.

"Look," said Thomas. "Snow."

Tiny white flakes had indeed started to mingle with the raindrops. There weren't many, but it was a sign of things to come.

I shivered at this revelation.

Although it probably made no difference in actual temperature, just the sight of it made me feel colder. I couldn't help remembering the warm fireplace at Sarah's, the way the firelight danced off the rock and wood. I dreamed of waking up in front of the fire and finding Jane and Sarah in conversation. I could almost feel the blanket wrapped around me and my feet toasting by the coals... *Almost* being the operative word. The slush falling all around us sent a thousand tiny drops of reality down upon me. Until this point, I believed returning there a possibility, that perhaps someday my wish would come true. But now, it seemed forever lost. My heart was saddened as I remembered those days.

Perhaps we could stop there on our way out for a few nights? I thought.

Then I shook my head. *Unlikely.*

The only reason Sarah was allowed to exist there in the first place was because it suited Lord Wright's plans. I shook my head again. He would certainly not tolerate it now.

I considered Syre, my little cottage with its warm little stove. For the briefest of moments, I entertained a fantasy that involved Jane living there as my wife. I imagined what life would be like, with her cheer brightening the walls of the little abode.

But reality kept falling all around me.

Even if the jury acquitted me, Syre still wouldn't be safe. Perhaps for the winter it would be, but come early spring, the soldiers would arrive. The only reason Syre wasn't now in their grasp was because Naehume and Lord Wright had their attention set on Alyth. Now that Alyth's fate had been sealed, where would their sight turn to next? A tyrants' lust could never be satisfied.

Perhaps Syre had already been in their clutches. Had I thwarted that as well? The memory of what Naehume had shown me returned. The images of other men like Lord Wright and Mr. Martin flowed through my mind—men eager to step forward and take their place in power. How far did that grasp reach? How far did they plan to extend it? And how far would one have to run to escape it?

I sat up in the saddle unexpectedly. My muscles tensed.

"What do you see?" asked Jane.

"A rider. And he's coming in fast."

Chapter Fifteen: What Once Was

Albert?"

I nodded.

Our little band trotted around the villagers and to the front. Henry was leading the procession, perched loftily on his mount. Charles, Marcus, and Lucy followed on foot, closely behind him.

They all looked at us disdainfully. We seemed to have interrupted a meeting—one where we weren't welcome.

"What?" Henry asked tersely.

"Albert," I said.

We all stopped to peer through the mist.

The tall, dark figure of the rider materialized through the gloom.

He drove his horse with great speed. Little clumps of leaves and mud were thrown up and flung behind the pounding hooves.

With wide eyes, Albert approached us.

Villagers huddled in to hear what he had to say.

We waited while he reined up.

"Well, what is it, son?" demanded Henry.

Breathlessly, Albert replied, "Large fires, blankets, tarpaulins for shelter. What General Pierce said is true. They have stew and cider warming over fires. There are six wagons, loaded with supplies, waiting for us. They even sent carriages to carry our sick and wounded. And there are soldiers ready to assist."

A bubble of excitement rose from the villagers.

"And father?"

"Yes?"

"Remember George Sawyer?"

Henry nodded.

"His oldest boy, Roger, is one of the officers."

Jane whispered to me, "You have met him as well. He was also with Lyman at the gate. He's a nasty one too."

"Aren't they all?" I asked rhetorically.

Henry turned his horse to face the villagers.

"There you have it," he beamed. "We are among friends. Relief has arrived."

A cheer erupted from the crowd.

Angus nudged his horse forward and addressed the company.

"This offerin' from Merrick comes at a very steep price. I urge ye to strongly reconsider what ye are doin'."

Henry, irritated with this affront to his new leadership, and apparently eager to solidify his position, rebuked Angus.

"Really, Angus, this is beneath you. Look at us. We are in need. What is the harm in accepting help on behalf of our women and children? Do you not see their suffering? I cannot accept that this generous hand of fellowship has any other motive than to relieve our misery. It makes no sense for the soldiers to feed us if their purpose is to kill us. No, we will go and partake of their generosity. I see no reason for us to suffer any more on account of your stubbornness."

"My stubbornness!" scoffed Angus.

"Yes, *your* stubbornness!" cried Lucy. "We need this! There is no cost greater to us than your leadership! They offer us shelter from this miserable rain; they offer us hot food and drink! We can leave any time we choose, and you still won't accept it. That *is* stubborn! Starve and freeze here if you prefer. I, for one, am going."

With that, she slogged away, carrying her cold, crying child.

"Join me, my friends," Henry said beseechingly. "At least come and dry yourselves. As Matthew said, once our bellies are full, and a fire has warmed our backs, then we can make a decision."

He turned his mount and set off after Lucy.

The villagers were already lost to us; I could see it. Their physical discomfort had won out. Some followed eagerly, others hesitantly, but in the end, they all left.

Even the men from Syre joined the procession. There had been a small debate between them, but as they had promised to do what was best for the company, they decided they should go.

Along with the women and me, Angus, James, and Thomas hung back. Surprisingly, Sabin and Sam stayed behind as well, although Sam had sent his wife on ahead.

"Well, what do we do now?" asked Hannah.

"We have to convince them not to trust the soldiers," answered Jane.

At this point, I felt indifferent. I was beginning to believe that it was pointless. It wasn't that I truly didn't care; I just couldn't see what could be done about it. The villagers didn't want to believe what we were telling them. On top of that, they were focused on the short-term problems of food and shelter. Which, granted, were big problems.

"John?

It was Sarah.

"Yes?"

"Well?"

"Well, what?"

"What do you think?"

"Oh…about what?"

"You weren't listening, were you?" accused Hannah.

I blushed. "No. I admit I wasn't."

"It's quite all right," said Sarah. "We all have much on our minds. I was wondering what you thought about the villagers. What do you think we could do to convince them?"

I sighed. "Not much."

"That's it? That's all you have?" said Hannah impatiently.

Ignoring her, I went on to explain, "They don't have it in them to fight through to Syre. They can't imagine that Marysvale is as bad as they've been led to believe…"

"We know all that," interrupted Hannah. "What we want to know is how do we change their minds? Aren't you supposed to have some kind of insight?"

"Unfortunately, there isn't anything we can say to change their minds."

"John," chided Sarah. "Do try to be more helpful."

"I would like to, but I don't see how. They won't believe a thing we say. It doesn't matter what proof we have; they will think that I've bewitched you. They will only believe what they see with their own eyes and hear with their own ears. By the time that happens, it will be too late. The soldiers are obviously putting on a show for them, and it won't change until they are all securely barred inside Marysvale."

I shook my head. "What I would suggest is what none of you want to hear, but I'll say it anyway. The villagers *will* turn on us and charge me with witchcraft—and most likely all of you as well. The soldiers won't hesitate to join them, and it will happen soon. I wouldn't even go to the camp. Now is the time to leave. We could easily disappear while our tracks are being washed away. If we stay, we will be greatly outnumbered. We will be in their hands. The villagers have chosen their path; now, it is time for us to choose ours."

"We can't just leave them," said Sabin. "They are our friends and family."

"Sabin is right," said Angus. "Perhaps we will nae be able to convince them, but we have to try one more time. At the very least, give those who desire to join us a chance."

It was a mistake to go any farther with the company. A good many of them believed that I was the cause of their tragedy and that Angus had grown frail in his leadership. They only followed us at first because there was no other option.

Now they had one.

They had just been given hope, deliverance, and the illusion of a better future.

Lord Wright ensured safe passage, food, and shelter—the three most important things to them right now. Deep down, the villagers may not fully trust Lord Wright, but they weren't distrustful of him either. They *wanted* to believe that they had found an easier way. They would rationalize the lies and deceive themselves. Once reality set in and the gates boomed shut behind them, only then would they realize what they had known all along. At least some would. There would also be some who would argue that at least it was better than the alternative.

"What do ye think, Jimmy?" Angus asked.

James, who had been looking down and appeared lost in thought, raised his head and addressed the group.

"Aye, it is rough. John is right. I can see the contempt that Matthew and some of our own have towards us. And no mind reading is necessary to see that we've lost them. Going back now may prove to be an error."

"But you can't just leave them," interrupted Sam. "My wife is among them!"

James raised his hand with his palm down to calm Sam.

"Let me finish. This is why it is tough: leaving now would be wise from a self-preservation standpoint but not from a humane one. We need to give them another chance and see who will join us. Going back could be tricky; we are now the outsiders. However, I believe we still have a wee advantage. The villagers may be quick to dismiss John, but not my father or Sabin. The respect *they* command is worth something. At the least, it will buy us time. With that said, I would not stay past morning. Don't give the soldiers too much time to work against us."

I studied James. There was something he held back.

He averted his eyes and looked away.

I didn't like feeling distrustful of him, but in that small act, I began to wonder. It was plain that he didn't want me to find out more.

"Good," said Angus. "Then, it is settled. We will go and try one more time."

Even though *I* felt uneasy, the others seemed in perfect agreement.

We set off, following the trampled and muddy path left by the company. Jane and Hannah rode to my right, and, to my left, a very ill-looking Thomas sagged atop of Shade.

We trudged on through the sludge. The rain still mingled with their white brethren. As soon as the flakes landed, however, they melted away.

I felt the cold and damp saturate more and more of my clothing. It had to be worse for those walking. Pushing their way through the wet foliage and sodden ground would certainly soak them faster and sap their strength. It would be difficult for those who did side with us not to heed the enticement of campfires, hot food, and shelter. I could imagine the turmoil that the parents must be suffering over their children.

At first, I didn't feel like talking. I believe the weather affected the others, too, as very little conversation took place. If not from the sleet, then from the fatigue that had culminated over the last few days. Again, I found it difficult to keep my thoughts from warm fires and beds in distant cabins.

It was then I decided to talk to Sarah.

She had been quiet during the discussion, and I wanted to know what she made of this entire mess. Did she still believe in our cause, or had reality set in?

I looked around and discovered that Sarah, along with James, had fallen subtly to the rear and were trailing the group by some distance.

Sarah noticed me, flashed a quick smile, and then averted her eyes. She said something to James. He glanced up, saw me, and he, too, quickly looked away.

Puzzled, I turned back around.

Perhaps I was wrong in my assumption, but I couldn't help feeling they were conspiring.

Were they afraid I might try to read them?

Again I peered back, but they were riding close together, lost in conversation.

Jane eyed me curiously but said nothing. She seemed tired, and I could see her shivering under her cloak. Hannah also shivered.

Wishing I could do something for them, I considered the tempting prospect of the soldiers' fires in a whole new light. And, with it came the hopeless realization that we didn't stand a chance against them.

I recalled the day before when I had drilled the shooting teams. I felt foolish now. How ridiculous for us to believe that we had any hope of winning. How deceived we had been.

In retrospect, it appeared obvious.

Of course, Lord Wright wouldn't send soldiers to kill us. Not when he can do what he has always done and simply ensnare us—send us comfort in a time of our greatest need. Isn't that how he had won Marysvale? Why would we try a different tactic now?

Unfortunately, this evident strategy of his had never crossed my mind until this moment.

Despair set in.

"Stop being gloomy," said Hannah out of nowhere.

"You were glum a moment ago," I shot back.

"Cold? Yes. Hungry? Yes. Gloomy? No. You look like we're beaten."

"Aren't we?" I asked. "We're certainly outfoxed."

"It's never over until it's over—you know that," rebuked Hannah. "But, I agree, we were outfoxed. I certainly didn't expect kindness from Lord Wright, and I never imagined that we would just roll over either. Quite brilliant, actually."

Thomas, looking miserable, asked, "Are you sure you have this Lord Wright all figured out? Perhaps he's not so bad after all."

Hannah shot him a look that said it all.

He raised a hand defensively. "All right, all right, just making sure. It's just hard to envision someone so evil."

"Is it?" I asked pointedly.

Catching my meaning, he replied sadly, "No, I suppose not."

I hadn't told him that his father was one of the men Naehume had shown me—one of those who had joined him. Nor would I ever.

"What do you suppose he would have done if you had rejected his hospitality?" asked Thomas.

"Fight," replied Jane. "The soldiers would have attacked and, quite possibly, the Brean, too. It would have been better for us than this, though. At least the people would know what he is really like."

She clenched her fists. "I will never go back and live like that again. I would rather die!"

"As would I," added Hannah. "We have to do something! We have to make them see who they are dealing with before it's too late. John, you can do it."

I shook my head. "I don't see how."

"Do what you did to Lyman. You have a way of bringing out the bad in people."

"Not entirely the compliment I would like to receive," I said dryly.

Hannah gave a little dismissive wave. "You know what I mean. All you have to do is get Matthew mad at you. He will explode and overreact. He will be exposed for all to see."

Shaking my head again, I said, "It won't work. Many of the villagers feel the same way about me as he does. They *want* to believe the worst in me. Anything I do will be seen as transparent as glass. They will know that I am trying to rile him. They will interpret it as a feeble attempt to get whatever power I had back."

"As much as I don't like to say it," said Jane. "I'm afraid John is right."

"But not all of them hate John," argued Hannah.

"No," I agreed. "Some believe in my sincerity, but they are suffering at the moment. In their eyes, the alternative is worse than Lord Wright."

"Believing is a start," she said.

"And then what? What do we do to convince them? We can't take on Lord Wright *and* the Brean. Even with all the villagers on our side, it's not enough. We were delusional to think so before. They will easily finish us off."

I thought about the dream I'd had. The images of the dead rushed back and haunted me. The memory made me feel as cold in my soul as their bodies had been. I didn't want to be anywhere near Marysvale.

"That is exactly what will happen," I stated.

Hannah gave another dismissive wave. "You give up too easily."

"I do not!" I snapped angrily. "I've seen what is going to happen, and I'm trying to make the best of it. Our cause is already lost. The only question is: what can we salvage? If we stay with the villagers, we will be dragged to Marysvale with them, and I don't believe throwing away lives at the gates of Marysvale, for an outcome we cannot achieve, is the proper course."

"And you believe running away is?" asked Sarah.

We all whirled around and found both her and James behind us. We'd been so engrossed in our conversation that we hadn't heard them approach.

I felt a little embarrassed that she had overheard me, but I still felt the same way.

"It's not running; it's facing the facts of our situation," I explained.

Sarah regarded me with a quizzical expression, then, to my amazement, she replied, "Perhaps you are right."

"I am?"

"He is?" said Hannah.

"Are you surprised?" asked Sarah.

"No, I'm just surprised that you would agree with me."

"As am I," added Jane.

"And me," agreed Hannah.

"I am not ready to quit just yet," said Sarah. "But that time may come quickly. We need to try to persuade our friends one more time. After that, if they insist on going to Marysvale with the soldiers, then we leave. We can't force them to believe us; they will have to see it for themselves. Perhaps next spring, with help from the good people of Syre, we will be able to enact a plan to help everyone there."

Returning wasn't exactly what I had envisioned, but at least we wouldn't all die at the gates of Marysvale. In my dream, the time had been winter, the ground frozen. At least springtime changed that part of the nightmare. Perhaps then the villagers would realize their mistake. Maybe Sarah was right; we could come back, smuggle some muskets in, and stage an uprising.

"I smell smoke," Thomas observed weakly. "We're almost there."

A pit grew in my stomach. I had felt it before. It was that old feeling that seemed to form when something terrible was about to happen—something usually involving the accusation of witchcraft.

Sure enough, the scent of campfire reached our noses. Despite the pit in my stomach, the additional aroma of food made my mouth water.

We passed a soldier acting as a sentry. He shot us a quick, dirty look and then turned away as if keeping a vigilant watch.

The sight of him made me angry. We all knew it was only an act. We had about as much chance of being ambushed as we had of Lord Wright giving up his power. If, by some slim chance, we were attacked, it would be a feeble one and likely only for show.

The camp soon fell into view. Large tarpaulins stretched overhead, each of the four corners tied to a different tree. They weren't large enough to provide shelter for the entire company, but they did give relief to many. Four huge bonfires blazed, along with a dozen smaller cooking fires. Soldiers warmed huge steaming pots of food over the flames. Some villagers stood in line, waiting to be served, while others warmed themselves around the fires. Many already held steaming mugs. I could see their mood and temperament improving rapidly; smiles and life had returned.

Sam nodded to us as he peeled away to find his wife. Sabin accompanied him.

One group of villagers, not lucky enough to find space around a fire, regarded us as if we were intruders—appalled by our audacity to show our faces.

The stares weren't lost on the others.

"I believe you're right, John," said Thomas. "I don't think they like you very much."

"I don't think they like *us* very much."

"Ah, I can see our prodigals have returned home," Matthew said for all to hear.

He walked toward us with an outstretched arm.

The sound of his oily voice made me cringe.

Villagers turned to stare from all directions.

I felt like a dog, throwing himself at the feet of a cruel master, hoping for a few scraps of food and a stayed hand. It was probably just what Matthew wanted.

My stomach churned again, both from the smell of food and from the dripping deceit taking place. This act of generosity would endear the villagers to Matthew and Lord Wright. They would view them as caring men who would freely give of their substance in times of want.

In that generosity, the people would understandably feel indebted to them. Little did they know the terrible price they would pay for this mess of pottage.

"Come," Matthew said magnanimously. "There is cider, tea, and stew warming on the fires, and bread as well. There may be a line of people, but fear not, we have enough for all."

"It is not yours to give," hissed Jane. "You have taken it from the people of Marysvale who are in desperate need."

The villagers watched their exchange with interest.

"Are these people not in need?" he asked piously. "Oh, that's right; you and John would rather they starve. Not very Christian of you."

Jane flushed with anger. "Which is crueler: to face hardships now, with the hope of freedom, or to give them comfort, before leading them to a life filled with misery, fear, and starvation?"

"Now, Miss Wolfe, you know that is not true."

"It is," she spat. "And the moment these people step inside Marysvale, they will realize their awful dilemma."

Now, almost all the villagers were watching.

Matthew, with a sad smile upon his face, addressed them. "Well, I must confess, Miss Wolfe is correct in that we don't have as much as we'd like. Unfortunately, it was a poor harvest for us this year. But, I assure you, with some belt-tightening, we will *all* have enough to last the winter. Mark my words, next year will be better."

"It was a good year," countered Jane with her hands on her hips. "But Lord Wright hoards the food in his stores. It's one of the many ways he controls the people. He rewards those who are obedient to him with food and punishes those who step out of line by withholding it."

Matthew clucked his tongue and wagged a finger at her. "Now, Miss Wolfe, you do spin yarns."

He gave a little laugh and then added, "Of course we must ration if we are to feed a whole other village of people. We can't have everyone eating as much as they'd like, or there wouldn't be enough to last the year. In these trying times, we must take from those that have, so those without won't literally die of hunger. Honestly, Miss Wolfe, you used to be so much more agreeable." His eyes flicked to me. "It is as if some strange force has a cold hold upon your heart.

"But that is not for me to judge," he said quickly. "I only wish to serve. And I certainly do not joy in this contention of yours. Take our help if you like; leave it if you don't."

Looking directly at me, Matthew added, "*We* aren't forcing anyone."

He made my blood boil with anger. I wanted to strike him down, which is likely just what he wanted me to do.

So, I did nothing.

Matthew smirked and then turned and sauntered back to a group of soldiers.

"To call him a weasel would be insulting to weasels," said Hannah.

I nodded in agreement while Jane clenched her fists tightly and fumed.

Hannah slid off her horse.

"That cider does smell good," she said.

"Certainly, you are not taking food from these wolves!" cried Jane with a look of disgust.

"As you said," she replied. "It's not their food; it's ours."

Part of me agreed with Jane, but a greater part of me agreed with my watering mouth and grumbling stomach.

"We all might as well eat," said Sarah. "You will need the energy and the warmth it will bring, and we don't know when our next hot meal will come."

We tied up our horses, but Jane still looked hesitant, held back by the loathing she felt at taking aid from the enemy.

"Come along," I said. "Sarah's right. Take what you can get. It may be a long time before we eat like this again."

Reluctantly, she took my hand, and we lined up with the others for stew and bread.

The man standing in front of us looked back. He was about to say something, probably a jovial comment about the food from the look on his face. However, noticing me, he snapped his mouth shut and quickly turned away.

We didn't talk while waiting in line with the other villagers.

The women were served first, then Thomas. Once he received his portion, I stepped forward.

The soldier, who had been dishing up the food, looked at me and then spat, "I'm a God-fearing man. And as such, I will not serve a *devil*!"

Chapter Sixteen: For the Love of a Woman

His comment, quite unexpectedly, stunned me. I should've anticipated something like it, but I didn't.

The soldier folded his arms across his chest, defiantly.

Jane thrust her food into my hands and ripped the ladle from the man's grasp.

"Oi," he cried.

He was about to take it back when James stepped forward. Placing his hands on his hips, he glared down at him. The soldier, observing the commanding frame of James Shepherd, stopped. Even more imposing were the undaunted, hard, and fearless eyes of the blacksmith. They conveyed the message that this was a battle the soldier would not win.

Perhaps sensing that very thing, the man stepped back.

With blazing eyes, Jane grabbed my plate and, while dishing up the stew, hissed, "My sister and I are the only two people here who have labored with our own hands for this meal. You and I both know who has made pacts with devils *and* monsters. And you all live lavishly behind stone walls, separated from the very townspeople who toil to bring you this food."

Jane handed the stew to James and then quickly dished up more for herself before she flung the ladle back at the soldier. He fumbled with it, desperately trying to prevent it from falling into the mud. He succeeded, but not before his uniform had been soiled in the process.

"Honestly, Miss Wolfe, I can't begin to imagine what has gotten into you," said a booming voice so everyone could hear.

I didn't have to look to know that it came from Matthew.

He feigned a concerned and disapproving face.

"These outbursts of yours are most unusual. We really must get to the bottom of what is *possessing* you."

Pointedly, Matthew regarded me and then looked away.

Before Jane or anyone else could retort, he spun on the heel of his boot and walked away.

From the looks of the villagers, I knew that it didn't bode well for me.

Jane's face flushed hot with anger.

For my part, I wanted to hit Matthew and lay him flat in the mud. However, it was obvious where he was going with his charade. Based on what I'd seen so far, he was well on his way to achieving his goal.

We had to leave, and it had to be soon.

Sitting upon a fallen log, we silently ate our meal. The stew was the best tasting I had ever eaten. Of course, being cold and hungry may have influenced my opinion.

After we had filled our stomachs, I turned to Sarah. "We should leave now."

"We will. But we must first give Angus another chance," she said.

"It won't work."

"Perhaps not, but we must try. None of us could live with ourselves if we didn't give the villagers every opportunity to see the truth."

I disagreed.

Sarah read the expression on my face.

"Fear not; you will be safe for the time being."

"I don't think so," I replied doubtfully.

She reached over and patted my arm.

"You have more friends than you know. They will stand with you when the need comes."

Hannah got up and disappeared without saying a word.

"I hope you're right," I replied, although I didn't believe a word of it.

Trouble has a way of thinning out so-called friends, and nothing caused as much trouble as being labeled a witch. I also feared that those who did stand by me wouldn't fare much better in the end.

"I am," she replied confidently.

"Well," said James standing. "I best go see how mine ancient is getting along."

Sarah looked up at him and their eyes locked. Some unseen communication passed between them. James gave a very brief and very slight nod, then walked away.

"What was that about?" I asked, curiosity getting the best of me.

With a dismissive wave, she said, "Angus is having a last go with the council, trying to persuade them to listen to reason. He decided it would be better if we weren't part of it."

"Angus is wise. It seems like that scoundrel Matthew has a way of making me look guilty, even when I keep my mouth shut."

"I shouldn't worry too much about it," Sarah said soothingly. "I'm sure this was all planned out from the beginning; they will do whatever they can to drive a wedge between everyone."

"And you wouldn't worry about that?" I asked doubtfully.

"Perhaps worry is the wrong term," admitted Sarah. "Try not to dwell upon it. They will prod us as much as they can in the hopes that we will make a grievous mistake in front of the villagers. We must do our best not to fall prey in the future."

Hannah returned. Remarkably, she carried six steaming mugs of hot cider, plus blankets for each of us, tucked under her armpits and draped around her neck.

"Oh," she said, looking around. "Where did James go? I have one of these for him."

"Off with Angus. They're hoping to convince the council to join us," replied Jane.

"Suppose that just means more for us," Hannah said, handing out the mugs.

Sarah and Jane each took a blanket and draped them around their shoulders.

Hannah wrapped one around Thomas, who didn't look well at all. Gratefully, he accepted her gifts.

Grasping my warm mug with both hands, I drank deeply. The hot, sweet cider felt like pure nectar flowing down into my belly. It, along with the food before it, warmed me from the inside out.

I couldn't help longing for Sarah's cabin. I closed my eyes and imagined myself sitting by the fire, watching the snowfall outside her windows.

"You're tired, John," said Sarah. "You should get some rest."

Opening my eyes, I observed Sarah holding her own mug with both hands.

"I don't know if I should," I said through a yawn. "Bad things seem to happen when I sleep."

"Do you think Angus will have any success with the council?" asked Hannah.

Sarah smiled, but it didn't extend to her eyes. "I always have hope."

"That sounds like a no to me," I said.

"Have faith," she replied.

"And what if he doesn't succeed?" asked Thomas.

"We leave."

I expected Jane or Hannah to protest, but they didn't. Perhaps now that they were here, they too could see we had already lost.

I yawned again.

Jane stood and reached a hand down toward me.

"The ground is wet, but there is a nice tree over here," she said. "Sit against it and get some sleep. It looks as if we may be here a while. If something changes, I will wake you."

Allowing her to pull me up, Jane took a blanket, wrapped it around my shoulders, and then led me to the spot.

***

While my slumber was not entirely devoid of sleep, it was, nevertheless, fitful, and I woke frequently. The tree against my back felt less than comfortable, aggravating the wounds from my flogging. Slowly, dampness crept through the blanket and into my britches, the cold seeping down into my bones. As rest gave way to misery, I gave up and stood.

To my surprise, the day had progressed more than I had expected. The rain and snow had stopped, leaving the ground covered with patches of slush, except where the villagers had trampled everything to mud.

Looking a little better with some food in him, Thomas sat leaning against a tree, busily carving a piece of wood.

Hannah watched him intently.

"What is it going to be?" I asked.

"A horse," said Thomas.

"Does the horse have a name?"

"Smoke."

"Not Shade?"

"No. Shade is a good horse, but he's no Smoke."

Thomas shrugged his shoulders. "Since you likely won't ever sell him to me, not to mention the fact that he doesn't even like me, I figure this is the closest I'll ever get to owning him."

"Of course he likes you. He lets you ride him, doesn't he?"

A sly, boyish smile played across his face.

Without taking his eyes off the wood, Thomas mused, "Remember the first time I rode him? I had to beg you mercilessly for days to let me."

"I remember," I said. "I was afraid you were going to die."

He laughed. "So was I."

"So was I," agreed Hannah. "Well, not the time you did, but the time Jane first rode him. I don't see what you all see in him. Smoke scares me."

"It's the fire in him that I like," said Thomas. "He's powerful, smart, and fast."

"How did you get him?" asked Hannah.

"From a farmer," I replied. "As you know, Smoke has a lot of spirit in him. The farmer thought it was stubbornness and mistreated him. The fool didn't know what he had or how to treat a horse, let alone train one. By the time I saw Smoke, he was a mean, distrustful animal. Always wanted to charge, stomp, or kick you."

"My, how some things don't change," commented Hannah.

Ignoring her, I went on. "It took a long time and a lot of patience before Smoke would even let me touch him, let alone ride him. But the first time he ran with me on his back..." I let out a low whistle. "That's an experience I won't ever forget."

"So he tried to kill you too," stated Hannah.

"Well, yes, but that's not the point. He was fast. I couldn't believe how fast. Things got better with him once I learned that trust goes both ways. Smoke may still be stubborn at times, but when it really counts... I owe him my life in more ways than one. Training him gave me a reason to exist. No one else wanted him, just like no one else wanted me. For a long time, he was my only friend."

"Well," said Thomas. "You have friends now."

"Yes," I agreed. "And of that, I am glad."

I looked around.

"Where are the rest of my friends?"

Hannah shrugged. "Don't know. Jane went off with Sarah shortly after you fell asleep."

"We stayed here to keep you safe," said Thomas.

"Does that mean you believe me?"

Thomas hesitated, weighing his feelings, and then nodded.

"And what tipped the scales in my favor?"

"The soldiers."

Feeling a little bewildered, I said, "But they haven't done anything but show kindness."

"True," he conceded, "But there is something off about them, and it makes me feel very nervous. Their generosity feels forced, like it isn't in their nature to be so. I'm sure others notice it too. I think you are right, John; they won't keep you around much longer. The more time that passes, the more others will spot the inconsistency between their speech and their actions."

"Let us hope they do it quickly," I muttered.

Thomas shook his head. "They won't recognize it fast enough. Look at them; they are still caught up in the moment. They have food, drink, fires, blankets, and some shelter. Once the euphoria dies, then they will see."

"If you're right, you're very perceptive for a lad."

He grinned guiltily. "I heard Sarah mention it to James—at least the euphoria part."

Then, adding quickly, as if he needed to redeem himself, "The first part about how the soldiers really are, I noticed that on my own."

"His neck is too big," said Hannah.

"What?" asked Thomas, puzzled.

She pointed to the rough wooden figure in his hand.

"It's not finished yet, silly."

"I know," said Hannah. "I'm just trying to be helpful."

I stood up. "I reckon I'll go check on Smoke and then see if I can find the others."

Walking through the throng of villagers, I made my way to the animals. I found Smoke safe and secure. As there wasn't much grass where he and the others had been tethered, I guessed that they had probably eaten it all. I unwrapped the reins and started leading him away.

"Fleeing so soon? And you weren't even going to say goodbye."

I recognized the sneer in his greasy voice.

Turning around, I saw Matthew, another soldier, and Daniel, the wagon master. Matthew wore an arrogant grin that I desperately wanted to wipe off his face. However, my eyes narrowed on Daniel. I hadn't forgotten how he had held Jane against her will. Daniel wanted to glare back, but he averted his eyes. The sight of him ignited the anger that now seemed to perpetually simmer inside me.

"Ah, so you two *do* know each other. Well then, you should thank Daniel here for the comforts you are now enjoying. If he hadn't informed us, well, where would you be now without Lord Wright's generosity?"

The fact that they were armed, with hands poised to use their weapons, was not lost on me.

Trying to stifle the desire to do something stupid, I led Smoke away to a better spot nearby.

They followed.

After tethering Smoke, I pretended to be checking his saddle but subtly tried loosening the crossbow still secured there.

"No, just leave that there. You won't need it," instructed Matthew.

I did so, but I had loosened it enough to where I could snatch it up if needed.

I turned my gaze back to the three men.

"I should congratulate you on your promotion," I said to Matthew.

The grin disappeared.

"Yes," he replied coldly. "It was unexpected. The fall of our last general was tragic, but of course, you know that. Rest assured, we will bring his murderers to justice."

My eyes narrowed, and I glared at him. I deeply desired to inflict the same fate upon Matthew.

"Now, we'll have none of that," he ordered. "No witchcraft, or I'll just have to shoot you here and now. And I'd be within my rights, wouldn't I, Roger?"

Roger nodded, a smile spreading across his face. Daniel betrayed no emotion.

"He looks as if he's trying to read our minds now," said Roger.

Jerking a thumb in the direction of the villagers, he added, "I doubt it would take much to convince them that you tried to bewitch me. Plus, I'd have two witnesses. I believe that would be good enough for a court."

"Now, now. We don't need to resort to such actions yet," said Matthew.

"Is there a point to your visit?" I asked coolly.

"Sadly, there is. I've been instructed to give you one more chance to join us."

I scoffed. "I don't have to read you to know that you're lying. Wright would just as soon see me dead. He would never offer me that. And if he did, it would be a trap."

"Oh, you are quite right. Lord Wright wants you dead at any cost, but there are others."

"And you'd have me believe that they would disregard Wright?"

Matthew rolled his eyes. "You are quite naïve and a bit slow; I can't imagine why anyone wants you."

I gritted my teeth, holding back the hatred that boiled inside.

"Lord Wright's power is not absolute. Other men wield considerable influence, as well. Perhaps individually, they are not as formidable as his lordship, but it's enough. Some of them would still like you to join our side. No, they don't really care about *you*—you are more of a fascination to them than something to be attained.

"No, this offer comes from he who is more powerful than them all. For whatever reason, Naehume has grown quite attached to you. He would like to finish the work he has begun."

"You still lie. Naehume wants me dead as much as Wright does."

Matthew shrugged his shoulders. "It matters not to me; I am simply fulfilling my duty and offering you one last opportunity. You would be a fool to turn it down, but then again, you are a fool. There is no conceivable way you can win. At my command, the forest will be crawling with Brean and soldiers. You will be under siege no matter the hour. Look at them." His arm swept back over the huddled villagers. "They are feeble, broken, and they beg for our mercy."

Daniel turned pale.

I looked at him incredulously. "You can't tell me you didn't know about the Brean and the soldiers; you were there at the meeting when this was all explained!"

"I…I just thought they were lies," stammered Daniel.

"No," I said, studying him. "You did know. You just didn't *want* to believe it. Instead, you had to convince yourself I was the evil one. Why? What were you promised?"

Matthew turned his head and looked venomously at Daniel. Smacking him on the side of the head, he barked, "Imbecile! He's reading your mind!"

"Jane," I said in horror. "She is your promised prize for betraying your friends."

I clenched my fists. Daniel took a step back. Matthew drew his pistol and aimed it at me.

"I still don't have your answer," he said through gritted teeth.

Ignoring him, I took a step towards Daniel.

"You wanted her during our expedition. You wanted to believe that she would come to love you. You'd sell your soul and your own people for a woman who despises you! But now you don't care, do you? It doesn't matter if she likes you or not; you'll have her regardless."

Matthew slapped Daniel again hard.

"Either block him out or stop looking at him, you fool!" he cried.

"Marysvale is the perfect place for that!" I hissed. "No wonder you're willing to help them."

Matthew cracked the butt of his pistol upon the head of the cowering Daniel.

"Block him out of your mind!" he shrieked.

I laughed contemptuously. "Don't worry, Daniel; whatever feeble conscience you have will soon leave, and you'll fit in there perfectly."

Matthew re-aimed the pistol at me, his face crimson with anger.

"Enough of your trickery!" he spat. "What is your answer?"

"No," I said. "I will never join the likes of you."

A malevolent smile broke across his face. "Perfect. Just what I wanted to hear."

He surveyed me in disgust. "The prospect of a lower-class dog amongst us is repulsive."

"Exactly what I was thinking," added Roger with a wicked smile.

"Then let's finish it."

Chapter Seventeen: What We Reap

I lunged for the crossbow, expecting the blasts of the pistols to end my attempt.

Nothing happened.

Snatching the bow up, I spun.

What I saw was not what I expected.

The two soldiers and Daniel were walking away.

Matthew looked back at me with an evil grin.

I leapt into his soul.

He promptly pushed me out.

His grin widened.

Matthew then put his back to me, and the three of them rapidly walked toward the throng of villagers.

This strange act terrified me more than any fight. In a fight, I had a chance. Perhaps not much of one, but at least my fate would be in my own hands.

This, however, was different, and it would be anything but fair.

I dashed back to where Thomas and Hannah sat.

Jane had returned and was sitting with them on the wet log.

They looked at me and saw the anxious expression on my face.

Instinctively, they reached for their weapons.

"What is it?" asked Jane.

"Time to go," I replied breathlessly.

"Why? What happened?" asked Hannah with wide eyes.

"It's not a matter of what happened, but what is about to happen."

"And what's that?" she asked, getting up.

"I had a run-in with Matthew, and he's up to no good. I'm positive they are about to execute some evil plan that involves me hanging or burning."

"Well, we won't have long to find out," commented Thomas, clutching his musket tightly. "Look."

He pointed to one of the bonfires surrounded by villagers.

Around it came Matthew, Roger, and Daniel. Henry, Lucy, and a crowd of villagers were in tow. Their demeanor and stony faces conveyed intense hostility.

Brutality would shortly follow.

Instinctively, I gripped my crossbow.

"Daniel," exclaimed Jane with disdain.

Her nose wrinkled, and a fleeting look of disgust registered upon her face. In the same moment, it was gone, and her composure returned.

"No getting to the horses now," muttered Thomas.

The mob stopped and faced us.

"What is the meaning of this!" demanded Jane.

Henry stepped forward, importantly.

"John Stone, you have been accused of witchcraft against these fine officers. What have you to say for yourself?"

He didn't waste any time getting to the bone of it, but I wasn't surprised. I had seen the eagerness in their countenances.

"This is outrageous," fumed Jane.

Matthew stepped forward and addressed the villagers sadly, "It is true. He has tried to break into our minds and put us under his control."

"I did no such thing," I spat.

"You yourselves heard the attack," continued Matthew. "Did I not just cry out moments ago to *block him out of your mind?*"

Some of the villagers nodded.

"I cried out because I could feel his evil spell being cast upon us."

"Lies!" I exclaimed.

"This is ludicrous!" exclaimed Jane. "John is here to help. He saved the men on the expedition; that is not the act of wizardry."

"Did he save my husband?" cried Lucy.

She glared at me, her eyes filled with loathing.

I felt an odd mixture of disdain for her and a little sorrow. I remembered her husband, Phillip. He had stood up against the others in support of me during my last trial, one of three men to do so. He had been the one to untie my hands so I could shoot the Brean, and he had fallen in that attack.

Sam pushed his way through the villagers. "I was there, and Jane is right. John tried to save us all, and he may have been able to do so if we would have listened to him earlier. None of us would be alive without him."

"Ah, that," said Matthew. "The famous John to the rescue. If only it had happened that way."

"And how else would it have happened?" growled Sam.

"My dear man, I have the utmost compassion for you. I do not blame you for unwittingly falling for a most foul deception. The fact is, every one of you who was on that unfortunate expedition was doomed from the beginning. Bringing a devil into your confidence unleashed an evil power that was out of your hands. In order to save his own neck, John cast a spell on you. But the spell was not as powerful as he planned. Some men were not deceived. Those innocent individuals he killed."

I shook with rage. "You are a vile and wicked brute."

Matthew puffed his chest out and raised his head defiantly. "I am a holy man, and I am not afraid of your black magic."

"We are not under his power!" snapped Jane.

Matthew looked at her. "That, Miss Wolfe, has yet to be ascertained."

He put a finger to his lips as if in contemplation. Then, as if receiving revelation, he said, "I know of a way. An examination of their bodies could possibly tell us more. Perhaps they have the mark of witchcraft secreted somewhere."

Daniel's eyes widened.

"You will not touch my sister or me!" hissed Jane.

"Do not discount such a thing; you may have no choice," said Henry. "It would not have to be intrusive. I and only a few others would be witnesses."

Gripping my crossbow threateningly, I growled, "Whoever touches either one of them will die, along with you, Henry."

Henry's face drained of color, but he hid his fear well.

242

Raising his hand, he declared, "Perhaps we will return to that later. For now, we have enough serious accusations to deal with—ones that must have some corroboration. Therefore, I ask you, sir," he inclined his head to Matthew, "What evidence do you have against this man?"

"I have one of your own," answered Matthew, turning to address the assembled villagers. "A trusted member of your community and one whom you all know."

He gestured to Daniel. "Daniel here, alone, withstood the power of the spell. He pretended to go along out of fear for his life. When he returned and saw the evil brought upon Alyth because of this witch, he sought our help. Is that not true, Daniel?"

Daniel looked at his feet, hesitated, and then nodded.

The utter disgust on Jane's face was complete and chilling.

Daniel remained incapable of meeting her intense gaze.

"I have never heard of such pish," boomed Angus.

He pushed his way through the crowd.

"With all due respect, Angus," said Henry. "We must listen to the evidence presented."

"Ye have the invention of one snivelin' wee coward versus the rest of… "

"I am not a coward!" cried Daniel.

"I must insist," demanded Henry with his frame erect and dignified, "that we have some order. All will get their chance to speak."

"If I may, fine sir," Matthew ventured politely, appealing to Henry's sense of importance.

Henry inclined his head significantly, and Matthew addressed the villagers.

"Good people, can you really afford not to believe Daniel's testimony? Can you afford to take the word of those under a spell? Look at all that has happened to you. It is no mere coincidence that when John shows up, death and destruction follow. And it certainly is not on our account. We have lived in peace as neighbors for many years. Furthermore, what will happen if you continue on this path of destruction? You know that no good will come of it. I have heard some of you express the same concern."

Many villagers nodded in agreement.

"This is sheer nonsense and complete foolishness," said Angus. "These soldiers represent the very men who would seek to brin' ye all into bondage. They would murder an innocent man who has fought to keep ye free."

He pointed to me.

"He who has kept many of ye alive, whether ye choose to see it or nae."

Matthew shook his head sadly. "I'm afraid I must take issue again with the insinuation and falsehoods being spoken. We are here to protect lives, not take them. If that were the case, we would leave you in the cold to die at the hands of the Brean. I desire the death of no one, not even John. I believe in redemption. If he confesses his sins and witchcraft and releases these fine individuals from his power, then I see no reason why mercy should not be extended."

"I have no one in my power," I growled. "And you know this. It is simply an excuse to rid yourself of an enemy by preying upon the fears of the people."

"I believe," Henry said loftily, "that these fine gentlemen are being very reasonable and have been more than generous."

"Ye are a buffoon, Henry," said Angus.

Angus turned and addressed the people.

"This conflict has been manufactured on yer behalf. Nobody demands change when times are peaceful. To gain power, they must produce chaos and blame others for that turmoil. Only then will ye demand change. And it only works if ye can't see through their lies."

Matthew stepped forward.

"The dark of winter is coming upon your people," he said. "You need our help. You can't do it on your own. Our common enemy prowls these dangerous woods. We can help, and we have helped. Look at what we can provide: safety, food, and someone to take care of you. The only thing we ask in return is your trust."

"The general is right!" cried Lucy. "We can't do this on our own. Where will we go? What will we eat? How will we stay warm? We have lost everything. It is perilous to continue. We will perish without their help."

The villagers turned to each other and whispered. Many bobbed their heads in agreement.

"It is true," cried a short and ragged-looking man. "Bad decisions from the past have caught up with us. Look at us! We can't possibly fight off another large Brean attack. They will tear us up, along with our women and children. Only a fool believes we can plan and execute anything other than desperation. We are shadows of our former selves."

"It is easier to keep yer freedom than to win it back," warned Angus.

"We won't survive the first major snowstorm," cried another woman.

"Yes," shouted another man. "And I won't be led to my death by a witch!"

The comments of the frightened villagers continued.

I turned and whispered to the others, "We've lost. We need to escape."

"It sounds to me like we have made our decision," said Henry.

A cry of accord rose from the villagers.

"Let's not wait any longer," said Hannah.

We backed away from the crowd.

"Where are you going?" Lucy shouted angrily. "You are the cause of all this, and you will answer for it."

"No," said Hannah, leveling her rifle at the villagers. "We are leaving."

"You cannot stop us," sneered Matthew. "We outnumber you."

He turned to Roger. "Summon the rest of the company."

Looking beyond them, I saw Sarah and James mounted and leading our horses.

"That isn't entirely true," Sarah said loudly.

The villagers craned their necks around to get a look at who had spoken.

"The riders of Syre are concealed in the woods with their muskets aimed at us right now."

"You're lying," said Matthew. "I saw them leave. They reported to the sentry that they had had enough and were leaving. You are all alone."

"Or, is that what we instructed them to say?" challenged Sarah as she approached us.

"Regardless, it won't matter for you," said Jane. "You, Matthew, will be my first shot. And I don't miss."

I leveled my crossbow, with its wicked tips, at Daniel. "You will fall at the same time. Followed by you, Henry."

Henry looked pale and shocked.

"Such treachery," he gasped.

"Yes," Jane agreed. "But not from us. The blood of the villagers will be from your own folly. We have escaped from what you now embrace, and we will not go back."

I held Matthew in my sights while Jane mounted Ember. Once in her saddle, she took up her rifle again.

"You will not get far," threatened Matthew. "We will pursue you. And when your horses are tired and spent, we will have fresh ones from Marysvale."

With Hannah and Thomas now safely on their horses, I lowered my crossbow and mounted Smoke.

"Father?" asked James with pleading eyes.

Angus shook his head. "Nae, my boy. My place is here. I will still try to get through to them."

He turned to me.

"Ye were right, laddie. For whatever it is worth, ye were right. They were nae ready for yer gifts."

Sadly shaking his head, he added, "I had so much hope."

Angus placed his hand on his son's knee. The look they shared conveyed more than any words could ever describe.

A brief moment passed, then Angus slapped the rump of James' horse, "Now off with ye."

With that, we galloped away.

"Get them!" shrieked Matthew.

Sarah led us as we sailed through the trees and angled away from the villagers.

A few muskets fired wildly, followed by more wild shouts.

Glancing back, I saw soldiers sprinting to their horses.

"This way," shouted Sarah.

She again made a course adjustment, and we galloped after her.

"Where are we going?" I shouted.

"To meet up with the others."

I scanned the forest as far as I could in front of us.

Nothing.

I looked to the right.

Again nothing.

Then I looked to my left.

"I see them," I shouted. "We're going the wrong way."

"No," cried Sarah. "We're not."

"But they are to our left."

"I don't know who they are," she yelled. "But they are not with us."

I studied them. Something about them bothered me.

"Whoever they are, they're coming at us from the side. They will intercept us soon."

248

"Then we have to run faster," shouted Sarah. "We have to reach the others."

I peered at the riders again.

What is it about them that's upsetting me? I wondered.

And then it hit me. And my heart sank.

They were riding in formation.

I looked back, and panic threatened to overtake my senses. I was right; the soldiers behind me were also riding in formation, with Matthew leading them.

Counting them up, I numbered sixteen from the left and twenty from the rear.

Panic gave way to anger.

I hated Matthew. I hated the soldiers. I hated that lying scoundrel, Daniel, and the pompous Henry. I even found myself hating the villagers. I had fought to protect them, their husbands, brothers, and sons.

How could they be so stupid? I wondered.

This was *their* fault. They would get what they deserved.

Even Angus' apology infuriated me. No one ever listened to me. If they would've, we would be safe on our way to Syre. Who knew what would befall us now?

The one thing I did know was that Matthew was going to be just as dead as the rest of us. I would see to it.

Matthew and the riders behind us did not gain, but those from the side angled in and were now in sight.

"We have to turn!" cried Jane.

"No!" replied Sarah.

"We have to stop!" I shouted.

Again, she called back, "No!"

"They will slaughter us on our horses. We won't get a chance to fight back. Let's at least turn around and take on Matthew. He has to be stopped," I yelled.

Sarah charged ahead without replying.

"John's right," called Hannah. "We won't escape this way. Let us at least fight."

Sarah ignored us and drove her mount relentlessly. But her course was off. We needed to turn and run away from both groups, not just one. She was bent on making it to the others, even though there was no hope in reaching them.

Musket fire rang out from the soldiers. On galloping horses, from this distance, they had little chance of hitting us.

Sarah drove on madly while the soldiers reloaded.

"Now! We can fight now!" I shouted. "While they're reloading."

The soldiers from our left fell in behind us. I could hear the snorts of their horses and the thundering of their hooves pounding up the ground.

"HALT!" ordered a soldier. "OR WE WILL SHOOT!"

Either out of blind terror or madness, Sarah wildly kicked her horse to go faster. Smoke could have gone faster, even Ember and the other two, but her horse and James' were already showing signs of tiring.

"HALT!" he shouted again. This time, there was anger.

Sarah ignored him.

Gripping my crossbow tightly, I readied for my assault.

We would not get another warning.

I spun around in the saddle, drew up my crossbow and...

A soldier fired.

His musket cracked to life, exploding its lethal projectile right at me.

Chapter Eighteen: Fool Me Once

The ball whizzed past my head before I could deliver my deadly bolt.

Other soldiers galloped with their muskets aimed right at us.

The message etched on their faces was clear: stop or die.

Of course, we were probably dead already.

Sarah, realizing the gravity, slowed to a trot.

I gripped my crossbow, ready to dispatch two of them once we stopped if I got the chance.

The soldiers spread out and flanked us on both sides, thereby ensuring that we would be caught in a crossfire.

Finally, Sarah halted.

I drew up next to her, with our backs to the soldiers. She looked at me.

I gripped the crossbow with eager eyes, waiting for the signal to begin the attack.

"Don't," she whispered.

"We're going to die anyway," I shot back in a whisper. "Might as well take as many of them as we can."

"We will not win this way. Trust me."

I still clutched the crossbow.

I couldn't understand her. Surely she knew what was going to happen to us, or at least happen to me. It was better to die this way than under the crushing, tearing jaws of a Brean or in the crackling of a fire.

She opened her eyes wide.

I blinked a few times at her, unsure what to make of her.

This was so unlike Sarah.

"Drop your weapons," ordered the commanding soldier.

Sarah and James dropped theirs without a word.

The rest of us hung on to them.

Clearly, we would not win. But to go without a fight…

"I assure you, you will not get the chance to use them. You will be cut down instantly," warned the commander.

Still, no one moved.

"I won't tell you again, and I'll start by shooting the young girl first."

Thomas dropped his musket.

Then Jane.

Finally, I relented.

Hannah still clung to hers.

"Please, dear," pleaded Sarah. "Don't let us watch you die. There is nothing you can do. All is not lost."

Hannah still didn't drop her weapon. Her grip tightened on the musket, and her finger eased into place over the trigger.

She looked at Jane. It was a momentary flash, but it was a look filled with love and sorrow. You could almost read the memories and the goodbye that were etched in her deep and endless green eyes.

Tears sprang into Jane's.

"No," she mouthed to Hannah.

Hannah smiled at Jane for one last moment and then spun around, drawing her musket with her.

Instantaneously, Sarah screamed for Hannah to stop, and Jane launched off her saddle, colliding with Hannah halfway through her swing.

Jane's momentum continued, carrying both her and Hannah off the saddle. They fell, with Jane landing on Hannah and the rifle discharging harmlessly.

Hannah yelled involuntarily from the pain of hitting her arm.

"Well done," Matthew crowed as he trotted up. "You just saved your sister's life...for the time being."

Sarah held her heart and looked about to faint.

Matthew snapped his fingers and pointed, of all people, to Daniel.

"You. Go collect the weapons. We wouldn't want any more mishaps."

Daniel obediently swung his leg over his horse and slid off.

"You might as well dismount as well," he said, addressing us.

Apprehensively, we each abandoned our horses and stood holding their reins.

Then, as if ordering a servant, he said, "Daniel, when you're finished with that, take their horses and lead them out of the way."

Daniel came over, picked up our weapons, and deposited them on the ground in front of Matthew.

The girls stood up and brushed off their clothes.

Hannah glared at Jane.

"Don't look at me like that," Jane whispered defensively. "I couldn't bear to watch you die."

"Better than being sliced up on a table in a dungeon," hissed Hannah.

"It won't come to that," assured Sarah.

"Oh, really?" questioned Matthew. "Any reason why not?"

Sarah looked at him in disgust. "So, you do plan on torturing us? Will the king of the Brean be there as well?"

Hannah's face drained of color, and her hands trembled.

Matthew shrugged. "If I want him to. And, if I want to hang you, I will. If I want to burn you, I will. The point is, I am now free to do whatever I wish with you."

Daniel returned and led the horses away.

Sarah raised an eyebrow. "And you want us to believe you were powerless before? Because of who, the villagers?"

Matthew leaned forward in the saddle. "Why, didn't John tell you? Of course not; he wouldn't have had time. Well," he began dramatically, "now that John has again turned down Naehume's gracious invitation to join him, I am free to dispose of you how I see fit."

"Is that true?" asked Sarah, looking at me.

I nodded, and then, addressing Matthew, I spat, "They wanted to use me and what I can do to further their own lust for power and enslave even more people. I would never have joined you!"

"And what do you plan on doing with the villagers?" asked Sarah. "Are you going to kill them too?"

He sighed. "That is none of your concern."

"Consider it a dying wish," she implored.

"No," he said. "It's more fun this way."

Matthew sighed. "I'm bored."

Then, raising his musket, he said, "Take aim."

The soldiers raised their muskets.

"So you do plan on killing them," persisted Sarah.

"Of course not all of them," he said irritably. "Only those who prove to be troublesome."

Daniel returned, walking in front of the soldiers toward us.

Matthew dropped his musket a fraction and exclaimed, "Good heavens, what are you doing, you idiot?"

Looking befuddled, Daniel said, "You promised Jane to me if I said what you wanted me to say."

"I will never go with you," Jane spat vehemently.

Matthew waved his hand. "And there you have it; she doesn't want you. Trust me; she's more trouble than she's worth. Find another girl."

"I don't want another girl," Daniel shot back angrily. "I kept my side of the bargain; now you keep yours!"

"No," said Matthew. "It's better this way. We'll just blame her death on John."

Matthew's eyes livened with dark cruelty.

"It's perfect!" he crowed. "We will bring him back, blame their deaths on him, and then burn him. There won't be any witnesses to refute it, and my revenge for Lyman will be so much sweeter."

My stomach lurched, and I felt the blood drain from my face. A wave of nausea washed over me. Fear swelled and surged through my body, cascading through me from my head to my toes.

Daniel turned around, anger blazing in his eyes. "I will refute it."

"Will you now," said Matthew with a wicked smile.

Daniel's eyes went wide.

His hand shot for the pistol in his belt, but Matthew was ready for it.

The ball from Matthew's musket slammed into Daniel. His back arched from the impact. His arms flew out wide.

He was dead before he hit the ground.

Daniel's ghost still grabbed for a pistol that was not there.

"NOW!" screamed Sarah.

She turned and threw her arms around me, hooked a leg behind mine, and, before I could do anything, hurled me to the ground.

James flung his arms wide, enveloping Jane, Hannah, and Thomas, knocking them off their feet.

As we fell, the ground all around us heaved upward.

A torrent of leaves flew into the air as if kicked up by a gust of wind.

But there was no wind.

The trap was sprung.

Chaos and pandemonium broke out everywhere.

Armed men emerged from the swirling leaves as if by magic.

The soldiers' horses panicked from the scare. Some reared and threw their riders.

Matthew was one of them.

A few muskets went off accidentally as they hit the ground.

Thinking they were being fired upon, the shooters unleashed a withering volley of rifle fire.

Stricken soldiers toppled and fell.

Through the thick cloud of gunsmoke, I burst my vision open and searched for someone in particular. During our confrontation, I had memorized Matthew's dark aura.

I found him scurrying through the melee on his hands and knees. He scampered over the bodies of the dead and wounded.

A horse nearly trampled him, but he rolled out of the way.

"I have to stop him," I cried, breaking free of Sarah's embrace. "We need him. He'll have information."

Struggling to my feet, I raced over and snatched up my crossbow where Daniel had laid it.

Matthew made his way over to a soldier about to fire on a man. He stood up, grabbed his comrade by his coat, and yanked him off his horse.

As he fell, the man shouted curses in surprise.

Matthew put a foot in the stirrup and swung a leg over. Hunching low to avoid gunfire, he galloped away from his men.

I sprinted to get beyond the fray.

My eye caught sight of Charles. He drew his rifle sight on the hunched figure of Matthew.

Angling over, I ran past him, knocking his rifle up before he could squeeze the trigger.

"I'll get him. I want him alive," I called back over my shoulder.

Clearing the men, I whistled for Smoke and said a silent prayer that he would come.

Somehow, Smoke had a keen sense to know when my call was desperate and when it wasn't. When it was, he came—mostly. Though I always feared that he wouldn't, my worry was unfounded. Smoke threw his head back and came running.

As he drew near, I grabbed the saddle, launched up onto his back, and promptly dropped the crossbow in the process.

I cursed and reined up.

Leaping off Smoke, I rushed over, snatched up the crossbow, and ran back.

With a little less flare, I managed to remount without dropping anything.

We galloped around what was left of the battle.

A musket fired, and half a dozen rifles responded. And then the field fell quiet.

The soldiers who hadn't been killed were surrendering.

Smoke streaked through the forest.

Ahead of us, Matthew was desperately whipping his horse into a frenzy.

He glanced behind him, fearful that someone was pursuing him.

Someone was.

I rose in the saddle, with my knees slightly bent and supple.

Hunching, I said to Smoke, "Don't hold back. Go get him, boy."

His magnificent stride lengthened, and the distance between me and my quarry steadily decreased.

Matthew looked back again and saw me. Rising up in his own saddle, he furiously beat his animal to go faster.

When he again peeked behind him, his eyes widened with fear.

We were close.

That's right, I thought savagely. *You should be afraid.*

Even more, I knew what his next move would be. Calmly, I secured the reins, trusting the rest of the chase to my horse. With my feet planted firmly in the stirrups, I stood up and pressed my legs against Smoke's sides for stability, allowing my knees to bend and straighten in rhythm with the motion of his strides.

I raised the crossbow.

Sighting, I aimed a little to the side of Matthew.

With a pistol gripped in his hand, Matthew spun around to fire.

Simultaneously, I pulled the trigger.

The bolt sliced through the air and embedded in Matthew's outstretched arm.

He cried out in pain as the pistol fell to the ground without ever firing a shot.

Matthew tried coddling his wounded arm, but the bolt made it awkward and near impossible.

Smoke finished closing the distance.

As we drew up next to each other, I moved Smoke in close, so our legs bumped and rubbed together.

Matthew looked at me with a mixture of terror, pain, and rage.

Plunging his good arm into his coat, he produced a long, ornate dagger with a hefty blade. It looked very much like the one Lyman had—the one that Jane had used to kill him.

Matthew slashed at me, but the movement was clumsy.

I swatted his hand away.

Still, he managed to keep hold of the knife.

Before Matthew could try again, I grabbed a fistful of his coat in my hand and, with a mighty heave, lifted him partially out of the saddle and shoved him backward.

His feet came out of the stirrups, and he fell off the horse.

Matthew dropped the dagger when he landed on his rump and began flipping and rolling through the wet leaves.

He screamed in agony as the bolt shaft broke in his arm.

Finally, he tumbled to a stop.

I reined Smoke and turned back.

Writhing in pain, Matthew alternated between cries of anguish and curses at me.

I couldn't help the smile that crept across my face.

Leaping lightly off Smoke, I walked over to him.

He looked up at me and cursed again.

"You fool. You have sealed your doom. The people will perish, and there is nothing you can do to stop it."

I hadn't forgotten my dream.

"Let's talk about that, shall we?" I growled.

Reaching down, I grabbed him by his clothes and yanked him to his feet.

Back peddling him, I slammed his back against the nearest tree.

"I won't tell you anything!" Matthew swore through gritted teeth, and then he spat.

I turned my head just as the spittle struck my cheek and oozed down my face.

"You'll tell me everything," I snarled.

I burst into his soul.

A smile spread across his face, and he shoved me out.

Matthew laughed mockingly. "I've been taught how to keep you out. You will get nothing from me!"

In that small moment, the fury within me exploded into a raging inferno.

I knew that I would enjoy this.

A sardonic grin crept across my face. "And who taught you that? Jex?"

Matthew spat again.

Slamming my forearm against his neck, I raised him onto his toes.

Again, I pushed into his soul.

I felt him gather and push back.

And then, I unleashed the raging serpent and shattered his defense.

Matthew's eyes went wild with surprise and then panic.

"That's right," I hissed scornfully. "And now you know my little secret. There is nothing you can do to stop me."

Matthew again mustered all his strength and tried to push me out.

I pressed deeper.

A tremor ran through his whole body.

"Too bad you won't get the opportunity to tell Jex about it. Was it he who taught you how to keep me out?"

"No," he croaked under the pressure from my arm.

But Matthew couldn't help the memory that rose to the surface, and my consciousness latched onto it.

It was of Jex addressing the men assembled around the table in the great hall where I had dined with Lord Wright and was offered Lyman's position. Except in this memory, Naehume sat at the head of the large table.

Jex was explaining how to block me. The men were confused about how it worked, and Jex was forced to admit he hadn't experienced it himself but quickly added that he'd seen it demonstrated.

"Apparently, it is quite easy," he said. "You simply focus on his presence in your mind and push back."

There was more to the memory. Much more. And I wanted to see it all. This was just the part that I had tricked Matthew into revealing. I wanted to know how Jex had burned down the town.

Matthew threw up his feeble attempts to drive me out.

The memory began slipping away.

"No," I hissed angrily.

In a rage, I tore through his mind after it.

Another tremor passed through Matthew's body as I dove down into his soul.

I snatched at the memory, and my whole being coiled around it. My power was fueled by my hatred for him, for Jex, for Lord Wright, and especially Naehume.

"It's mine," I jeered, and I yanked on it.

Oddly, it seemed to come completely clear from his soul.

"What have you done?" Matthew shrieked.

I had seen terror before, but not like his. It was exquisite and complete. It cut through his face and throughout his whole soul.

"It's gone," he wailed.

Tremors of pain now constantly racked his body.

"It's not gone," I spat irritably. "It's right here, as clear as day..."

Suddenly, the realization of what had just happened hit me like a bolt of lightning.

The memory wasn't in his mind; it was in mine!

I recalled every detail. I saw Jex explaining how he had killed the guards and let the soldiers in. How, together, they used oil to ignite the village. Jex explained how he jammed the water towers shut. Everything he said was right there. Everything about that meeting was mine!

Hungrily, I dove back into Matthew's soul for more.

I could sense the hole where a part of him had been ripped away. I could feel the terrible violation.

Matthew sobbed, "Leave me, and I'll tell you everything. Please!"

A hand touched my shoulder. It was gentle and non-threatening.

"John," said a distant voice. "Let him go."

The gates of Marysvale! I have to know about the gates! I thought.

Ignoring the hand and the horror of my aggression, I pushed back in.

The hand on my shoulder grew forceful, and tried pulling me back. It wasn't strong enough.

I was determined to know. I had to find out their plans! I had to stop the future from happening!

When the villagers were on Matthew's side, they were not a threat to him. They were safe, and Jane was safe. She would have left with me. But now that the villagers knew the truth, the tables had turned. Lord Wright would not allow them into the town, and there would certainly be a battle. Jane would surely stay to help, and she would die, just like in my nightmare.

"John!" cried Sarah from a hazy distance. "Let him go! You are hurting him!"

I have to find out!

Putting my mouth right up to Matthew's ear, I whispered low and menacingly, "You will show me everything I want, or I will take it all. Every memory will be ripped from you until you don't even remember who you are. I will leave you with nothing! You will be like a baby, not even knowing how to speak."

"James!" cried Sarah. "Stop him!"

Chapter Nineteen: The Rest of the Soldiers

Two hands, like vices of steel, gripped my shoulders; and then I was flying backward.

My link with Matthew broke.

The anger raging inside of me subsided some, but not entirely.

I felt more frantic than ever about the future, and I had to stop it.

The hulking frame of James Shepherd stood over me. He reached an arm down, offering me a hand up.

I looked at him, then past him. Matthew had crumpled to the ground. The sleeve of his coat was drenched in blood. He whimpered as Sarah tried to help him sit up.

"Sorry, lad," said James. "I didn't mean to throw you like that, but you had quite a grip on him."

I glanced back at James and took his outstretched hand.

Gingerly, he lifted me to my feet.

Jane was instantly at my side, along with Hannah, Sabin, and Charles.

"Are you hurt? What happened?" she asked breathlessly.

"I...I don't know."

I did know, but I didn't want to talk about it. Not because I was ashamed; after all, Matthew had tried to kill us. No, it was because I didn't want to concern her. Perhaps, to be more honest, I didn't want a lecture.

Walking past her, I approached Matthew. He cowered at my sight.

"Let me have a look at your arm," said Sarah.

Matthew held it close to him doubtfully.

"I won't hurt you," she reassured him.

Slowly he offered it to her.

"You will need to remove your coat for me to inspect it."

"Why are you helping him?" I asked.

"Because he needs it," replied Sarah.

"But why? He was going to kill us. Let him rot. It's what he would do."

Sarah looked up at me and calmly said, "We are not like them. We do not seek to destroy, imprison, enslave, or otherwise dominate and control."

I didn't say anything in return. I didn't want to argue in front of Matthew. So, I settled on glaring at him.

He refused to meet my eyes.

Sarah looked back up at me.

"Must you do that?"

"I want something from him."

Matthew shrank at my words.

"There will be a proper time to *ask* questions, but not now," Sarah said sternly.

I squatted down next to him anyway.

James moved behind me, prepared to stop whatever I was about to do.

"I'm not going to hurt him," I reassured James. "At least not yet. I just want to tell him one thing, and then I will let Sarah mother him all she wants."

Sarah shot me a look that conveyed she didn't appreciate my tone.

I wasn't bothered in the least.

Taking his chin in my hand, I tilted his head up. He closed his eyes, not meeting mine.

"Do you remember what I said before we were separated?"

He nodded.

"Good, because that was a promise. If you do not cooperate and tell all that you know when the time comes, then believe me when I say that no one will be able to keep you from me, and I will do all that I vowed."

I let go of his chin and asked, "Do you understand?"

Matthew immediately nodded his understanding.

Rising to my feet, I turned and then stopped.

Looking back over my shoulder, I warned, "The same promise will be fulfilled if I hear you say anything more about witchcraft."

I removed myself from the group and stood with my arms folded across my chest while glaring at Matthew intently.

He didn't look at me but continued to shake like a scared kitten. I relished having him in my control.

Jane came to my side.

"What did you say to him before you were pulled apart?"

Without taking my eyes off Matthew, I said, "That I would hurt him in ways that no other person could."

After a silent moment, I glanced at her.

She was regarding me curiously.

"You disapprove?" I asked.

Jane shrugged. "Not necessarily. Although, I believe Sarah is right. I do not desire to be like them."

"Of course, I'm not saying we should be tyrants, but look at where we are. We are losing. And we need help. Something inside of me is changing. I feel my power growing. I've held it back for too long, and I can see I've been wrong in that."

"Growing in what way?" she asked uneasily.

"Don't be concerned," I reassured her. "I believe it to be for the best. My whole life, I have hidden from who I am. I've sought and been taught to keep my gift quiet. I've been afraid of it. I've been afraid of where it would lead and how people would react if they knew about me. But in holding back, the things I dread come true anyway. Restraint hasn't made any difference; I'm still feared and persecuted. Maybe I've been going about it all wrong. Perhaps I should have been using my gift with impunity—developing and strengthening it. If people knew what I could really do, they would respect me."

"You mean fear you."

"But that's just it; they fear me now. Fear, respect..."

"And what about love? I fell in love with you the way you are. I don't want you to change into someone to be feared."

I took her by the shoulders and turned her to face me. Her green eyes met mine.

"Nothing will change between us. I still love you."

Jane shook her head sadly. "No, it would have to. You cannot serve two masters, John. You cannot split who you are in two. One will surely spill over into the other, and you will end up hurting those you love. You will hurt me."

I tucked a lock of hair behind her ear. "I could never hurt you."

"And what if you were angry with me? It will happen; it is inevitable. If you are accustomed to letting yourself go, will you lose control and break me like you did Matthew?"

"Of course not. That's different. You haven't tried killing me," I said with a smile.

The corner of her mouth turned up in a suppressed grin. "At least not yet."

Jane quickly forced the grin away.

"I am serious, John. I don't want you to change."

"But what if it keeps us alive?"

She placed her hand upon my heart.

"I would rather lose your body than your soul. I want the John I fell in love with. Is it not better to cultivate love than fear?"

"Perhaps," I said unconvinced. "Sarah says it's more powerful, but I haven't felt it. At least not when it comes to my gifts."

"But in life?" Jane asked.

I didn't get a chance to answer.

Hannah cleared her throat and trotted up on her horse, with Smoke and Ember in tow.

"You two do realize that you're not alone?"

Then under her breath, she added, "I just don't understand young people these days."

"Your turn is coming," I muttered.

She ignored me.

"Whatever you did to Matthew seems to have worked. He sure is chatty all of a sudden. You should do that to all our enemies."

"Hannah," snapped Jane. "Don't encourage him."

She shrugged. "Could come in handy."

"See, Hannah understands," I said.

"No, she just thinks she does."

Hannah rolled her eyes.

"Well, you two can stay here if you'd like, but we're leaving."

Indeed, Matthew had been placed upon his horse, and the rest were mounted and walking away.

As our group rode back to the scene of the battle, Jane and I stayed to the rear. It didn't take long for Sarah to join us.

She looked at me, but I didn't meet her gaze.

"Would you like to talk about it?" asked Sarah.

"Talk about what?" I replied, knowing full well what she meant.

"About what happened back there with Matthew. The others saw you physically taking your anger out on him, but it was more than that. I have never felt anything like that come from you before."

"No," I said. "I don't want to talk about it. What I want to talk about is why you didn't tell me what you were planning. It would have saved me a lot of worry."

"I am truly sorry about that. At the time, I deemed it necessary. Perhaps it was; perhaps it was not. We had little time to prepare. We could see that the soldiers hoped to turn the village against us. Accusing you of witchcraft would be easy—even easier than they realized, as many villagers already blamed you for their misfortunes. And you told us not to trust Henry, so we didn't."

Sarah continued, "It was you who gave us the idea. You said the villagers wouldn't believe us unless they saw the horror with their own eyes and heard it with their own ears.

"James thought we could use the blankets that the Brean had hidden under and had his men ride back to retrieve them. Meanwhile, we convinced people in your shooting groups to help. We put as many of your men on horses as we dared. They rode out under the guise that they were the men from Syre. And, as they were unneeded and had had enough, they were going back home. We risked that the soldiers wouldn't know how many men had really come from Syre and that they wouldn't be able to tell the difference between them and the villagers.

"I knew Matthew would confront you. What I wasn't prepared for was the speed of your conviction. Our original plan was to bargain with Henry to let us go peacefully, with the agreement that we would not interfere with his leadership decisions. Then we could ride to where the ambush would happen and wait. We knew that the soldiers would never let us leave, no matter what the deal was. Especially not you. Again, I do apologize; but I didn't know how well you could act your part. I was afraid that if your reaction didn't appear genuine, they would detect deception and take caution."

Sarah paused a moment in thought. "Upon reflection, it was a blessing everything unfolded so quickly. There were a lot of

271

things that could have gone wrong. With too much time, the few villagers left behind who knew about the plan might have grown nervous and tipped off the soldiers.

"I think the speed threw Matthew off as well. I believe the outlying soldiers were meant to cut off our exit immediately. With our rapid departure, they didn't have time, and it gave us a chance to reach the ambuscade. It would have been better for us if our horses hadn't been so tired; that's why we couldn't outpace them. However, in the end, I suppose it all worked out."

"I still wish you would have told me," I complained stubbornly.

"I tried to. I hoped you would read my mind as we were fleeing. But, I suppose to your credit, you didn't."

"I told her not to tell you," said James, falling back to join us. "You were defeated in your own mind, and that is never an asset. However, the fact that you are not like Matthew is. He is a devious character, and you are not. And, in this case, that part about you may have worked against us. If Matthew did not see a genuine reaction in you to what he said and planned, he would perceive a trap. And we needed the villagers to know what was going on before they were locked away behind the walls of Marysvale, and it was too late."

Then, in a tone that conveyed the message to stop sulking, he added unapologetically, "Like it or not, lad, we made the correct decision."

James was, of course, right. Their plan had worked, and it was hard to argue that.

Notwithstanding, I still felt angry, although I didn't quite know why.

We rode in silence.

Resentment continued to simmer under the surface, despite my efforts to stifle it. It seemed everything caused me aggravation, regardless of whether or not it was reasonable.

After a while, Sarah signaled for me to fall back, and I obeyed. Jane and Hannah both looked like they wanted to join us, but they didn't.

We slowed until we were a considerable distance behind.

I didn't say anything. I knew she wanted to tell me things that I had no desire to hear. And truth be told, I was irritated with myself for feeling bitter.

"John," she said patiently. "You have to let the anger go."

"I suppose," I replied. "But there is power in it. When I feel angry, I can do things that I can't do otherwise."

"Yes," she agreed. "In the short term, it may appear that way. Rage certainly is powerful. When you choose to use it against another person, you may find yourself inflicting things that you could never imagine yourself doing. Anger is a demon. It is the mother of hatred. It consumes the wielder of it and hurts everyone around you. It destroys and ridicules unnecessarily. It doesn't take pleasure in accomplishment; it is only gratified when the object of the anger is crushed."

"Doesn't Lord Wright deserve to be destroyed?" I asked.

"Stopped, yes. Brought to justice, yes. The object of our hatred, no."

"I don't see how that's possible. Look at the misery he has caused. He has murdered and spread suffering everywhere. I don't see how you can remove the emotion from that."

"You may feel passionate about the cause; just beware of unchecked rage. It will mislead you. You will feel that your wrath is justified. But unchecked, you become consumed with vengeance instead of what you really set out to accomplish."

"Isn't the goal to stop him? Isn't that what we are trying to do?"

"Our goal is peace. Our goal is to return to our farms and live our lives how we see fit—to be free! Stopping Lord Wright is only a part of that. John, hatred is bondage. If you let it, it will rob you of everything you hold dear."

Feeling defensive, I clenched my jaw and silently stared ahead.

"I know you may not believe me," she continued. "But love is a much better motivator. Though darkness can yield an imposing force, the smallest beam of light can pierce it. Love is light. Love liberates the mind and stills the soul. It frees you to see things for what they really are."

"But I do love. I love Jane dearly, and I care a great deal for you and Hannah."

"And the villagers? Do you love them?"

I hesitated.

"They are why we are still here," she continued. "We are trying to help them."

"But they tried to kill me!" I shot back.

"They are scared, John. And blind with grief. They are grasping for any hope, even false hope. They would not have tried it if they knew what we know."

"But they did. Am I just supposed to forget that?" I spat angrily.

She sighed. "I am only trying to help, but I can see you are not ready for this. I will not press further. But as a friend, let me caution you: hatred will change you, whether you want it to or not."

Sarah nudged her horse forward and joined the others, leaving me to myself.

After a few minutes, Jane fell back.

To my relief, she didn't say anything. She just rode by my side.

Soon, we reached the battleground. Nearly a dozen soldiers lay dead on the field, along with several horses. About fifteen soldiers were wounded. A few of our own men had been injured in the fight, but they looked like they would live. The unscathed soldiers had been rounded up and were under heavy guard.

James, Thomas, Sarah, and Hannah were talking to Charles. Jane and I went over to join them.

"Any get away?" I asked.

Charles shook his head. "Nope."

"Good."

He scratched his beard. "But, as I was explaining, we have another problem."

"And what is that?" I asked.

"Well, I figure the soldiers back at camp aren't going to like what we did with this lot. How are we going to deal with them?"

"I have an idea," ventured Jane. "Remember what you did to those soldiers in Marysvale?"

I furrowed my brow, trying to narrow it down. "I did quite a few things to them."

"The ones that harassed the old man, Simon?"

"Wait, what?" said Hannah. "I didn't hear about this. What did you do?"

"I stripped them of their clothes and gave them a dose of their own medicine."

"What does that mean?" asked Hannah.

"I dressed up as a soldier, acted like a soldier, and took them to the market."

"Oh," she said.

Then, as what I said sunk in, she repeated, "Ohhh. You sold them?"

I nodded.

"We can do something similar," said Jane. "Well, at least you men can. If you look like a soldier when you arrive back in camp, you can quickly surround the others before they even know what happened."

"That's not a bad idea," said Charles while scratching his chin.

The others agreed, and we set about making the change.

While we were getting ready, I remembered a question that I wanted to ask Jane.

"Are all these men from Marysvale?"

She looked at me curiously. "What do you mean?"

"Are they all original citizens from Marysvale, or did they come from other places?"

"Oh," she replied. "No, they are not all from Marysvale. Lord Wright has recruiters to go out and find the right type to join up. At first, they claimed we needed help forming a proper army. It was easy to convince us. The Brean had increased their activity and had been seen in larger numbers. All staged for our benefit, no doubt. Now that they have total control, they don't explain anything."

When we finished donning the soldiers' uniforms, their hands were bound so that the women and a few others could keep guard until wagons could be sent back for the wounded.

I didn't want to be gone long. As it was, it would be night before they could be brought back into camp. I suspected the Brean would leave well enough alone, but I didn't want to chance leaving them unprotected in the dark.

As the sun was in the process of setting, we didn't have much time.

When everything was ready, and all the shooters were mounted, we set off at a brisk pace.

Daylight faded rapidly. Which, in a sense, was good; the dark would aid in concealing us from the more keen-eyed soldiers.

Before long, we could smell the campfires, and soon after, their bright orange light came into view.

I instructed the men to get ready. We formed up into two columns and rode in formation like I'd seen the real soldiers do. The plan was simple. Upon entering camp, we would quickly surround the remaining guards. Knowing how they felt about the people, I didn't expect them to be mingling, but one never knew for sure. If they were scattered about, we'd just have to deal with them the best we could.

We passed the first of the villagers. Some looked at us and then looked away. However, as their brains caught up to what their eyes had seen, they quickly snapped their gaze back. They wore expressions of recognition and surprise upon their faces. Apparently, a bunch of scruffy men in ill-fitting uniforms was no replacement for well-groomed soldiers.

It was time to move quickly.

Gripping my crossbow, I gave the signal. The columns of two riders fell into a gallop and split.

Twenty soldiers were gathered around their own fire, near the wagons.

The column I led cut between the villagers and the soldiers. People scurried to get out of the way of our horses. The other column of horses dashed around the outer side.

Perhaps my plan wasn't the best one. Uniformed riders, charging in, immediately drew everyone's attention. Moving in at a slower, leisurely pace would've been less conspicuous. But it didn't matter now.

Something did work in our favor, however. The soldiers were more curious by our strange entrance than alarmed.

It was after we encircled them that they finally realized what was going on.

One soldier shot a hand up into a wagon, snatching at a musket.

My crossbow came up quicker.

With a twang, the bolt sliced through the air, into his outstretched arm, and embedded into the wood. He howled in agony as the bolt held his arm fast.

Another soldier reached for a pistol in his belt and then screamed.

Unfortunately for him, in his panic, his finger had squeezed the trigger before he could get the pistol clear. He fell to the wet mud writhing in pain. Through gritted teeth came a mixture of cries and curses.

His leg sustained the second injury of the hour.

As threateningly as I could muster, I informed the lot, "The first shot was a warning. The next ones will be to kill."

They all stood stark still.

"Matthew is still alive," I said. "And if you wish for him to remain so, I would drop your weapons slowly to the ground."

Nobody moved.

Scanning them again, I discovered that, for many, nothing had changed in their feelings. While interesting to note their lack of concern for their general, I suppose it wasn't surprising. He wasn't the one they were afraid of. Matthew was merely a puppet. It was the hand that controlled the puppet that struck fear into them.

I instructed my men to shoot anyone who twitched.

I locked another bolt into my crossbow.

"We are not afraid of death!" one soldier cried defiantly.

He may have been certain in his convictions, but others were not so sure. They highly valued their own necks.

"Very well," I replied.

"Wait!" cried a soldier. He stepped forward with his hands raised. Like most of them, he had no weapon on him.

Motioning with my crossbow, I said, "Step aside then."

No sooner had he done so, then another did the same, and then another. The ones valuing their lives were soon segregated.

The next to surrender were the soldiers who tried desperately to figure out how they could retaliate. Upon seeing that they had no chance, they finally accepted their unfortunate position. They weren't happy about giving up. Most likely planned to escape later, or some other scheme.

Four proud soldiers remained defiant. They looked upon their comrades in disgust.

"We would rather die at your hands than surrender to a witch," spat the same soldier who had proclaimed they were not afraid to die.

"Oh, you won't die at our hands. At least, I can promise that two of you won't."

They looked perplexed.

I patted my crossbow. "I'm sure I can stick two of you with this and stop you before you can shoot. Those two unfortunate souls will live—at least for a while. You will be tied to a tree. At that point, if you're lucky, you will either freeze to death or, worse, starve to death. It could take days. However, I'm guessing the Brean will find you first. How do you think they'll treat you?"

Outwardly, they appeared unfazed.

Inwardly, I knew I'd struck a chord.

I emphasized my point.

"From what I understand, the monsters will take their time with you. It's not a pleasant sight, but then I suspect you already know what they can do."

Their faces turned white.

One of the soldiers immediately disarmed, and I motioned for him to step away.

"Well, that narrows it down a bit. Your odds of survival are not improving," I said coldly.

And with that, the remaining three threw down their arms.

The weapons were collected, and the soldiers' wrists were bound behind them—all but the wounded one.

With the newly accumulated firearms, we could now double our little village army.

When I felt sure the soldiers didn't pose a threat, I left with James in a wagon to bring in the wounded from the battlefield. Sam drove another.

Charles and the rest of the shooters spread about the villagers to relate what they had heard while they were concealed.

The sky was now completely dark.

Our long, long, eventful day was drawing to an end, or at least I hoped. I felt depleted. Fortunately, I had a nice bench to sit on, and James had offered to drive the team. I volunteered to keep a watch, but James just smiled knowingly, and, before the camp had even fallen out of sight, my head slumped to my chest. I fell into a restless slumber, awakened only occasionally by the jostling of the cart.

In what seemed like only a few minutes, we reached our destination. The wounded were loaded into the wagons, and we returned without incident.

Arriving back at camp, we gratefully warmed up by a fire and ate, mostly in silence, as everyone seemed to be in a similar state of exhaustion.

There was a brief discussion on the possibility of an attack, and we concluded that it was unlikely. As far as our enemies knew, we were in the capable hands of the soldiers. The Brean may put up a show to illustrate how valuable the soldiers were, thus driving us further into their arms of safety. Still, we considered it a very remote possibility.

However, since we couldn't be sure, we established a watch. Thankfully, I was not a part of it.

With everything decided upon, James retrieved a large tarpaulin. We laid out our blankets, climbed in, and then folded the other half of the tarp over the top of us.

Instantly, I was fast asleep.

***

I walked through the vacant, moonlit streets. No light streamed through the windows of the homes and buildings. The only sounds were those of my boots scraping on the cobblestones and the biting wind that whistled through the empty town. The frigid air invigorated my senses.

I was alone. But it didn't matter; I would always be alone.

I was different now, and I felt as empty and cold as Marysvale itself. I preferred it that way, as there were no others like me and none that I cared about—except for one.

There was one I hungered to find—one who consumed every waking moment of my thoughts. I would make it my life's mission to seek after that one, the king of the Brean, and kill him.

And if I found any others of his kind, I'd kill them too.

My crossbow rested easily on my shoulder. The fresh blood that covered the tips of my bolts was beginning to freeze.

Powerful strides carried me over the bodies of the fallen monsters, villagers, townspeople, and soldiers who littered the ground.

I looked at their faces. Most of them I didn't know. I didn't care. People, Brean, they were all the same to me.

I held no fear of either, and I would never fear them again.

Quite the contrary, they all feared *me* now. They had seen what I had done to the soldiers and had fled in terror.

I continued stepping over the bodies, making my way up to the garrison of Marysvale. Its polished gates stood open, welcoming me home.

Passing the threshold, I walked by a pile of dead, frozen soldiers. When it warmed, and if I still lived here, I would burn them.

I strolled past the vacant keeps and on to my own. Once occupied by the former Lord Wright, they proved to be fitting chambers for the new me. It was here, in one of the high towers, where I was forced to watch the Brean sweep over the walls and through the broken gate. It was here where I witnessed the soldiers join the Brean in the destruction of the people. They had streamed into the town, raking down the innocent with muskets, clubs, and claws. Their blood flowed down the streets in rivulets, staining the cobblestones and soaking the ground. Not even children had been spared.

It was here where I had finally embraced the demon that had grown inside of me.

The rooms in the castle were all empty now.

At first, there had been some soldiers who had stupidly thought they could elude me, but I had found them. All of them were guilty, and I had made each one pay for his crimes.

Reaching my chamber, I closed the massive door behind me and bolted it. Although alone, it was in sleep when I became truly vulnerable. The stone walls and the heavy door would keep me safe.

Tossing my crossbow on a table, I walked past the great expanse of windows that overlooked the ice-covered forest and passed into a small washroom. Pouring water into the basin, I splashed my face. Everything was freezing. But the cold had ceased to bother me since the fever had set in.

By embracing my demons, I was able to draw upon great and terrible power. It coursed through my veins, giving me strength that I couldn't possess otherwise. Both Lord Wright and I had discovered my new might in this very room.

For Wright, it was to his mortal destruction.

I splashed more water.

Then, taking a dirty linen cloth, I patted myself dry and gazed into the silver mirror that lay on the table.

A beard now adorned my face, wild and unkempt. Above it, hollow red eyes stared back at me. A fitting representation of the fever that filled my being, as if my soul itself were being consumed in the very pits of hell.

Chapter Twenty: Thomas' Sacrifice

Throwing the coverings aside, I sat up and buried my face in my hands, trembling from the emotions that flooded through me in the aftermath of another nightmare.

Why show me that? I wondered. *What did it mean? Is it a picture of things to come? What was the purpose?*

I abhorred the thought of becoming such a being, so callous and cold. Yet I found myself, even now, feeling hollow and hopeless.

The crackling of flames, the chattering of voices, and the smell of food drifted through the air.

Lifting my head, I looked around and discovered that the rest of our party had already risen. Indeed, I appeared to be the only one in the whole company who was still in bed.

Dawn was breaking, and already most of the camp had been taken down and packed up. Everyone was busily preparing to leave.

Jane walked over to me, carrying a steaming mug.

"Why didn't anyone wake me?" I asked.

"I tried but couldn't. I was afraid that you were under some kind of attack, but Sarah didn't detect anything and insisted I let you rest. She said it would do you some good. Your sleep didn't look very restful to me, though."

She offered me the mug. "This will warm you."

I stood and gratefully took it, raised it to my lips, and sipped hot herbal tea.

Crinkling my nose from the bitter taste, I asked, "Sarah?"

Jane nodded.

"She said it would both 'warm you up and soothe your aches.'"

Truth be told, I didn't feel very cold. I knew I should, but I didn't. In fact, I felt slightly warm.

I observed the villagers all huddled around fires. Many were wrapped in blankets; others were warming their hands over the flames.

Taking another sip, I reflected upon my dream.

I recalled that a demon had grown inside me and that a fever had given me strength. It had happened in Lord Wright's tower.

I furrowed my brow, trying to remember all the details.

Were the fever and the demon the same thing?

I didn't particularly like the idea of embracing a demon.

However, I couldn't deny that I felt physically better. I was somewhat startled to note that my pain was virtually gone.

Is it a coincidence? I wondered.

"What is it?" asked Jane. "What troubles your mind?"

"I'm remembering a dream I had."

"Another one? Like before?"

"Yes."

"Of the future?"

"Yes," I said darkly. "I believe so."

"From the sound of your voice, I gather it isn't good."

"No, not at all."

"Tell me about it."

"It was horrible. Everyone died, people, soldiers, monsters. The only two left were Naehume and me."

Jane patted my arm.

"You mustn't worry about such things. You don't know for sure it will come to pass."

"It feels like it will. I feel like a ship tossed before a great storm, powerless to change my course."

Jane nodded in understanding.

"Perhaps what you saw will come to pass, perhaps not. What *is* important are the decisions we make. You know that this life is not the end. Whether we live or die, it is *how* we live that matters most. Perhaps we are a ship in a tempest. Do we blame the captain, or anyone else for that matter, for putting us in the storm? Do we set the rigging ablaze and jump ship, saying all is lost? Or, do we trim the sails, grab the wheel, and throw her prow straight into the storm? Isn't this a fight worth fighting?"

"And what if the storm is too great? Will fighting matter?" I asked.

Jane stepped close and looked up at me with her deep green eyes. "In one case, the result is guaranteed. In the other, it is not."

Placing her hand upon my chest, she added, "In your heart, John Stone, you know this."

She was right, of course. I had nearly given up before, only to be redeemed when all seemed lost.

Jane's words reminded me of our last moments before reaching Alyth, how bleak and hopeless it had seemed. And yet, here we were.

My face softened, and I smiled.

She smiled back. "I like that."

"You sound like Sarah," I said.

"Thank you. She is a person worthy of emulation."

Jane took my hand in hers. "Come, it is nearly time to leave."

She led me to where the others stood.

James, Sarah, Angus, Sabin, Charles, and Hannah surrounded a buggy that had already been hitched up. Thomas sat on the front bench. Behind him reclined three wounded men. Two looked either asleep or unconscious.

Thomas looked up at me and smiled. It was a good sign. His face was bruised and appeared particularly black around the eyes.

"It's getting better," I commented. "Today, you only look like a horse kicked you."

He grinned. "Oh, don't worry about me. It feels much worse than it looks."

I smiled. "Decided not to ride Shade?"

"I rode him enough yesterday. Since we have space, and this looks like such a splendid coach."

"Good, you should. How are you really feeling?"

Thomas shrugged. "My face, chest, and leg hurt. Other than that, I'm fine. I'll live. It could've been much worse. And Sarah gave me something to drink for the pain. It seems to be helping."

Remembering my bitter liquid, I said to him conspiratorially, "Should've let you have mine."

Sarah gave me a disapproving look.

"It's not that I'm not grateful," I said. "It's just that I think Thomas could've used it more."

"You're not fooling anyone, John Stone," said Hannah, on behalf of Sarah.

"I suppose not," I agreed with a defeated sigh. "Just wish it tasted better."

"How are the villagers?" I asked no one in particular.

"Do ye mean by that, how are they holdin' up? Or how are they feelin' about ye?" questioned Angus with a raised eyebrow.

"I suppose both."

He shrugged.

"Well, the food, supplies, and wagons help a wee bit. However, they know they have a difficult road ahead of them still."

"And the other part?" I asked, this time looking directly at Charles.

"Ah," Charles scratched his beard. "It is a hard thing admitting you're wrong. Some readily declare it, as I do. Your standing has improved with most. As for the rest, well, they need some more time."

"And we're still heading to Syre?" I asked.

"About that, laddie," replied Angus.

Worry swelled inside me.

"Why? Why go there?"

"Do you think they will let us slip by?" asked James.

Without waiting for a reply, he continued, "You know they won't. It's better to bring the fight to them on our terms than to be caught out in the open against an army of men and monsters. With surprise on our side, they will be expecting us, just not in the way they think."

As much as I dreaded going there, I knew James was right.

"What is our plan?" I asked with a sigh.

They all stared back at me expectantly.

Worry grew to fear.

"Wonderful," I muttered.

"Do ye have any ideas, laddie?" asked Angus.

"Pray," I suggested.

Angus' eyes twinkled. "Aye. Already done. Well, I suppose we have a wee bit of time to work out the particulars."

The group dispersed, and we went about preparing the villagers, animals, and wagons to leave.

When everyone was finally ready, we set off. The morning sky was clear, though the ground was still sodden from yesterday's rainstorm.

Hannah had volunteered to drive the buggy for Thomas. He had argued that it was unnecessary, but she insisted.

Noticing that the soldiers carried supplies, I asked, "Whose idea was that?"

"Mine," replied Hannah. "It will tire them out and make them less likely to give us trouble. It also frees up some wagons for the wounded and those who can't walk. Genius, don't you think?"

I had to admit that it was and told her so.

Then, I added, "Since you're so full of brilliant ideas, what should we do when we get to Marysvale?"

Hannah thought about it for a moment and then ventured, "Ask them nicely if we can come in?"

"Oh, I'm sure they'll be happy to let us in…if we forfeit our weapons. Perhaps it will come to that in the end."

"It will never come to that," Jane said flatly.

"And what if it does?" I asked. "What if our only option is to surrender?"

"I'd rather die," she said resolutely.

In my mind's eye, I could see the two girls battling it out as a tide of Brean swept over them—all while soldiers watched on from the wall.

Would they truly be able to stand by and do nothing? Could they be so cold?

Then I recalled the control that Lord Wright wielded over the people.

Of course, they would. Even if some wanted to help, what could they do?

I had to come up with a plan, and soon. By my reckoning, we should arrive at the gates of Marysvale sometime this afternoon. It left little time to organize any sort of a siege, not that it would work anyway.

I gently pounded my fist against my forehead.

Think! I screamed to myself. *You're missing something!*

"You needn't beat yourself up," said Sarah, who was riding behind me with James.

"If I don't, then you will all die," I said sharply.

Sarah didn't seem to mind the edge in my voice, and she replied calmly, "You are allowing fear and stress to affect your judgment. Take a few deep breaths and then list our assets."

"Even if we throw everything at them, what good will it do? We won't prevail, not against their forces."

"Then perhaps we should consider something other than a fight."

"I don't believe asking nicely will get us in."

Sarah sighed, not out of frustration but out of disappointment.

"What are they expecting, John?"

Her question caught me off guard.

"I'm not sure I understand."

"What are the guards of Marysvale expecting to see when we arrive?"

"I suppose a group of bedraggled and desperate citizens."

"Bedraggled, maybe, but not desperate."

"Aren't we desperate?"

"Perhaps, but not in their eyes."

"Soldiers!" cried Hannah.

Jane stepped in to save me from my confusion.

"The Marysvale guards are not anticipating a group of desperate refugees on their doorstep. What they are most likely expecting to see is a company of grateful and submissive villagers being led dumbly to the gates by their saviors, the soldiers."

I raised my eyebrows in comprehension.

"I can see you understand," said Sarah.

So perhaps we can trick them, I thought.

I furrowed my brow.

"What is it?" asked Jane.

"How do we know if that's what they're expecting? They could be preparing for the worst."

"It is possible," admitted Jane. "However, we have you. And you are uniquely qualified to find out exactly what they have planned."

"That's true," I said.

I turned Smoke around, and Jane followed on Ember.

"John," warned Sarah. "Don't hurt him."

I didn't meet her gaze.

As I passed the wagon, Hannah leaned over and added with a wink, "At least don't hurt him too much."

"Hannah!" exclaimed Sarah reprovingly. "Don't start down the path of becoming like them."

I had no intention of becoming like them. However, I did intend on getting the information we needed. I'd rather sacrifice one disgusting, evil man than an entire village of innocent people. And even more important to me were the lives of Jane and those I loved.

The soldiers marched behind everyone else. Well-armed guards, mounted on horseback, kept a watchful eye on them.

Matthew, free from carrying a load on account of his wounded arm, led them. I had to admit I was a bit disappointed to see that the bolt had been removed. His arm, now bandaged, rested in a sling.

Jane and I dismounted, and I handed her the reins.

Matthew glared at me as I strode purposely over to him.

Without any formalities, I grabbed him by the coat and flung him out of formation and onto the ground.

He cried out in pain as he landed on his arm.

Immediately, I fell upon him, rolled him onto his back, and knelt on his chest. In consideration of Sarah, I avoided kneeling directly on his wound.

He looked up with terror in his eyes.

I pressed into his soul. Matthew tried keeping me out, but I was getting stronger and better at this. I crushed through his feeble defense.

"You're going to answer some questions," I stated.

He trembled under me.

"I'll answer anything, just stay out of me," he pleaded.

"That's not how it works," I growled. "But if you cooperate, I'll leave your memory intact. Deal?"

Matthew nodded quickly.

"What will they do when we show up?"

His mind dug up the answer, and I knew what he was going to say before he said it.

"It depends. If they don't get word, they will assume the worst and post soldiers in place of the town guards. If they…"

I stopped him from finishing. "Let's explore that first option. If that happens, what will they do? Will they fire upon us?"

He shook his head. "Not necessarily."

Images of Brean filled his mind. He imagined them attacking the villagers, pinning them against the wall, and cutting off any retreat.

"And the soldiers will just watch?"

"They will let you in if you disarm. But they don't expect you to. If you fire on the town, they will return fire."

"And if they do get word?"

"That is what they hope. They wanted me to succeed. They don't want to alarm you or lose any soldiers or Brean, if possible. They want me to disarm you at the gates. A contingent of officers will be on hand to instruct the town guard. We believe the town guard looks less threatening and easier to trust. Once you're disarmed, they will let you come in."

"And what if we follow you all the way there, but then we refuse to disarm?"

"Then we go back to the first plan. The Brean will be ready, and they will attack."

"How will you send word?"

This part, I could guess, but I wanted to be sure.

"I will dispatch a soldier to inform them of the situation."

"Any soldier?"

He nodded, but he also held something back. I could sense it.

"Not very bright of you," I hissed.

Lifting my knee off his chest, I repositioned it and ground it down upon his wounded arm.

Matthew howled in pain.

"We had a deal," I growled. "And you just broke it."

"Don't hurt me!" he wailed. He turned his head and closed his eyes.

A tear broke free and streamed down the side of his head, disappearing into his hair.

I grabbed his head with both my hands and jerked it back. With my thumbs, I pried his eyelids open a sliver. It was enough to slide back in.

"One last chance," I spat. "If you fight me, I'll start taking things. And I'll start with your family if you have any."

Matthew stopped fighting and opened his eyes fully. The image of a young boy involuntarily flashed into his memory.

"Your son?" I asked. I knew it was.

He nodded.

"Then speak if you don't want to lose all memory of him."

"There is a code phrase."

I could tell he didn't want to say it, but his fear of losing his son motivated him.

"John is dead, or John is not dead. It doesn't matter which one. It will just notify them so they can prepare accordingly."

"And what do they plan on preparing for me if I *am* alive?"

"I don't know," Matthew wailed.

A hand gripped my shoulder and gently tried pulling me back. She wasn't strong enough to force me.

"Let him go, John," said Sarah. There was no anger or threat in her voice, just pleading.

It didn't matter now. I knew he was telling the truth. So, I stood up.

Another question popped into my head.

"When do they expect to hear from you?"

"Sometime this morning," he squeaked.

Not feeling like a lecture, I turned and walked past Sarah and James. Taking Smoke from Jane, I mounted and trotted past the villagers. They watched me with what? Fear?

297

Admiration? Curiosity? I didn't care to find out. It didn't matter. My first goal was to protect my friends, even if they disagreed with me. In the end, I felt confident that they would.

Again passing Hannah in the wagon, she asked, "Did you get it?"

I nodded.

"Good."

There was no contempt from her, no look of disapproval. She understood what was at stake.

"Tell me about it," she said.

With Thomas listening, I conveyed the information I had received.

When I had finished, Hannah let out a low whistle.

"If we plan on trickery, we have a few problems. The first being, there isn't a lot of time left; the morning is almost over. The second problem is that they are expecting a rider they know."

"I considered that too," I said. "If we leave this moment, we may have a chance if we don't spare the horses."

Then I shook my head. "But I don't see a way around the second problem."

"I do," said Thomas.

We both looked at him.

"I can play the part of a soldier."

"You can't," I protested. "It will be a hard ride as it is, let alone for someone in your condition. You will be dead from the pain alone."

"Listen to me. I *can* do it. I don't have facial hair, so I look like one of them. And look at my face. It's so black and swollen; they wouldn't recognize me."

"But you're too young to be one of the soldiers," said Hannah, clearly not liking this plan.

Thomas held up his hand. "I'm not much younger than a few of those fellows. And I have a similar build. As I said, they won't recognize my face. I can get away with it."

"It will be dangerous. If they do recognize the trick or become suspicious, they will kill you."

"I know," Thomas said simply.

Gritting his teeth in obvious pain, Thomas climbed out of the wagon.

While we wanted to stop him, we also knew he was our best chance.

"He could use another dose of that tea of yours," I suggested to Sarah.

"It will be a little cold, but I'll make some right away."

"Come along, laddie," said James. "I'll help you with your uniform."

"James, will you tell Sabin to take the rest of the uniforms from the soldiers who are still wearing them?" I asked. "Have them dress like villagers and vice versa. We might as well look the part as best we can."

Pausing, I added, "Except for Matthew. Have him keep his uniform. We'll need him later."

Hannah watched Thomas depart with concern etched in her face.

"He's not going alone, is he?"

"No, I'll go with him. However, I'd better round up some different horses. I don't imagine they will recognize Smoke and Shade, but just in case."

"Do you want to ride Smoke for me?" I asked.

"No, I think I'll not risk my life just yet. I'm very happy right where I am."

"I'll just tie him to the wagon then."

Sidestepping Smoke, I drew next to her, leaned over, and spoke into her ear.

"You know he is not a prince or magistrate or anything like that."

"Yes, I know that. But his dad was a magistrate before.... Oh, sorry, John. I didn't..."

I raised a hand to stop her.

"No offense taken."

"How did you know? Have you been reading me?" she asked accusingly.

Not answering her question, I said, "Well, I better get our horses ready."

I dismounted and proceeded to tie Smoke's reins to the back of the wagon.

"John, you haven't found a way to read me without me knowing it, have you? Who else knows?"

I just smiled. "Don't worry; I won't tell anyone. However, I might have to chaperone you two from time to time."

Glancing up, I saw her glaring at me.

My smile widened.

I turned to scout out two suitable mounts.

I had another reason for switching horses. If two animals had to be sacrificed for the sake of reaching Marysvale in time, I didn't want them to be Smoke and Shade.

Thomas returned looking smart in a soldier's uniform.

"Say hello to Private Ash," he said with a crooked grin. "He's the soldier I resemble most in the lot."

Before leaving, I took the opportunity to consult with Angus about our whereabouts and the distance left to Marysvale. His answer was not encouraging. There was a good possibility we wouldn't arrive in time. However, depending on how hard we drove the horses, there was a slight chance we could make it.

With another cup of Sarah's concoction down Thomas' throat, we set off, pushing our mounts as hard as we dared.

I wondered what they would do if we arrived late, or rather if Thomas arrived late. Would the guards accept him, or wouldn't they?

I considered his mother. If we failed, there was a good chance she'd never know what happened to her son. And the thought of breaking the tragic news to Hannah filled me with dread.

And what if Thomas does convince the guards? I wondered. *Then what?*

The problem of getting the villagers safely into Marysvale was a daunting responsibility. Even if we succeeded, there were still all the soldiers in the garrison to deal with.

I tried not to think about it further. There was nothing else we could do. Our hand was dealt, and all we had left was to play it out and see what happened.

Remembering my own advice to pray, I did just that.

Although Thomas rode stoically, I could tell he was in great pain. The few parts of his face that weren't covered in bruises were stark white. I could see that it took all his concentration and effort to simply hang on and endure the grueling ride. I wished there was something I could do for him, but there was nothing.

The miles melted away.

I had picked good horses, but they were showing strain. They dripped in sweat, and steam swirled off their bodies, but we drove them anyway.

As it stood, we wouldn't make the morning deadline, but we wouldn't miss it by much.

I hoped it was close enough.

Before long, and using my special vision, I could see figures on top of the wall.

I signaled Thomas to stop.

"Do you need a rest first?" I asked.

He took his time considering. I could tell he desperately wanted to slide off the saddle and lie down, but he finally shook his head.

"I doubt I could get back up. Plus, I don't think there's time. I just want this over with, and then I'll find a nice place to collapse."

I nodded in understanding.

We walked the horses a short distance to the edge of the woods. Concealed in the forest, I wouldn't be spotted by anyone at the gate.

"Do you remember the passphrases?" I asked.

Thomas nodded.

"What are you going to do if they question you more?"

"I don't know."

He didn't look good; even his bruises looked pale. Was it from fear? Pain? Fever? Perhaps it was all of them.

"Thomas?"

"Yes?"

"Good luck."

Without saying a word, Thomas straightened up in his saddle, trying to appear stronger than he felt, then kicked his horse into a trot.

From behind the cover of the trees, I watched him cross the open fields toward the gates of Marysvale.

On account of the approaching rider, a flurry of activity ensued on the wall. Men conferred with one another. One man disappeared for a moment and then returned, leading another.

From the way the second man carried himself, I presumed he was the officer assigned to wait for the messenger. I also assumed that he would relay the message to Lord Wright, who would either signal the Brean to attack or not.

Recalling the Brean, I took a few moments to scan the surrounding woods.

Nothing.

But that didn't mean they weren't there.

They could be hiding on the backside of Marysvale. It wouldn't take long for them to run around the town and attack. They could even split their force and come at us from both our flanks.

Briefly, I debated riding around Marysvale and checking. In the end, I decided against it.

Our horses were spent. If spotted, there would be no outrunning a Brean.

Thomas approached the gate.

The officer waited with his arms folded across his chest.

My attention was drawn to Thomas as he addressed him.

I watched intently.

Thomas' simple message was taking a long time to deliver.

This should only take a few moments. A single phrase was all that was required. The officer must detect that something is wrong.

I drew my rifle and prepared to... To do what?

One rifle against a dozen muskets—what use would that be? And I was on a tired horse to boot.

Thomas would be dead before I got halfway there.

Watching him, I felt a pang of guilt, realizing that I was powerless to help.

Could I live with myself if I don't at least try?

I hated this predicament.

I found myself detesting the soldiers, but mostly I despised Lord Wright, his followers, and Naehume. Oh yes, the Brean shared in the blame too, but they wouldn't be where they were if they didn't have help from those evil beings. I hated them all.

I had to warn the villagers.

But why? I argued with myself. *What will that change? They will still come, and they will still die. Then what would be the reason for all of this?*

Instantly, I knew the answer to my question. Lord Wright would be my reason.

If the villagers still insisted on coming to Marysvale, then I would use their sacrifice to crush him.

At that moment, I vowed vengeance in my heart. I would make Lord Wright and the lot of them suffer for all the hurt they had ever caused.

And what about Jane? queried the voice inside my head.

Should they all die at the gates for nothing? I countered. *If I can't dissuade her, there has to be purpose in her death. Wright will win without paying any consequences. He cannot get away with slaughtering an entire village. Where would it stop?*

Inside, I knew he would not stop. There is no end to a tyrant's lust for power. After conquering Marysvale and destroying Alyth, Syre would be next to fall, and then another town, and then another.

In the wandering of my mind, I had neglected Thomas.

When I looked, he was already riding back.

With arms still folded across his chest, the officer watched him depart.

And then I had a thought.

Can I read the soldier from this distance?

My powers had grown over the past few weeks. Other than becoming a little more tired, what could be the harm in trying?

I leapt across the expanse and into his soul. I was pleasantly surprised to discover that I could actually do it. The impressions weren't strong, not like they would have been if he'd been standing right in front of me, but they were there.

Searching quickly, I found that he did believe Thomas. Still, there, in the back of his mind, was misgiving. Not enough to change his report. He may not even consciously recognize the doubt. It would probably be one of those things that, once our ruse was up, he would think back and acknowledge that something had felt off about this moment.

I let the vision close.

As soon as Thomas was safely out of sight, he slumped in the saddle, nearly falling out of it.

I hurried to his side to support him.

"What passphrase did you use?" I asked.

"John is dead."

"Did it take some convincing?"

"Not particularly. The officer seemed pretty confident in their plan."

"Then what took you so long?"

"He wanted to know how you died and what happened to my face. They were one in the same story. Apparently, you beat me and a few others before you were subdued. It's why I was chosen to be the bearer of the good news, despite my injuries."

"And how did I die?"

"Shot into submission and then hung. You put up quite a heroic effort," he said with a weary grin.

But his smile didn't reach his eyes. They were filled with pain and exhaustion.

"Come, just a little longer, and then you'll rest. When we're safely away, we'll wait for the others to catch up to us."

After a mile, we stopped.

When I went to help Thomas out of his saddle, he fell into my arms. Carrying him to a soft bed of leaves, I laid him down gently.

"I'm cold," he said weakly.

Despite the frigid air, I removed my coat and wrapped it around him.

He looked up, his eyes dull.

"I'm sorry I ever doubted you, John."

"Don't be," I replied. "I always knew you would stand with me when the time came."

"If I don't make it, you will let my mother know, won't you? She'll worry."

"You will see her again. Sarah will be here soon. We'll put you in a wagon, with lots of blankets and some of her tea inside of you."

He smiled weakly. "That drink will wake the dead."

"And by nightfall, you'll be in a warm bed," I added.

But he wasn't listening anymore.

His eyes had closed, and he was gone.

Chapter Twenty-One: Marysvale

Hannah leaped off the wagon and ran to us.

Falling to her knees by Thomas' still body, she cried, "Oh, no! Not you!"

Her eyes welled with tears as she stroked his hair.

Watching her, I said, "He's not dead, you know."

Confused, she looked up at me and blinked.

"He isn't dead," I repeated.

Hannah made a fist and slugged me in the arm.

"Ouch, what's that for?" I said, rubbing it.

"Why didn't you say that sooner?"

"I did say it sooner. I said it as soon as I could."

"Besides," I added, "you could've asked instead of assuming the worst."

"But he looks so pale."

Jane, Sarah, and James were hurrying over.

Standing up, I said to Sarah, "He could use some of your tea to warm him."

She nodded.

"James..."

Sarah was about to ask him to light a fire, but he was already collecting sticks.

"And how about you?" she asked.

I made a face. "No, thank you. I don't need any tea."

"Make him drink it anyway," said Hannah, glaring at me.

"I wasn't inquiring if you would like tea; I wanted to know how you are feeling. Although I suppose you could use a warm drink after a hard ride."

"Oh, I'm fine," I assured her.

Sarah surveyed me, doubtful if she should believe me.

"No, really; I'm quite fine. I feel better than I have in days. And I'm not cold at all; so, I won't need any tea, thank you."

Sarah's eyes narrowed as she reached up and placed the back of her hand against my cheek and forehead.

"You feel warm."

"Well, I feel fine."

"Aches? Pains?"

"No. Like I already said, I feel good. It's Thomas you should be worried about."

She gave me one more look of concern and then turned her attention to Thomas.

Gingerly, Sarah inspected him. As she worked, Thomas' eyes fluttered open.

"How do you feel?" she asked while inspecting the bruises on his chest.

"Awful, but I think I will be fine. I'm a little cold."

Sarah nodded. "James is heating water. I'll brew something to warm you and help with the pain."

Thomas made a face and groaned.

"Honestly," exclaimed Sarah. "It is not that bitter, and any relief has to be better than no relief."

"I suppose that's true," conceded Thomas.

James returned and, in no time, had a small fire blazing right next to Thomas. Sarah crushed herbs into a small kettle of water that sat warming over the flames.

While the villagers rested, I grew restless.

Using my vision, I peered through the trees and studied the guards standing at their posts. Not much had changed. No stream of soldiers poured down through the streets. There was nothing remarkable or different.

Or was there?

I studied the town.

Marysvale looked utterly ordinary, at least from what I could see.

Then, with a sudden shock of awareness, I realized that the difference was in *me*.

My gifts had grown in strength.

While we weren't terribly far away, it was farther than I could normally see with my sight. And it was easier to keep open. I even sensed Sarah's gift gently reaching out, connecting her energy with everything around us.

For a moment, I marveled at my increased power and Sarah's gift before refocusing my concentration on the trouble looming before us.

Until now, the dilemma of Marysvale was something to worry about in the future, but the future had now arrived.

In my bones, I knew what would happen at her gates. I'd seen it.

Just as surely as winter would suck the warmth from the world around us, the path ahead was filled with the cold sting of death. Thomas had, perhaps, been delivered a reprieve, but it wouldn't change his fate in the end.

Even if our plan went well, the facts of our situation remained. We'd be stuck between two walls and trapped between two armies. They had the food stores and the weapons. They could fight and crush us, or they could hold out and starve us. Either way, their victory would be sure. Unless…

I reflected upon my nightmares. They had not only shown me the fate of my friends, but they had also shown me my own future. I was powerful—a force to be reckoned with. Maybe there was more I could do; something left untapped. Was that wrong? It didn't feel wrong.

Sarah had told me that my coming here was no accident. She believed I would somehow overthrow Lord Wright. According to my dream, I would do just that.

But at what cost? Was this my destiny all along? Capable of defeating my enemies but powerless to protect the ones I loved?

I felt a surge of anger.

It seemed such a cruel joke to come so close to happiness, only to have it ripped away from my grasp.

Clenching my fists, I shook with hatred.

What could I do? Nothing that I wasn't already doing. The die was already cast. The pieces were coming together, and there was nothing I could do that would change their shape.

So be it, I thought bitterly. *Lord Wright will indeed suffer for this!*

Sensing the change that had come over me, Sarah stopped her work and looked at me.

Seeing her concern, I concentrated on stifling my rage. It ebbed but didn't dissipate completely.

Sarah handed a mug of tea to Thomas and then stood up.

"Come and walk with me, John."

"We should be moving on," I said.

"I thought you didn't want to go to Marysvale."

I shrugged. "It is inevitable now."

Sarah started walking.

I stood there stubbornly for a moment and then reluctantly fell in by her side.

"John," she began carefully.

I cut her off. "I know what you are going to say. So, you can save your breath."

"And what was I going to say?" she replied patiently.

"That I shouldn't give in to anger or fear. But I'm not afraid."

It wasn't entirely true. I was terrified of what was about to happen to the women I loved.

"I can't change our fate," I conceded. "I see that now. And I see the part I am to play. I will make sure Lord Wright is stopped and that he will pay dearly for all the suffering he has caused."

"Ah," she said and fell silent.

We took a few more steps.

"And what is *ah* supposed to mean?" I asked irritably.

"It means that you are treading a dangerous path, John. Anger changes people. I can feel it working in you."

"I'm only doing what you all expect," I shot back. "I'm going to Marysvale. I'm going to stop Lord Wright, just like you want."

"No, not like I want. I don't wish to make Merrick Wright suffer."

"You don't?" I asked incredulously.

"No. Merrick, or even Naehume, is not my goal."

I started to protest, and Sarah raised a hand for me to be quiet.

"They may be part of that goal, but they are not the focus. What I want, what Jane wants, goes far beyond two individuals. We want peace…"

This time I cut her short.

"Getting slaughtered, or doing nothing, does not equal peace," I snapped.

Sarah sighed. "Already, your anger blinds you, John. That is not what I was saying. I know lack of war does not necessarily equal peace. I can see that the people in Marysvale do not live in peace, despite not being in a state of war. And I know that dealing with Merrick is a large part of what we need to accomplish. What I'm saying is, don't be so bound by rage and revenge that you lose sight of what we are really striving for. You focus on the individual brushstrokes instead of the painting. Stopping Merrick and Naehume are merely brushstrokes. The painting we are creating is much larger than that.

"We desire freedom. We want to live our lives free from tyranny, from *all* those who seek to enforce their will upon us. We want to go home and live free from fear. We want to do what we choose to do without having to beg or bribe a minister, lord, or magistrate. However, real freedom, freedom for our soul, is as much a product of our choices as it is our circumstances—perhaps even more so. I hope you can see the picture I am trying to paint for you."

"I do," I said hesitantly.

Sarah stopped and faced me.

"Do you?"

"Yes," I replied.

"I don't think you do. I still sense hatred and fear inside of you."

"I am not afraid," I said defensively. "I have come to terms with what will happen."

"Accepting your fear and not being afraid are two different things. You are not at peace with yourself, John; you have simply embraced the turmoil. The same goes for your anger. You are embracing it."

"And I don't see how you *can't* be angry. I know you say love is more powerful, but I don't see how."

"You haven't tried it," she replied.

"I do love. I love Jane."

"But do you love Merrick? Or Naehume?"

I was shocked. "How could you love them? They need to be crushed, not hugged!"

"And therein lies the problem with you, John, and the problem with hatred. Compassion doesn't mean you have to condone. I feel sorrow over Merrick. Sorrow for the misery he has sown, both for his victims and himself. I am passionate about helping free those whom he has oppressed. You, John,

314

can be part of the healing. But when you focus on revenge, you not only lose sight of the goal, you become bound to the great enemy of *all* our souls. Our enemy and their enemy is one and the same. Hate is our common foe."

I looked down, unable to meet her gaze.

I didn't necessarily disagree with her, but I deemed her argument to be a distinction without a difference. Defeating Lord Wright and Naehume was necessary to achieve what she described. Once they fell, the rest of what Sarah wanted would surely come to pass.

If I had more time, I could experiment with love, but now it was too late. We were already at the gates of Marysvale. Like it or not, my power grew with rage, and right now, we needed all the strength that we could get.

Sarah sighed and took a step forward. She stood on her toes and kissed me on the cheek.

"I love you, John, but you must decide for yourself. I cannot force you, nor would I. Realize you do have a choice. Please don't fall captive to the enemy of your soul."

She walked away.

I stood there for a long moment in silence and contemplated what she said.

A hand touched my arm.

Looking down, I met those large, beautiful green eyes that I loved so much.

"Have you come to lecture me too?" I asked.

Jane raised an eyebrow. "Do I need to?"

"No."

She smiled. "Then, no. I came to inform you that we are nearly ready to make the final push to Marysvale."

I nodded.

Jane slipped her hand into mine and began walking further away from the company.

"Where are we going?"

"Do be quiet, Mr. Stone," she said with a smile.

Jane led me off into the forest and behind the trunk of a large tree where we couldn't be seen.

Facing me, she threw her arms around my neck and drew us together.

Touching her cool lips to my burning ones, we kissed.

The kiss was short but passionate. It was wonderful and exhilarating.

I pulled her in close to me, feeling her warmth.

My heart ached terribly.

As she looked up at me, her smile dimmed just a bit.

"In case we don't...I mean...It may be some time before we get the opportunity again."

"You believe my dream then?"

"Of course not! Your dreams may be important, but I don't believe they are absolute. We still have a choice in our fate."

"I hope so," I replied, but there was no conviction in my voice.

***

The column of villagers trudged onward.

Soon, Marysvale lay clearly in sight for all to see.

My heart beat rapidly as the first Brean showed up. Then others arrived, and still more.

No one else would be able to detect them at this point, except perhaps Sarah.

The monsters were not sufficient in number to warrant a dire threat. They unnerved me, but they let us be.

I guess it makes sense. Why attack us if Wright's plan is working?

The soldiers were in the rear, dressed as villagers. The riders still surrounded them, fanned out in the formation I had seen the soldiers use. The problem was, not one of them resembled a soldier. Their grooming, or lack of it, was sorely evident.

If the officers looked too closely, our game would be over.

There was one soldier, however, who did belong. Matthew rode in the lead, his wrists securely bound in front of him and fastened to the saddle.

I rode by his side, ready to stop any treachery he might try.

Taking the opportunity of our last few moments before reaching the gate, I reminded him of my previous threat.

"I know you want to warn them. I can see it in you."

He glared at me.

"Get those ideas out of your head, or I will rip them out of there myself."

Fear flashed in his eyes, and he complied.

"It will not work," said Matthew. "Even if I do my best to help you, and you do fool the town guard, you will not fool the officers who have been placed there. It is not too late to free me and save the villagers."

I scoffed, "You and I both know your promises are worthless."

"For you, that is true, but not for them. They can have a life."

"Your definition of *life* and how we define it is vastly different."

"At least they will be alive. And it will not always be like this; it will not always be necessary to live behind walls."

"Yes," I said. "Naehume showed me. Take territory after territory until all are under your control. And how many will die in the process?"

"People die every day. They have to be led by someone; you can't trust them to themselves. They are stupid, uneducated..."

"Enough!" I snapped. "The only thing I want to hear out of your mouth is an order to open the gates."

Matthew shrugged and fell silent.

We crossed the field.

The walls of Marysvale seemed even more formidable than before. On top stood about twenty of the town guard. I saw no foot soldiers, which was a good sign, but there were a half dozen officers spread throughout the guards. I didn't like seeing them there, but they were expected.

One officer stood at the gate, accompanied by Captain Smith, the commander of the North Wall Regiment. I was heartened to see Captain Smith, for I knew him to be a good and fair man.

They waited for us as we drew up to the gates.

The officer standing with the captain hailed us.

Matthew turned to me and said, in both a sneer and a wicked grin, "Either way, I'm dead. And so are you."

His head snapped around to the officer on the wall, and he yelled, "It's a…"

I slammed the butt of my pistol savagely into the side of his head, cutting off the warning cry. He toppled off his horse, but as his hands were still tied to the saddle, his body flopped awkwardly down. Limp arms stretched above his unconscious body.

Captain Smith looked confused.

The officer did not.

His hand snatched for a metal horn slung over his neck while my hand seized the crossbow.

The sound of the horn pierced the air, a clarion call for whoever was listening.

I loosened a bolt.

It struck the horn, ripping it from the officer's lips and cutting short his call.

"Open the gate!" I ordered while looking directly at Captain Smith.

The officer turned and shouted right into the captain's ear. "You'll do no such thing!"

A similar horn responded from the garrison.

And then came the sound that I dreaded.

The high staccato-like cry of a monster rolled across the fields and echoed off the hills. It was followed by another similar cry and then another. They rang out until the whole forest seemed to be filled with the battle cries of the Brean.

"You hear that, Captain Smith?" I shouted. "Your master there not only called the soldiers; he also called the Brean."

"That's a lie!" shouted the officer.

"Then open the gates!" I bellowed.

Captain Smith looked at the officer expectantly. I could see that I had made an important point.

"You will not make a move unless I say so," ordered the officer.

Hurriedly, I scanned the forest.

Already I could see the dark vortexes of the Brean sprinting through the trees. A constant stream of them flowed into my sight.

The villagers didn't need special sight. They could hear the cries, barks, and roars that rumbled through the trees.

We were running out of time.

Frightened villagers spun about, trying to determine where the first monsters would appear.

I could see they would come at us from all sides.

Another officer walked down the wall and joined the first to add his support.

I gave the signal for the shooting groups to fan out and protect the villagers.

Panic began to set in. Children cried; women embraced and tried to comfort them. The men without rifles took their crudely carved spears and knives and put themselves behind the shooters.

"You see?" I called up to Captain Smith. "Your masters will not tolerate armed villagers in the town. They would rather kill the innocent to protect their power."

"It is a lie," cried the other officer. "A lie from a devil."

Instantly, anger flared inside me. I could feel a surge of power rush through my being.

I welcomed it.

"If you execute the witch," bargained the first officer while pointing at me, "then we shall let you in. Only then may we be sure that the spells he has cast will be broken."

He lied.

He had no intention of letting us in, even if they did kill me. He was merely stalling for time. The Brean would be upon us soon, and then he'd claim it was too late to safely open the gates.

No, they would never open the gates, even if it meant shooting Captain Smith and any others who tried. Soon, soldiers would be on their way down to reinforce that decision.

He was the foulest of humanity.

And my hatred of him spiked like the growing fever within me.

Chapter Twenty-Two: The Battle at the Gate

The officer leveled his musket.

"What do you say?" he said with a smug grin. "Sacrifice yourself to save the rest?"

Sensing he would shoot without waiting for an answer, I snapped my bow up and...

A rifle boomed to life.

The shot hit the officer with such force that it picked him up and hurled him off the wall.

"Enough talk," said Hannah, as gunsmoke trailed out the end of her rifle.

At least, I think that's what she said. I couldn't be sure through the ringing in my ears.

"Hannah!" snapped Sarah. "Stop overloading your rifle. One of these days, you'll blow yourself up."

The second officer was furious. It was just the excuse he needed.

"Shoot them!" he screamed, or that's what he would have screamed if he could have remembered what it was he meant to say.

I crashed into his soul.

Rushing in, I found the thought and tore it from his memory.

A tremor of pain wracked his whole being. I felt the revolt, the violation, and the violence that I had committed against him.

And I was horrified by it.

But there was something else.

It was also thrilling.

The electrifying power the act generated flowed through me and made me feel invincible.

I didn't stop there.

I ripped the memory of why he was even there and who we were straight out of his mind.

He looked at me with fear and horror.

He knew what I was doing.

I tore that from him as well.

The officer may have forgotten what I was doing to him, but there was no taking the defilement and the pain away.

Stumbling back and shrieking, he ran down the stairs and disappeared from my sight.

Captain Smith looked dumbfounded at the man. He simply believed the officer a coward.

The few remaining officers left their posts, running to see what had happened.

I called to the captain, "We are out of time! Let us in, or we will die! You know some of these villagers; they were your friends and neighbors once. They can be again. You have no love for what has happened to your town. Now is your chance to change that. That call was just as much for the Brean as it was for soldiers. They are in league with each other. But you know that already, don't you?"

Perhaps he hadn't recognized that he knew it or even consciously considered it. Still, deep down inside him, Captain Smith knew something was wrong about the relationship between the Brean and the garrison.

"You know that wall up there isn't to protect them from the Brean; it's to protect them from you! That is why they don't allow the people to arm themselves. It's not to protect you from that foolish curse that comes from killing monsters; it's to keep you all from rising up against them. You outnumber them."

I felt him waver.

"You won't get another chance in your lifetime to change your lot. Your children may not get a chance either. Do you really want them to continue living like this?"

With that consideration, Captain Smith made a decision.

"Open the gates," he ordered.

The officers returned, screaming, shouting, and yelling for them to stand fast. Pulling their pistols and muskets, they threatened death to any who disobeyed. They also threatened their families.

And then, they all fell silent.

One fell, struck by a bolt from my crossbow, and the rest by the shooters.

"Open them," I said forcefully to Captain Smith.

He nodded to his men.

In a flurry of activity and a moaning protest from the iron hinges, the gates swung stubbornly open.

More rifles barked to life.

I spun Smoke around and saw the first of the monsters stream out of the trees.

"Hold them off while the others get in," I shouted to the captains of the shooting teams.

Sliding off Smoke, I snatched my rifle, aimed, and fired at one of the brutes.

It yelped in pain as a chunk of its arm blew off. Then it changed to an angry roar.

In an instant, Jane, Hannah, and Sarah were at my side.

Jane finished the beast in one fantastic shot.

Through the forest, I could see many more on their way.

The most swift were snarling and sprinting towards us.

Jane and I both loaded our guns while Sarah and Hannah took their shots.

All around us, shooters were firing their weapons while villagers scrambled through the gates.

Jane fired again and hit a monster. It didn't kill it, but it did stop it. Falling to the ground, it writhed in agony.

I thrust my rifle into her hands; she put it to use while I loaded hers.

Hannah fired and hit one from a great distance. She, too, was about to load her gun when a hand reached out and grasped it.

She looked up and into the eyes of Thomas.

He looked pale and sick, but he stood there resolutely.

Hannah flashed a beautiful smile at him, not unlike Jane's, and released her gun.

Thomas handed her his musket and began loading the rifle.

Nearly all of the villagers had made it inside.

But time was up for the shooters.

The main bulk of the Brean now broke into the clearing. Like a mighty wave, they would soon crash into us and sweep us away.

"Run!" I shouted, mounting Smoke.

The monsters' roars and barks sounded all around us.

Looking up, I was thunderstruck.

Not one of the town guards had fired a single shot. They looked nervous and uneasy.

"What are you waiting for?" I screamed. "The only curse that will fall upon you is that of our ghosts, as we will surely haunt you if you stand by and do nothing!"

Captain Smith hesitated, but only for a moment.

His musket came up, and he fired.

It was the permission the others were waiting for.

A salvo of musket fire erupted from the town guard.

Balls whizzed by overhead, striking the oncoming Brean.

"Through the gate!" I ordered.

Shooters scrambled and sprinted for the now-closing gate.

Sarah, Jane, Hannah, and Thomas made it safely through.

Behind me, I heard a terrible scream.

Spinning Smoke, I saw a monster snatching at a young woman.

I recognized Hannah's friend, Skye, from the All Hallows Eve festival.

She scrambled about, trying to dodge the beast.

It caught her by the hair and dragged her back.

Skye cried out in agonizing fear.

There wasn't time to reload the rifle or the crossbow. And I'd probably hit her instead of the Brean with the pistol.

The last of the shooters had made it safely inside, all except for the poor young woman and myself.

I looked imploringly at Captain Smith.

He nodded and raised his musket.

Other monsters closed in fast.

Kicking Smoke, we galloped straight at the oncoming tide.

I heard the crack of the captain's musket.

The ball whizzed by my ear.

Blood erupted from the Brean's head from the impact.

The monster reeled and then fell forward.

Skye tried scurrying away, but the lifeless beast collapsed on top of her.

She cried out as its weight crushed her to the ground. Her torso, head, and arms stuck out beneath the massive carcass.

Desperately, she pawed at the ground, trying to extricate herself.

A volley of balls shot past me.

Another monster crashed into the ground nearby, plowing up a pile of dirt before it finally slid to a stop.

In a moment, nothing would be able to keep the oncoming wall of fangs and claws from us.

Leaping off Smoke, before he even stopped, I grabbed Skye's hands and pulled.

She barely budged.

With more time, perhaps, I could've freed her by myself. But there was no time.

Letting go of her, I ran for Smoke and grabbed his reins.

"Don't leave me!" she wailed fearfully, tears spilling out of her eyes.

Another barrage erupted from the town. Balls whizzed over my head.

I didn't have time to look at their intended targets, but I could hear the cries, yelps, and snarls from the beasts.

Frantically leading Smoke, who was clearly frightened but hadn't yet bolted, I reached down and snatched her by the wrist.

"Hold fast," I instructed.

Skye grabbed my wrist with her other hand.

I gave Smoke the order to back up.

He obeyed.

With his strength added to mine, we pulled.

Skye cried out in pain as she slid from under the beast.

She came free.

"It's my leg," she said through gritted teeth. "I think it broke in the fall."

Without a word, I grabbed her and tossed her into the saddle.

In my panic, I nearly threw her over Smoke. But she caught hold and managed to hang on.

I leaped up behind her.

Without further prompting, Smoke spun around and launched forward, taking off like a startled deer.

The force of his speed toppled both of us backward, and we nearly fell off.

I clung precariously to Skye while she gripped Smoke's mane. Neither of us held the reins, but it didn't matter. Smoke knew where to run.

We sailed through the opening. Villagers parted as we galloped by.

Men swarmed behind us and shoved against the gate.

The rusty iron hinges groaned as the heavy wooden doors swung slowly together and closed.

But they didn't bar it fast enough.

Suddenly, Brean crashed into the doors.

The impact sent men stumbling back.

More men flocked and clambered to add their strength.

But the Brean were stronger.

The gate began to slowly open back up.

However, it wasn't enough for any of the brutes to get through. They snarled and snapped their teeth through the opening.

More men flooded to the gate, and a war of strength ensued.

The only thing keeping the gate from opening all the way was that we had more men against the doors than Brean. That would change very soon.

A hairy hand shot through the opening and snatched angrily at anyone it could grab.

Men ducked and scrambled to avoid the vicious claws.

After a few futile attempts, the monster succeeded in grasping the arm of an unlucky fellow.

He cried for help and fought frantically as the beast started pulling him through the open slot.

Another man grabbed hold of the victim and fought to keep him on our side.

Several women surrounded Skye.

I leaped off Smoke, dashed over, and put my strength to the tug of war.

As the monster twisted and pulled angrily at the man, the bones in his arm snapped, and the man screamed in agony. Despite it, he still braced a foot against the door. Whatever damage was done to his appendage would be small compared to what would happen if he slipped through the opening.

Shots from the wall rained down upon the Brean.

More angry snarls and howls of rage and pain erupted from the beasts.

Suddenly, the hairy arm that had hold of the man fell limp to the ground.

Unfortunately, it still protruded through the open slot of the gate.

More shots and more howls filled the air.

Two men grabbed the monster's massive arm and heaved it awkwardly up and back through the opening.

Under fire, the Brean weren't able to put enough strength into the battle; and the doors finally slammed shut.

Heavy timbers quickly dropped into place.

The Brean pounded furiously, and the gate trembled under their assault.

But it was short-lived.

The constant barrage grew unbearable, and the Brean quickly fell back out of range.

The men pushing on the door relaxed in a collective sigh of relief, and shooters victoriously informed us of the monsters' retreat into the forest.

I searched for the women and found them running down the stairs from the top of the wall, carrying their rifles.

They ran over to me.

"Well, that was close," I said with a triumphant smile.

Sarah, looking grim, said, "It's not over yet."

"What do you mean?"

She pointed toward the garrison.

Turning, I observed a stream of armed soldiers marching through its open, polished gate. They snaked down the cobblestone street, led by sword-wielding officers mounted on horseback.

Chapter Twenty-Three: The Dark Ones

My heart fell.

We were hopelessly outnumbered.

I looked at Hannah inquiringly.

She straightened up and said firmly, "We can do this. They will line up like traditional forces. We can shoot at them from behind buildings and other objects of safety."

The rest of the shooters gathered around us, along with Captain Smith and many of his men.

They all looked at me for direction.

She was right. We had no other choice.

"As Hannah said, we'll fight all right, but not in the open. Stay behind the houses and any other cover you can find."

I felt a sense of disgust pass through many of the men. Like me, they deemed it cowardly to hide from what they considered a fair fight.

On the other hand, I was beginning to see things differently. Nothing up to this point had been fair. Lord Wright hadn't been fair in deceiving the people. He hadn't been fair in governing his people. And he certainly wasn't playing fair now.

I felt irritated with the men surrounding me but downright furious with the soldiers. I allowed these emotions to flow through me, feeding my fever.

"Do they treat the people of Marysvale fairly?" I snapped. "Is it fair what they did to Alyth? Do you deem it fair what they are about to do to us? If so, then, by all means, feel free to step out into the open and die fair and square by their hands. I am not the one marching trained soldiers against farmers, innocent women, and children. As for me, I'm going to do whatever it takes to stop them."

I pointed to the oncoming soldiers.

"Do you think for one moment that they will forgive you for what has happened today?"

They shifted from one foot to another. My question unnerved them, just like I knew it would.

"Whether you like it or not, you *and your families* are now involved."

I studied the men.

"You know in your hearts that Lord Wright will not stop at these walls. There aren't enough of you to support how large and numerous they are growing. You yourselves have wondered why he needs so many soldiers—many of whom you don't even recognize."

I recalled the men that Naehume had shown me in my dream—greedy men whose lust for power drove them for riches and glory at any cost.

"They hope that by helping Lord Wright obtain what he wants, they will get what *they* want—untold wealth and power to lord over all of you."

My words struck a chord with the men. They may not believe all I had said, but they believed enough.

"We have only two options: fight tooth and nail for the freedom of our loved ones, or die stupidly for their slavery. Which do you choose?"

Hesitating a moment, I let my words sink in.

I didn't have to wait long.

Captain Smith looked at his men, and, seemingly to read their thoughts, he stepped forward.

"You are right. We are with you. Where do you want us?"

Scanning the hill, I watched the progress of the soldiers as they steadily marched through the open space between the garrison and the homes of the wealthy high on the hill. I took in their auras and the light that attaches itself to each one. In particular, I was drawn to the dark ones. Their cold souls lacked natural affection and love. They regarded other humans—not as people with feelings, hopes, and dreams—but as objects, property to be sold or discarded as they saw fit, according to how useful we were to them.

A plan began to form in my mind. Admittedly, it wasn't much of one, but it was all I could come up with. I needed to get closer, where it would be easier to probe the soldiers more thoroughly.

They were now passing the larger homes and were nearly to the densely populated town and narrow winding streets.

"The way I figure it," I said. "They need a space where they can establish an area of operations. My guess is that they'll drive as far as they can toward us, but at the very least, they will hold the town square. From there, they can stage and organize their troops."

"If they even believe it will come to that," said Sabin.

334

"True," I agreed. "I doubt they think we'll put up much of a fight, but they will still take the square. They have to have soldiers *in* the town, and the square is the only open space. When they take it, they will also cut off half the town from us and remove any support we might get. We need to get there first."

"That's going to be a tall order," exclaimed Smith. "Even if we leave this moment, we still won't get there in time."

"I can slow them down," I said.

"We can't possibly hope to hold the square," exclaimed one of the town's guards.

"We aren't going to, and there isn't time to fully explain what I intend to do. You will need to trust me."

Turning to Jane, I asked, "Will you assemble all the shooters who are on horses that you can muster? We need them now; if they aren't ready, we can't wait for them."

She nodded and hurried away.

"Captain Smith?"

He looked at me expectantly.

"Gather as many men as you can, but make haste. Go to the square, but do not enter. You won't win if you're in the open. Fire at the soldiers from behind anything that will protect you from their muskets."

He nodded in understanding.

"Shoot any soldiers that come in. Hold your position for as long as you reasonably can. If you're overwhelmed and must fall back, then do so in stages. Put up as much of a fight in your retreat as you possibly can."

"And after that? If they keep coming, what then?" he asked.

"Keep falling back until you reach this spot, and make your stand here how best you see fit."

I didn't feel it necessary to explain that my plan would have failed if it got to that point, and we'd most likely all be dead.

"What about me?" asked Thomas.

"Stay here. Rest if possible. And if it comes to it, do what you can to protect the women and children."

He was in no shape to run around the streets of Marysvale, and he knew it.

This time, he was the one to wish me luck.

I flashed him a brief smile that was meant to comfort him, but it came out a little sadder than intended.

"Someday soon, this will all be over. You will be healed, and then we'll take a nice long ride together. Who knows, I may even let you ride Smoke."

At least, that's what I wanted to say, but the words were never verbalized.

Instead, I turned and dashed over to Smoke as Captain Smith barked orders to the guards.

"Don't be foolish," yelled a voice to my right.

Noticing the band of prisoner soldiers, I spied Matthew's arrogant crony, Roger Sawyer.

"You won't succeed," he continued. "But if you release us, we will plead your case."

I glanced into his cold soul. He had no intention of helping us in the slightest. His comment was designed to demoralize and emphasize our inferior force. He believed that he would be liberated shortly, and then he would make us, our women, and our children pay for our defiance.

Fueled, as if driven by a hot wind, the hatred burning inside me sprang into a raging inferno.

I relished the surge of power flowing through my veins.

Snatching my rifle from Smoke, I quickly strode over to him.

Roger glared at me defiantly.

But not for long.

The butt of my rifle smashed into his head. My actions were so swift that he barely had time to register surprise, let alone defend himself against the savage attack. The blow crushed the bones in his face and sent him flying onto his back.

He came to a rest in a crumpled heap.

His soul flickered, threatening to extinguish.

I didn't care. I knew what he was capable of and what he would do to us if he could.

His side started this fight, and he got what he deserved.

I felt a shadow cross over my countenance.

Scowling at the other soldiers threateningly, even eagerly, I growled, "Anyone else?"

Power coursed through me in a throbbing fever, and I hungered for more.

That sat in silence, cowering at my feet.

"Very well," I hissed. "Perhaps another time."

And without wasting another precious moment, I sprinted to Smoke and jumped upon his back.

Jane returned with the men from Syre and as many shooters as could find horses. The three women wordlessly took their places with James and myself at the front.

"Lead the way," I said to Jane.

She kicked Ember to a gallop. The rest of us followed.

The horses' hooves clattered upon the cobblestone street, reverberating between the houses.

Townspeople scurried out of our way, ducking into the buildings nearest to them. Anxious faces peered out through windows as we charged on.

Jane led us through the twisting streets that made up the labyrinth of Marysvale.

Before long, we reached the square.

As we entered, I could picture the slave market in my mind. It sickened and incensed me, but I had no time to dwell upon it.

Jane halted.

"Now, what do we do?" she asked.

Rapidly, I divided the riders into three groups and selected a captain over each.

"Your job is to slow them down. Keep them from getting here before our men do."

I quickly explained this part of my idea, which in its basic form was similar to what our main force would do. I positioned the groups strategically throughout the route the soldiers would take. The first group would blast at them as long as they could, without risking serious casualties, and then fall back to the cover of the next group. The overall hope was to kill as many of them as we could before being forced to make a final stand.

If we could do that, we'd be on more equal footing for whatever happened next.

At least that was my hope.

As for me, I had another card to play.

When the last group was in position, I turned to James.

"Are you an expert with that?" I asked, pointing to his musket.

He nodded.

"Good. I wager you won't be leaving Sarah's side."

He shook his head. "Nae, where she goes, I go."

"Very well. The two of you, along with Jane and Hannah, will come with me. I need your marksmanship."

The rhythmic sound of marching boots on the cobblestones was growing louder and louder.

"What are we going to do?" asked Hannah.

"You'll see soon enough. We need a house or a rooftop where we can get a good line on the soldiers."

"I know just the place," Hannah said excitedly.

"Lead on," I instructed.

Hannah guided us over one street and then turned up the hill. After a short distance, she came to a stop.

We hopped down from the horses and secured them in an alley close by so we could make a quick exit when the time came.

Hannah then led us a short distance to a corner house.

"From the top floor, we can get a clear view," she said.

I tried the door.

"Locked," I said.

James stepped forward and, with a mighty kick, splintered the door from its lock and sent it crashing open.

Inside the cramped two-story house stood a young man about my age, brandishing a large stick like a club. Behind him, a woman holding a small child stood trembling.

Sarah stepped forward and said, with compassion but urgency, "I am sorry. We will be using your house. Take your family and flee toward the gate. Find another place to hide."

"I'm not leaving my own home. I know you're not soldiers," the man said stubbornly.

"Don't be a fool, man," I growled. "We are using your house regardless if you like it or not. And when we're done here, soldiers will come. I suggest you consider your beautiful wife and child. The soldiers sure will."

Without any more deliberation, I pushed by him and raced up the narrow stairs. In the small room above, I shoved a makeshift bed away from the two windows. Only one window had glass; the other was boarded up.

I knocked both out without issue and gazed upon at least two hundred soldiers snaking their way through the narrow street. They marched four abreast, as their heads bobbed up and down in unison, to the cadence of the march.

The spot was perfect for my intention. It had a clear view of the street and beyond the first few rows of soldiers.

The others entered the room.

"They left," informed Sarah.

I shrugged.

"We'll need other places just like this," I said. "Be thinking about where to go next."

The soldiers continued their steady march, drawing ever closer.

Scanning the column of men, I selected five of the darkest souls. They were all officers. Two were on horseback, leading the procession. The other three were interspersed amongst the regular soldiers but wore different hats, which made them stand out.

I pointed them out to the others.

"I'll take the officer on horseback on the right side."

He was the easiest to hit, and I figured I'd let the better marksmen try for the more difficult ones bobbing about in the sea of soldiers.

The others called out their targets.

"Are you ready?" I asked.

"Ready," replied Hannah.

The others nodded.

"On the count of three," I said. "Three, two, one."

Our guns roared to life.

Acrid smoke and jets of flame exploded their lethal projectiles into the selected men.

We all hit our target.

"Load!" I ordered unnecessarily.

Confusion struck the soldiers. Men threw themselves to the aid of their collapsed leaders. The column ground to a halt as soldiers tried to avoid stepping on the fallen and those giving aid.

Seeing the mess of men, I realized that I could've delivered a far more devastating attack had I kept my riders together. Between the two-story houses, the soldiers were like fish trapped in a barrel. From the rooftops, we could've decimated their first lines in no time.

Unfortunately, I hadn't thought of it.

Other officers noticed their predicament as well and were beginning to shove their way forward, barking orders.

There wasn't time to point out the darkest souls, so I ordered the others to shoot any of the officers.

"Ready," I called.

We sighted our weapons the best we could through the cloud of smoke that now hung in the air.

"Fire," I shouted.

Four men fell. One officer fell by two balls as I saw his body jerk twice—one ball from my rifle and another from someone else's.

Acrid smoke now completely obscured our field of view, except for myself.

With my vision, I noticed that the soldiers could see the smoke from our position.

They took aim.

"Get back!" I cried.

Grabbing Jane and Hannah, I flung them to the floor. James did likewise, throwing his body over Sarah's.

The soldiers fired.

Balls struck everywhere, tearing through the flimsy walls and window frames.

The room exploded with wood splinters. Dust and debris rained down on us.

"To the horses!" I shouted and pushed the girls forward.

They crawled over to the stairs and then sped down. Sarah, James, and I followed right after them.

We sprinted through the house, out the door, and around the corner to our horses.

Leaping on, we galloped away, with Hannah once again taking the lead.

We rode only a short distance to the next location.

Storming the second house, we gave the occupants a brief warning as we raced up the stairs.

Again, I knocked out the windows and selected another five dark souls.

However, this time, we were farther away, and our shots would be more difficult.

I had confidence in the others but not in myself.

It couldn't be helped.

"Ready?" I asked after we had each selected our man.

They indicated they were.

"Three, two, one…"

Again, we dispatched five of the darkest souls to the afterlife.

Unlike the first time, the soldiers were ready to retaliate.

They wasted no time in locating us.

Through the gunsmoke, I saw the enemy raise their muskets.

Another squad of soldiers broke off and sprinted to our location.

"Out!" I shouted.

The others instantly bolted for the stairs.

Behind us, the room was shredded by musket fire.

We flew out the door and to our steeds.

Not far away, the sound of more gunfire erupted. It was answered with a withering response.

The sound echoed and rolled down the empty streets, filling the air with a sense of dread. Although they weren't the first shots fired in this war, they hung ominously, signaling something momentous.

They signaled death.

They signaled the end.

I knew that the blood of our people, no matter how careful they were, was now flowing.

Men, and even women, were being violently taken from their loved ones and hurled into the afterlife. They would not be alone there, but their families here would be without them.

Just assuredly as their blood seeped into the ground, bitterness and anger seeped into my soul.

I hated the soldiers with a vengeance. I hated Lord Wright. And I hated Naehume.

It cankered my heart, but I didn't care.

What mattered most was stopping all of those monsters before they could spread their misery over all the land.

The sound of the fight lasted for only a moment before dying off.

"They've reached the first of the groups," Sarah declared grimly.

We hesitated, noting the significance. But we didn't have time to dwell on it.

"The big place by Patience Miller?" suggested Jane.

Hannah nodded in agreement.

We wheeled our horses and galloped through the empty streets.

Turning a corner, we ran into a squadron of soldiers, just as they were marching two by two around the corner at the other end. At first, there were only two, then four, but more were behind them.

We skittered to a stop; the horses' hooves scraped and slid on the stones.

Both Jane and Hannah instantly snapped their rifles up.

So did the soldiers.

The girls fired first.

The two soldiers in the lead of the procession fell, their muskets banging harmlessly on the cobblestones.

We all swung our horses about as more soldiers poured onto the street.

The next two soldiers stepped over their fallen companions and drew up their muskets.

Sarah spun and aimed her rifle between Jane and Hannah, who were now at our rear.

Holding my breath, I cringed.

The girls leaned far apart, giving Sarah as clear a shoot as possible.

She squeezed the trigger.

Another soldier cried out before falling.

I exhaled, but there was no relief in it.

James' musket thundered in my ear. The little ball sped between Jane and Hannah, finishing off another.

Two more soldiers turned the corner, and then another two.

Those in the lead were raising their muskets, taking aim.

Perhaps it was instinct. Perhaps it was the fever.

Regardless, I did it.

As they sighted down their muskets, I struck as quick as a viper. My power plunged into their souls, biting into the thoughts that hovered at the forefront of their minds.

Like tearing flesh, I savagely ripped their intention to shoot us right out of them.

Tremors of pain rack their souls, caused by the gaping holes I had left in my wake.

That strange feeling of elation filled me as I inhaled the rush of power that the violation had created.

Though I still felt horrified by my actions, it was not as sharp as before. I was getting used to it.

Before any more attempts on our lives could be made, we galloped around the corner and out of sight.

More gunfire erupted across the town.

"I need a high place where I can get a good view of the soldiers," I called.

"That's going to be difficult," shouted Jane over the clattering of our horses.

Hannah reined up, and we stopped.

"I know of a place," said Hannah. "But it's behind the enemy."

"Where?" asked Jane.

Hannah explained the location.

The names they used meant nothing to me, but the location would be a good one. As Hannah explained, it had a clear view of many streets, including the square, and a way to access the rooftops.

Jane knew the place. It was in a part of town at an intersection of sorts. The houses there were a bit taller than most in Marysvale.

"That will be a big risk just to get off a few shots," observed Sarah. "They may be there already, and they would certainly hear our horses."

"I will risk it," I said. "I need to see as many of their troops as I can for my idea to work. Take us as close as you think we can get without being heard. Then I will go the rest of the way on foot."

Sarah looked concerned but said nothing. We all knew that, from this time forward, no one would be safe, and risks had to be taken.

If I failed, we'd all fail.

Hannah nodded and set off at a fast gallop.

We raced across the town and turned up toward the garrison. After a short ride, we stopped.

"This is as far as I dare go," she said.

Intense gunfire rang through the town.

"It sounds like the soldiers have reached the final rallying point of the riders," observed James.

"I do hope they were able to slow down the advance," said Sarah.

Dismounting, I grabbed my crossbow and the remaining bolts. I counted twelve of them and wished it was double that.

"Tell me how to get there," I said. "I will go alone. Your muskets will give me away, so there's no sense in you coming. Wait here for me to return if you can. If you can't, fall back to the others, and I will make my way there on foot when I am finished."

Jane dismounted.

"I will come with you and show you the way."

I was about to protest, but I saw the determined look in her eyes and allowed it.

Sarah looked at me, and her eyes seemed to pierce through my soul.

It wasn't fear that I saw in them but sorrow.

For the briefest of moments, it gave me pause.

Why was she sad? Did she have a premonition?

At this point, it didn't matter, and the moment quickly passed. Turning away, I steeled myself for what I had to do. It was either succeed or die in the attempt. There would be no surrender.

With a rifle in her hand, Jane set off. I followed, armed with only my crossbow and a pair of pistols tucked into my belt. The pistols would probably be worthless in a real fight, but then, if it were a real fight, it wouldn't matter what weapons I had. We would be outnumbered.

As Jane approached each corner, she stopped and stealthily sneaked a peak before proceeding.

The gunfire across the town died down.

From our position, I could hear the clamor of marching boots. The sound seemed to come from all directions, and I guessed they would be fanning out about now.

I was sure our riders had thwarted a speedy drive to the square. Out of necessity, the soldiers would split their forces and take alternate routes, lest they pile up under an ambush and halt all progress.

I wondered if Wright and his puppets had ever imagined an armed response from their cowed subjects. We probably already caused more casualties than they could think possible. Perhaps, they were even beginning to have doubts.

I planned on furthering those doubts.

Reaching another corner, Jane took her careful glance and then flew back in alarm.

"Did they see you?" I whispered nervously.

"No." Then, decisively, she added, "There is still a chance, but we must be quick."

She turned, ran back a few houses, and cut through a narrow alley to another street.

Barely stopping to make sure our path was clear, she dashed out and down the street.

The cadence of marching soldiers in front of us grew louder.

In moments, we would be trapped.

I reached out to grab her and haul her back before we were spotted, but she turned and dove into some hollowed-out ruins that had once been a home.

There were no windows or doors, only half walls and rubble, and the partial remains of what had been a second level.

Jane ducked low, grabbed my coat, and pulled me down as well.

We squatted and pressed our backs to the outer walls of the adjacent house.

The sound of boots on cobblestone grew louder and louder. Until, finally, the bobbing heads of soldiers passed the house, advancing two by two.

From the side, they couldn't see us.

However, if any one of them chose to look back over his shoulder, we'd be spotted.

I gripped my crossbow anxiously and watched the columns pass.

My hands grew sweaty despite feeling cold.

Any fight we might wager would be feeble. I could get two, Jane one. With our pistols, possibly a couple more, and then it would be over.

No help would come. And I could only hope that they wouldn't take us alive.

We waited. And then we waited some more.

We waited until the last two fell into view and then disappeared.

Even though the whole column took only a few minutes to pass, it felt like an eternity.

Slowly, I let out my breath, unaware that I'd been holding it.

I turned to look at Jane.

She wiped her forehead as a sign of her relief.

"We're here," she whispered, pointing up.

Following her finger, I noticed a rickety staircase leading up two flights of stairs. Not much of the roof remained, and through it, I saw a darkening sky. The daylight was fading.

"We can get to the roof from here and then make our way to the spot where Hannah had in mind."

I nodded and stood, offering Jane my hand. She took it, and I pulled her up.

Hand in hand, we crept carefully up the stairs to the top floor.

Against the decaying wall leaned a crudely built, wobbly, weather-beaten ladder.

"Children built it. From the roof, they watch the activity and slave trade in the market," she explained.

Gingerly, I scaled the ladder.

Each rung groaned and creaked under my weight, threatening to collapse. If I fell, I doubted the rotting floor beneath us would stop me.

Not even daring to breathe, I slowly pulled my way up.

Finally, miraculously, I cleared the last step.

Swinging myself over onto the roof, I reached back and took Jane's rifle while she climbed.

Suddenly, massive gunfire erupted from everywhere. It rolled over buildings and echoed through the streets.

Shouts, screams, and cursing filled the air, along with the endless thunder of battle.

A thick cloud of choking, acrid smoke rose eerily over the houses. It looked as if the town itself was gradually sinking into the vapors of hell.

Indeed, it was.

Jane's head momentarily emerged. I took her hand and pulled her up.

Hastily, we crawled up to the crest of the roof and peered cautiously over.

Dozens of soldiers lay dead in the streets. Amazingly, only a few of our people had fallen thus far.

That would soon change, however. Perhaps even before our very eyes.

Hundreds of soldiers were forming up in the square, preparing to volley a withering response.

Officers barked orders to their men, who were still falling prey to the barrage of our people.

Farther up the street, safely in the narrow confines of the buildings, and behind the other soldiers, were the dark souls whom I sought.

They were the ones I was interested in; they were the ones most like Lyman and Matthew.

There were three of them conferring together.

Two had their backs to me. One did not.

I leapt through the window to his soul.

The man jerked, at first unbelieving what he felt.

It couldn't be, he thought.

It was just like he had been warned.

He tried pushing me out, apparently having been schooled by Jex.

It was a fruitless attempt.

The fever raging inside gave strength to my cause, and I tore my way through.

I sensed the surprise and confusion he felt.

Clearly, he had not expected or been taught that I could slice past his resistance.

Plunging deeper, I searched for anything that could be of use.

A thought surfaced in his mind.

I felt the man's desperation to keep me from seeing. He spun around, putting his back to me.

Our link broke.

Despite it, a brief smile crept across my face.

Perhaps I didn't have all that I wanted, but I had enough. I knew their plans.

Through the smoke rising from the battle in the square, I sighted the crossbow between the buildings and down the street to where he stood—no doubt discussing what had just transpired.

He didn't have time to explain much before the bolt struck him square in the back. He fell forward just as my second bolt pierced his comrade.

Snatching another bolt, I hurriedly slid it into the crossbow and set it.

Quickly drawing the weapon up, I searched for the third man. I caught a fleeting glimpse of him dashing away.

Cursing, I took the time to load the second bolt.

"What is it?" asked Jane.

"They are planning on taking part of their forces and circling back towards the wall. They will drive up behind us."

"What are we going to do? We have to warn our people, or they will be caught unaware in a crossfire."

I considered our situation for a moment.

"If we can move quickly," I said, "this situation may be to our advantage."

"How so?"

Before I could answer, she answered her own question.

"They will split their forces. We could lay an ambush for those at the rear and instantly take out half of them. We must hurry!"

Jane started to get up, but I put a restraining hand on her.

"Not yet. We will still be outnumbered, and I got the impression that more troops in the garrison will soon join the battle. This is only a preliminary force, just what they had on hand. Undoubtedly, we surprised them the way we entered the town. I'm sure they never dreamed that the town guard would defy the officers and open the gate."

"What are we to do?"

"Soften them up; rot away their support, and then we move."

"How?" she asked.

"Keep giving me these, two by two, as I need them," I said while handing her my remaining bolts. "I only hope they will be enough."

One after another, I sighted ten of the darkest auras. I checked them against where they stood in relation to the other troops. I needed to make sure they were the ones I wanted.

The first two fell instantly. And then, one after another, the others dropped in rapid succession.

All that is, but the last one. As my wicked bolt was about to silence him, he abruptly turned.

The bolt left only a superficial wound.

The man cried out and pressed his hand to his chest. Drawing it away, he looked at his blood-covered fingers.

He scanned for where it could have come from, but as the square was thick with smoke and the potential sources were nearly limitless, he gave up and fell back while barking orders.

"Well, that's that," I said. "*Now,* we must hurry."

I discarded the crossbow. Without proper bolts, it was nothing more than a club.

We dashed along the rooftop, making our way to the ladder.

"Up there!" cried a voice.

Glancing over the edge, I observed a half dozen soldiers passing along the street below.

One had seen us.

In our rush to reach the others, we had given ourselves away.

Muskets roared to life.

A ball whizzed by perilously close.

I grabbed Jane and flung her back with me.

More balls struck the edge of the house, blasting splinters into the air.

Drawing my pistols, I worked my way to the edge. Jane joined me.

A series of grunts and a few shouts could be heard from the soldiers.

"They must be reloading and coming up after us," I said.

"They will have to come up one at a time," said Jane. "We can hold them off. At least for a little while."

"Until they set the building ablaze," I muttered. "Is there no other way down?"

"Jump," she replied.

It was too high.

We were trapped, and there slipped away our chance of warning the others.

It fell quiet below.

"Wait here," I said.

Warily, I crawled on my belly to another part of the roof, at a place where they wouldn't expect me. Perhaps another plan would present itself in the process. I could at least get a peek and empty my two pistols into the soldiers.

With guns ready, I took a deep breath, sprang to my knees, and commenced my assault.

Chapter Twenty-Four: Into the Fire

Oi you goin' ta stay up there all day? Fight'ns down here, y'know."

The soldiers were not where I had anticipated them to be. Nor did they stand as I had expected. In fact, they didn't stand at all. It took me a moment to take in the scene below.

At first, with bewilderment, and then with a grin, I stood and shoved the pistols back into my belt.

"What is it?" asked Jane, noticing the expression on my face.

Walking over and offering her a hand up, I said, "See for yourself."

"Simon!" cried Jane beaming.

The old man swept off his hat and bowed low.

Jane laughed.

Together we scampered down the ladder, the stairs, and over the soldiers' arrow-ridden bodies to greet the old man and the dozen others with him. All had bows and quivers full of arrows.

"Saw young John up there shootn' like a madman and thought we'd come and join 'im."

"I could just kiss you!" exclaimed Jane. And she did, right on his cheek.

The old man blushed.

"T'was nuttin', Miss. John saved me from these nasty buggers once."

Simon kicked a soldier unceremoniously with his boot.

"Just wanted ta return the favor."

My mind flashed back to the soldiers who had attacked Simon and how I'd sold them into slavery. I briefly wondered what became of them.

"Is this all of you?" asked Jane.

"Aw, no, Miss. We gots another fifty comin'. Should be here soon enough. I know t'ain't much. Folks is too scared ta join. But, fear not." He patted his bow. "Since they took our guns, we made these. Every one of us has had years ta practice."

"Besides," said an eager-looking man. "We can shoot these much faster than if we had to reload muskets."

"Excellent," I beamed. "We're going to need you. But first, we have to get back to the main group. I'll explain on the way."

"What about Hannah and the others?" asked Jane.

"Aw, they had ta flee, Miss. Saw 'em a headin' back ta the others, leadin' rider-less horses." Simon touched his nose conspiratorially. "Tis really how we knew where ta look fer ya. Guessed where you'd be. Best place ta view the battle."

"We have to go," I said with a renewed sense of urgency. "If we're to be successful, we must act now before the enemy can get into position."

"You lot go with 'em," ordered Simon to the rest of his men. "I'll find the others an' get 'em where they need ta be."

"It's too dangerous to go alone," said Jane.

Simon winked. "I know lots of ways ta get through this town without bein' detected. Now off ya go."

Running through the town, down back alleys, and even cutting through houses, we came upon our forces.

The battle raged, and I was glad to see they still held the square. Well, actually, the soldiers held the square, but at a steep cost, and our forces hadn't yet retreated.

Hannah saw Jane and ran to embrace her.

"I was so worried! We heard the soldiers coming and had to leave. You can't leave me again!"

She looked desperately into Jane's eyes. "Promise me!"

"You know I can't promise that. But I will try. Now we must find the others."

Hannah led us to Sarah, Sabin, and Captain Smith.

I quickly gathered them together and explained what the soldiers had planned.

After I finished, Captain Smith groaned and shook his head.

"Then we are lost. How can we possibly defeat them? Even if we stop those circling behind us, more will still keep coming at us from the garrison."

"We don't stop those from coming behind us," I said. "At least not yet. We drive those in the square back to the garrison first. That will dispirit the enemy and cause them to reconsider their plans. And, it will then give us time to deal with those to our rear. Plus, others are coming to help."

I told them about Simon.

"I believe even more will come to our call," added Jane. "We just need a little bit of time."

"We won't have time to drive them all the way back," said the captain. "The others will be upon our rear before we can accomplish that. *If* we can accomplish it."

"It will be easier than you think," I said. "Trust me. If we storm the square and get them to fall back, they won't stop until the garrison."

"It won't be that simple," contended the captain. "We should concentrate on the ones behind us. They will be easier to defeat, and it will give us a place of retreat."

"It won't be easier," I snapped. "And if we stand here arguing about it, we'll be dealing with both at the same time."

Captain Smith looked ready to debate, but Sarah stepped in.

"We have made it this far with John. I trust him."

"As do I," added Sabin.

One by one, the others added their support.

Captain Smith hesitated a moment and then conceded, "Either way, it probably doesn't matter. The outcome will be the same. I'll do as you please."

"Hurry, Jane," I instructed. "Get the rest of the riders. Once the soldiers start falling back, we will drive them all the way to the garrison."

"They will regroup," Smith said doubtfully.

"Perhaps, but I don't think so. A few dozen men on horses, chasing them down, can be intimidating."

The captain shrugged. "I don't think it will work, but have it your way."

I could tell he was beginning to regret letting us in. At this point, the captain's feelings mattered little. Indeed, it may turn out to be worse for him and the people of Marysvale. But it certainly wasn't worse for us.

"Once we get the soldiers in the square retreating," I advised, "waste no time, as you will have none to spare. Take your men, divide them into two groups, and conceal yourselves back in the town. Once the rear troops pass between you, ambush them. They won't be expecting it. If you can, hide on rooftops; they give you cover and allow you to shoot down upon them. The trick will be to know what route they will take."

"Leave it to me," replied Captain Smith. "There are only a few ways for them to come. I'll send my swiftest runners to spy right now."

"Good. Now hurry; spread the word among the men. As soon as they hear the signal, they are to charge the square."

"And what signal would that be?" asked Hannah.

Sabin withdrew the horn the officer had used at the gate.

"How about this? Figured it might come in handy, and I didn't think he would need it. A bit dented, but should still work."

"Brilliant," I said. "Then, the plan is simple. On the first horn blast, our shooters stop what they are doing and reload if they need to. On the second blast, they are to charge into the square and fire. And keep firing until they run. Understand?"

They all nodded.

"Good. Now go. Report back and let me know when we're ready. And for all our sakes, be quick!"

Captain Smith shouted for his messengers. He gave them instructions and sent them on their way. Jane and Hannah set off rounding up the riders and getting them back on their horses.

While that was going on, I wanted to take one last look at the square.

Walking up one of the side streets, I went to where I could get a glimpse. All the while, I stayed close to the houses and out of sight.

Although shots from both sides rang out frequently enough, the majority of the gunfire had died down.

I would soon find out why.

Near the opening to the square stood a dozen men pressed up against the homes.

Watching my approach, one of the men warned, "Careful. They have a nasty habit of killing you when you stick your head out."

He indicated one of the fallen men sprawled on the street, his eyes open. There was no light in them.

"I'll keep that in mind," I muttered.

Getting down on my belly, I slithered along until, with one eye just peeking around the corner, I could take a quick glance.

I hoped the soldiers wouldn't expect that. They were most likely looking for a musket from a man crouched or standing, not just an eyeball next to the cobblestone.

A good two hundred soldiers firmly held control of the square. Although they were in the open and in a precarious position, *we* were the ones who were pinned down.

They were lined up and organized into small groups. Vigilantly, they kept their eyes and muskets down the open streets that led to the square in all directions. Four officers

362

stood in the center, like the hub of a wagon wheel. From where they stood, they could quickly and effectively give orders.

The only reason we were still able to put up a fight was likely because they weren't in much of a hurry. The troops were waiting for their comrades to come at us from the rear. And time was on their side. Reinforcements would also arrive from the garrison.

I gazed at the scene and the soldiers' auras for a brief moment before pulling back.

It was just in time. A ball struck the cobblestone nearby and ricocheted up into the house on the opposite side of the street.

Although I'd drawn back before they had a chance to hit me, it was a warning that I had been seen.

I walked back while summing up our forces.

We had about the same number of men, including the riders. Muskets and rifles were our limiting factor. After the battle, we'd have more. Thinking about it, I had doubts about the validity of my strategy. I had planned on us pinning them, not the other way around. But as it stood, our casualties would be significant in the opening charge.

There was no getting around that.

By the time I returned, our forces were ready.

Taking the horn from Sabin, I mounted Smoke.

Jane, Hannah, Sarah, and James drew up beside me.

"What are you doing?" I asked Jane.

"Joining you, of course," she replied.

"Oh, no, you're not!"

"If you're going to charge into the thick of things, I will be at your side. Besides, I am not entirely sure I want to go on without you."

"If I die in the opening volley, then you will have plenty of opportunities to join me before this is all over."

"John," Sarah said firmly. "We are coming."

"Not in the opening charge!" I fired back.

I knew what would happen, and I couldn't bear the thought of losing them. I couldn't watch it. Perhaps it was selfish of me to want to die first, but I was unyielding.

"Quit arguing!" exclaimed Hannah. "You're wasting time we don't have."

"You are the ones wasting time."

"Then a compromise," offered Sarah. "You need as many men in that fight as you can get. We will be with you but will take up the rear."

I still didn't like it, but I knew the riders in the rear held a better chance of survival. So, I nodded in agreement.

"That's not fair!" exclaimed Hannah.

Jane also started to protest, but I raised my hand.

"Please," I said. "I won't be able to concentrate as I need to with you there. I'll be more worried about you than about what *I* need to do. It's the best you're going to get."

Although Hannah squawked up a storm about them being better marksmen than me, Sarah led them to the back.

I looked at James. "Good shot on horseback, are you?"

I knew he was, and I wasn't really asking that. I was asking him to be with me in the opening charge.

He nodded.

I asked the same question to the men behind me. One of them was Charles.

They all nodded.

"Very well, then there are two men in that group who must die."

I described the officers. While there were four of them, there were two that I was most concerned about.

As soon as we entered the square, James and I would take one. Behind me, Charles and his partner would take the other.

They nodded in agreement.

I took a deep breath.

In my original plan, I would signal for my men to load, wait until the enemy loosed a volley, and then charge as they were reloading. But as we were in a standoff, both sides were likely already loaded.

Nevertheless, I took the horn, pressed it to my lips, and blew, signaling for them to load.

It also gave me a moment to steel my nerves.

I reached down and patted Smoke's neck affectionately and whispered, "Well, boy…"

I planned on saying more, but I couldn't think of anything to say. I stroked his neck. His head was down, and he pawed on the stones under his hooves. He could sense the impending charge and was anxious to get on with it.

With a sad smile, I thought, *Well, if you're ready for it, big fellow, then so am I.*

Raising the horn again to my lips, I blasted it long and hard.

Tossing it aside, I snatched up my rifle.

Without having to be told, Smoke powerfully drove forward.

365

As one, our men whooped and shouted in a chilling chorus.

The buildings to our sides seemed to blur as we galloped past them.

To the sounds of the battle cry and hooves pounding upon stone, we shot down the narrow street and on to the waiting soldiers.

Chapter Twenty-Five: Ghost of the Past

Muskets and rifles fired everywhere. They cracked and boomed, rolling into one great unending cacophony of thunderous sound.

In my mind, I envisioned everyone converging upon the square at precisely the same time. The reality was that our charge hadn't been timed very well. Men reached the square in their various groups at different intervals.

The unlucky ones who got there first paid for my mistake. Perhaps I would join them soon.

Smoke's unconquerable spirit and powerful strides propelled us forward. He ran faster than the other riders. Letting go of the reins, I trusted my course and fate to God and Smoke.

Rising in the stirrups, I grasped the rifle and readied myself, anxious for the moment when I would be able to spy the dark souls I sought.

Smoke charged into the square.

The sight that greeted me took my breath away.

I thought I had seen battle before, but in this moment, I realized I had only seen feeble skirmishes.

Gunsmoke polluted the air. Brothers in humanity, who should be neighbors and friends, were now locked in deadly combat, seeking to snuff out the light of their enemy.

Men fell on both sides at a sickening rate.

Red blood soaked the ground.

Wounded cried out in pain.

Amid the melee and thunderous roar of guns, I saw that it was also raining arrows.

Simon!

Arrows soared through the air, plunging into the soldiers. They flew from rooftops and windows. Townspeople, who had waited perhaps a decade for this moment, now took retribution upon their captors.

A ball whizzed by, and the cries from a fallen rider behind me refocused me on my task.

I found the dark, evil soul and...

He jerked violently from the impact of someone else's ball.

Leaving him, I honed in on the other dark one.

As best as one could upon a galloping horse, I steadied my aim. Drawing upon my lessons with Jane and Hannah, I squeezed the trigger.

The ball struck his leg. A split second later, as he was falling in agony, another ball hit his side.

The little light that his soul still possessed extinguished.

The battle raged for just a little longer before I saw a handful of soldiers break and run.

A moment later, more soldiers fled the field.

Under the onslaught from the people of Alyth, Marysvale, and the men of Syre, the enemy's ranks were speedily collapsing.

Soon, all the soldiers were in full retreat.

Shouts of joy and victory filled the air.

I spun to shout an order to Charles, but he was not there.

A brief search told me he would never be there again.

Instead, I found James.

"Take the other riders and keep on them. You don't need to follow so close as to put yourselves at risk, but keep firing on them and drive them back to the garrison."

He nodded.

Sarah had leaped off her horse and had already begun attending to the wounded.

Jane and Hannah rode to my side.

"Stay with Sarah. I'm going to join the riders," I said. "The danger will come from the soldiers approaching from the rear."

"Be careful, John," said Jane.

I smiled. "Don't worry. I know what I'm doing."

"That's what we're afraid of," quipped Hannah.

"As soon as I'm sure the soldiers are going to retreat all the way, we'll be back to help Captain Smith with the rear assault."

Without waiting for a reply, I turned and found the captain. He barked orders to fall back to their other positions. His arm hung limply at his side. Blood trickled down and slowly dripped off his fingertips, splattering upon the cobblestones below.

I caught his eye. He answered my unasked question.

"Already on it. You just make sure those fellows don't circle around and come at our flanks."

I nodded and galloped after the rest of the riders.

The occasional body of a fallen soldier lay in the street. It told me what I had hoped for. They were in full retreat, every man for himself and all desperately running for the safety of the garrison.

Following the sound of rifle fire, I quickly caught up.

The riders were doing what I would have done exactly. Back far enough to not force the soldiers into taking a stand but still shooting at them—reminding them that they were there and ready should the troops decide to regroup.

The town below us again exploded with the sounds of gunfire.

The second assault had begun.

After passing through the narrow confines of Marysvale's poor section, we entered the sprawling estates of the wealthy. The fleeing soldiers ran past the last of the mansions and out into the open space before the garrison walls.

Galloping to the front of our column, I halted the riders.

"No farther," I said. "We don't want to get too close."

The gunfire from the clash below started dying down.

"We should go see what happened," said a rider.

I agreed. Choosing a few scouts, we quickly searched for houses where they could keep an eye on the garrison. One of the locations had occupants. They were adeptly persuaded to leave.

I instructed the scouts to keep their horses inside with them, as I feared any returning bands of soldiers would spot them.

With that affair settled, we set off.

On our way, we met up with Jane and Hannah. They bore the good news that, with the help of Simon and the archers, the ambush had been complete. They now held many soldiers as prisoners.

Riding back toward the square, the men told battle stories and shared in their sorrow of the fallen.

I found myself at the back of the group with Jane and Hannah.

As we rode in silence, I pondered on the incredible events of the day.

We had won a battle, but the war was just beginning.

We had rallied faster and better than Wright's army had anticipated, thus taking them off guard. An advantage we would not have again.

Lord Wright had sent a few hundred men, but he had hundreds more at his disposal. They would come at us with disciplined soldiers, who would be well fed, well trained, and well supplied.

Though we could rally more people and were lighter and more maneuverable than the soldiers, we could never match them in the open or in their strength. We'd have to fight from alleys and rooftops.

Where the soldiers had a fortress to retreat to, we had nowhere to go.

They would hunt and fight us day and night.

Not taking into account how they will utilize the Brean, I thought grimly.

My head slumped to my chest.

True, we had won a battle; but the war would be different. Despite our victory, nothing had changed.

After a moment, I realized that the girls were no longer with me. I turned about in the saddle and spied them gazing down a street.

Without a word to each other, they turned their horses and followed it.

Curious, I turned Smoke around and trailed them.

They traveled for some time before turning onto another side street.

It was then that I realized where they were going.

They stopped in front of a house—their house.

It was the house where their father had died.

Wordlessly, they dismounted.

Slowly, lovingly, Jane placed her hand on the door and rested it there for a moment.

She took a few deep breaths and then gently pushed it open. The door creaked on its wooden hinges.

I slid off Smoke and silently watched them.

Jane entered the house first, followed by Hannah.

They stepped cautiously into the hallowed home and looked around. Cleaned out by other needy residents, nothing was left of their sparse furnishings.

Their eyes fell on the spot where their father had spent his last moments—the place where he had finally stood up to evil, even knowing the price he would pay.

A dark stain, where his blood had spilled, marked the location on the wood floor.

Hannah knelt by it and placed her hand gingerly on the spot.

Her shoulders slumped as she bowed her head to her chest. Her long hair shrouded her face as wrenching sobs tore from her with uncontrollable anguish.

With tears flowing unreservedly from her own eyes, Jane knelt by Hannah and wrapped her arms around her.

Night had firmly taken hold before we arrived back at the square. The moon bathed the town in its subdued light, and stars twinkled above the clearing sky.

The dead had been cleared off the streets. And, under the expert guidance of Sarah, the wounded were being transported to more suitable quarters.

When she finally noticed us, Sarah hurried over.

She looked like she was about to scold us for making her worry. But, even in the torchlight, she could see the lingering grief upon the sisters' faces.

Sarah immediately softened. "Oh girls, I'm so very sorry."

They each dismounted, and she embraced them both.

"Would you like to take your mind off it?" she asked.

They nodded.

"There are many wounds to clean and care for. I could use some help if you feel up to it."

"It will do us good to focus on someone other than ourselves," replied Jane.

With a silent nod, Hannah agreed with her.

To me, Sarah suggested, "You best go find the others."

Then she told me where they were.

The women set off to their work while I went in search of Angus and Captain Smith.

I found the captain first. He was talking with his men. His arm still hung limply at his side; dried blood caked his fingertips. A hastily torn scrap of cloth bandaged the wound.

"You should get that looked at," I said.

He turned to face me.

"The shot passed through," he said simply. "I can wait my turn."

Then leaving his men, Smith came over to me. I slid off Smoke.

"Was it a clean shot?" I asked.

He shrugged his good arm.

"Still here, aren't I? Haven't bled to death yet."

"Well, that is something."

"Been looking for you."

"So it would seem," I replied.

While we walked to where Angus had established headquarters, he filled me in on the ambush.

"We didn't lose as many as we could have or as many as we should have. I don't understand something. How did you know they would retreat all the way back to the garrison? They should've regrouped and mounted a counterattack."

I smiled. "I was busy hunting their officers, or at least the key ones. I wanted to make sure that when they started falling back, there would be no one there to order a halt and form up ranks again."

"And how did you know which ones to get?"

I sighed, mostly because I was tired of explaining myself.

"I suppose you'll find out sooner or later. I have the ability to see into the souls of men. I looked for the dark souls, the evil ones—like Lyman and Matthew. I figured Lord Wright would put officers in charge like them. I simply had to find them and then silence them."

"Appears you were right."

I grunted noncommittally.

"It won't be that way tomorrow, though," he said softly.

"No," I agreed.

We walked a bit before the captain asked another question.

"Do you think it will all be worth it?"

His tone was as a boy inquiring of his father, almost pleading for reassurance.

I hesitated as I found myself wondering the same thing. I wanted to flee, not fight a war we couldn't win.

In my uncertainty, Captain Smith had his answer.

"That's what I thought. I'm not sure I made the right decision joining you."

"Either way," I replied. "Your fate is now tied to ours."

"To be sure."

"There is always hope," I said, trying to comfort him, and perhaps myself. "I never believed we'd make it this far. And here we are."

"That is true," he agreed.

We found Angus, Sabin, and the other leaders relating their battles and discussing stratagems.

The next few hours passed in discovering how many men we had, recruiting others to join us, taking inventory of our weapons and resources, and dividing them amongst the shooters.

The strategy was simple: break into small groups and spread out, and then harass the soldiers as much as possible. We would conduct lightning-fast raids, fighting from houses and rooftops, always with a way of escape, and then falling back before we could incur heavy loss. They would fall by our whittling their forces down as much as possible, not from one decisive, fatal blow but from a thousand tiny cuts.

More captains were chosen to lead the small groups. Boys would be used as runners to relay messages back from those groups to a central command that Captain Smith would run. That way, we could move quickly and stage forces where they were needed.

All in all, it wasn't a bad plan. In small groups, we would be difficult to find and flush out. The psychological effect would be nerve-racking for the soldiers. Every house, every street, could be a possible ambush.

The candles burned low before we finished our preparations. In a few hours, dawn would be upon us.

In truth, we weren't wholly prepared. However, we all desperately needed some rest, albeit short.

I rode back to the square to find out where the women had taken the wounded. With the aid of a boy who acted as a runner, I learned that they were not far from Angus' headquarters.

Sighing, I backtracked to the given location.

I found the women sitting on the floor of a sparsely furnished home, exhausted. They warmed themselves by the heat of a small stove.

Their garments were covered in blood. Two buckets filled with blood-soaked rags sat beside a small table that held a saw, several knives, needles, and thread to stitch up wounds. An oil lamp, which was the source of our light, took up the remaining surface of the tabletop. Piles of bandages, and Sarah's depleted medicine pouches, lay on the floor beneath it.

Two other tables had been brought in and pushed together, which appeared to be where the injured had lain to be treated. A few extinguished candle stubs lay on top.

The floor had been cleaned but deeply stained with blood, particularly around the table.

"The wounded?" I queried.

"Close by in surrounding houses, should I be needed," replied Sarah. "Have you eaten?"

"No," I replied. "But I'm more tired than hungry."

Sarah got to her feet. "I have a small loaf of bread. I'll make us some tea, and then you can tell us about your night while we eat."

"Oh," Hannah said wearily. "I used the last of the water."

She got up. "What's one more trip to the well? I've seen it so many times today, we're on a first-name basis. His name is Dale, in case you're wondering."

Jane gave a tired smile.

"Well, I'm up," said Sarah. "Might as well keep you company."

Hannah picked up an empty water bucket, and they slipped out into the night.

Jane slumped down onto her side and used her arm as a pillow.

"Was it horrible?" I asked.

She closed her eyes and nodded slowly, already succumbing to exhaustion. In seconds, she had drifted into a deep sleep.

I reached over and brushed a lock of hair away from her mouth and tucked it behind her ear. Then, seeing she didn't have her coat, I removed mine and covered her with it.

Lying down on my back, I turned my head and watched her sleep.

***

With a jolt, I awoke.

Everything was dark, and it took me a moment to remember where I was.

As my eyes adjusted, I realized that the darkness in the room had lost its edge. A very dim light tried creeping past the shuttered windows, barely pushing back against the grasp of night.

Day must be approaching.

The room was cold, although a bit of warmth still radiated from the iron stove.

Reaching out, I felt Jane still sleeping exactly as before.

The only sound was that of her breathing.

I listened to her for a moment.

And then it hit me.

There were no other sounds!

I couldn't hear anything from Hannah or Sarah.

My eyes burst open.

Nothing.

The room was empty.

I went up the stairs.

Again, there was no sign of them.

Retreating down the stairs, I knelt by Jane, shaking her urgently but gently.

"What?" she asked groggily. "What is it?"

She tried opening her eyes, but the best she could do at the moment was a few bleary-eyed blinks.

I was about to answer her when another sound caught my attention.

Smoke snorted outside.

But that wasn't the sound that woke my senses.

There it was again. I recognized it.

A boot scraped across the cobblestone out front.

"Where…" started Jane.

Placing a warning hand over her mouth, I pressed a finger to my lips.

Instantly, she was fully awake.

She nodded once to indicate she understood.

Removing my hand, I silently stood up.

Jane did, likewise.

Drawing the two pistols from my belt, I kept one for myself and handed the other to Jane.

Noiselessly, we crossed the room to the door.

She stood off to the side while I pressed up against the wall next to the door latch.

A boot again scuffed the ground outside, and I looked at Jane expectantly.

She understood and nodded.

In one movement, I flipped the latch and threw the door open.

In that instant, in the earliest dawn of the coming day, I knew what had happened to the women.

Chapter Twenty-Six: A Shadow

My stomach sank, and my anxiety mounted, but as I stared at the man, my fever burned hot.

Although he wore a black cloak, under it, I could see the clothing that was afforded to those in Lord Wright's service.

"Greetings," he began to say, his hand still poised to knock on the door.

But before he could finish his salutation, I grabbed the little man by the coat and flung him into the house.

He fell on the floor, sprawling. Before he could protest or get to his feet, I reached down, heaved him up, and slammed him against the wall.

I pressed the pistol hard against his cheek while pinning him with my other forearm.

"Go ahead," he croaked. "Have a peek."

The man looked up towards his forehead and then back at me.

"I'm curious how it works."

I did exactly as instructed and pressed inside, finding a memory right at the forefront.

"Ah, John," said Lord Wright in the little man's memory. "Good to see you again."

He chuckled at his little joke.

Illuminated by the torches on the wall, Lord Wright appeared downright evil.

"What's that? But I can't see you, you say. Fear not; that will be remedied soon enough. You see, I'm extending an invitation for you to join me. A family reunion of sorts, shall we say?"

Wright started walking. The little man's gaze followed him.

I couldn't repress a snarl as Sarah and Hannah fell into view. They were in a stone room. Their wrists, ankles, and waists were strapped to thick wooden chairs with armrests, and a gag bound their mouths.

"No, don't thank me," continued Lord Wright as he stood behind them.

Spreading his arms wide, he gripped the back of their chairs.

"It was really no trouble for me to arrange our little get-together."

Wright clucked his tongue disapprovingly. "You should be more careful; the town is no longer safe. It was fortunate for these two women that it was only a few of my soldiers dressed like common rabble at the well. Otherwise, with all the violent rebels about, it could have been quite tragic for them."

He sighed forlornly. "It used to be such a peaceful town. Of course, we'll have plenty of time to discuss that later. Not too much later, mind you. You see, John, I expect you to come right now. No time to scheme, plot, or otherwise disrupt my domain—at least more than you already have."

While leaning forward, he cupped a hand to an ear.

"What's that, you ask? What if you don't want to come?"

He stepped away from the women.

A table came into view with an assortment of knives, hammers, hooks, and curved instruments upon it.

"Miss Wolfe remembers these tools quite well. Don't you, child?"

He stroked Hannah's cheek with a finger.

She shrank from his touch, and tears welled in her terror-stricken eyes.

Suddenly, Lord Wright grabbed a hammer off the table and, without warning, struck her forearm with demonic fury.

In the little man's memory, I heard her bones crack.

The gag muffled her scream.

Sarah struggled helplessly against her bonds. She tried telling me something, but she, too, was muffled and made no sense.

My utter hatred for Lord Wright burned hot and furious.

The little man quite enjoyed this spectacle of torture. I pressed hard against his throat, cutting off his air supply.

"Oh, and John," said Lord Wright over Hannah's muffled sobs, his tone returning to his usual sanctimonious self. "For the sake of Miss Wolfe, let us leave my manservant unmolested, shall we?"

He leaned forward conspiratorially. "Only the messenger, you know. And, please, do hurry, or there may not be much left of Miss Wolfe to recognize."

I shoved harder against the little man's throat.

"Only the messenger," the little man squeaked.

I wanted to tear the memory from his mind. The one thing keeping me from doing so was Hannah and Sarah's wellbeing.

Releasing my hold on the little man, he slumped down, bent over, and commenced a coughing fit.

"Tell me what you saw, John," demanded Jane with fear in her voice.

Bowing my head, I said, "He has them. Lord Wright has Hannah and Sarah."

"Oh, no!" cried Jane, covering her lips with her hand.

Her eyes were wild with horror. "What do we do?"

"I'm to go with him," I said.

"Oh, no. No, no, no!" sobbed Jane. "Oh, please, no."

Tears sprang from her eyes.

Throwing my arms around her, I drew her in.

"It will be all right," I said soothingly, stroking the back of her hair.

Then, whispering in her ear, I said, "If the Brean aren't here already, they will be soon. Get the horses out if you can and wait for me behind Lord Wright's castle where the cave entrance used to be."

"None of that," said the little man, who was still bent over but eyeing us now that his coughing fit had passed. "And really quite disgusting. Have you no morals?"

Letting go of Jane, I handed her my pistol. I wouldn't need it now.

Spinning to face the little man, I grabbed him roughly by the coat. I was about to haul him up and toss him out when he squealed, "Unmolested!"

Instead, I spun him around by the shoulder and shoved him out onto the street.

The early dawn cast its dim light into the shadow-filled room.

Grasping the door, I took one more look back at Jane. Tears streamed down her cheeks. She stood with both hands now covering her lips in a state of shock; her green eyes filled with her greatest terror. She looked so alone and so afraid, standing there in the darkness of the cold, bleak room.

"I love you," I mouthed.

Then, pulling the door closed, I walked away.

Smoke whinnied as I passed by. I ignored him.

The only thoughts I allowed myself were those that fed the fever.

I *needed* the anger.

The little man bounded along beside me as the daylight grew in strength.

"It won't be all right," he said.

I made no acknowledgment of him nor his comment.

The man repeated, "When you said it would be all right. It won't, you know, at least not for you. You are a fool to think you could possibly win. You may be a witch, but you're not that bright. You're certainly no match for the magnificent Lord Wright."

I remained silent while the little man prattled on.

Lapping up every word, I savored each bitter morsel.

I felt my muscles begin to ripple with power as the fury inside of me mounted. I hungered for more.

The fact that I hadn't reacted emboldened the sorry little man.

"As for the war... What war? Your forces will be crushed before the morning is over. The streets will run with the blood of those traitorous scums. But don't worry about the girls; they will be taken care of. There will be a good use for two as pretty as they."

The fever burned my flesh. Every fiber in my body seethed with vengeance. I felt incredible strength coursing through me as if I could snap this little man in two with just a thought.

A dark shadow entered my body and shrouded my soul with its deathly cold embrace. And I received it with ravenous affection.

Only one feeling withstood the icy chill—complete and absolute hatred. It blazed white-hot, consuming my whole being.

"Oh, yes," said the man. "It will be a glorious victory."

I halted.

The little man continued a few steps before realizing I wasn't with him.

He stopped and turned back.

He was about to say something, but he froze in alarm. Wide-eyed, he looked at me fearfully.

My body felt immortal and huge—I seemed to tower over the little man. Whether it was real or not, I didn't know. Nevertheless, I stood erect, fearless—invincible.

"You are wrong," I said quietly.

The words came out of my lips, and he heard them with his ears. But they also came from my soul, and it spoke directly to his soul. Even if a battle had been waging, with muskets blasting in our ears, I knew he would've heard my words as clearly then as he did here, in the still, cold, early dawn.

"There *is* a war coming," I continued.

The little man stumbled back, falling right on his rump. Immediately, he threw his arms up as if to ward me off.

"My forces may fail this morning," I said. "But come afternoon, it will be the blood of your soldiers that bathe the streets. I have foreseen it, and *I will make it happen.*"

I took a step forward and offered him my hand.

He recoiled as if I were about to strike him.

"Are you certain that you are on the winning side?" I asked.

As he scooted away from me in terror, I let my hand drop.

"I won't forget those who are with me—and those who are not."

I continued walking. "Come along, little man. I have my destiny to meet, and I wouldn't want Lord Wright to worry that his servant was *molested.* At least, not *yet.*"

I didn't have to look back to know that he had obeyed. He scurried behind my long, quick strides. He dared not walk by my side or meet my eyes.

We continued on straight past the sentries. They were well concealed, but I could see them. They knew me and didn't stop us.

Approaching the gate, it opened for us on well-oiled hinges. We passed through.

Inside the garrison, troops were in various stages of preparation. Columns and squads were forming, marching, and drilling their musket and bayonet techniques. Soldiers, wearing long, shiny riding boots and swords, led horses out of stables—a cavalry, no doubt. And from their demeanor and confidence, they would be a terrible force to reckon with.

Both curious and disdainful looks followed me as I walked past them. I had no need to be shown the way; I knew my destiny waited for me in the towers of Lord Wright's keep.

Before the doors of the imposing castle, I stopped.

The little man hustled around me and squeaked, "Wait here."

He shuffled past the two guards at the door and slipped inside.

The guards regarded me with contempt.

I could tell that killing Lyman, escaping the garrison, capturing Matthew, and starting a revolution had won me some notoriety.

The hatred was mutual.

Glaring at one of them, I welcomed the darkness and the demons as they slithered deeper into my soul.

My eyes narrowed, and my lip curled up into a silent snarl. I fought the yearning to bore into him and rend him to pieces.

But I didn't. I entered softly. I took nothing, watched nothing. I was simply there inside him, and he knew it.

The sneer faded from his face as I continued my withering gaze. He quickly grew uncomfortable, and his defiance gave way to nervousness and self-doubt.

Shifting uncomfortably, he averted his eyes.

That's right, I purred silently. *I will remember you. We'll meet again before the day is through.*

I then turned my attention to the remaining guard. He also quivered, like a mouse in the presence of a mighty lion.

The doors flung open, and Lord Wright, Jex, and a cadre of guards strode out of the castle.

I glared at Jex for a moment before fixing my gaze on 'his haughtiness'.

"Ah, John, how nice of you to come," Lord Wright said sardonically.

"Afraid, are you?" I asked, sweeping my arm over the assembled guards. "All this just for me?"

Lord Wright paused for a moment, taking in my countenance.

"My, my, how you have changed," he said in contemplation.

"You have no idea," I growled low and menacingly.

Jex involuntarily took a step back.

"Bind him," ordered Wright with a hard look.

The guards rushed forth and, with strong cords, tied my hands behind me.

Lord Wright leaned forward a bit and explained, "We can't be too careful. I must admit, John, you did take us by surprise."

He shook his head regretfully. "To lose the town so quickly. It was quite a shock to realize no officers survived; on your account, I am sure."

"There were some who came back," I countered.

Wright gave his hand a dismissive little wave. "Return, perhaps. But survive? Oh my, no. The few who dared to return have paid for their gross failure."

A look of disgust passed over my face.

Lord Wright noticed it. "And that, John, is why you are destined to fail. You will not do what it takes to succeed. You are just a foolish little boy. Here, on the dawn of your defeat, you come to the aid of two worthless women. You, the most valuable person in that miserable force of yours, and you throw your opportunity away."

"Have I thrown it away, or am I embracing it? Are you so sure I've already lost?" I asked with a raised eyebrow.

He looked at me with a sneer. "Oh, yes, John. I'm quite sure you have lost."

"Then perhaps you should tell Jex. He seems a bit doubtful and unusually quiet," I replied evenly.

Wright's demeanor instantly boiled into fury.

"Oh, John, I shall relish in *showing* you just how much you have lost. Bring him," he ordered.

Two guards flanked my sides. They hooked their arms through mine and propelled me after the arrogant lord.

Jex, on the other hand, held no boldness.

He glanced at me as we strode through the castle. A confused look crossed his face.

"It's not too late for you, Jex, or for any of you," I offered. "You can join me. Unlike your tyrant here, I will deal mercifully with you."

In one fluid movement, Lord Wright stopped, spun around, and backhanded me across the face.

We all came to a stop.

Closing my eyes, I basked in the fury washing over me. Loathing cankered my soul, and power cascaded through my body.

Wright grabbed my chin violently, jerked it up, and dug his nails into my skin.

My eyes flew open.

With our faces inches apart, Lord Wright spat, "You have no idea how unmerciful I can be. Fortunately, you and your friends will not have to wait long to find out. I am not afraid of your parlor tricks, boy. Jex has taught me how to keep your vileness from defiling my mind. Care to put our wits to the test and see who is the strongest?"

He widened his eyes tauntingly.

It took all my self-control to restrain myself. Whatever had been forecast in my dreams had not come yet. I didn't know what was brewing inside me, but I knew it still needed more time to incubate. If I unleashed it now, I could tear the mind of the despicable lord to shreds. But then what? I'd be gunned down, and all would be lost.

No. The dream had shown me victory; albeit a shallow one, it would be better than nothing. I may lose everything, but at least Lord Wright would too.

He released my chin with a jerk.

I felt a trickle of blood drip down my neck.

"Just as I thought. You are a coward—weak and pathetic."

We resumed our march and arrived at a circular stone stairwell, where we ascended the steps. Reaching the top, Wright lifted a latch on a heavy wooden door and stepped inside the room.

"Bring him in," he barked.

I was shoved into the room.

Before me stood four heavy, wooden chairs with thick leather straps affixed to where the arms, chest, and ankles would go; two of the chairs were occupied. Sarah was bound in the outer chair, and Hannah was strapped next to her in an inner chair. They were both gagged.

The women still wore the blood-soaked clothing from the night before.

Hannah's arm was swollen, black and purple, from where Lord Wright had inflicted his savage blow. Her eyes were red and puffy from tears of pain.

"Sit him down there."

Lord Wright pointed to the chair on the other end.

The guards unbound my wrists, only to throw me forcefully into the chair and strap me down.

An empty chair remained between Hannah and me.

"I had a fourth chair brought in," explained Wright, "should the other Miss Wolfe decide to join us."

Addressing the guards, Lord Wright ordered, "You two remain outside the door. I'll need you to remove the bodies when we are finished. The rest of you are dismissed."

The soldiers bowed and retreated out of the room, closing the door behind them.

Sarah looked at me with pleading eyes.

Lord Wright noticed her expression and said mockingly, "I am certain, if our dear Sarah could speak, she would say to you, 'Fool! How stupid of you to come! We are already dead. And now you will join us.'"

Her eyes flicked angrily to Wright.

"Ah, I see you still have some fire in you yet. Well, you won't for long," he said wickedly.

Picking up a long, thin knife, he pressed it to her cheek.

A trickle of blood oozed from the cut.

Then, checking himself, he pulled the knife away.

"Still, we mustn't rush ourselves. I would hate for you to miss the show we have planned for you."

Laying the knife down, he swept his arm around the room.

"What do you think?" he asked.

Tapestries, swords, and horns adorned the walls of the square room. Facing us were two large doors that led presumably to a balcony. To our left was the table that I had seen in the memory. It held the instruments of torture.

Behind us stood Jex.

"I had to make a few minor adjustments to this room," explained Wright. "As you know, the previous chambers for my craft have been damaged. Would you like to know what this room used to be?"

He didn't wait for a reply.

"It was a sitting room. On pleasant days, I enjoyed looking down on the town and to the country beyond. From here, I can see my future kingdom. Soon, everyone, everywhere, will all bow and call me *your majesty*."

Wright waved his hands up and down as if to calm us.

"Fear not; the dungeon and the Brean's tunnel will be restored, and this room will return to normal."

Silently, I glared at him.

With an evil gleam in his eye, he took the palm of his hand and pressed it against Hannah's broken arm.

She cried through the gag in agony.

I strained at my bindings.

A low, inhuman, guttural growl rumbled through my chest.

I could feel the demons inside me emerging.

For the briefest of moments, fear flashed in Wright's eyes, but he quickly regained his composure.

"Well, well, this will be fun. But wait! I haven't shown you the best part yet!"

He spun around, walked over to the double doors, and flung them open.

A blast of cold air rushed into the room.

Hannah shivered.

Sarah trembled as well. Although, for a very different reason.

Perhaps I, too, should have been chilled and horrified, but I wasn't. I was simply witnessing the fulfillment of my fate and what I already knew would happen.

The opened doors revealed the rising sun on a crisp November morning. White frost glistened off the roofs of Marysvale. From our vantage point, we could see the soldiers lined up and ready at the gates.

However, what I suspected truly frightened Sarah was what swarmed in the forest far away.

Lord Wright leaned close to my ear and said quietly, "Do you see them?"

I could see them.

Hordes of monsters gathered. I had seen them amass at the fall of Alyth, but that was nothing compared to this.

Many of the great brutes wore helmets and breastplates. Their armor glinted in the sun. They carried large spiked clubs. A dozen of the largest Brean heaved a massive tree as a battering ram.

"That is right, John," he purred. "The gates of Marysvale will splinter and be torn asunder. They were never truly designed to withstand those magnificent creatures. The Brean will pour through those gates as my forces surge through these."

He stood up erect. "And they will suffer, John. All those people will suffer because of *you*. You will watch their annihilation. Their agonies will burn your eyes, and their screams will scald your ears. And you will know that *you* were the cause of it."

Town guards stood along the wall. I knew many more men, women, and even children were concealed within the town. They waited to either throw themselves into the battle or upon the mercy of the soldiers.

Taking a long, straight horn off the wall, Wright walked out onto the small balcony.

"Are you ready, John? Are you ready to hear their screams?"

He looked at me.

"No?"

Then adding, in a malevolent jeer, "When it's over, those who are left will hear *your* screams."

Pressing the horn to his lips, Lord Wright blew a long, loud call.

A mighty shout went up from the soldiers below.

Across the fields and over the walls rolled the bone-chilling roars of the monsters.

The garrison gates swung open.

The Brean streaked across the frozen ground.

In the lead ran the biggest and most armored brutes. They carried the massive battering ram. The rest fanned out behind them as if completing the tip of a spearhead.

Lord Wright surveyed the scene before him with a puffed-out chest and pride in his heart.

"Beautiful isn't it," he said admiringly.

He drew in a deep breath and then turned to look at me.

My blazing eyes narrowed on his.

"What's that, John? Care to have a look?" Wright leaned forward. "Go ahead, take a peek, for I have something special to share with you. Something that will make your miserable defeat all the more…"

Sweeter was what he was going to say.

I rushed in with such force that Wright staggered back. His feeble defenses went up in alarm as he tried to throw me out.

But it was too late.

I surged in and—

I froze.

Both Lord Wright's eyes and mine were locked in each other's horror.

Chapter Twenty-Seven: And Then There Was One

Lord Wright had two memories to show me. They came instantaneously and shocked me as keenly as I had stupefied him.

The first memory immersed me in a forest. It was that of a younger Merrick Wright before he had proclaimed himself a lord. He held a musket and was aiming at the back of a hairy beast—a Brean.

He hesitated, but only for a moment.

He wondered how it would taste. He'd never really seen one before, but he'd heard rumors of their existence, and he was hungry.

Relishing the trophy he would boast, Merrick Wright pulled the trigger.

The Brean fell.

For a moment, Merrick watched as it writhed in agony, its howls rising above the trees. Then, quickly, he loaded another ball, aimed, and shot it in the heart.

The beast quit screaming. It twitched and moaned for a moment, then lay still.

Merrick was trying to decide if it was finally dead. He was about to investigate when he heard a sound.

It was the snapping of a twig.

Quietly, he shrank back into the undergrowth and watched.

A man approached. Walking over to the fallen beast, he knelt and examined the body.

For a moment, he placed a hand on the Brean's belly.

It was bulging.

Tipping his hat back, the man looked around for the shooter. "Hello?" he called.

Merrick recognized him. He didn't know him personally, but he knew he was married and had a boy about the same age as his son.

Unsure of what to do, Merrick stayed quite still. But he didn't have to wait long.

The man stood and took one more look around.

"I know someone is there," the man called out. "I don't want your kill."

Wright didn't even breathe; he held perfectly still.

The man shrugged. "Have it your way."

He turned and left.

After a while, when he was sure the man would not come back, Merrick started toward the fallen animal.

But he stopped as the hair on the back of his neck bristled.

The air felt cooler, and the stench of something horrid reached his nostrils.

It was then he felt the hot, putrid breath wash down his neck. He spun and….

The gigantic beast grabbed his neck and lifted him clean off his feet.

Wright dropped his musket and clung to the monster's steel-like grip.

"No," he croaked.

"It...wasn't...me...can...prove...it...footsteps...leading...away. I...can...help you."

Miraculously, the man-like beast loosened its grip and said something.

The sound of it stunned Merrick. He certainly didn't expect this. It was pure panic that made him even try to speak to the monster.

The Brean repeated one word several times before Wright could make it out.

"Who?"

Swiftly, an idea began to form in the dark and twisted mind of Merrick Wright.

The first memory left me shaking with rage, but it paled in comparison to the next one. Although shorter, it shook me to my core.

A cloaked man, wheezing, stood in front of the new lord. In his hand, he held a highly polished mask of blackened metal, resembling that of a Brean.

"Were you successful, Jex?"

"Uh, not entirely, my lord," he confessed nervously.

"And what exactly does that mean?" hissed Wright.

Jex took a tense step back.

"We shot the man," he gushed. "But the boy...the boy got away. It's not our fault; he never came back."

The lord was furious.

"For your failure, you will be the one to go with our enemies to their new town; you will be our spy. If you do your job well…"

I didn't finish the memory. It was too much.

It was they who had started all of this. It was these evil men who had killed my mother, grandmother, *and* my father.

The memory of my father's ghost burned in my mind. It was his spirit that had warned me to flee.

I felt dizzy with the fever consuming my being, and, at that moment, I realized I had been holding back. I had been chaining the demons inside, afraid of what they could do. Afraid of what *I* could do.

That is right, they whispered. *Let us help you.*

The people in the town may be doomed. But I would see to it that these men, and every soldier, and every last Brean would pay. They would be stopped. No more would they live to oppress and terrorize others. No more!

Whoever survived would either fight for me or against me. There was no middle ground. Fear them, or fear me; that was the choice. It was the way the world worked.

With all my soul, I embraced the demons and let them rule.

Shaking off the final shreds of restraint, I flew into Lord Wright's soul with impossible power, as I could never have dreamed. Unabashed, I surged forward into every recess of his mind, absorbing everything that was Merrick.

In an instant, a serpent, born from the fever raging in my soul, uncoiled itself and struck Lord Wright with such venomous force, he was paralyzed to respond. The consequence was immediate.

I possessed *his* soul.

Lord Wright was mine!

All my life, I had been using my eyes to connect to and interpret what I saw in someone's soul. I didn't need my eyes or his now. My power was absolute.

I was invincible.

An unnatural growl rumbled through my body, penetrating all those in the room.

My restraints began to give as I struggled to pull free. The leather creaked, and the wood cracked.

Cocking his pistol to my head, Jex asked a pleading question, but it wasn't to me.

"My lord?"

The wood snapped and broke around my ankle as the fire completely consumed me and gave me boundless strength.

"MY LORD?" cried Jex with more panic.

I stopped struggling and fell quiet.

"It is quite all right," said Merrick.

Merrick had said it, but it came from my mind.

I stretched out my hand, but it wasn't my hand that moved. It was Wright's.

"Hand me the pistol," he said. "I'll deal with him myself."

Jex hesitated.

"Give it to me!" I hissed through Merrick.

Reluctantly, Jex reached over my shoulder and placed the pistol in Wright's hand.

I could feel the cool metal and wood in my grasp.

"Thank you, Jex," I said.

Except, this time, I allowed it to come through my own voice.

"Now, you shall have your reward."

I caused Wright's hand to fly up and pull the trigger. I sensed the impact of the ball as it slammed into Jex behind me, and I felt his blood splatter upon my neck and arms.

He groaned and then hit the floor.

Without having to be told, Wright immediately responded to my wish.

He unfastened my buckles.

I stood and faced the women.

Their eyes were filled with horror.

"It's all right," I said with a strange, hollow voice. "Everything will be fine now."

I unbuckled Hannah first.

When I went to Sarah, she cringed and shrank from my touch.

Tilting my head to the side, I looked at her blankly, trying to comprehend her.

Hannah, though terrified, squeaked, "I'll do it."

She pushed me back a step.

With gritted teeth and her one good arm, she unfastened the buckles on Sarah's wrists. Sarah then freed herself.

"Come," I said. "Jane will be waiting for us."

They hesitated.

Finally, Sarah nodded to Hannah and said, "We will go."

Retrieving a knife from the table, I opened the door.

The guards took one look at us and raised their weapons.

Instantly, I stole their minds and gave them a command.

Obediently, they turned their weapons upon each other and fired.

Pausing, I had an idea. I had scarcely to think it before Wright crossed the room in obedience. He stepped over the bodies and started down the stairs.

Hannah shot me a nervous glance. I paid her no heed.

I felt exhilarated! Power coursed through me as if fire flowed through my veins. My supremacy would finally right the world. I smiled in spite of myself.

We passed down the stairs and through the corridors. People acknowledged Lord Wright and bowed. When they saw me, they shrank back. No matter; I would deal with all of them in time. For now, they were just objects in my way.

I looked back at the women only once. Sarah clung to Hannah, helping her. Fear still played mightily in their eyes, and I knew that I was the reason they were afraid.

It didn't matter. I knew what was best, and I knew there was no other way. There was business to attend to, and I would do it.

We eventually came to Wright's private chambers—the very ones where I had waited before that fateful dinner.

Upon entering, I bolted the door from the inside, using a key that was in the lock.

Wright stood patiently, waiting.

The women still clung to each other tightly.

"John," pleaded Sarah.

I looked at her, waiting for her to continue.

Releasing Hannah, Sarah crossed over to me and took hold of my arm. I jerked away from her.

There wasn't any more time. The battle had begun. Didn't she realize that I, alone, could change the tide?

Although there was apprehension in her eyes, she grasped my arm again.

I started to pull away, but she held me firmly.

"If you are still with us, John, you will come with me."

She tried to lead me away, and I stiffened.

"Please," she begged. "I don't want to lose you."

Indulging her, I allowed her to usher me to the small washroom.

Placing her hand on my back, Sarah guided me in.

"Look," she instructed.

I gazed into the mirror that she held in front of me.

From sockets that were dark and sunken, blazing red eyes, devoid of all humanity, glared back at me. A ravenous brute filled the hollow void of my icy soul.

My whole countenance was consumed in darkness. Cold. Dead.

I was not surprised. I had seen those eyes before in my dreams.

But there was something unexpected. And what I realized horrified me to my feverish core.

My soul was not my own. A stranger was looking back at me.

I took a step back, but Sarah put a restraining hand on my shoulder.

"Behold your adversary," she said softly.

Gazing through fiery eyes, I regarded the demons of hatred and anger that I had fed so hungrily and embraced so willingly. For the first time, I understood true coldness, true dread, and true repulsion. They scowled at me, defiantly.

Come, John, they hissed. *It is time to destroy your enemies. Everyone is at our command. You can make them all suffer for their wrongs.*

No, I thought.

But they deserve it! Look at what they have done! Look at the misery they have caused! They must pay!

Again, I felt the tug—the terrible temptation to comply.

I considered the people dying at that very moment and all those who would die before this day was over, and I felt incensed with the terrible waste of life. Then I remembered my family, and the fierceness of hatred and anger boiled within me.

I felt the bond tighten, pulling me like a marionette.

Yes! they hissed gleefully. *Avenge your mother and father! Crush them all!*

I looked again into the eyes of hatred. And in them, I saw the same soul that possessed Naehume.

I had become *our* enemy.

"No," I whispered.

You are nothing without us! You need us! The demons ranted and shrieked in a terrible tantrum.

"I thought I needed you, but now I don't want you. I don't want to be like him. Leave me alone," I said, barely audible.

A howl of inexpressible horror screamed from the fiery hell of my soul as the demons fought their ground.

There is no turning back. You ARE us! We ARE you! You cannot change that.

I sank to my knees and covered my face with my hands. I was lost. There was no way out. Harrowing fear seized my heart.

I had done that which God himself would not do. I had possessed another and stolen his free will. Oh, one could threaten, tempt, deceive, and torture someone into submission, as Lyman had done to Jane and Hannah. But in the end, their resolve to act or to be acted upon was still their own.

Not me; I had occupied my victims so completely that they had no choice. I seized their intelligence and crushed it, twisted it, and made it obey *my* desires. I had imprisoned them in their own minds.

As the reality of my heinous crimes washed over me, I was racked with exquisite guilt. It burned into my soul, branding me with inexpressible horror. I wished I could sink into oblivion to stop the torment.

Sarah knelt and put her arms around me. I felt her presence push beneath the piercing ice that penetrated my being. She enveloped me, and I felt the hold of my enemy begin to slip away.

"I can bear to lose your body, but not your soul," she said. "Despair is also the enemy. There is nothing you have done that cannot be healed in here."

She pressed a warm hand to my chest.

Somewhere inside the icy casket of my heart, I strained to feel Sarah's words. Hungering to believe her, I searched the darkness of my prison for any hope of redemption.

The chains that bound me felt so heavy, so cold—cold as death.

Sarah's presence began to separate the ice from my heart. I felt her love flow into my soul, stirring my senses.

"You still have a choice, John. Forsake the bitterness and welcome the light. It is already within you if you choose it. Let it heal you."

But if I do, we will all die. We cannot win otherwise.

"Love is stronger than anger, John. It is stronger than hate."

Her hand upon my heart gave me courage. I felt its warmth and the life it offered me.

Then, I saw it—a tiny beam of light that seemed to pierce the darkness.

Anger and hate began to recoil, cowering away from the growing lumination inside me.

As I clung to this infant hope, fear struck from the shadows of despair with vicious ferocity.

Everyone will die now because of you! Lord Wright will win. You are a coward, selfish, powerless.

I listened. It was right. Who was I to argue? I was everything despicable and more! Fear began to overwhelm me, threatening to extinguish the tiny hope.

You think you are worthy? Look at you! You are nothing! Less than dust! There is nothing you can do to change your fate. We are your fate!

For a moment, I wavered.

But I had already felt life and love awaken my soul, and I wanted more of it.

With all of the energy I could muster, I focused on the light. And as I did so, the tiny spark of hope began to grow, warming my heart, and enlightening my mind.

No, I said. *You are wrong. I now know what I have to do, and I am not afraid anymore.*

You will die without us! fear hissed.

Yes. But I will be free when it happens.

I felt a surge of love as Sarah hugged me tighter. The chains that bound me slipped away and fell back into the awful pit from whence they came.

Mercifully, tenderly, the light continued to grow, purging every recess of my being and dispelling all the darkness within me.

With my head bowed, I breathed in new life.

Sarah waited a moment and then asked, "Are you with me?"

I nodded.

"Welcome back," she said and kissed my cheek.

"Uh, Sarah? John?" called Hannah anxiously.

Sarah stood. "It appears we are needed."

Slowly, I got to my feet and entered the main chamber.

Hannah looked at me.

"Oh, good. I like that color of your eyes much better."

Then she pointed to Wright.

He was cowering in the corner, moaning.

I took a step toward him, prepared to offer him a hand up.

I felt truly sorry for him. For the grand emptiness he'd built around him, and for the darkness he embraced in his soul.

Wright tried scrambling away. As his back was already against the wall, all he could do was cover his head and tremble like an abused animal.

"No!" he wailed. "Stay away! I will do anything. Please don't hurt me!"

I hesitated.

Sarah, placing a reassuring hand on my arm, said, "Perhaps I should take care of this."

Unsure what else to do, I stepped back.

She walked over, plucked a vase off a table, and smashed it over his head.

"That should help," she said as Wright crumpled to the floor unconscious.

Speechless, I gaped at her.

"Well, don't just stand there," she chided. "You do have a plan of escape, don't you?"

"I do."

Abruptly unfreezing my body, I exclaimed, "Jane!"

Had she made it?

I hurried over to the huge windows and flung open the glass door. Running to the stone railing, I peered into the forest.

Seeing me, Jane waved vigorously. Relieved, I returned her greeting.

She rode over on Ember, leading Smoke and two other horses.

Hastily, I pulled down the tapestries from the wall and, with the knife that I had taken from the tower, sliced them up and made a rope.

"I can't go down that," protested Hannah in terror.

"I'll lower you," I said.

"Absolutely not!"

"There is no other way," I explained, tying the rope to the stone railing.

"I believe Hannah may be right," said Sarah. "I'm not sure it is wise. Our death may come more assuredly leaving here than if we stay put."

Inhaling, I was about to argue when Sarah said, "We'll be fine. The door is locked, and we will secure Merrick. He will be our prisoner, so we will have something to bargain with. We'll wait for you to send help, and if needs be, we will go down with a real rope."

I looked at her with sad eyes and said, "I don't want to leave you."

There was more to my meaning than leaving her here in Lord Wright's chambers. There was something I had to do, and Sarah knew it. I suspected she'd known it for a long time and had finally succeeded in getting me to see it.

Sarah came over and drew me into a long, tight embrace. When she pulled away, there were tears in her eyes.

She peered at me and whispered, "The rewards for the brave are vast and worthwhile. You will never be lost to me, John. I see your light. Go now, and fulfill your destiny."

I couldn't meet her gaze. I pulled her back to me as I fought to control my sorrow.

"I love you," she said softly.

We separated as the tears broke and rolled down her cheeks.

Hannah, sensing a change in us, came over. She, too, put her good arm around me.

"Do be careful, John Stone. Without me by your side, who will save you?"

"I've already been saved," I said.

"Yes," she said tenderly and kissed my cheek. "Now go save my sister."

I nodded silently.

Without another word, I shimmied down the makeshift rope.

Jane dismounted and threw her arms around me.

I hugged her back.

"I was so worried," she said.

Then, releasing me, she asked, "Where are Hannah and Sarah?"

"Up there. Safe for now. They will need you to bring back help and a proper rope."

"There is no help coming; they will all be in the fight. I saw the army of Brean amassing even as I left the gate. And besides..."

She trailed off when she noticed me looking into the forest.

Then, fearfully, she said, "I've been followed, haven't I?"

I nodded. "It was inevitable; there was nothing you could have done. It's me he wants, not you."

"Naehume?"

I nodded again.

With eyes that burned like fire, the mammoth monster watched us from far off, his armor gleaming in the sun.

He was alone.

"Go hide in the woods. It will be over soon," I said quietly.

I was unable to look at her, afraid my eyes would betray what I felt.

"Oh, my love, I know that look. You can't possibly win."

"No," I replied softly. "But at least I can make it an even fight for the others. There is still a chance for them."

"How? He's too strong. You will surely lose!"

I looked into her beautiful green eyes and explained, "The battle that we will fight will not be one of strength."

"You will still lose! He will not fight fair nor alone."

"No," I agreed. "It is a trick to draw me away—one that I will fall for. But it doesn't matter; I won't need long."

"There has to be another way; we just have to think of it. I can't lose you! Please, John!"

Tears welled in her eyes, glittering in the radiant morning sun that brought no heat or comfort to the heart.

"Don't cry. And don't be afraid," I said comfortingly. "Our die is cast, but that doesn't mean all is lost. If I fall, it will still be well for our side. As long as Naehume and I stand, everyone between us will die. I cannot return to Marysvale. Even now, I feel our true enemy calling me—tempting me to enter the fray and strike down all who oppose. If I succumb, and we survive this battle, you will still lose me, and that is more than I can bear."

The whisperings of her soul told her that I spoke the truth.

Jane wiped the tears from her face.

"Then, I will go with you. If a little time is all you need, I can help buy you that time."

I saw the determination in her eyes.

"Hannah told me to keep you safe."

"Is there anywhere that is safe?"

Of course, there wasn't. And, for all I knew, the battle was already lost. Regardless, I would have argued with her if, for one moment, I thought she would actually stay behind.

Seeing my hesitation, Jane seized upon it. "Then, it is settled."

I put my arm around her waist and pulled her in close. Tucking a piece of hair behind her ear, I looked deeply into her eyes.

"I love you, Jane Wolfe."

"I love you, too, John Stone," she whispered.

Then, placing her hand on the back of my head, she drew me to her, and we kissed passionately.

All too soon, Jane slowly pulled away.

With tears in her eyes, she said, "And that will have to do, Mr. Stone."

My heart breaking, I helped her onto Ember.

Jane retrieved her rifle.

"Ready?"

I nodded, mounted Smoke, and turned him to face the king of the Brean.

Closing my eyes, I took a deep breath and bowed my head for just a moment.

Memories of the cabin, my friends, their laughter, and their love washed over me. My heart burst with gratitude, sadness, and deep, abiding love.

Steeling myself, I kicked Smoke into a gallop.

He responded with tremendous power as we charged forward.

Naehume saw us coming, turned, and ran.

We shot after him, around the hill, and toward the front of Marysvale. The gates fell into view. They lay open on broken hinges.

Monsters swarmed the wall. The great beasts swung their clubs at the guards, sending men hurtling through the air.

Men and women of all ages streamed out of the houses, brandishing cooking knives, pitchforks, clubs, anything they could get their hands on, and sprinted toward the fight.

Even over the rush of wind as we galloped, I could hear the muskets and rifles bark their report from all over Marysvale. Gunsmoke rose from different quarters of the town.

It was a dreadful sight to behold.

Tremendous heaviness and sorrow enveloped me.

I stole a glance back at Jane and Ember; they were holding their own. Seeing her at my side sent a pang of yearning. As much as I wanted her with me, I wanted her to live. I wanted her to return to Sarah and Hannah and experience days they had glimpsed but had never truly known. Happy times at Sarah's cabin, free from fear. Free to sit on the porch swing and sip tea on a pleasant spring day, with the smell of blossoms and sweet wildflowers filling their senses. If there was a chance of making it happen, even a small one, I wanted to try.

Leaning low in the saddle, I said, "Run, Smoke! Go as fast as you can!"

And he did.

That magnificent animal surged forward as on wings of lightning.

"No!" cried Jane. "Wait for me!"

Burying my head, I gave one last instruction to my horse.

414

"Don't let her catch us!"

I couldn't really call it running; it was more like flying. Smoke flew so fast that his hooves barely touched the ground. They peddled the air, only dipping down as if to check and make sure the earth below was still there.

We soared over the fields and leaped into the woods after Naehume.

With each gallop, the distance between us shrank.

Naehume ran upright. His heavy armor made him less agile than usual, but his speed was still something to behold.

The trees were mere blurs to my vision as Smoke sailed through the forest.

Our end was near. I wasn't sure how I knew it, but I did.

I think Smoke sensed it too.

A change seemed to fall all around us as if the forest shared our foreboding. Despite the pounding of Smoke's hooves, it grew quiet, cold, and lifeless.

Soon, the stench of monsters filled the air.

I had known it was coming. I even knew how it would happen.

There was no getting around it, no escape.

It had to be. I had to confront him.

Naehume was sure he would win. But he didn't know what I now knew, or he never would've come close to me again.

I caressed Smoke's neck for one last time.

And with that, the trap was sprung.

Suddenly, Naehume dropped to his hands. His claws dragged through the frozen ground as his feet spun about.

Facing me, he bellowed a terrifying roar.

His muscular arms rippled as he reversed his backward slide and charged forward.

The ground all around me exploded upward.

Five gigantic, armored monsters flew from their concealment. Throwing off the blankets and leaves, they lunged for me, snapping their jaws and twitching their claws.

My rifle came around to the brutes on my left. Selecting one, I pulled the trigger. Flame and ball blasted out the end. It slammed into the breastplate of the Brean and bounced harmlessly away.

I couldn't even see the mark where it had struck.

A split second later, we collided.

I sailed through the air and came crashing down onto my side.

The Brean wrapped its massive arms around Smoke, and they plunged to the ground.

The fall broke the monster's grip.

Smoke scrambled up just as the monster leaped to its feet and sprang.

My mighty horse tucked both hind legs up and then kicked out.

With a dull gong, Smoke's hooves struck the brute.

It stumbled back, but the armor protected it from any harm.

Other monsters rushed in.

"NO!" I cried.

I was on my feet and running, desperate to get to Smoke.

The Brean piled on top of him—first one and then two.

Claws and teeth tore violently at his body.

A third monster jumped into the fray, and they finally knocked Smoke down, pinning him under their considerable weight.

Smoke struggled to free himself, whinnying, kicking, and twisting.

Even as I moved, a giant form loomed at my side.

I knew who it was.

Instantly, the stone-like fist of Naehume crashed into my ribs.

Bones snapped as I was lifted and flung backward.

I slammed into the ground; dizzying pain washed through my body.

Each breath brought with it searing agony—they came shallow and ragged.

I heard a girl scream and then a rifle crack.

A ping rang out from a ball striking armor.

Oh, please, no, I pleaded.

Naehume bellowed a terrific roar, bursting with rage.

Chaos reigned all around.

I looked at Smoke.

The monsters tore at his body.

His thrashing grew weak.

"SMOKE!"

My heart shattered, and I cried in raw anguish for my friend.

He looked at me.

And, for the first time in our lives, I *understood* his language.

I love you too. I replied. *Thank you for saving me.*

Smoke's chest heaved once and fell in a long sigh.

Jane screamed again.

I turned and watched helplessly as a monster swatted her out of the saddle.

Like a doll, Jane was spun around, her back pressed to the beast's great armored chest. Its arms wrapped around her in a crushing embrace.

Ember bolted as a Brean charged at her.

With my arm across my chest, attempting to stem the searing pain, I rose to my knees and started for her.

I didn't make it far.

A devastating weight fell upon my calf.

With a snarl, Naehume transferred the whole of his mass to my leg.

The bone snapped.

Despite the stabbing pain in my chest, I screamed wretchedly and fell to the ground.

Tears of agony blurred my vision as I looked for Jane.

Our eyes locked.

Love, sorrow, fear, and longing all played in the fathomless depths of her stunning green eyes.

I yearned for her.

Love coursed through me, releasing a power and a wonder I had never felt before.

Instantly, my soul soared to hers. We intertwined, embracing and absorbing each other.

"I feel you," she said in her mind.

And, in that tiny instant, everything that made us who we were transferred to the other.

I knew what it was to be Jane, and Jane knew what it was to be me. The good, the bad, the hopes, the dreams, and even the sorrows were laid bare for each of us to experience in the other.

I flashed her a smile. I could feel that she sensed my sorrow and suffered the pain from my tortured body, just as if it were her own.

"No, don't leave."

I heard her thought echo through our growing distance as I pulled away.

The crushing weight lifted from my leg.

I rolled on my back to face Naehume.

The force of our souls crashed into each other.

It was the moment I had been waiting for.

The same power I had felt with Jane overcame me again, born not of hate but of compassion.

I soared into his soul as he burned into mine.

We locked.

Naehume's eyes blazed triumphantly.

"You have lost, John Stone," he snarled.

It was not said in his guttural, animal-like voice. It came clear in my mind, confident and articulate, unencumbered by the limitations of flesh.

Perhaps I couldn't quite bring myself to love Naehume, but I did feel compassion and even sorrow for his bondage.

When I looked at him, I saw what I came so close to becoming. And I wanted to free him.

"No," I said sadly. "You have already lost. You lost a long, long time ago."

I flashed him the memory of Merrick Wright, killing his mate and unborn child. It transferred to him instantly.

A violent shudder ran through his soul.

I had struck a blow, although that was not my intention.

The demons of anger and hate flared furiously.

He lies! He is deceiving you! His father killed your mate!

"You lie!" he growled.

Sympathy flowed from me in response.

"It is not I who have deceived you," I said. "All these years, you have been helping the very man who stole your life from you. He took from you the last being you ever loved. And for that, I am truly sorry."

Another convulsion surged through him.

He wavered. A seed of doubt had been planted.

Let it be enough, I prayed.

Naehume knew what I had shown him to be true. He knew that Merrick Wright was perfectly capable of such a lie.

You need us! hissed the familiar demons. *Without us, you are nothing!*

"These are your enemies," I said. "They are the ones who deceive and bind you with bitterness."

I felt the turmoil in his soul.

"You can be free," I implored.

But he had hated so long that he could not bring himself to accept the horror that now confronted him. Even more, he *wanted* to believe the demons. They were old companions, and they felt comfortable. What I offered was new, unknown, and he judged it to be a weakness.

Naehume misunderstood, as I had done, the real power of love. It took tremendous strength and courage to develop, and though it is more subtle than anger, it is much more potent.

Instead of embracing the truth, however, Naehume decided to silence it.

He couldn't face the message, nor the messenger who bore it.

The demons raged, and any doubt Naehume felt quickly slipped away.

Look what he tries to take from you! Avenge your mate and end it!

With crazed fury, Naehume bunched his hands into fists and raised them high over his head.

"Both you and the girl will die!" he snarled.

"Then I am sorry for you," I said. "You will never be free and never experience true joy again."

He felt my sincerity, and it infuriated him.

With a tremendous roar, Naehume hurtled his fists downward.

Instantaneously, I flew into him and swooped through his soul. I found the illuminating tube of twisting glass and followed it down into the depths of his core.

Another tube joined the first, and then another.

I dove until I saw hundreds, if not thousands, of translucent tubes converge into one glowing, white-hot ball.

In an instant, I surrounded them, isolating them from the darkness that consumed their space.

At the exact moment that Naehume's iron fists crashed into me, I heaved the tubes free from his soul.

An unseen, otherworldly explosion shattered our link, hurling us apart.

Blinding pain tore through my body as I rolled over and over.

Then blackness washed through my consciousness.

As I slipped into darkness, I heard terrible roaring, snarling, and the tearing of flesh.

The Brean swarmed over me.

Chapter Twenty-Eight: Healing

Someone moaned.

Who is that moaning? I wondered. *Whoever it is, I wish they would stop.*

Whoever it was didn't stop.

He groaned again.

As the pain grew in my consciousness, I realized that it was me.

Blearily, my eyes cracked open.

Jane hovered over me.

She said something.

I couldn't understand her.

She turned and spoke to someone.

A moment later, Sarah's head appeared.

Everything looked hazy.

My chest and leg burned with unquenchable fire.

It was then that I realized that I had not died.

As my suffering grew, I started wishing I had.

Gratefully, unconsciousness washed over me.

Welcomed oblivion dragged me into relief.

***

My body was damp and burning hot, raging with a natural fever.

I felt a cool washcloth caressing my face.

The blurry images of the women appeared again, talking to me, but I could not hear.

Scorching agony consumed my whole frame.

As before, relief came at the gentle hand of unconsciousness.

***

The blackness parted again. Pain still racked my body, but this time, my eyes blinked open, and I became aware.

Jane gently stroked my forehead.

I focused on her face.

Her head was bowed, her eyes were closed, and her hair fell about her face in long tresses.

She looked exhausted.

I watched her for a moment.

Sunlight beamed through large windows, falling upon her in golden streams.

She was the most beautiful sight I had ever seen.

With tremendous effort, I reached up and brushed a lock of hair from her cheek. I tucked it behind her ear so that I could see her better.

Jane's eyes opened, and she gazed upon me.

She sighed and said, "Please tell me this is not a dream. Are you really here with me?"

I smiled.

"I am."

Immediately, footsteps could be heard running down a corridor, and, in a moment, Sarah and Hannah burst into the room.

"We heard voices," Sarah said anxiously.

As I saw them, I took in my surroundings for the first time.

I lay in a large bed, in a room built of stone. Tapestries hung on the wall, and a fire burned on the hearth.

"Where am I?" I croaked.

"In one of the castles," replied Sarah.

Thomas, noticeably less bruised, came in, followed by James, Angus, and Simon.

"What happened?" I asked.

"We were going to ask you the same thing," said Hannah.

"There will be plenty of time for that later," chided Sarah. "John needs food and rest. He's been out a long time."

"It's all right," I said. "I want to know."

Jane glanced at Sarah. A look passed between them.

"Where to start?" asked Jane with another sigh.

"How about with you?" I suggested. "What happened to Naehume? Why are we still here?"

She took my hand in hers.

"Why indeed," Jane mused. "That is what we all want to know. As for our part, *what* happened is quite simple. *Why* it happened...well, that is something else entirely."

I waited.

"It was quite amazing, really," she continued. "You were on your back, and Naehume had just brought his fists down to smash you. But as soon as he touched you, you were thrown apart. Like some invisible force picked you up and tossed you away from each other. You flew back and rolled several times before you stopped. You didn't move at all; I feared you were dead.

"Instantly, the Brean that had been crushing me let go. I thought he was going to go after you.

"Naehume was in a terrible rage. I had never seen anything like it before. Nor do I want to see anything like it ever again. It completely terrified me. He pulled himself up and flew at you again. But he never made it. My Brean threw himself between you and Naehume…"

Jane's voice trailed off, and a shudder ran through her body as she recalled the scene.

"It was the most dreadful battle you could ever imagine. It was all the more awful on account of their armor. The whole ground seemed to shake as they fought. The other Brean joined in the fray. *They were all protecting you!* Two were killed before the others could restrain Naehume.

"And when they did…" She closed her eyes as if to block the image. "They tore him to bits."

Opening her eyes, Jane caressed my cheek with her fingers.

"Aye, our experience was much the same," added James. "One moment, the Brean were utterly destroying us. Then suddenly, they stopped as if in a daze. Then, just as quickly, they ran for the soldiers.

"Poor devils didn't realize what was happening until many of their comrades had perished from the unexpected turn of events. The Brean relentlessly pursued them throughout the garrison and the castles. After the soldiers had been destroyed, the Brean wearing armor removed it; then they all simply dropped their clubs and left."

"The Brean who killed Naehume also removed their armor," noted Jane. "One gently picked you up and cradled you. He carried you all the way back to Marysvale while the rest followed. It was incredible! They were so peaceful! They *were* fast, though; I couldn't keep up with them for long."

Sarah added to the narrative. "They laid you at the gates of Marysvale and left. That was four days ago. Nobody has seen one since."

"But that doesn't explain *why* it happened," said Hannah.

They all looked at me expectantly.

Suddenly, a great tremor of pain shot through my whole frame, taking my breath away.

Instantly, Sarah said, "That's enough for today."

"No," I gasped. "I'll tell you now, and then it will all be over. I need it to be over. There really isn't much to say anyway."

Of course, that wasn't true, but I had no energy nor desire to relive the events and the changes in myself that had led me to my conclusion. So, I shortened it.

"I discovered that Naehume had a supernatural ability as well, except that he used his gifts to control the Brean. In essence, he stole their free will. I simply used my ability to reach into his soul and set them free. I had no idea what would happen after that."

I left out the part that I knew all this because I had *become* Naehume.

However, as I thought more about it, I felt as if I had, deep down and subconsciously, known it from the beginning.

"Handy gift of yours," Angus said brightly. "Aye, we may need it still. Of the enemy that survived, many are claimin' that they were forced to act against their will. Of course, we suspect they're just tryin' to save their necks now that their empire has fallen."

"Naehume's power only extended to his own kind," I said.

As mine only extended to humans, I thought to myself. However, somehow, he and I could connect. Perhaps it was because our gifts were so similar.

"To what extent Lord Wright was involved in their claims and what he threatened them with," I continued. "I'm afraid I will not be able to help."

"But ye have to, laddie!" exclaimed Angus. "How will we know if they are tellin' the truth?"

"It's not that I'm unwilling."

Even though I was entirely unwilling.

"It's that I no longer have the ability."

"What?" Hannah exclaimed in surprise.

The others looked at me in equal astonishment.

"Something happened between Naehume and me. The explosion of sorts that occurred between us stripped away our abilities. I'm sorry. Even if I wanted to, there is nothing left. I can no more read you than you can read me."

They all looked at me in stunned silence for a long time.

It wasn't true. I knew my gifts were still intact, but they would never be used again. Not that I couldn't. It's that I wouldn't.

I had seen what they could do, the damage they could inflict. The gift in itself was not evil; it was simply a tool. It was up to the wielder on how the instrument would be used.

And I could not trust myself.

Even now, I could hear the siren call of the enemy. I could feel the appealing enticement to exercise it for personal gain. I could easily become the new lord of Marysvale.

I shuddered.

"Ah, such a pity," sighed Angus.

The others in the room seemed to accept this explanation—all, that is, but Sarah and Jane.

However, they never questioned me about it. Ever.

Epilogue

Wildflowers sprang to life in the meadows; fruit trees bloomed in the orchard. A gentle springtime breeze erased the lingering chill of winter. Blossoms drifted lazily on warm currents of air, bringing with them the sweet scent of life itself.

The sun glistened brilliantly off the deep blue water of the lake. It was so alluring that I imagined myself rocking languidly on Sarah's rowboat, basking in the radiant, warm sun. That is, assuming I had the courage to climb into the rickety, old craft, which I did not.

So, instead, I turned my gaze upon the gathered people. These were friends from those dark days—alive in this peaceful setting. Simon, Sam, and even Sabin were here, along with many others. I felt joy being in their presence.

Much had changed in the time following the fall of Lord Wright. The newly appointed territorial governor, the honorable Simon Mays, had convened a court. Many were tried for their crimes, and those found guilty, including the late Merrick Wright, had been hanged.

After the people had mourned their dead and the criminals had been tried, Angus and Simon had deemed it necessary to hold a celebration in honor of a new beginning.

The wall was torn down.

Teams of horses and swarms of people descended upon the once imposing structure and, with hammers, stones, ropes, and any other implement they could find, they demolished their prison cell. Townspeople hugged and cried and cheered during the weeklong demolition. A great feast and dancing accompanied the event.

Or so I was told.

I spent long days in the castle recovering. It suited me just fine. The only celebration I needed was a mug of tea with friends. Not one of those nasty healing brews that Sarah tried sneaking in every once in a while, but a soothing cup of something sweet.

I relished the many hours I spent with Thomas, James, Sarah, Hannah, and, of course, Jane, sitting in my room by the fire, laughing, and even crying, as we reminisced and created new memories.

As soon as I was able, we traveled to Sarah's cabin.

It was late spring by then.

Those who had farms returned to them and began the arduous process of restoration. Others built homes and barns on new land, using the material from the castles and walls of Marysvale. Some chose to leave the territory altogether. Very few chose to stay in the town itself.

The one remaining castle, or the portion of it that hadn't been torn down and plundered, had been reconstructed as a church. The surrounding grounds were marked with the graves of all those who had fallen in the final battle.

Within a year after the wall came down, a fierce lightning storm had ignited an abandoned house. It spread like wildfire and destroyed most of the remaining buildings. Marysvale quickly became a ghost town.

Eventually, a new town was built, but not in the same location. It was a town without walls that took in a territory of farms and cottages that were free and peaceful. Angus had built a home in the heart of it and had another church constructed, similar to the one in Alyth. Along with conducting worship services there, he also performed his duties as the newly appointed justice of the peace.

From where I stood, I could just make out the steeple in the distance.

It had taken some time to decide what to call the settlement, and, in the end, Angus' proposal of the name Anam was bestowed. It was an old word, he said, that meant Soul.

Memories of the past and what I had almost become still plagued my thoughts from time to time. I often remembered Naehume and regretted that I hadn't been able to reach him. I was saddened that he wasn't able to see through Wright's treachery from the very beginning, both for himself and the scores of other people who suffered from his deeds.

I pushed the thoughts from my mind.

Not today.

Today was a celebration—the union of two souls in blessed matrimony.

And the bride looked radiant.

My eyes wandered to Sarah and James' cabin. The sweet memory of returning, and the ensuing months, still filled me with warmth. It had been the fulfillment of a dream.

I continued surveying the nearby area. Another cabin had been completed, and a third was beginning to take shape.

An elbow jabbed me in the ribs.

"You are not paying attention, are you?"

I gazed down into Jane's beautiful green eyes.

"No," I admitted with a grin, only now realizing that Angus had started the ceremony.

She looked at me sternly, but her eyes twinkled, and a smile soon broke across her face.

"Do try to pay attention, my love. Occasions like this don't happen very often."

"No," I agreed.

Then under my breath, I muttered, "Thank goodness."

Jane again elbowed me playfully in the gut, just as Angus gave the groom permission to "Kiss yer bride."

To which Thomas, with trembling hands, took Hannah in his arms and bestowed a tender kiss.

With no trepidation, Hannah threw her arms around him and returned it.

Mrs. Martin wiped tears from her eyes while the rest of our gathering erupted in cheers.

Across the meadow, a yearling whinnied as if joining in the celebration.

It then turned its attention to frolicking around its mother. The young horse tried to coax her into a game of chase, but Ember was having none of it.

She simply kept her head down and grazed on the lush green grass.

Finally giving up, the yearling took off like a bolt of lightning to harass the cattle.

And just like his father before him, Fire was the fastest horse I'd ever seen.

www.ingramcontent.com/pod-product-compliance
Lightning Source LLC
Chambersburg PA
CBHW051513250626
47156CB00001B/73